Holden Gate

Holden Gate

Sally Corrie

Published by Kearton Books

A CIP catalogue record for this book is available from the British Library.

ISBN 978-0-9931588-0-3

Book layout and cover design by Clare Brayshaw

Prepared and printed by:

York Publishing Services Ltd
64 Hallfield Road
Layerthorpe
York
YO31 7ZQ

Tel: 01904 431213

Website: www.yps-publishing.co.uk

For my boys, Bruce and Xander

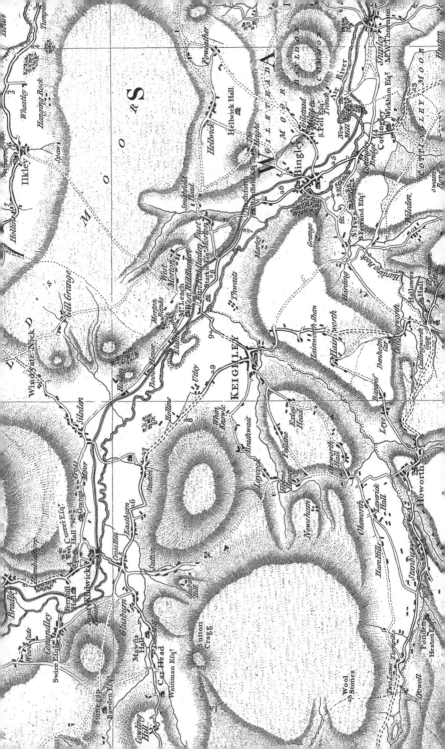

A Short Glossary

Barghest   A monstrous black dog of legend, particularly in the north of England. It appeared only at night and was thought to foretell a death. Descriptions mention its fiery eyes and accompanying howling, baying and rattling of chains which drew a following of all other dogs in the area.

Dash   In a plunger type butter churn, the dash is the staff which is raised and dropped within the wooden churn to agitate the separation of fat from the buttermilk.

Ginnel   A narrow passage or alleyway.

Ings   An old Norse word still in common parlance in the north of England meaning water meadow/marsh by the banks of a river.

Intack   Moorland which is improved and brought into cultivation.

Lady Day	The feast of the Annunciation (of the blessed Virgin) 25th March. It is first of the four Quarter days of the church year. Before the mid eighteenth century (and the adoption of the Gregorian calendar) this was the beginning of the year when, traditionally, new leases were drawn up between tenants and landowners.
Lye	Potassium hydroxide is a strong alkali derived from the water leaching of wood ashes. The resultant liquid or lye was used to launder linen.
Offshut	A small side room leading off from the main living chamber of the house.
Pentice	An overhanging roof and the rain-protected area beneath.
Quarter Sessions	Local courts that sat four times each year (Epiphany, Easter, Midsummer and Michaelmas). They were convened to discuss petty crimes and other matters of civil jurisdiction including the administration of the Poor Rate, the repair of roads, the setting of rents and the organisation of militias.
Quoin	Corner stones, sometimes decorative which are a feature of Yorkshire vernacular architecture.

Holden Gate. July 1689

*F*rom up here I can see the whole world stretching out before me. I am sitting atop the bank looking down over the roof of the barn, and the house in which I was born. This is my fifth summer, and I am hot and uncomfortable in my heavy linen. Mother says that I must not remove my dress though I long to wait in the looseness of my cotton shift.

Margaret is wailing, I can hear her from here. Mother will be running a cloth about her neck and ears, or pulling a comb through her knotted curls. I know this, for I have already endured the same. I do wonder whether God really minds if we have clean faces and tidy hair. I mentioned this to father once and he laughed. God sees us as we are Eliza he said, but we wash our faces for the people at church. I don't understand this, but whoever we do it for, it is the same each Sunday.

Ann prefers to keep her dress clean so will be in the parlour with mother. She will not be persuaded to join me here on the bank even though I have with me a new kitten. I have stolen her from her mother. She is black as night, and though I cradle her to me, she will not be still. Her claws *have drawn a stripe of blood across my thumb which I am sucking for fear it marks my dress. I will return her to the nest behind the barn before we leave for church. I shall name her Bet, and she shall be mine.*

I wonder where father can be? I didn't see him leave the house this morning, but he will be away on the moor checking on his sheep. I think I hear the dogs now. Come Bet, you shall have to go back to your mother. She will protect you from the dogs.

It is too lovely a day to be in church. The Reverend Pollard is a nice man but he talks and talks of things I don't understand. Ann pinches me when I fidget, and when I try to pinch her back mother takes my wrist and gives me that look. The church is always dark and cold, even on a day such as this. I shall be thankful of my heavy linen when I get there.

Father reads to us all from his big heavy bible each night and I know that it's important to listen and maybe learn. I'd rather learn of God from father than the Reverend Pollard. I'd rather be here at Holden.

1

November 1703. Marley

The wind could not get stronger Eliza prayed: its wild cry amplified her own animal cries of pain. The baby was fighting its way out into the world. A world of fury and noise and destruction. Where was John? Pray God he was safe. Her mother Mary kept witness, mumbling, cursing and startling as, out in the darkness, the storm tore up trees and tumbled walls as it made its violent progress north across the land. Above the roar, window shutters and doors chattered in their frames, and unheard in the black, the sheep called in terror to one another.

The storm had arrived three days past. The dimming of the November sky that morning had raised little comment. This month often heralded rain in sharp violent starts. Wet freezing fog rolled along the valley floor, deadening sound and lingering for days. Snow was not unknown, indeed, so harsh had been the winters these past ten years that if the first flakes fell after the beginning of Advent, it was seen as God's blessing.

This day was different however, and the livestock seemed to sense it. The sheep knotted together beneath the hawthorn hedge, and in the barn, the chickens continued to roost in the low rafters. All day the rush lamps had been lit and from every angle the room was pierced by the wind like ditchwater finding its way through old boot leather. It was impossible to know the coming of the night for so black was the sky. Not a drop of water fell from the heavens. Inside her belly the child seemed to recognise this change, twisting in anticipation and fear.

John had been gone four days now. He was making the journey on foot to see his father and brothers in the place of his birth. It was a day hence across the rough high moorland that stretched north from where she now sat gazing into the flames of the open hearth. Word had come that his father ailed and was unlikely to see the winter through. His mother had lain in the churchyard four years now, and her passing had seen John set forth to find his way in the world. He had enjoyed seventeen summers in the family homestead, but as the youngest of three, knew that his future life lay beyond its nine acres. As Ann, his mother, lay gasping her breath like thistledown in the wind, he had clasped her papery hand to his heart and pledged to honour her memory. So tiny a woman to have borne three such fine strong sons. As the candle guttered so her soul rose to the Almighty.

Richard, his father, had paid the sexton and turned his face towards the dark lane, heavily overhung with oak and ash. In his wake Benjamin, Samuel and John walked in single file and silence. He would not seek another wife. Benjamin at almost twenty years had already pledged himself to Susanna, and before the year was out, was planning to lead her back to the same church from whence they now departed. Samuel, in time, would also find himself a wife, and for this generation, at least, the farm would sustain them all. John had seen, without being told, that his future lay elsewhere. Mindful of this, he had approached his father some days later as he led his cows towards the byre in the late afternoon haze. He asked that he be allowed to leave. His friend Nathan Gill had, the summer last, left the valley to seek work across the moor in the valley of the Aire. He had returned briefly at Easter with news of his impending marriage and his new life as a tenant farmer within the manor of Harden. For all his talk and good humour, Nathan's face carried fine lines like autumn leaves and his hands appeared knobbled as pignuts. His father had eyed him without speaking, but in the knowledge that Nathan Gill had gone before and would be John's bondsman, he gave his blessing.

John had gathered up his few worldly goods: a short blade knife, a good linen shirt, a soft felt cap, and a cross of straw fashioned by his mother a Palm Sunday long ago. He drew all up in a thick woollen cloak which he threw over his shoulder. The month was August, and behind the cottage, wheat was beginning to ripen. As he embraced his father and brothers, swifts screeched their farewells as they flew in and out of the open barn. When he had walked on for several minutes, he glanced back towards the farmstead. As his brothers moved like ants across the yard, and out towards the low pasture, his father remained close to the

3

open door, screening his eyes towards his departing figure and the rising sun.

As the pasture gave way to the high open moorland, he began to hear the mournful cry of curlew, as across his path, grouse bustled and awkwardly took flight. Against the heavens, skylarks rose in song. At his back, carried on the light summer wind, the slow rhythm of the church bell announcing the laying in earth of a neighbour's baby. The child had breathed but a few hours before it was called back to God. John mouthed a silent prayer as he walked onwards. After a couple of hours with the sun at its zenith he threw down his pack, and from his leather jerkin took out his kerchief containing a hard fist of dark bread and sour white cheese. Replenished, he lay back in the soft purple heather and, for a short while, closed his eyes. Behind his eyelids, in the soft pink glow, he pictured his mother's face, not as she lay dying, but in the closeness of her evening kiss. He needed to remember her features before they dissipated like clouds in the summer sky.

The afternoon wore on, so too the miles, and ere long the land began to fall away towards the white ribbon of the Aire. Ahead, the smoke from cottages could be glimpsed. He had passed no one walking the moorland track, but in the air came the voice of a shepherd and the confused reply of his sheep. Glancing left he was distracted at the sight of a rocky bluff atop which two stone tables appeared silhouetted against the sky. He remembered with a warm sense of reassurance that these were the giant toadstools of which his father had spoken. From where he stood they were surely the work of man rather than nature. Ancient as time itself, the firestones marked the boundary of his future. As the track rose from a shallow hollow, the grey ling roof of a low building took form. Outside its open door two figures, heads close, warmed their backs against the ancient stone. He was now walking the drovers' road, worn into the landscape by the hooves of countless beasts. As he approached the building, the two men broke off from conversation and nodded to John; he shyly raised his hand in acknowledgement. The drovers' inn was positioned as a final staging post for the weary men who had for centuries walked stock down through the wild lands of the north, before their descent into the valleys and markets.

With the rhythm of his step, the untamed moorland began to give way to pasture, mill and quarry. Cottages and farmsteads and rough dressed tracks began to form the lacework of communities, and for the first time since he had begun his journey, he discerned the toll of a church bell. As he followed a tumbling beck down the hillside, the land began to level, and he found himself amid a scatter of low houses. Many of the doors were open, and in the dry dirt, a child rolled and sang. He startled as a squat grey pig eased past him, pursued lazily by a lad of about nine years. Birch twig in hand and clay pipe clamped between his thin lips, the lad chased the animal down the lane leading from the hamlet. By now the sun was beginning to lose its warmth as it touched upon the dark shoulder of the distant hills. In an insect haze and long feathery grass, John at last found himself at the bank of the Aire. In the company of tufty red cattle he bathed his feet in the silty shallows. Wanting to reach his destination before the fall of darkness he followed the riverbank past a churning water mill until he reached the narrow stone sweep of the pack bridge. Crossing the near silent water, he arrived in the cluster of houses known as Keighley. Through low mullioned windows he saw the soft glow of firelight, and heard the sounds of life within.

Only then, within a scant mile of his destination did he stop to enquire the way to Marley. By the lychgate two women chatted, a small child grasping the rough woollen skirt of his mother. The older woman, whose cheeks and nose were crazed with a filigree of tiny veins, smiled and pointed at a narrow ginnel that passed between two cottages. In the last vestiges of light he was aware of the flashing circle of a family of bats, feasting on the bounty of the night sky. A dog barked, and out in the hills came the scream of a fox cub. Hard by a rising blister of land, he finally arrived at the Gill homestead.

* * *

Mary alighted from the low stool and walked the short distance to the inglenook. Outside the storm raged so hard as to force the smoke back down the chimney. Even the pot swung like a corpse in a gibbet above the flame. She prayed to God that her family high up on the moor at Holden were safe. Robert, her husband, would not want for nourishment as her daughters Ann and Margaret could keep house in the ways she had schooled them. Maria would tend her youngest, John, barely four years old, and surely now weeping in terror in her arms as the force of natures power crashed down upon them.

Eliza no longer heard the storm, nor feared God's retribution. Upon her finger tight as twine was a wedding band. This baby would be baptized in the name of her father, but was it God's will that the baby be born at all? She thought of her father Thomas who had died when she was but a small child. She remembered standing at his graveside, her three sisters about her and her mother Mary dry eyed and silent. She had not wanted to leave her father in that place, and had wept in ignorance and futility. Mary had been sharp with her which had only added to her misery. The walk back to Holden was a long one, the month was June and though the sun shone, the air was unseasonably cold. Thomas had left this life in the cruellest of circumstances, taken by the fever that claimed infants and the infirm; Thomas had been neither. He had risen one morning before the sun, as was his way, but as Mary and the young girls had awoken with the crowing of the cock, they found him by the dying embers of the fire. His thirst could not be assuaged nor his body warmed. The beasts in the field and the sheep on the high moor became Ann and Margaret's concern. By the third night he began to cry out to his maker. The priest was called. They had heard the passing bell carried up from the valley so often that year, and the sexton was rarely idle, but none had supposed that when death came to Holden, it was Thomas it sought.

Yes, if the baby be a boy it would be Thomas. She had told Mary of her intentions, and her mother's eyes had brightened as she summoned his face. Perhaps he would have the dark Fowler eyes of his namesake and hair as dark as peat. Mary, whose own colours were muted as a winter's day had wished the same for all of her children, but only Eliza was so bestowed. As if communing with her, the baby pitched and her belly rose and fell.

Mary ladled pottage into a small wooden bowl; the night was to be a long one, and she would face whatever came alone with her daughter. John would not return this night. Not even the wild creatures of the hills would leave the safety of the deep earth in this tempest. It felt like the end of days, when all but the righteous would be eternally damned. How she wished that her family were with her, Robert and the children.

Eliza was growing weary, but again she refused to take a little broth when Mary proffered it. In the dim rushlight her face shone slick, and dark tendrils clung to her temples and neck. Her cotton shift twisted round her body like river weed about a pole, and her lips shaped silent words. Mary reached for her hand and gently stroked it. She could make no promises, but could offer up prayers that the life of her daughter and the child be spared. Low like a growling cur came the rumble of distant thunder, and then as though in the presence of angels, the room was filled with silver light. With the first thunder clap, the rain at last began to fall.

2

August 1699. Keighley

The Reverend Gale took up his quill with the intention of writing to his friend and physician Dr. Martin Lister. The pain in his stomach persisted, and he feared it was the stone. He would not ride out this day, but would send word to his clerk to attend to parish business. He had slept very ill the night past, and Margery had found him, framed by moonlight, his eyes towards the dark form of his church. Was it sickness of the body or mind that tormented him? In vexation at himself, he crept quietly down the spiral stone stair and across the moonlit hall to his library. Here, unwilling to light a candle, he ran his hands across his desk until his fingers found the rock. His excitement at receiving this latest sample that day was probably the cause of his unrest. Jabez Lambert had arrived at his door that morning with the stone he had carried back from a lonely moorland watercourse. Within its rugged fabric could be discerned a shell-like form, set like a reed in winter ice. Knowing that the Reverend Gale was a learned man who found pleasure in novelties such as this, he had slipped it into his jerkin knowing that his reward would be a free breakfast. Gale had spent the rest of his day pulling volumes from his shelves, and poring over steel point drawings. Frustrated by the noise of his four young children and his inability to identify to his satisfaction the creature trapped within the stone, he had resolved to write to Dr. Lister.

Margery knocked lightly on the door, and with a small dry kiss to his bristly head, delivered his warm milk and the small bottle of syrup of roses. This, he hoped, would relieve the pain in his belly. In a rambling missive he described the symptoms of his malaise and the remedies he had administered on his friend's recommendation. On the whole he was feeling better now that the faintness had passed. He cursed his constitution and this place that had brought him so low. Of more importance, he went on to write of the new rock sample and the site of its discovery. He sketched in the margin a map of the moorland and made particular mention of its lying in the shallow brook. He would carefully wrap the stone in cloth, and have it delivered to Lister in York. Here the great scientific minds of the day might be confounded, and conclude that indeed this was something never before seen. In time the new discovery could bear his name, guaranteeing immortality. His grumbling innards however made him think, sourly, likely not.

It was almost twenty years since he had arrived in Keighley to take up his appointment as Rector on the resignation of the previous incumbent. With his young wife Margery, and a baby on the way, they had travelled from his father's seat at Farnley, across the wild uplands and heath until they had reached to valley of the Aire and the ancient church of Keighley parish. In his youth, Miles had been an ambitious man. As a younger son, he would not inherit the family estate, so, as was custom, a career in the church was settled. During his Cambridge years his eyes had been opened to the worlds of science and philosophy in addition to his theological studies. As the country settled again under its King after the tumult of the civil war, the future promised much for a man like Gale. His sights were set on the city of York, as a seat of learning and ecclesiastical import; he had often walked its warren of gates and prayed at the great church of St Peter. With its many parish churches, he saw himself as a gentleman priest who, at leisure, could indulge his passion for knowledge. When word had come from the bishop of the vacancy at Keighley, he had swallowed his bitter words and accepted the post with all the grace he could muster.

Only the arrival of his first born son in the early months could sweeten the bile he felt at his fate. His parish seemed like a penance. The straggle of some hundred houses about the ancient church represented the town itself, though the extent of the parish boundaries stretched some ten miles end to end. Tiny hamlets turned in on themselves, renouncing the world, lone farmsteads not fit for beasts, and everywhere, cattle and sheep.

The Rectory was at least commodious, and of recent design. He was cheered by the horse at his disposal in the stable. Margery, with her gentle disposition and sweet nature, had declared it a fine house, though at the time, the arrival of the child preoccupied her. The first Sunday, he rose from his bed and walked the across the green to the church. His parishioners numbered barely thirty, and he rued the hours he had spent on his sermon. His theme had been the fall of man, from the book of Genesis. It seemed an appropriate place to start, and, he like Adam felt cast down. As his words rose and fell he would, at intervals, glance up, and catch the eye of one of his flock, an elderly woman almost bereft of hair. It seemed the rest of the congregation were more intent on looking at each other. Even as his voice rose to the dramatic exile from Eden, it was met by a blanket indifference. The service ended with an exasperated benediction and his parishioners seeping from the church, mostly to the ale-house.

It took many weeks to learn that his congregation was small mainly because of the popularity of the Quakers and other dissenters. The valley's wild nature seemed mirrored by its people, who had, in former days, rejected the King, and also the established church. Their ways were to stand in fields and wild places to hear the words of their preachers, or meet in upper rooms in silence like rats behind panelling. His mood darkened as the days shortened and winter approached. Even his rosy cheeked son and merry wife could not raise his spirits.

More than anything he missed the quick minds of his fellow students. Here, where books were as rare as pearls, any intellectual discourse would have to be at a distance. Anxious that his brain did not turn to cheese, he sent to Farnley for his books which arrived some weeks later. He spent less time on writing sermons, preferring instead to write letters to his Cambridge friends. With the arrival of that first spring, and despite the many invitations he had written to family and friends alike, he had had no visitors. Sorrowfully, he compared himself to St Jerome in the desert, at which Margery merely smiled. In darker moments he wrote letters to the bishop, bemoaning his lot, but it was felt best that Miles remain in Keighley, to seek to increase his congregation.

The beauteous countryside about him did not compensate for the wretched lives of his parishioners which filled him with despair. Although they lived by the seasons, and toiled gainfully in the fields, mills and mines, their ignorance made them no better than beasts. With the birth of each base child, and the end of each life unmarked, he began to feel that God had forsaken, these, his people, and in turn, they had forsaken God. He enquired of his clerk, George Heaton, if there was anyone who was able to sign his name with more than a mark, or able to read the catechism. Aside from the gentlemen whose manor houses were scattered thinly about the valley, Heaton was able to name but six.

The following Sunday at the end of service, by the church door, he quietly asked members of the departing flock if they would be interested in learning their alphabet. Most eyed him with suspicion and shuffled away, but James Crossley, with his plump wife and two fair sons seemed to consider the notion. Although his days were spent scratching coal, he hated to think of his sons' golden hair for ever black, their faces streaked with dust and grime. He could not offer them money or land, nor even a home that was not tied to the mine, but an education would be some small inheritance.

The Crossleys lived in the hamlet of Thwaites, on the valley road to Bingley. The Reverend Gale visited their cottage. It consisted of a single fire house with a ladder up to sleeping quarters, and little in the way of furniture. He had brought with him two small slates and chalk, and his own childhood alphabet. Sarah could barely raise her eyes to him, and offered him bread and ale for his troubles. He politely declined. The boys, James and Michael, uttered not a word during the hour he spent with them, but followed his instruction with diligence.

For the next few months he called upon the Crossley's twice weekly, and his spirit rose to see how the boys progressed. By his third visit, they even thanked him. Returning to Keighley one evening, he was heartened to see bold letters scratched into the sandy dirt. He was being shown what God wanted from him, and though the immensity of the task seemed hopeless, he could but try to rise to the challenge.

Over the ensuing years, the word began to spread, and indifference gave way to curiosity. James and Michael proved themselves worthy of his efforts. Although James did become a miner like his father, Michael left the valley to seek his fortune, and in later years became a shopkeeper in the town of Manchester. The Reverend Gale began to gain the trust of parishioners, and, in ones and twos, they began to arrive at his door, or linger after church and ask that they might learn.

His days began to fill, and in spite of his initial disdain, he grew to admire his flock, for although taciturn, they learnt their letters with the enthusiasm of Trinity scholars.

During the long summer evenings, he would saddle up the horse and take to the hills with his books and a small portable desk, visiting his widely scattered class. Margery relished those evenings when he returned, red of face in the dying light, full of tales and contentment.

3

November 1697 Holden Gate

Robert Gawthorp leant against the porch of the great barn and breathed heavily. Behind him, and, beyond the oak door, he imagined that he could hear her weeping. The wind tore at his thin hair as it gusted up from the valley, the lone tree at the gate dancing wildly. The light would be gone in a couple of hours, and he needed to get to Ghyllgrange before nightfall. Wiping his face, still wet from her tears, he called for his dogs and took the track that led away from house and climbed onto moorland edge. Over and over in his mind he pictured her and convinced himself that he had seen the same desire in her eyes. When she had tried to pull away from him, it was her shame at betraying her mother. He'd forced her to look him in the eye and assured her that Mary should never know of her wickedness. As he'd walked away her arm still bore the marks of his fingers, like cinders in the snow. He told her that he would return from Ghyllgrange in the morning at first light, and that she was to tell Mary that she had stumbled whilst crossing a ditch. With her hands full of fire sticks and the bank treacherous with moss, who would question it?

Gawthorp had arrived at Holden some five years past. Mary, the widow Fowler, had struggled to maintain the farmstead after the death of Thomas, relying on her brother Francis and his men to help with the crops, whilst Thomas had left her funds to pay a stockman. The girls, all aged under ten, helped their mother about the house, their faces solemn as they watched silent tears slide into Mary's lap as she worked her spindle in the firelight. It was clear that Mary had to find a new husband, for she could not for ever rely on Francis.

The Gawthorps were sheep farmers in the low hills on the far side of the Aire. Robert, the youngest son stood a head higher than his father and brothers, and in spite of his prodigious appetite, his spare flesh clung tight to his bones. He had been born on a cold February morning, and was thought unlikely to last the day. His eyes, dark as the winter night and full of fury, conveyed his intent to survive, but he did not, or would not cry. His silence marked him out, and defined his boyhood. His brothers laughed together as they worked in the fields alongside their father and at night as they crawled up to their bed in the rafters. But Robert kept his counsel. He listened as his mother fretted over the son who laboured hard yet sought no reward in the company of friends or conversation. As the years passed and the boys grew to be men, Robert spent his resting hours walking the hills until darkness blotted the sky, and smoke from the chimney became a dancing figure in the moonlight.

He said little, as each Sunday, the family would walk down to the river, across the stone bridge, and on to the church at Kildwick. Although the ancient church was large, its many pews remained empty and forlorn, and even on summer mornings those attending divine service shivered in their Sunday best. The Reverend Pollard, who had known Robert since he was but a boy, was always heartened and yet unnerved by his presence. Unlike the rest of the congregation, who bowed their heads during the sermon, in reverence, or possibly reverie, Robert held his gaze. His dark eyes, that blinked slowly, seemed to seek out the hidden corners of his soul. One day, at the church door, the Reverend Pollard had enquired whether Robert was considering a life in the church, for he seemed to show such interest. The thin smile and cold rebuke confirmed that Robert's weekly presence had nothing to do with God.

In spite of his quiet ways, there was little that Robert did not know of other people's lives, joys and tragedies. A stranger to the ale-house, which his brothers often frequented, he paid great heed when they came home, animated with tales of people's fortunes and misfortunes. His preference when not walking the hills was to carve and whittle small items in holly and hazel wood. Sitting on a low stool where shadows met the fire's reach he would listen to their stories, as he worked with his knife, and store them like a squirrel preparing for winter.

One day he had crossed the old stone bridge, and carried on walking to the hills that rose up on the far side of the Aire. Going by the village of Silsden, which echoed with the urgent hammering of the nail makers, he took the moorland track until he arrived at Holden. In front of the huge porched barn, two small girls chased an angry black chicken in a wild dance across the broad stone pavement. They stopped at his approach and called out to their mother. Robert greeted them sombrely, and the three figures remained motionless until Mary appeared from the low, front door of the house. She recognised him at once from church, but as they had never spoken a word to each other, she was puzzled as to his presence. Removing his felt cap, he offered his services as a labourer, to help with the sowing of the oat crop. Blushing and awkward, she thanked him for his offer, but explained that she would be unable to pay him. Undeterred, he insisted that it was his Christian duty to help, and that his efforts were no longer needed at the Gawthorp farm. Although proud, Mary was pragmatic and agreed that in return for his help, she could offer him food and shelter. With a smile that barely graced his lips, he promised to return the following day. That night as Mary kissed her children before sleep, she offered up a silent prayer to a God that had seen fit to reward her piety with this blessing. That night as his family finished their evening meal, Robert announced that he was leaving, and would not be returning.

Gawthorp arrived at Holden in the heavy dew of a warm spring morning. Mary watched from the window at the tall thin figure approaching and disappearing as he made his way along the undulating road from Silsden. Much of the land was given over to cattle, and on the higher pastures her sheep roamed as far as the Doubler Stones on the top of the moor. In front of the farm, in the gently sloping land that faced into the valley, Thomas had cultivated oats, hay and some holly, which fed the cattle and sheep throughout the long dark winter.

Mary ushered Robert into the parlour where the fresh laid fire crackled and spat, and offered him some bread and pottage. He declined, but said he would avail himself of a small beer. Afterwards, she walked him across to the great barn where her horse was tethered and Thomas's plough was kept. Examining the rough splintered handle, Robert pronounced that before he began work in the field, he would repair the plough. She pointed to a forlorn rack of tools that had not been removed from the wall since Thomas's death. As she reached the open doorway of the barn, returning to the house, she looked back to see him running his long fingers over the blades, chisels and saws.

As the morning had worn on her chores about the house kept her occupied. Her girls brought in eggs they had hunted from around the yard and under the low hedge. Together they had washed linen shifts and tethered them with stones on the springy grass behind the house, to dry in the spring sunshine. As the sun stood at its highest point in the sky Gawthorp emerged from the barn, dragging the great plough. Its blade glistened afresh, its handles pale where new wood had been spliced in. Leading out the horse, his fingers ran the length of its flank as he fitted the leather harness and yolk, attaching the creature to the plough.

He took small refreshment, then began leading the horse across the track and onto the stubbled grass that sloped gently down towards the valley. As the plough broke the earth, the sun momentarily disappeared behind a thin gossamer cloud, and the figure of Gawthorp fell into the rhythmic tread of the horse. Throughout the day, Mary paused in her work to observe him, his figure bent slightly as a wind-fashioned tree; he paused only once when she brought small ale, but seemed unwilling to pass the time of day with her. She returned to the house where her girls gathered near the open doorway.

By the end of that first day, the ground was one third ploughed; by the second day, it was finished. On the third day, he asked for her hand in marriage. His proposal was direct and terse. She laughed, believing it mischief, but he assured her that he was in earnest, and the smile faded from her lips. She asked his age, and when he replied three and twenty years, she retorted that she had lived his life and half again, had buried a husband, and had four young daughters. He swore that he could be a good husband to her. He had proved himself to be strong and hard working, and would ensure that the future of Holden was secure.

She studied his face, so unlike that of Thomas which, though ridged and wind worn, had a softness about the eyes. Pinkened by the weak spring sunshine, Robert's face was as sharp and unyielding as a quoin. She thanked him, and begged that he allow her time to dwell upon his offer. That night as the children drowsed, she stared into the peat flame and pondered if Gawthorp be an angel sent from God, or the temptation of Satan.

He no longer walked down to the church in Kildwick on Sunday mornings, instead toiling with the land and animals of Holden. Mary attended service with the children each week, silently seeking the answer to Robert's offer. One Sunday in May, prayers were offered up for the soul of Esther Gawthorp whose body had been laid to rest earlier that week. On her return to Holden, Mary had found Robert stacking peat to dry against the barn, and had carefully asked when he had last heard from his family. He studied her face so long and without reply, that she reach out and took his hand, and explained gently that his mother had died. His expression did not change, but she saw a slight clenching of his jaw. He thanked her for letting him know and then turned back to his work. This was the last time that his family was ever mentioned.

As the summer drew on and the land softened green and gold, Mary approached Robert one late afternoon as the air shimmered with dancing insects. She had watched him toil these many weeks; he had left the farm only to walk the high moor to tend her sheep. In return he had taken but meagre refreshments, and had bedded down in the great barn at the close of day, declining to sit with her at the hearth and talk about what the day had brought. The children had, at first, viewed him with the curiosity they may have shown for a newborn lamb, or a nest of tiny eggs glimpsed through a hedgerow. Ann, the eldest, had asked questions of him, of his family, of his home, but he would only smile and hold her eye for so long that she became ill at ease. Before long, the girls knew to keep their distance from him as they would a feral cat. Mary had spoken with her brother of Robert's proposal. Francis had not had cause to visit Holden as often since Robert's arrival. The two men had spoken only of farming matters, and whilst walking the land each focused their gaze on the distant violet hills. Francis reassured Mary that Robert would safeguard the future of Holden, but in her belly she sensed the flutter of unease that she had felt from the morning of his arrival.

Putting aside her worries, she held his gaze as she offered her hand in marriage.

The wedding took place in the parish church of Kildwick on an early September morning. The crops had been gathered and the church was still garlanded in thanksgiving for a successful harvest. Mary had removed the simple gold band that Thomas had placed on her finger so many years before. She carried it with her in a small purse at her waist. The church danced in the dust of the long dead as Robert placed another ring upon her finger, and in the company of her girls, her father and brothers, she became his wife. That evening they had sat together in front of the fire for many hours, their company punctuated only rarely by talk. As they climbed into bed an owl could be heard somewhere close at hand, its spectral cry signalling the beginning of the night's hunt.

4

October 1699 Marley

Nathan Gill and John walked beneath the arched gateway of Marley Hall, and there they were met in the paved yard by a squat woman of indeterminate years who asked of them their business. From an aisled barn to the left, a handsome mare was being led out by a lad who barely reached its withers. Its head nodded in appreciation of the light and its hide gleamed like polished oak. Nathan enquired of the woman as to whether Mr Parker was at home. She replied that he was at present, but the horse was being saddled for his departure to Bingley. Nathan introduced himself as a tenant who required but a few moments of his time; she bade them follow her. As they entered through the low porch, their eyes struggled to become accustomed to the dim light of the panelled hallway. Leaving them alone as she went to seek Mr Parker, they glanced about them, admiring the pewter flatware on the low table and the ornate candle stems and sconces. Grinning nervously at each other, they removed their caps and smoothed down their shirts.

Presently the woman reappeared and indicated that they should follow her. She led them into a parlour illuminated from either side by broad leaded windows. In front of a fireplace so finely carved it seemed alive stood Mr Robert Parker. Although not a tall man his presence was amplified by the brightness his coat and the neatness of his wig. The blue and white were the colours of a summer sky. He sucked away at a thin briar pipe which he tapped at intervals into the fire.

He recognised Nathan as one of his tenant farmers who had rented from him the small cottage and land that lay at the point where the sloping hills met the valley floor. The other man was a stranger to him. Nathan introduced John Asquith, a boyhood friend who had arrived two months past seeking work. He had helped Nathan bring in the harvest, and they were now building stone walls marking the boundary of the land. He could vouchsafe for John's character and strength and his willingness to work. Could Mr Parker find work for the boy around his estate? Mr Parker liked Nathan Gill and his pretty young wife. The land he had been given was poor, stony and sloping, but he had watched him gathering rocks from the land and piling them up to form a new hill close by the cottage. Together with his land agent, Mr Parker had paced out the extent of Nathan's land, and marked it with wooden stakes.

The land had for centuries been rough pasture for sheep and cattle but with work and enclosure, he could see how crops could be grown and money made. The cottage which had not been built in living memory required a new roof which Nathan had attended to with cheerful purpose. Only then had he been able to take a wife. He had arrived with a letter from his village priest attesting to his reliability and hard-working nature. This he had presented to Mr Parker when he had first arrived in Marley. It could, however, have declared him the greatest rogue in Christendom for all Nathan knew, as he could neither read nor write. Mr Parker had read the letter with interest, and, admiring his enterprise, had given him a chance.

John was almost the same height as Natahan and as dark eyed as Nathan's grey eyes were pale. Both were broad about the shoulder and strong in leg, their skins darkened from hours spent in the fields. Mr Parker asked of his family. John explained that his mother was dead and his father's farm was too small to support three sons. Although only seventeen years old, the boy had a maturity and purpose about him that impressed Mr Parker. There was much work to be done about his estate. With the burgeoning population, even the poorest tracts of land could be improved and farmed. There were stones to be cleared and lime to be spread. If the boy could tolerate a winter of hard labour, and if Nathan could feed and house him until then, he could not see a problem. He was to spend half the week working with Nathan, and the rest of his time at the disposal of Mr Parker's estate manager. With a nod of the head they were then dismissed into the hallway.

The day was bright and becalmed, and although there was work to be done, Nathan suggested that they celebrate John's good fortune with a little sport. Stopping only to collect netting at the cottage, the pair headed down towards the river. They chose a spot where the Aire swept wide and drove slowly across the rocky floor of the valley. In the shallow margins, minnow and dace flicked in and out of the shadows. Casting off his boots, Nathan edged slowly into the water; his breath caught at the chill of it. Three tall posts roughly hewn of tree branch had been staked out into the river, about which he festooned his net. John, holding the other end of the net, anchored it under a large rock. As Nathan splashed his way out of the river he looked along the Keighley road, where, trailed by a low dust train, a horse approached. The creature moved slowly, but even at a distance noisily. A figure dressed entirely in black bounced rhythmically in the saddle, and at either flank clattered wooden boxes. As the horse neared, Nathan recognised its rider. It was the Reverend Gale, with his small white collar flapping at his neck like a butterfly. On seeing the two young men at the riverbank, he touched his broad-brimmed hat. The boys raised their hands in acknowledgement. As the horse drew level, and then passed them heading towards Bingley, Miles Gale began to sing, his words in time with the clatter of the boxes that beat a tattoo into the distance.

The afternoon wore on, and Nathan and John collected firewood from beneath the ancient oaks that ranged along the margins of the riverbank. Though they knew the old tale of Satan amongst the brambles forbidding the eating of the fruit after Michaelmas, the plump blackberries that studded the tangle proved too tempting. The boys crammed them into their mouths until their chins ran purple. As the sun began its slow descent over the treetops, Nathan again removed his boots and waded into the water. Swiftly drawing in his net, he laughed with delight at his bounty, a large eel that seemed to writhe in anger at its own stupidity. Still swathed in the netting, he dashed its head against the large rock, thrilled at the prospect of a good supper.

Days began to fall into a pattern for John. Rising with the first intrusion of light and the choir of birdsong, he would join Nathan and Jennet around the fire. Rubbing his hands, he waited until Jennet served him a bowl of pottage and pelt-like oatcake from the ceiling rack. Together the three would take breakfast in the gloom of the parlour, feeling warmth spreading through their bodies. On the days John worked with Nathan, they would first attend the mound that marked the lime pit. For half the week, lime smouldered away in the pit, for two days it cooled. The finished lime was collected and spread the following day, and the pit refilled and fired the day after. Although he feared the lime pit and knew its dangers, John was also fascinated by its alchemy, the ancient miracle that converted rock into this material that enabled crops to grow where before nothing thrived. Nathan was now literally reaping its benefits, but there was yet more work to do. The clearing of stones that scattered the land was wearisome, but his labour kept him warm as the wind swung in from the north bringing the certainty of winter. On the days spent working for Mr Parker, John worked on the intack, the upsloping land being reclaimed from the moor. Alongside three other labourers, he cut turves of heather, turning and stacking it in preparation for the elements to begin the progress of decay. Ditches were dug, latticing the land, a back-breaking task that seemed to provide little obvious result for the effort expended. The ground would be sown the coming year with grass for cattle pasture, and so sweetened that eventually crops could be grown.

Bending into the wind that barrelled off the high moor, growing more vicious and wet with each passing week, John felt the season change. Each day brought a straggle of strangers, picking their way wearily down from the high moor: men from the north where, word had it, the harvest had failed yet again. They trailed the drovers the long trek southwards, whip thin with faces tanned the colour of peat, seeking any work anywhere. Dreadful rumours went about: the Scots would eat their own kin it was said. The incomers were, for the most part, ignored and feared. People had long memories, and the Scots were not to be trusted; most continued the journey south beyond the parish boundaries. John wondered at their fate, but thanked God for his own good fortune.

With the coming of the first hard frost, which hurried in with a mighty fall of snow, livestock became the concern. Sheep on the high moor had to be fed, together with cattle in the lowland pastures. John loved being away from the intack. Although he walked many miles with the hay-laden pack-horse, once up on the high moor his step quickened, his soul lightened. He called out to the flock scattered across the land like an army , and laughed as they pitched towards him as though charging into battle. As he spread the hay, he loved the feel of their urgent bodies seeking food, and the damp warmth of their breath that engulfed him like a rising cloud. Making his way down the slope, he could see that the sun in its passage had wiped the frost from the roof of Marley Hall like dust from a dresser. The horse, sensing the comfort of the barn, hastened its step.

Advent was marked by the gathering of holly and ivy, which Jennet placed about the windows. The days were now so short that John spent evenings picking through oily fleece, removing thorns and teasels ready for Jennet to spin. Other times, Nathan and he would work at a cradle being fashioned of oak gathered in the autumn from a great fallen bough. In the darkest hours, he lay listening to the soft cries of Jennet and Nathan in their pleasure, which would surely bring a new life to fill the cradle.

5

December 6th 1699. Keighley

The Reverend Gale was in an ill-humour. The day had begun, as happened each Wednesday, with the family being woken before dawn by the setting up of the market at the market cross. The Rectory overlooked the market square where, each week, a congregation gathered, far greater than that which worshipped each Sunday. With the clatter of handcarts and chorus of voices animal and human, the town mustered about the ancient stone cross. The caccophony of whistles, bleats, laughter and obscenities, tore him from slumber, and into the bleak reality of another winter morning. Carefully alighting from the bed, he reached down for the chamber pot. At the sound of his water Margery stirred, and from the chamber next door he heard the boards creak as the children arose.

His thoughts turned to his eldest child Christopher who, some months past, had departed for the New World. As yet there had been no word, though in his heart he knew he was unlikely to hear anything for many weeks. In Christopher he saw himself as a young man. He had been a contented child who sometimes accompanied Miles about the parish and had a deep interest in the natural world;

his sharp intellect obliged Miles to continue the boy's education elsewhere. A career in the church did not appeal, and quietly Miles was glad. When he expressed a desire to study at law, his father had no objection.

For three years he had been articled to a practice in Lancaster, where he had proved himself a popular if argumentative student. That summer he had returned to the Rectory. One late afternoon in his father's study whilst examining fossils, he had expressed his wish to seek his fortune in the American colonies. Miles was at once surprised, and a little angry. On reflection, he realised that the rage he felt was at his own lack of fulfilment that endured like a stain on linen. The following day he had given Christopher his blessing and apologised for his disagreeable temper. Margery's tears had sprung purely from fear and love. Her anger at Miles was to endure unspoken down the years.

His boys Miles and Thomas would be arriving home the next week at the end of Michaelmas term, Thomas studious and taciturn, Miles, restless and funny. The sense of excitement had been growing amongst the younger children of the house, especially in Marianne who missed them both dreadfully. Each time there was a knock of the door, she would appear at the head of the stairs, her small round face tight with expectation. Her grief at their departure to school had seemed almost boundless, in particular for Miles, whose presence filled the house with brightness and mirth. In the days after he left, the great clock in the hall seemed somehow louder, the shadows of the house darker.

The Reverend Gale dressed with haste as the morning was chill. Downstairs in the parlour, Sarah the house girl clattered and swept about the kitchen. The scent of bread rolled up the stairs and under each door. Perhaps a little coffee and eggs might improve his disposition. Gathering up his wig from the stand and adjusting it to his satisfaction, he leaned in to give Margery a faint kiss and then headed down to the parlour. The room afforded a little respite from the noise of the market, being at the rear of the house, nevertheless above the crackle of the fire in the grate he could still hear the orchestra of commerce being conducted at his doorstep. Sarah appeared at the door with a bob, her eyes not meeting his. He requested a pot of coffee, eggs and a little cheese, though he knew, shamefully, that his physician Lister advised against it.

As he waited he thought about what the day would bring. That morning he had two funerals at which to officiate, winter's savagery wheedling out the weak and infirm. The ground in the churchyard was so frozen, and the steady arrival of the dead so unrelenting, that the sexton had been digging for over a month. Having officiated, he would return to the Rectory for dinner.

Today the family would be joined by the overseers of the parish. Talk of the poor relief, which was being sorely stretched by the influx of Scots migrants would be postponed until after the meal and the departure of Margery and the children. He found these meetings to be almost unendurable in their length and hostility. He prayed that God would grant him the patience to maintain his humour and good grace. The monthly meetings would often end in acrimony and raised voices that not even a good claret could rectify.

Depending on the length of the meeting, which he was always able to end with his call to evensong, he planned to speak with Samuel Greenwood who lived in a small house just off the market square. Samuel, it was said, had fathered the child of Martha Chambers. A comely girl of twenty years with hair the colour of winter beech, she swore that Samuel had promised to marry her. He now denied any such contract and was indeed seeking the hand in marriage of Elizabeth Woodhead. Miles had sadly recorded the baptism in the name of Samuel, the base son of Martha. It was common knowledge about the town that Samuel was indeed the father, and he had been heard boasting in the ale-house of how he had lain with Martha in his own father's hayloft. Miles had now to persuade Samuel, who had already made it known that he would not marry Martha, that he would have to pay to the parish maintenance for the child. Although he rarely saw Samuel in church and had never had the occasion to speak with him, Miles knew his father to be a reasonable man. It would be an uncomfortable conversation nonetheless.

Before supper, Miles had a number of letters to write. He was eager to entreat Ralph Thoresby, the notable historian and antiquarian of Leeds, to visit. Having lately abandoned his long association with the dissenters, he now embraced the established church. Miles was eager to make his acquaintance and to impress him with his substantial collection of curios. He must also write to his cousin Thomas Gale who was in failing bodily health yet still keen of intellect. Over the years they had enjoyed a lively correspondence on matters both spiritual and esoteric. Given his cousin's precarious health, Miles knew that he must try to make the journey to York to see Thomas before it was too late.

Supper was the favourite meal of the day. That evening it was to be mutton pie and a good beef broth, and already Miles could imagine the taste of it. With the children abed, he and Margery could then spend a little time in domestic discourse, flimsy and light, which somehow calmed and eased him into gentle sleep.

In the event, the day had not progressed in the way he had imagined. The funerals had been conducted in haste, largely due to the inclement weather. The church was little warmer than the graveyard, and the mourners' breath billowed over the pews, jagged with each muffled sob. Leaving the churchyard to the sexton piling earth and snow noisily into the open graves, Miles made his way through the market. Picking his way carefully among the carpet of straw, dung and ice, and the traffic of geese, chickens and dogs, his passage was halted by a broad swaying figure. He recognised the obstruction at once as Michael Pighells. A fellow overseer of the poor and shortly to be dinner guest, he seemed eager to engage Miles in conversation. Michael had a face that seemed scrubbed raw by the winter wind which also appeared to have removed much of his hair. Vestiges of grey twine flapped about his face, catching his eyes and causing them to water. For such a large man his voice was alarmingly womanly and shrill. He took the Reverend by the elbow and steered him through the crush of bodies towards the ale-house, insisting that he had to speak in confidence of a pressing matter in advance of the meeting. Dipping their heads and removing hats, the men entered the ale-house.

The air was grey with pipe smoke and heavy with the scent of wet woollen cloth. At the sight of the Reverend, a group of men gave up their settle close to the fire. Out of the corner of one eye, Miles could see the figure of Samuel Greenwood disappearing out of the door and into the market. Armed with tankards of ale, Michael leaned in towards Miles and began speaking. At several points, Miles was forced to ask him to repeat himself, as his words were smothered in the blanket of other voices. It was clear that Michael had a grievance, and the issue was Miles himself, and his plans for the church renovations. Although Michael was a regular churchgoer, accompanied each Sunday by his wife, children, and grandchildren, his attendance was one of convention rather than conviction. In his opinion the repairs to the church were a luxury that the parish could ill afford to meet, particularly when the poor rate was being stretched almost to breaking point with the arrival of the itinerant Scots. In addition, the parishioners could not be expected to provide even more statute Work at this, the darkest time of the year, when they struggled to fulfill their own necessary labours.

Miles could feel his neck growing red as his frustration and anger mounted. Each year it was the same; as he sought to improve the fabric of his church, he was met with howls of indignation. In their ignorance, these people could not see beyond the immediacy of the seasons, content to live as their forebears had lived. Michael was the personification of this intransigence, unwilling to meet change for the common good. Miles was being warned off raising the subject of church repairs, and though couched in gentle tones, the meaning was as sharp and jagged as ice. Miles could not trust himself to remain Godly, and thus rose to his feet, bidding Michael good day, promising to continue their discussion within the hour at the Rectory.

Miles was thankful for the slap of cold air that met him as he opened the door back into the market. With a little time at his disposal, and his senses keen, he decided to pay an early visit to Samuel Greenwood. His ill-humour increased when, in spite of his loud hammering at the Greenwood door, there was no reply. Father and son, like as not, could now be found in another of the town's taverns, like foxes buried deep in the earth.

He had little alternative then but to return to the Rectory, where he stamped about in cold and anger, slamming his study door to the rest of the family. He then attempted to begin his written correspondence, but found that the words would not come, lost behind images of the broken church windows and the womanly simper of Michael Pighells repeating in his head.

Outside in the passage, he heard the front door opening and shutting, announcing the arrival of his dinner guests. He determined that he would keep them waiting, justifying himself by attempting to assuage his bad temper. There was nothing to be gained by arguing his case with his fellow overseers, they outnumbered him five to one. He directed a silent prayer to God, seeking the fortitude to deliver him of his troubles, and the reassurance that his purpose was indeed divine will.

Some hours later, having taken the evensong witnessed by a congregation of six, he reflected that perhaps God had not heeded his prayers that day. The meeting had been long and fractious, all mention of church repairs, the founding of a school and an increase in statute work had been deflected into the new year – new century, he thought wryly. His fellow overseers had been happy to drink his claret and enjoy his food, but declined to listen to his ideas. Shamefully, his voice had grown louder as the afternoon had worn on yet could not compete with the chorus of naysayers. God's divine presence had not been a guest at dinner that day. So weary was he that, after evensong, he returned to the Rectory directly, postponing his visit to Samuel Greenwood. He managed a perfunctory letter to his cousin Thomas, and demanded an early supper. Dismissing his children at the soonest opportunity, he sadly reflected that he could find no joy in the mutton pie that evening. Margery, who could read his wordless countenance, suggested they retire to the chamber early, citing a headache. For this kindness alone he gave thanks to God.

6

December 6th 1699. Holden Gate

Mary knew that the baby in her belly was growing impatient to greet the world. Each day was becoming a greater struggle, and in her heart she knew that this child would likely be her last. She had seen forty summers and hair that once held the colour of stones in the moorland stream now was as grey and coarse as the Doubler Stones. Each night she questioned God on why she had been undeserving of a son. Six daughters had been her blessing, all strong and fair, though only Eliza dark as Thomas, who still haunted her dreams though it was almost ten years since he had been laid in the earth. Together they had produced four daughters, yet he had always believed that she would, one day, produce a son. With each birth he had kissed her forehead and given thanks to God. Any disappointment he may have felt he kept hidden deep within his heart. Since her marriage to Robert there had been two more children, both girls. His attitude towards them had been different than to her girls. The older children were by turn scolded and ignored, the younger children simply ignored. It was clear that she had to produce a boy; for Robert, it was the only way he could maintain his claim on Holden.

In many ways God had been bountiful she reminded herself. She could not imagine what would have become of them all had not Robert arrived as he did. In the darkest corner of her soul, however, she berated herself for her impatience. Had she not leapt with indecent haste at his proposal? Had he known that she would?

She walked across to the window, her youngest daughter Hannah grasping at her skirts. The older girls Ann and Eliza had walked down to Keighley that morning to the market. They had taken a basket of eggs and some butter that they hoped to sell. If successful, they had been told to buy a little salted pork, and some linen from the draper's. The baby would need a shift, as the robe which had served six children was now little more than darned holes. The light would soon be gone, and Mary sensed that the girls would likely delay their journey home. There had been a moon the past two nights but the sky was now heavy with snow. She lit a rush lamp and placed it on the mullion frame.

Ann and Eliza had woken at the crow of the cock, but remained in each other's arms. Their breath curled about them as they whispered to each other, trying not to waken the younger girls. When at last they heard their mother bid farewell to Robert, and the heavy oak door slam shut, they bundled out of their bed. Dressing quickly, they made haste downstairs to the warmth of the parlour. Mary was setting platters about the table, and the room was gently scented with fresh oatcakes warming above the fire. Her movements were slow, her steps small and her face set hard against the day. She had already gathered the eggs and placed them in a deep basket which she had carefully lined with straw. The butter, neatly wrapped in muslin strips, was in a shallow trug. The girls knew that there was not time to linger over breakfast if they were to ensure a place beneath a pentice in case the threatening snow began to fall.

As they made their way down the hill, picking up the track that wound its way to the town, they were joined by other folk old and young, making their way to the market cross. At the hurry of footsteps the girls turned to see Rebekah and George Snowden making up ground to catch them. The Snowdens lived up at Ghyllgrange, almost the highest point on the moor. Tenants of the Rishworth family, they had maintained sheep for three generations on the moorland pastures. George, the eldest child, would continue their tenancy of the farmstead, which clung like a gall to the side of Ghyllgrange itself. Today he appeared as a giant with a great cargo of woollen yarn, spun throughout the quickening days of autumn, held in a blanket and tied at his chest. He and Rebekah would sell the wool to Edward Sharp whose livelihood was the weaving of cloth, which he practised at a loom which clattered ceaselessly in his tiny parlour. With some of the money they received, George and Rebekah would visit Leach the grocer to purchase soap, tobacco and flour.

As the four figures picked their way down towards the town, their steps hastened. The market square was already alive with the crush of morning commerce. Continuing their journey past the church to the house of Edward Sharp, Rebekah and George bade farewell to the girls, Ann's gaze following them until they were lost in the crowd. Finding a narrow window ledge on a corner which offered shelter from the snow but not the wind's icy pinch, the girls camped, clutching their baskets in their laps. The crowd, a great serpent, flexed and twisted about the confines of the square. Violent laughter ended in a viscous rattling cough as an old woman selling coneys hung from a frame greeted a neighbour.

Ann and Eliza sat together, speaking only when making a sale, huddling into each other, and drawing their late father's camlet cloak about their shoulders. They remembered the times when their mother would bring them as young children down to the market. As she sold eggs, cheese and butter, and sometimes bilberries gathered from the moor, they would weave between legs like mice through the grass. They knew to avoid the geese that drew themselves tall and flapped and chased, but greeted each dog as an ally in their miniature world. If Mary had managed to sell her wares, or at least a good portion, there might be a sweet treat for the children, spice cake or apple bread, which they savoured as they made their way back up to Holden. Everything had changed with the arrival of Gawthorp, however. He forbade Mary from visiting the market, and, as he seldom had cause to be in Keighley himself, it became the work of the children to sell at market each week. They could only now savour the memories of the sweetmeats, the delicate scents of which hung in the air.

Eliza, in spite of her tender years, knew to fear Gawthorp. She was not sure what it was that made Ann stiffen in his presence, but like meeting the geese in the market, she knew to be wary. She had also begun to notice the time Ann was spending alone in the great barn at his direction.

Though there was kindling to fetch, cows to milk, eggs to collect, Eliza was told to remain with Mary and the other children in the parlour. Was she the only one to notice that Gawthorp would absent himself from the hearth, often without word? Eliza would watch him cross the flags to the great barn and close the door to the evening light. After a time he would emerge, calling for his dogs and marching away up the moor, behind Holden. When Ann returned to the parlour it was always without word, her eyes cast down. Eliza was troubled for her sister, but hesitated to speak with her mother on the matter. There was something in Mary's countenance, an unspoken anger she had known when, as a young girl, she had grown restless in church. It was the same look which now bound her to silence. Those nights, as they gathered for warmth beneath the rafters, Eliza knew by her stillness that her sister did not sleep. Though she begged to know what passed between Ann and Gawthorp in the great barn, her entreaties met with no reply.

From the church gate to their right, they saw the figure of the Reverend Gale emerging to the sombre toll of the bell which sounded for the burial of the widow Beanland. A woman so bent with age that, with the turning of each season, she had seemed to dissolve into earth. How much of her was there left to bury? Eliza followed the thin black figure of the Rector weaving his way through the crush of people until he was abruptly stopped in his passage by the burly figure of Michael Pighells. At this point her view was obscured by two women who leaned in to her, eager to buy butter. When she looked up again the Rector was gone.

As the sky grew heavier with the menace of snow and the crowd thinned until they could see the entrance to the ale-house at the far side of the square, the girls knew that they were unlikely to sell any more. Women and children had seeped from the market down the narrow alleys leaving only the men who gathered in clusters, stamping feet in the fog of pipe smoke. Many of the vendors had packed away baskets and carts, counted coins, so fleetingly held, before passing them on in the shops and ale-houses of the town. Studying their baskets, Eliza was happy to find that she had sold all but two slabs of butter; Ann had barely a dozen eggs left. It was a rare day indeed when they returned to Holden with empty baskets, but today's sales would allow them to visit the butcher and the draper.

From the butcher's shop where they purchased a thin creamy slab of salted pork, it was a short walk across the square to Teal the draper. Stepping carefully over the raised threshold, the air dancing with fibres and dust, the girls were at once transported into a world apart. From floor to low ceiling the room was filled with fabric of every description. At floor level, great bales of kersey and drab, above which rolls of serge and coarse linen created a soft landscape of muted colour. Upon the narrow trestle was a tangle of laces and ribbons, and shelved high, the ghostly sheen of silk and satin.

As the only customers, they were able to linger a while as John Teal selected a fine gauge linen cloth the colour of buttermilk from which he rent a narrow length. All the while the girls ran fingers and eyes over the array of fabrics, taking in each distinct scent: earthy, animal, homely, strange. Eliza held up a slash of crimson ribbon; as she ran it through her fingers, she shuddered as the image of blood finding its way into a culvert filled her head. Replacing the ribbon she smiled shyly at Ann as she handed over the coins in return for the linen.

Once outside in the fading light of the narrow lane they knew that they should take the road back to Holden, yet Ann was hesitant, insisting that they should return to the market cross. With no reason given, Eliza was unsure, but agreed, not wishing to anger her sister. Only a few figures now peopled the square, most hugging the doorway to the ale-house. Dogs tussled over mutton bones carelessly tossed, and everywhere straw was kicked into filthy drifts. Taking Ann's arm, Eliza wondered at their business and delay. The answer soon presented itself in the shape of George and Rebekah whose animated voices grew louder as they emerged into the square. The smile that bloomed at Ann's lips was the first that Eliza had seen in many weeks, and in that moment she understood. George, relieved of his great woollen burden, towered slight above the girls. With the opening of the ale-house door, a wave of laughter heralded the beginning of their journey home. As they passed Teal's drapery, two young men emerged from the shop into the lane. With a start Eliza noticed that one dangled from his hand a length of the crimson ribbon that she had, not five minutes past, held. Laughing, they headed back towards the square, and Eliza's head turned towards their departing forms.

Only the wind's cold sting and the fulfilled promise of snow hastened their journey up the moorland track.

Rebekah walked ahead filling Eliza's ear with the course of her day, the deafness of Edward Sharp, and the plump currants to be seen at Leach's grocery. In the gathering darkness, and close in their footsteps, George and Ann walked in near silence. As they neared Holden the travellers bid farewell and the Snowdens continued their journey up to Ghyllgrange. At the parlour window a rush lamp glowed, a faint star in the vastness of the dark moor.

7

December 6ᵗʰ 1699. Marley

It was Wednesday, and the hour early. John's sleep that night had been dreamless. With a vigorous shaking of his shoulder, he was cast abruptly into the day. In the blackness he could make out no form, but as he moaned, he heard Nathan's excited voice entreating him to rise. Throwing on his britches and jerkin and feeling for his boots, he crouched his way across the floor ensuring that he didn't crack his head on the low oak beams, and followed Nathan down the ladder into the dim parlour. Jennet had not yet risen, and the room was pungent and smoke-filled as the peat fire began to take hold. Nathan held out a bowl of pottage from which a thin curl of steam rose. Together they stood in the hearth, wordlessly breaking the night's fast. When John attempted to speak, Nathan drew his forefinger to his pursed lips, and pointed towards the door.

Gathering cloaks and hats, they stepped out onto the ice-glazed cobbles, closing the door fast behind them. The air was still and keen, the purple stain of first light edging the distant hills. Nathan took John's arm and led him away from the cottage and towards the lights that defined the outline of Marley Hall, dim as stars. Once away from the cottage, Nathan could contain his excitement no more. In a cascade of words and laughter he announced that Jennet was with child. Her courses had not arrived the past two months, and she was struggling to keep food down. In his innocence, John could not understand the meaning of his friend's words. It sounded to him as though Jennet ailed, and how could this be a cause for celebration? Clasping his shoulder, Nathan grinned, explaining that she was perfectly well, and that these were the signs that foretold the birth of a child. That, and the enormous belly, he added.

As they walked together along the track towards the lime pit, Nathan explained to his friend that the baby would be born, like as not, in the high days of summer, before the business of harvest. He reassured him that his help would be of great benefit to them in the latter days when Jennet would become heavy and slow, and there would be much to do about the cottage. At this John beamed, for although he had been given no guarantees from Robert Parker that his employment would continue come the spring, his friend Nathan clearly intended him to stay.

There was also another surprise in store for John that day. Nathan was going to take him to the market in Keighley. Mr Parker had sent word that he required provisions from Leach the grocer. Normally, this would be the job of the cook, however with the coming of Christmas, there was to be much entertaining, and the cook had not the time to spare. Fattened geese in the field approached their final days, the larders were stocked with puddings and pies, hams and bacons, and on dank stone shelves cheeses aged in the darkness.

The festive preparations began before Advent, and as the days shortened so the kitchen work increased. In the oily steam of the kitchen, the cook toiled from first light until sleep overtook her as she lay back in the hearthside chair, her head drooping like a spent rose. She would wake again with a start at the noise of the kitchen lad banking the great fire in the kitchen hearth. Christmas required the stamina of youth, but with each passing year her aching bones reminded her of her fleeting mortality. After the great feast of twelfth night, the culmination of her efforts, Mr Parker was generous in his remuneration; as the guests departed she could help herself to whatever food remained. Her family dined like yeomanry a day later.

Nathan had been given a long shopping list of provisions which would require an extra pair of hands, and so it had been agreed that John would accompany him to market. Port and claret had been ordered in advance for collection together with a cask of finest brandy. Seventy beeswax candles, a pound of tobacco, lamp black, lump sugar, dried peas and flour had also to be bought. Mr Parker would settle his account after the festivities. It was decided that they should pannier one of the pack-horses to bring home the groceries, and so they made their way towards the Hall where lights already glowed in the stable yard.

As they made off towards Keighley in the thick grey light, the colours of the land muted and watery, John had many questions. He had not returned to the town since the day of his arrival autumn past, and his recollections of the place were slight. He had only ever visited a fair once, and that was with his family many years ago. As a child of only four years, his memory was of noise, colour and being hoisted high on his father's shoulders when almost lost in the crush of people. The day had been hot, and from his lofty station he looked down on the heads of his brothers, feeling in that moment a perfect happiness. At the thought of his family, tears pricked at his eyes: this would be his first Christmas away from home. He wondered about his father, for the first time without his wife for the festivities. At this, a surge of longing overtook him, and he allowed the sharp tears to roll and pool at his chin. Nathan noticed his friend's silence and glanced over, sensing his sorrow. He suggested that they should make haste to allow time for a tour of the town. John lengthened his stride and ran his fingers through the straggled mane of the pack-horse. Ahead in the road, blackbirds bounced and hopped, tugging at worms, taking to the air in low flight. In the near distance they could see grey figures in groups and alone, their voices just heard, making the same journey towards the nearing town.

As they approached the outskirts of Keighley, passing the water mill clashing as it churned up the icy water, their attention was caught by the sight of a heron flying low along the track of the river, trailing its legs like a fragile train. Its gaze was unbroken as it divined the small silver fish that skirted the frothy water thrown up by the creaking wooden wheel. Above the sound of the mill, the morose measured chime of the church bell echoed across the valley, the sound announcing some poor soul's departure from the world. Nathan led his friend along a narrow lane between houses crowded like teeth, until they came to an inn. They entered a wide low gateway which opened out into a small stable yard about which a number of other horses were tethered and grinding at hay from wooden mangers. From amid the steaming flanks a short man with the complexion of a toad appeared. Nathan greeted him with a friendly grin and handed him a small coin, at which the man took the rope bridle and tethered their horse next to a tall grey cob with the shaggy coat of a wolf. As they left the yard, Nathan explained that his friend Joshua, the innkeeper, had lighted upon a way to make money on market days, opening his yard, for a small fee, to traders and shoppers alike. Although some folk chose to leave their horses tied at the church gate or tethered to trees at the town limits, there had been thefts, which many blamed on the Scots, and Nathan could not take that chance with Mr Parker's horse.

John wanted to walk as slowly as he could in order to take in his surroundings, the tiny thin houses almost adjoining each other as if for comfort or warmth, and in between, the glimpse of a yard, the low snuffle of a pig. Above, the passing bell echoed about, growing louder as the lane grew wider, and they approached the church green. John was totally unaccustomed to the volume of noise, the discordant music of people and animals. The smells, sour and vegetable, sweetened at intervals by notes of cooking meat and bread, and underlying, the base note of excrement. For the second time that day, John felt his friend take him by the shoulder, this time leading him towards the church cross itself. Ranged about it, perched market traders, hawking rabbit, wood pigeon, chicken and pheasant. Nathan explained that it was the unwritten law of the market that these traders of flesh would always take the central place at the cross itself, and that families had held their positions for generations. Looking into the glassy eye of a pheasant, its majestic plumage as foolish as motley as it dangled from its twine noose, John shuddered.

Approaching them from the church gate, and at a brisk pace, came the stygian figure of the Reverend Gale. Clearly in a hurry, he touched the brim of his hat at intervals as people greeted him, though he seemed at pains to avoid meeting their gaze. His face was mottled with cold beneath his snowy wig, and from his pocket he drew a dainty kerchief to contain the drip at his nose end. Nathan drew John aside to allow the Reverend Gale to pass and wished him a good morning, which was acknowledged with a tip of his hat. The Rector had not progressed much further towards his house when he encountered, and then was diverted by, the imposing figure of Michael Pighells. Nathan's attention was taken by their meeting , and he smiled at the sight of the Parson being led towards the overflowing door of the inn. Nathan knew Pighells as an occasional visitor to Marley Hall. He also knew that Robert Parker had not a good word to say for him. It was rumoured that he had fathered three children about the parish, and that he boasted when full of ale that the church had yet to catch up with him. Nathan mused that it was unlikely he was about to seek confession.

John and Nathan continued on their way through the crush of traders and shoppers until they reached the far side of the church green, where they were able to walk directly on to a broad lane, the main artery of the town. A short distance along this street they came to the double fronted facade of Leach the grocer. John had never seen such an establishment, nor the huge array of goods for sale, many of which he could not identify. As they stepped inside, he was at once assailed by the warmth, and heavy scent of coffee, lavender and other mysterious delights. Jonas Leach had been expecting a visit from his patron at Marley Hall. Robert Parker was a valued and profligate customer. He smiled as Nathan handed over the list of provisions required. Though Nathan had not the vaguest idea what the list might say, being unable to read, the great number of words suggested that there would be much to take back to Marley. It was agreed that Jonas would gather together their requisites, and that the boys would return at three of the clock with their horse.

The boys were then at liberty to continue to explore the town, which Nathan clearly knew well. He led John the length of the main street, pointing out the various shops, inns and workshops. Along the way they were greeted by other men, some of whom John recognised from Marley, others that he had seen on the Bingley road. Nathan introduced his friend, and could not resist telling all who enquired of her that Jennet was with child. At length they arrived at the old stone bridge that forded the river, and that John recalled from his first arrival. Here, the wind buffeted down from the hills carrying the cries of cattle on the moorland track. The boys turned and made their way back towards the church down Back Lane, feeling the need for refreshment. Along the narrow length of the lane, figures clustered in dark doorways, and the laughter and shrieks of children could be heard from within. At present they arrived at a narrow ginnel down which they ducked; it opened into a tiny yard enclosed on three sides. Stooping to enter a small parlour in which bodies were crammed like apples in a barrel, Nathan assured his friend that this was the finest tavern in Keighley. John had not cause to doubt him as they enjoyed a fine lunch in the dusty upstairs chamber.

Thoroughly warmed and replete, the boys made their way back towards the market cross, threading this way and that along the maze of tiny streets. By now the light was fading, and the market traders beginning to pack up their remaining wares. Nathan had one further task before heading home, for which he required John's assistance. As they stepped into Teal the draper's shop, Nathan asked that his friend help him choose something for Jennet. He had saved a little money, and though extravagant, he wanted her to have something that would express his love. While eager to tell everyone of his impending fatherhood, he was frustrated at himself when he had not the words to tell her what she truly meant to him. John ran his fingers over the smooth skeins of silk ribbon and coarse yet fragile lace, his eyes drawn to a length of scarlet that draped from the open basket on the trestle. She would look well in this, he declared to his friend, and smiling, Nathan agreed.

Out into the lane a group of four figures stepped aside to allow them out of the shop. Nathan laughed with excitement at the thought of Jennet's face when he gave her the scarlet ribbon. John's attention was momentarily taken at the sight of a girl, one of the four people in the lane; he was sure that he had seen her face before, though could not place it. She had startled at the sight of them, though her friends had not. John was still thinking of her pale round face as they led the heavily burdened horse along the road in the gathering darkness back to Marley.

8

March 1700. Holden Gate

"Eliza, fetch your father's bible, make haste girl."

Mary sat by the hearth, her young son at her breast. The child mewled quietly as he fed, and Mary cradled his tiny body gently to hers. Eliza set aside her besom and made her way to the furthest recess of the parlour where stood her father's desk. The dark oak sloped box, deeply carved with heavy iron hinges, had been placed on a straw sack to preserve it from the dampness of the flags. Her eyes checked the door, anxious that Robert should not return. Lifting the lid she smelled at once the old leather and dusty pages of her father's small cache of books. She was transported back to her childhood, nights when she would grow drowsy in the firelight at the gentle lilt of his words. She almost imagined that she could catch his scent, held like a pressed flower in the pages of his books. Robert had wanted rid of them when he had married Mary; he saw little point in keeping them as he professed to neither read nor write. He was threatened by Mary's literacy and that of her older children; it linked them for ever with Thomas. When he had moved to sell the books together with the desk, Mary had been forced to ask her brother Francis to intervene on her behalf. The books had remained, though exiled to the furthest corner of the parlour so that Robert should not have to see them. He had grudgingly acquiesced as an acknowledgement of his wife's piety. What Robert was not to know was that Mary was committed to continuing Thomas's work, and educating her children.

Eliza reached into the desk and removed the largest of the volumes, the Fowler family bible, its gnarled embossed cover worn smooth by the oil of many fingers, its pages fanned by decades of damp. She carried it over to the hearth, ears pricked to the sound of Robert's step. Mary reassured her that he would not return for several hours having business with William Rishworth at Ghyllgrange. Their meetings entailed long walks over the moorland to Rishworth's tenant farmers; he would often stay for supper, though Robert seldom joined his host in drinking. That day, he had left shortly after breakfast, and Mary had stood in the front yard watching his departing figure disappear over the brow of the hill. She had little reason to suppose she should see him again before nightfall.

"Bring it close and sit at my side that I may watch you read."

Taking up a low stool, Eliza drew together her skirts and balanced the heavy book in her lap. Opening the volume at random Eliza held her finger above the beginning of Proverbs Chapter 18. As she began reading aloud, Mary smiled, for these were words she knew well.

"Through desire a man, having separated himself, seeketh and intermeddleth with all wisdom. A fool hath no delight in understanding, but that his heart may discover itself. When the wicked cometh, then cometh also contempt, and with ignominy reproach."

Over the past few years, she had snatched moments to tutor her children when Robert was away from the house. Ann and Eliza could now read with ease though they still needed practice with their writing. Paper was almost impossible to come by as Robert controlled the family purse strings, but Francis provided a little when he was able. This Mary secreted in the back of the desk beneath Thomas's smaller volumes and goose quills. Ink was made up in small quantities from soot and ground charcoal. In this way the girls had been able to practise their scripts in a necessarily tiny hand. It was understood that Robert should know nothing of their learning. Early in the marriage he had come upon Mary tutoring Ann in her reading. The girl had received a boxing of the ears, and he had threatened to throw the bible into the fire; it was only the unheralded arrival of Francis that averted disaster. He had subsequently spoken to Robert of the books, pointing out that they meant much to Mary, and of course, were of not inconsiderable value. Recognising the last point, Robert had conceded that they should be kept.

Though Mary was keen that all her children be educated, in practical terms this was impossible. Ann and Eliza had begun their learning with their father Thomas, but Margaret had been only three, and Maria a babe in arms, when he had died. It was her dearest wish that Ann and Eliza might pass on their knowledge to their younger sisters, but in practice they had little opportunity. Robert seldom left the farm, and then only to call upon his near neighbours. He avoided visiting the town wherever possible, and was a stranger to the church and the ale-house. He was as proprietorial as a dog with its sheep, his eyes ever watchful, his intent, threatening.

Mary looked down; the baby's lips had fallen away from her breast, but as he slept, he continued to suck at the air. That God had finally granted her a son reassured her that she continued in his grace, that he forgave her for deceiving Robert in continuing the education of her children. Her labour had been mercifully short, and as the child slid into the world, his face contorted with fury, she thanked God that he had bestowed such a blessing upon her. Robert had come to her bed some time later to greet his son, and for the shortest time she had seen what she imagined was love in his eyes. His gaze was, however, only directed towards the baby.

The sun cut suddenly across the room, golden ribbons of light, sharp edged, casting across the flags and the corner of the broad oak table. A moment later it was gone, dissolving into the dullness as a charcoal edged cloud skittled across the sky.

"Eliza, please take the child, there is something I must do."

Mary rose as gently as she could and passed the sleeping infant to her daughter. The baby gurned silently before settling into repose. Eliza drew the child close and watched her mother walk over to the corner of the room and open the lid of the desk. Rummaging amongst the volumes, she presently produced a small sheet of paper and a goose quill. From the floor behind the straw sack her hands found the small pot of fire black ink that she had made up that morning before Robert had risen from his bed. Taking the items over to the table, she directed Eliza towards the door to ensure that none of the other children entered. It was unlikely as it was Wednesday, and Ann had been tasked with taking the younger children to market. Robert's girls Jane and Hannah required boots, and Ann had been trusted with selling enough butter and eggs to allow the expenditure. Standing at the window Eliza watched the cloud shadows race across the fresh ploughed land, and crows, buffeted and angry in the spring air.

At the table, Mary paused to collect her thoughts before committing them to paper. Her letter was short, the quill catching at the rough paper sheet as her words formed on the page. With haste she signed her name in tight cramped characters, cursing wordlessly as the ink blotted. When she was sure that she had written what was necessary, she rose and walked towards the fire. The grate sizzled gently as she cast the ink into the flame. She then took the small pot and returned it to its dark confinement behind the straw sack, and, lifting the lid of the desk, replaced the quill.

"There is something I must ask of you Eliza."

"Of course, Mother."

"Do you know the Reverend Gale?"

"Yes, Mother, I have seen him at market and watched him go into the church. I have heard others speak of him kindly."

"I need you to give him this." She indicated toward the sheet of paper which she now scrolled and fastened with a short length of twine.

"But, Eliza, no one must know of this, not Robert, nor even any of your sisters."

At this, Eliza's face grew anxious. Why could Ann not be told? Why had she been asked rather than Ann? Mary recognised her concern and silenced the questions before they could reach her lips.

"I am trusting you because Robert watches Ann closely."

In the silence that followed, both mother and daughter reached an understanding of each other. Eliza, so like Thomas in both looks and manner, sensed the darkness in Robert. Mary could never speak of what she knew, of what she had guessed, confirmed that day as she had listened at the barn door.

Taking the scroll in exchange for the sleeping baby, Eliza held her mother's gaze. The directness of it caused Mary to gasp. She recalled Thomas whose eyes would follow her around the parlour as she laboured in her mundane duties. She remembered how his hand would reach out and catch her skirts as she passed, gently drawing her in for a hasty embrace. All the while his eyes would scan her face as though seeing it for the first time and committing to memory its folds and contours. She blinked back the tear that threatened to escape and turned to the hearth. Eliza tucked the letter into her apron and took up her broom once more, the conversation being at an end.

Later that day Robert returned to Holden Gate, surprised to see Eliza clashing butter at the oak table, Mary sewing at the fire, the baby slumbering in the cradle. Before he could enquire as to why Eliza had not accompanied her sisters to market, Mary began to complain of the sharp pains that had beset her arms that morning which had meant she had been unable to fulfil her household chores. She had thus asked Eliza to stay behind to help her with the laundry. The day had been blustery and fine and, making the most of the weather, they had ensured that the family would all return to clean linen that evening. As an afterthought she added that her pains had now subsided and she was sure that by the morning they would have disappeared entirely. Robert seemed to accept the tale though he said nothing as he peered into the cradle at his sleeping son.

A short time later as the sky grew heavy with rain cloud, voices could be heard approaching the door. With a rush of chill air the girls entered the parlour, their clothes infused with the scents of the market scoured by the fresh air of the heath. Their cheeks glowed pink, the noses of the youngest girls running and dripping. Robert demanded to know how much they had sold that day, and Ann was happy to report that they had returned with empty baskets. With Easter approaching, the pious of Keighley observed something of the strictures of Lent, avoiding meat entirely but taking their fill of eggs and butter. Ann had sought out the cobbler Shaw who made the journey from Colne each Wednesday to the market at Keighley to sell his sturdy leather boots. Jane and Hannah were now furnished with new boots which had been purchased large to last, but which had worked up angry pink blisters at their heels as they had journeyed home. They complained bitterly to Mary of their pain, but were silenced with just a glance by their father.

In the fading light there were still jobs to do before the family sat down to their evening meal. Margaret and her sister Maria went without bidding to collect eggs from underneath the hedges, Hannah and Jane helped lay the table whilst Eliza tidied the baby John, who grizzled in discomfort in his cradle. Gathering up the empty market baskets, Ann left the house for the barn to collect firewood. Only a short time later Robert made for the door in silence. Mary paused in her labours to glance at his departing figure before turning her attention back to the thick broth bubbling in the grate. Eliza felt her entrails twist and she fought back the desire to run after Robert, to see what passed between him and Ann behind the doors of the great barn. In her wretchedness a sudden thought occurred: whatever their secret may be, she now had a secret of her own. Her mother had trusted her with something that set her apart from the rest of the family. She consoled herself with this thought as she drew up a taper from the fire and began lighting the rush lamps.

9

March 1700. Marley

John's day had been one of mixed fortunes. He contemplated this as he gathered sticks in the fading light by the banks of the river. With the coming of spring, his working day grew longer. He rose with the sun and the increasingly noisy song of birds. These days he saw little of his friend Nathan. They breakfasted together and walked the short distance to the Hall, at which point their paths diverged. Nathan was about the business of sowing crops. The winter had been harsh but mercifully short, and as the ground thawed, the task of ploughing had been completed quickly. He was collecting oats from the Hall barn to spread about the fresh-turned earth. It was a job that Nathan enjoyed as, with only a keen audience of birds in his wake, he imagined the arrival of his child with a warm excitement.

John had waved farewell to his friend at the gate to the Hall, and taken the moorland path. With a dog for company that rushed to meet him from the stable yard, his spirits were high. Mab was his favourite of all the dogs at the Hall. Though she belonged to no one person, she had spent so long in his company on the high moor that John felt that they had developed a mutual understanding.

Enthusiastically she ran ahead, ears pricked to the cry of the sheep carried by the wind, but waited, sentinel like, at the brow of each ridge. It was known that she was in pup, and John had delighted in feeling the flesh of her side rise and fall as he ran his fingers through her coarse hair. If it were possible, he would love to have a dog of his own, perhaps one of her pups?

As they climbed higher towards the summit of the track, the wind pushed and buffeted, capturing lapwing and plovers, alarmed at being held in its vortex. At intervals they passed solitary trees, bent like ancient travellers by the wind's relentless force. Seemingly dead in their black skeletal form, from their finger ends sprouted the first green of hawthorn and holly. Spring was at hand, and John had now to find the last of the lambs to be born on the moor. Most of the sheep families were now complete; only a few ewes, mostly those in their first year, had yet to lamb. He wondered at the mystery of birth, the God-given knowledge that enabled the ewe to lamb alone in the wilderness.

It didn't take long for John to find the first of the day's new lambs. Wobbling on settling legs, it bleated in alarm at the sight of Mab. Checking it over, running his hands through wool tight wound, still brown streaked with the process of birth, John was happy that it seemed strong and healthy. A good distance further, they came upon a pair of sheep yet to lamb, and, by their appearance, in no hurry to do so. It was unlikely to be that day, experience told him. Looking back into the valley, he saw the sheep gathered in drifts like spring flowers by the riverbank, motionless at a distance. With only a couple more ewes to find he turned his gaze back to the broad expanse of the moor extending to the horizon where the white sky began. With a shrill whistle he drew Mab to him before casting out an arm, which she understood to mean that she must seek out sheep in the dips and folds of the moor. With an excited bark she bounded across the heather, pausing at intervals to read the language of scent carried on the wind.

Within fifteen minutes they had come across a ewe still off her feet having just given birth to a tiny lamb. Calming the dog, John drew closer, at which point the sheep attempted to rise, the tiny lamb in confusion nudging at her side. It became immediately obvious that there was a problem, as the ewe slumped to the ground breathing hard. From the base of her tail two tiny feet protruded, rigid and bloodied; the ewe in exhaustion had been trying to push this second lamb out for many hours, and could go on no longer. Crawling towards the sheep, John whispered gently as he took hold of the tiny legs, beyond which he could just make out the tip of a nose. The lamb was at least facing out into the world he saw with some relief. With three sharp tugs, the narrow body slid to the ground, stretched long and motionless.

Acting quickly, John cleared its nose and mouth of the thick mucus coating. Still the animal lay unmoving, its eyes closed to the world. Snatching up the lamb's hind legs, and jumping to his feet, John swung the animal round and round, causing the first-born lamb to stumble in haste and alarm and the ewe to rise to shaky feet. Laying the newborn lamb back in the soft heather John was dismayed to see that it still did not draw breath. Suddenly, as though wracked from within, the animal shuddered and with a splutter it breathed its first. For several moments John sat back and smiled with relief as the ewe gently licked the face of the shivering lamb.

Then Mab stiffened, hackles raised. John jumped to his feet and followed the direction of the dog's gaze. As quietly as he could, he walked a little way out from the hollow where the ewe and lambs lay. In the near distance he could see two figures, one of which he knew to be George Snowden. He had met the boy many times in the past weeks, as their paths had crossed upon the moor. George was also seeking to find new lambs amongst his flock that roamed the high heathland. The Snowdens were hill farmers and their flock greatly outnumbered that of Mr Parker. George had told John when they had walked together some days back that he still had thirty-five ewes yet to lamb. He had many more days of walking the moor still to come.

John did not recognise the other man who towered above George. His coat flapped about his gaunt frame, his thin hair caught in the gusting wind like the ravaged hawthorn trees he'd earlier passed. The stranger's voice, raised in menace, carried to where John and Mab stood, though his words could not be made out. Sensing trouble, John made towards the pair, Mab running ahead. At the sound of his approach, the thin man turned, his eyes flashing with anger.

"Call your dog away before I thrash it, and back the way you came, you have no business here." The man raised his stick, intent on carrying out his threat.

"Mab, here! George, does this man mean you harm?"

Before George could utter a word, the angry stranger began walking away in the direction of Ghyllgrange, the slope of the land causing him to disappear from view within moments. For some time George seemed unwilling to speak as though afraid that the man would return at the sound of his voice. After a time John spoke again.

"Who was that man, and what did he want of you?"

"He is Robert Gawthorp of Holden Gate. It lies a distance below Ghyllgrange. He was giving me a warning. I am to keep away from his daughter."

"Will you heed him?"

"I have no choice, he is a dangerous man, not to be crossed. Ann fears him greatly and I do not want her to come to harm. May the devil take him!" spat George.

John was taken aback to see his friend so angry, tears threatening to spill, jaw clenched in frustration.

"Come, walk with me a while, and tell me of your troubles."

George hesitated at first, continuing to watch the space on the horizon where Gawthorp had stood. Eventually he turned and nodded, falling into step with John. As they walked along, and with some coaxing from John, George began his tale.

He had known Ann and her sisters all his life. He and his sister Rebekah had often sat in the parlour at Holden Gate whilst their own father had shared the day's news with Thomas and Mary Fowler. The Fowlers and Snowdens were good neighbours and friends, both hill farmers through generations. When the weather was fair, the children had played together in the yard, running in and out of the great barn, inventing tales of fairy folk that lived in the shadows.

In the long evenings of midsummer, the Fowler girls had been allowed to run up to Ghyllgrange, taking eggs and butter to the Snowdens, enjoying the company of George and Rebekah as their reward. This had all ended with the death of Thomas. In the early days after his passing, the two families became closer still, as George's parents tried to help Mary in the running of the farm. The arrival of Robert Gawthorp had changed everything. When Snowden arrived at Holden Gate one morning he was met in the yard by Gawthorp, who, unsmiling, thanked him for his regard, but assured him that his assistance was no longer needed. George's mother still missed Mary's company, and he and Rebekah stopped visiting the parlour, and playing with the fairy folk in the barn.

As the years had passed, and the children grown, so they had been allowed to take the butter and eggs down to market each week. This had allowed George and Ann some small time together, and he had discovered that she had bloomed into a girl he hoped one day to marry. As a child, he remembered, Ann's lively mind could always produce a story or a song; these days however she seemed increasingly guarded and sombre. As they walked together to and from the market, he would occasionally catch her eye and see that the spirit still glowed, though dimly. When he had tried to speak of her step-father she had beseeched him not to, and out of respect, he had ceased.

Last Wednesday as he and Rebekah had journeyed down to market, they had neared Holden Gate, and had seen Ann and Eliza some distance ahead. Racing down the hill in pursuit, he had barrelled into the figure of Robert Gawthorp, emerging as if from nowhere into his path. He had apologised hastily and profoundly at his clumsiness, but Gawthorp seemed not to hear him, his gaze distracted by the diminishing figures in the distance. George and Rebekah continued more slowly, mindful that they were being watched, and did not catch up with Ann and Eliza until almost at the river. Later that evening he had thought uneasily about what had transpired, but had not reckoned on any consequence. Today, however, he had been proved wrong. Miserably, he conceded that Gawthorp was not a man to cross, and in future he would have to accede to his demands.

As George and John talked, they were surprised that they had almost reached the Doubler Stones, and in the hollow of a wind-blasted tree they came upon the last of John's ewes. At her feet lay the remains of her lamb, upon which crows had begun to feast. The animal had been born several hours since, its tongue blue and swollen, hung from lips that had not drawn breath. The ewe, uncomprehending, waited for the lamb to stand.

"Leave it be," said George, "drive her down to the others."

"I must go," replied John, "and I'm sorry for all your troubles. I shall not speak of this."

George shrugged, raising his eyes in frustration and hurt. Before turning towards the Doubler Stones, he thanked John but cautioned:

"Be wary of that man, he knows your face, and a friend to me makes you his enemy."

With that George turned and continued his upward trek. John considered his words as Mab gently guided the sheep away from the dead lamb and back towards the track that traced its way down to the valley. Reporting at the Hall in the late afternoon, John was met by the estate manager in the stable yard. Mab, his faithful companion the day long, seemed delighted to be home, the other dogs excited and noisy at her return. John was able to report that all the ewes had now lambed, and though he had found one dead, he had helped in the delivery of twins. The estate manager clapped his shoulder in approval and had news for him from Mr Parker.

"He had hoped to speak to you himself, but he has been called to Bingley. He tells me that you have proved yourself worthy of employment and hopes that you might stay with us."

This was as unexpected as it was wonderful. He imagined that, in years hence, he would see this as the day that he became a man. He pondered this as he gathered firewood at the river, eager to tell Jennet and Nathan of his news. As they sat together around the fireside, wearied by the fullness of their days, they shared details large and small. John was delighted and proud that he was to be retained in Parker's employ; at the news, Nathan clasped his friend's shoulder and grinned. Jennet teased that it was well that Robert Parker did not witness John's untidiness; should he see the state of his sleeping quarters perhaps he would not be so keen to employ him. Together they laughed and talked until the pull of sleep called them. John did not, however, mention his encounter with Robert Gawthorp. He had sworn to George that he would speak to no one of it. Even in the company of his dearest friends, he was beginning to learn when to keep his own counsel.

10

March 27th 1700. Keighley

The Reverend Gale sat alone in his study. He stared with disappointment into his cup where only the dregs of his chocolate remained. He was contemplating a letter to Dr Lister regarding his continuing ill health. He was treating himself for the symptoms of melancholia, craving all things sweet, insisting that Sarah add a little fennel seed to her pottage. He had forsworn all meat for the duration of Lent, but could not even find joy in the plump brown trout, shining with butter, she had served that day.

The letter from his son Christopher in the colonies had arrived two days past. Written in the first weeks of his arrival in the New World, it painted a picture so beyond the imagining of Miles that he found himself reading and rereading the text. Christopher's passage across the Atlantic had taken fifty-four days. For the first two weeks of the voyage, his stomach had pitched with the rise and fall of the ocean. He had found the salted pork, hard tack and shingle hard beans almost impossible to digest, and he had feared that he would starve before he ever glimpsed the Americas. Life in the Rectory, and the ancient panelled hall of his school and been woeful preparation for a life at sea. His ship, the *Agnes*, had sailed from Tilbury in the calm waters of an autumn day, deceiving Christopher into believing that patience was the only requisite of the journey to come. Sickness was only the first of the miseries to be faced. As he spent dark hours suspended in a hammock that never completely dried, his clothes began to take on the fetid reek and dampness of their surroundings. Reading was completely out of the question, and his beloved books in their travelling slope bloomed and bulged like mushrooms in the darkness. Unable to sleep a night through, in desperate moments he cursed himself for the folly of his enterprise.

Awoken by a slice of bright light that reached down through the deck and warmed his cheek, Christopher had risen from his hammock and found, to his surprise, that his first desire was not to retch. The sea still swayed in the same disordered dance, but something had changed. It was day sixteen of his journey and he had finally discovered his sea legs. In view of what was to come, the timing was most fortuitous. As they reached the mid-point of their crossing, they bore witness to the might of God's power. The waters boiled, stirred by winds unimpeded by landscape, the ship clung to the surface of the sea, the fragile place between the cold fathomless deep and the vastness of space. All was darkness and the travellers hid below deck, startling with each creak and sway, as animals in the earth. When finally the storm abated they had lost three of their number, two that succumbed to sickness, and a cabin boy who, unobserved, had been swept from the deck.

How sincere had been the prayer he offered up when at last birds against the sky had heralded the first sight of land. The day had been the longest he'd known as the faint grey shadow on the horizon seemed not to grow. The light was almost gone as they finally sailed past the outer banks and into the broad calm waters of the Pamlico Sound. Sinking a depth, the captain had insisted they drop anchor for the night, experience having taught him the danger of making landfall in the dark. Standing on deck, Christopher could just make out the scent of woodsmoke carried offshore, the light of fires faint as stars.

As he had planted his first footstep on the silty earth of the riverbank, his first emotion was that of elation. God had protected him in his travels, he had a purpose for him here in this new land. He had fought down the urge to laugh. If he had expected strangeness here, he was somehow surprised by the familiarity of what he could see. Though the vegetation was lush and unknown to him, the chickens and pigs scrabbling in the dust around squat wooden houses reminded him of the scattered moorland hamlets of home. In the still waters of the Pamlico river, boats of sail and oar anchored off, small tenders running back and forth between vessel and shore. The bustle of animals and folk at the river's edge reminded him of the Wednesday market of home.

His letter went on to describe the fledgling community that was being established in the Carolinas. Although trade with the native Indian populations had been established some years, furs and tobacco in exchange for cloth, rum, tools and sugar, as yet nothing so much as resembling a town had been established in this area. He had already made the acquaintance of one John Lawson, recently arrived from Charlestown, but originally of Yorkshire stock. Did his father know of the family? He claimed a distant and fleeting knowledge of Dr Lister through his father's friends at the Royal Society.

The letter ended with warm endearments, a desire that he be remembered to his dearest mother, brothers and sister. Miles felt frustrated at the lack of detail; all these weeks he had waited and, though thankful that Christopher had arrived safely, he craved to know more. Margery had wept in pain at the thought of her eldest boy enduring such horrors, for so they seemed to her. Miles could sense that she held him responsible for Christopher entertaining such ambitions. Why else would he seek to journey to the furthest ends of the earth were it not for his father's thwarted ambition? He had felt the tightness in her shoulders as they'd lain last night, and could only imagine the thoughts she harboured.

Sliding back his chair with a flourish, he resolved not to write to Lister that day. He had completed his letter to Christopher before the trout was served. Satisfied that he hadn't missed any news from home, he had been overwhelmed by a feeling of wretchedness. Perhaps a little fresh air might clear his head he mused. The church green would be emptying, the market drawing to a close. As he opened the study door he could hear reedy voices in the parlour, Margery and Marianne, doubtless discussing supper with Sarah. Sliding his arms into his black overcoat and gathering up his hat he stepped out into the glare of the spring afternoon.

The hour was probably three of the clock, and sellers now outnumbered buyers on the church green. Keeping his head down, he marched briskly towards the church gate, managing to avoid the eye of anyone. He noticed with exasperation a collection of mutton bones, recently cast, that littered some of the more ancient graves near the church wall. Had these people no respect at all? He would have the sexton remove them, and would raise the issue in church that Sunday.

As he closed the church door behind him, blackened and dull by years of filthy hands, he found himself exhaling deeply. His breath billowed and hung in the chill air. His steps carried him past the pitch dark box pews that reached almost to his shoulder. He gazed to the dark shadows where the wall met the ceiling which marked the ghost of the rood screen, long gone. He sometimes wished it were still there, a sanctuary from his congregation. Today however he was unlikely to be disturbed by anyone, the clerk and sexton would be in the ale-house warming their calves by the inglenook. Miles, with effort, descended to his knees in front of the altar rail. Attempting to empty his mind of all but God, he found that Christopher's revelations overwhelmed his thoughts. Try as he might, he could not find room for Jesus. He attempted to recite out loud the *Credo* followed by the *Agnus Dei*, but Christopher's pallid face in the space behind his eyes filled his being.

"Keep him safe, Lord, keep him safe."

The simple incantation he repeated again and again until he was satisfied that God would heed his prayer. Rising to his feet with the stiffness of his old cat, he crossed himself and nodded with a final gesture of thanks to the crucified Christ who hung in perpetual agony and cold upon the altar.

At the back of the church he noticed a great dark pile of yew boughs which had been gathered for the coming Sunday to mark the entrance of Jesus into Jerusalem – his triumphal arrival in the city which presaged his death only days later. Again he thought of Christopher. In the time it had taken for his letter to reach home anything could have happened.

"Keep him safe, Lord, keep him safe," he wordlessly pleaded as he drew the door shut with a clap.

The wind was blowing off the hills from the north, its sting counteracting the weak spring sun. Miles fastened the top three buttons of his coat and steered a course over the church green towards Leach the grocer. He required carbon black and a stick of sealing wax, but had also determined to treat Margery to a little of her fancies, a cake of soap and a pound of plump raisins.

Making towards the narrow passage that led off the square he felt a gentle tugging at his arm, about which he turned. Expecting to see his nemesis, Michael Pighells, and feeling sufficient ill-humour to do battle, he was surprised to see the slight figure of a young girl.

"Begging your pardon, Parson Gale, my mother beseeched me to give you this."

He felt the marble cold of her skin as it pressed a tiny scroll of yellow paper into his hand. With that she turned away, walking at speed, her black hair escaping in twisted vines from her mob cap. He could not recall having ever seen her face before, certainly she was not one of his congregation. He turned again to where the girl had departed, but could only see the meat sellers at the market cross beginning to pack up their remaining wares. Without his spectacles he would not be able to read whatever was written, so he carefully placed it inside the breast pocket of his coat and continued on his way.

It was almost an hour later that he returned to the Rectory, by which time the air had grown quite raw, and his nose dripped as he entered the warmth of his hall. At the sound of the door, Marianne's impish face peered out from behind the parlour door, and the scent of baking bread hung invisible in the passage.

"Father, where have you been?" Marianne enquired.

"Why, hiding from you of course," he laughed, scooping her up into his arms. Her warm body wriggled in mock terror.

Only much later as he sat again at his desk, the embers of the fire failing in the grate, he reflected on the day. His temper was greatly improved, and the family had enjoyed a convivial supper. For the first time in weeks, Margery's smile had reached her eyes. Perhaps God had truly heeded his prayer, and granted that Christopher be protected. Perhaps Margery had found forgiveness in her heart, and did not hold him responsible for their son's leaving. Certainly the kiss she had placed on his cheek when he surprised her with gifts had fluttered with warmth. He would follow her to bed shortly.

Holding a candle to the sealing wax, he positioned it carefully over his letter to Christopher, stamping it fast with a slender intaglio. Rising from his chair and taking up his candle, the pool of light followed his step to the door. He remembered the scroll in his coat pocket. At the sight of Mary it had been forgotten. The hour was now late, and his eyes weary. He would be sure to read it in the morning, though it would likely be of trifling significance. He would then write also to Lister of his improving health.

11

March 27th 1700. Keighley

"Where is Ann?"

George had emerged from the dark passage that led into the church green from the river. He had been watching Eliza and Margaret for some time, jumping at each passing figure that eased past him. He had never seen Robert Gawthorp in Keighley, let alone at the market, but after their recent encounter, he had no desire to renew their acquaintance. When he felt sure that the coast was clear, he dashed the short distance to the market corner where the girls sat. At his approach, Eliza began scanning the green in the unlikely event that Gawthorp was watching.

"Where is she, why is she not with you?"

Eliza lowered her eyes. She felt a rising panic and irritation. What if someone was to see them together; William Rishworth, in particular, was a regular visitor to the town on market days. She was also afraid that she might miss the Reverend Gale. How would she explain to her mother that she had failed to deliver the letter?

"George, you must go, we cannot speak. Ann remains at Holden with mother, she is quite well, but please go!"

As he attempted to remonstrate, Eliza's eyes flashed; the conversation was over. Miserably he turned to depart in the direction from which he had come.

"Eliza, why can we not speak with George?" wondered Margaret.

Eliza, not wishing to explain her reasons, floundered.

"Perhaps you could follow him and see if Rebekah is at market today, I haven't seen her as yet. I think that we shall head home soon, I doubt we shall sell any more today."

Margaret did not enjoy market day, and would have favoured spending the day at Holden with her younger sisters. A quiet soul, who preferred the company of animals and small children to that of adults, she cheered at the thought of their departure. As she scurried away in pursuit of George, Eliza's eyes flicked between the doors of the church and the Rectory. Of the Reverend Gale there was no sign. Would she dare knock on his door and deliver the letter? No, she had promised Mary that she would deliver it in person, and she would make good that promise.

The green was beginning to empty of traders and buyers, and glancing at the church clock she saw that the hour was almost three. The wind was picking up and divining its way through the lanes of the town, under doors and through ancient casements. Across the green, head bowed, came the slight figure of Margaret. Only ten minutes had passed.

"I couldn't find George. I walked as far as the bridge but he wasn't there. Can we go home now?"

Eliza hid her dejection as she gathered up her basket and tucked her shawl into her apron; there was nothing she could do but wait another week. Although Mary had not

82

indicated that there was urgency in delivering the letter, she sensed that it was of great import, and that she had failed her mother.

As they crossed the green, snaking between baskets and carts, avoiding puddings of dung and discarded rags, Eliza saw the door of the Rectory open. The stygian figure of the Reverend Gale emerged, walking briskly towards the church. In a matter of moments he would be gone.

"Margaret, wait a moment, I have a stone in my boot."

Eliza sat down on the stone mounting step and made great play of the pain in her foot. Margaret, impatient at the delay, offered to help.

"It's fine, Margaret, I can attend to it," she snapped.

Removing her boot and feeling within for the imaginary stone, she then proceeded to gently rub at the sole of her foot, all the while peering up through her cap at the door of the church. Where could he be? Unless he appeared in the next couple of moments, her distraction could not be maintained indefinitely. Fussing and adjusting at her boot, standing, stamping and then removing her boot once more, Eliza waited but there was still no sign of the Rector. Having prolonged the charade for as long as credible, Eliza replaced her boot a final time, rearranged her shawl and picked up her basket. The girls recommenced their walk across the green, Eliza feigning a limp. As they turned into the lane, she had one last glance over her shoulder to the church. To her distress, the great door began to open.

"Margaret, I am such a goose, I think that when I sat to remove the stone, I have dropped my kerchief. Wait here, I will be back in an instant."

Without giving her sister the chance to reply and dropping her basket at the girl's feet, Eliza turned and raced back towards the church green. The Reverend Gale was heading towards Back Lane. Covering the ground with the swiftness of a deer, Eliza reached out and caught the sleeve of his overcoat. In the briefest of moments her task was complete, and turning tail, she made back towards Margaret, remembering as she drew close, the imaginary pain of her tender foot.

"Eliza, your kerchief is in your pocket, I tried to tell you, but you had gone."

"Of course it is – whatever made me think I could have dropped it? Perhaps it's fairies whispering mischief in my ears." The relief of having delivered the letter caused her to laugh at the nonsense of her own words. Gathering up her basket she reached for Margaret's hand, and together they turned into the wind and towards home.

John had come across George by the river. He sat on the bank amongst a carpet of celandine, a host of tiny radiant suns in the tussocky grass. He was casting stones into the water with an aggression that reflected his temper. John was in no particular hurry that day, having been sent into the town on something of a fool's errand by Tobias Green, groom to Mr Parker. He had been asked to acquire a particular camphor liniment, but had been told by a handful of people that he was unlikely to find it in Keighley. Nevertheless, he enjoyed his visits to the town as respite from the monotony of his days, and had happily accepted the task.

John dropped down onto the riverbank next to George and enquired what troubled him. Without looking up, George had recounted his meeting with Eliza at the market, and the absence of Ann that day. Suddenly a thought occurred to him.

"Do you know Eliza? Would you recognise her? She sits at the corner of the market and sells butter and eggs, she and Ann, though today it is Eliza and her sister Margaret."

He looked hopefully into John's puzzled face, searching his memory for how best to describe her.

"Her hair is black as pitch, her eyes dark, her skin pale." George sighed at his inability to find the words to describe the girl he had known all his life. "She's just Eliza."

But in spite of the ill-sketched image, John knew exactly who Eliza was. His eyes had sought her out each week on the market corner – the solemn moon faced girl who reminded him of an image in glass he'd once seen long ago. He recalled from childhood days, the Stevens family. Though Papist, his mother had no time for religious intolerance, and counted Tamar Stevens a trusted friend. One day she had taken John to visit Tamar who had shown them both the tiny image of the Madonna and child, centuries old, that had been recovered from the parish church. After the Parliamentarians had ridden away, villagers had returned to the church to find Christ dashed from the cross, lying among the shards of the ancient window, headless saints desecrated in their niches, and the rood screen smouldering in the churchyard.

Tamar's father had gathered up the remains of the window, the image of the virgin and child miraculously intact. He had kept the relic safe, and at his death it had passed to Tamar. As John had held it up to the light, he had wondered at the beauty of the Holy Mother and her dark, searching eyes, and the motives of those who had sought her destruction.

"I know her," he said, his eyes meeting George's.

"Then I ask you as a friend, please help me. Speak with Eliza, ask of Ann. I cannot rest until I know of her wellbeing. I fear Gawthorp's spies are about the town and if I am seen speaking with her, word will get back to him."

Shaking his head He added: "I do not know where else to turn, my sister Rebekah fears Gawthorp too. She will not return to Holden. Will you help me, John?"

"Wait here," said John, springing to his feet. Moving swiftly along the back lanes of the town, he began to approach church green. His heart was pounding, in excitement at his part in the secretive task, but also at the thought of speaking with the girl Eliza.

As he reached the market place he sought her out, but was dismayed to see that her usual space on the corner was unoccupied. As his eyes darted about, he saw the Reverend Gale making his way across the far side of the green and then the figure of Eliza running swiftly towards him. Momentarily, the two were in conversation, but as John made towards them, she turned heel and began to dash back the way she had come. Anxious at the thought of failing George, John began to run in pursuit, but as he neared Eliza and her sister in the lane, he realised that he had no idea what he should say or do. Remembering suddenly the purpose of his visit to town he cleared his throat.

"Begging your pardon, but might you know where I might purchase camphor liniment?"

Eliza and Margaret turned at the sound of his voice. Eliza recognised the tall figure of John, though Margaret did not.

"I am a stranger to this town and do not know where I might find a grocer or apothecary. Can you help me?"

Eliza held John's gaze without blinking. Why was he lying? A chill of suspicion and fear ran through her, but she recalled the first time that she had seen him, stepping out from Teal's drapery, the gash of crimson ribbon trailing. She had observed him since on market days and on one occasion their eyes had locked at distance.

"Margaret, wait here with the baskets, I shall be but an instant. Come, this way."

"Eliza … !"

Margaret's exasperated entreaty hung in the air as Eliza dashed down a side lane towards Teal's, John in her wake. When she was satisfied that they were out of sight and earshot, she paused in a doorway, her eyes flashing.

"My name is John, of Marley, I am a friend of George Snowden; he has sent me." His words silenced Eliza. "He worries for your sister Ann and seeks reassurance that she is well."

Studying his face, his eyes wide set, the corners of his mouth deeply sunk, she replied at length.

"Gawthorp will not allow her to come to market. He forces her to stay at Holden. I don't understand what she has done and why George's name cannot be mentioned in his presence. I hear her weeping at night and despair at her unhappiness. Please tell George to keep away, for I fear that he will be seen speaking to me and …" Her words failed at this point.

"Let me help you both. I will seek you out next week at market. Trust me, I am a friend."

"I must go, thank you, thank you … John." Her words lingered in the air as she ran back to Margaret. Again the image of the tiny fragment of glass came to him, the face of the virgin, the memory of which he had carried through the years.

John walked with George a stretch of the road to Bingley in the late of the afternoon, the drill of a woodpecker carrying from a nearby copse on the strengthening breeze. The pair resolved to meet at Doubler Stones the morrow. George had something he wished John to carry, to give to Eliza. As they parted company near the corn mill they clasped hands in friendship and conspiracy. It was only as he neared Marley, his thoughts infused with Eliza, that John remembered the camphor liniment.

12

June 1700. Holden Gate

Mary entered the barn, flooding the great space with summer morning. Above, swifts screeching in frantic pursuit, sweeping low over the mossed stone tiles. Weariness like a heavy cloak slowed her step. The baby John had mewled the night long and she had enjoyed little sleep. Though he had suckled long, his tiny sighs marking the transition to rest, she fretted at the damp chill of his brow. Before long, spars of morning sun were cutting across the chamber and her day was beginning. She had left the baby swaddled tight upon Ann's knee at the hearth side, and instructed the girl to come find her the moment the child woke.

Checking on the great mash tub, there was ale to flagon that day and, later, cheese to be made. Gawthorp had left the house early that morning, the land still dark. He had saddled the mare to make the journey across the moor to Ilkley. Three times a year he made the same trip to visit his cousin Isaac, the only member of his family with whom he maintained contact. Mary had never met Isaac, but in the early days of their marriage she had made enquiries amongst her friends. Though no one had made his acquaintance, word of his character spread far beyond the bounds of Wharfedale. A tailor by profession, he worked from his house in the centre of the town. He was a Godless man who tyrannised his wife and children. It was said that he so feared spending money, his wife could not leave the house, for shame at the holes in her gown. His sons and daughter had never married, all working long hours at his great sewing table. It was however said that he produced very fine clothing with which he supplied the yeomanry of Yorkshire. Gawthorp, when he returned from Ilkley, would say little, indicating only that Isaac and the family were well, that business was even better. Mary had tried to elicit more from him, on one occasion even suggesting that she should accompany him on his next trip, he had sneered at the very thought.

In her darker moments, Mary wondered at the stranger she had taken to her bed. Though they had been married eight years, he seemed little more familiar to her as the day he had first arrived unbidden at her gate. She had long since ceased in talking to him of the children or herself, his only interest being the running of the farm. Her world was now so small, being denied visitation to the market and the church, that she saw little of her neighbours and friends. Her children were her eyes and ears of the world beyond Holden, the bible and books, her soul's comfort.

When the family gathered about the table at supper, it pained her not to speak the grace, instead the children would wait until Gawthorp took up his first mouthful before following suit.

Sometimes he would ask the wellbeing of the sheep, if the cows should be moved to new pasture, which chickens were ready for the pot. The girls would be sure to have the answers to his questions. He would allocate the next days labours to be divided amongst the family, and inform them all of his own intended tasks. At the end of supper he would rise from the table, his chair rasping the stone flags, and leave to make final check of the animals. On long summer evenings he would walk up to Ghyllgrange to meet with William Rishworth.

Rishworth was a haughty man, tall of stature, broad of girth whose family could be traced back to the Conqueror, centuries before. Though Mary and Thomas had exchanged pleasantries with him at the church gate and moorland track, Mary always had the feeling that he did so under sufferance. In conversation his eyes always sought some indefinable object on the distant horizon, he was always in haste to some other meeting, his words brittle as ground frost. Though Gawthorp spent much time in his company, Mary could not understand the nature of their friendship. The two men spent hours walking the high moors together, sometimes seen silhouetted against the sky above Holden; he almost never graced their parlour. On occasions he rode his great grey horse past their very gate on his way down to Keighley, never stopping or even glancing in their direction. Returning from Ghyllgrange, Gawthorp would often seem agitated, and in anticipation of this, she would ensure that the girls were to bed early. Not wishing to discuss his visit, Mary would follow him to the chamber where, in the darkness, they would couple swiftly and in silence.

As Mary drew off the first of the flagons of small beer that trickled musically from the great tub, Eliza's footstep alighted the threshing floor.

"Mother, I am away to Riddlesden to visit the widow Bell. She ails after her fall and can no longer make her way to market. I shall take her some butter and a little cheese."

Though Eliza spoke the truth, Mary was aware that this was not the sole purpose of her visit. Having delivered the letter to the Reverend Gale, Eliza had made mention of John of Marley and the kindness he had shown. She had seen the flush of her cheek as she had spoken his name that lingered even as the conversation had ended. Mary did not wish to know the true purpose of her visit to Riddlesden, for in not knowing, she would not be forced to lie if challenged by Gawthorp.

"Make haste then, Eliza, for we must finish the cheese-making today."

Eliza, her small basket ready packed, bobbed in thanks then ran to the gate, taking the track that hugged the hillside the way to Riddlesden. She had woken, like Gawthorp, in the darkness, and lain still in the quiet punctuated only by Ann's mouse-like breath. Soon she heard Gawthorp leave the house; she paused to hear him saddle up his horse whose hooves danced briefly on the flags of the yard. Only then could she be sure he had departed. In excitement, she had dressed quickly in a cap and apron freshly laundered, heather scented. Dispensing with her domestic duties as quickly as she could, she would be able to report to her mother that the floor was swept, the oatcakes fresh made and the youngest girls dressed, if challenged. She was meeting with John, away from the market where they had snatched brief conversations over the past weeks. Her eyes now sought him out in the knot of the market square; as she yearned to see his shy smile, and they had managed to share a word when Margaret could be distracted. But with their growing association came the danger that Gawthorp should hear of it. This was something they must avoid at all costs.

Her step quickened as the rooftops of Riddlesden came into view, clinging as it did to the pitch of the hill. She would first visit the widow Bell, a tiny wraith-like woman whom Eliza had known all her life. Until her recent fall on her journey home from Keighley, she would seek out Eliza at market. Smiling, she would say that the girl's mother made the best butter in the whole of Airedale, and she should know, as she was as old as the hills and had tasted more butter than most. If she was so inclined, she would tarry a while and recount tales of her youth, the wild days of the war, the madness that had for a time stalked the land. Eliza was both frightened and beguiled by her stories, minding not that she had heard some of them many times over.

When she arrived at the old lady's house, an ancient cottage scarce big enough to house a sheep, she knocked gently at the door. A wisp of smoke from the chimney told her that the widow was at her hearth. Entering, and allowing her eyes to grow accustomed to the gloom, she picked out the tiny figure in her fireside chair, swathed in layers of wool in spite of the warmth of the day.

"Eliza, dear, so nice of you to visit. I see you have brought me some of your mother's good butter. Did I tell you that she make the finest in all of Airedale?"

Eliza crouched at her feet, taking her spidery hands in her own, shocked at their icy touch.

As she listened to the familiar tales of long ago – a King's man left for dead in a ditch, children emboldened to take the fine feather from his hat – she pitied the relict whose only company was now the shadows of her youth. By the by she took the penny from the old woman's papery hand, glancing a dry kiss in thanks and promised to return the next week bringing more butter and news from the town. As the door gently closed behind her she could hear the widow Bell continuing the conversation, laughing at the memories that sharpened each day shared only by her company of shadows.

The scatter of houses along either side of the track began to thin as Eliza left the hamlet of Riddlesden behind. Her journey's end approached, and so her excitement to be meeting with John increased. Just out of the village there was a small copse which screened a spring that trickled its way down into the valley. Where the land folded in on itself like a crease in paper they had arranged to meet when they had spoken last at the market. The day was Saturday and the hour well before noon. Eliza hoped that John was already there for the loneliness of the wood made her afraid.

Leaving the track and entering the green canopied glade she felt her skin cool as the sunlight was sieved as though through sacking. Her worries were dispelled as she made out the figure of John plucking at the new leaves of a hawthorn bush. At the sound of her footfall he leapt to his feet, smiling shyly as she approached.

"Eliza, I am so glad that you could come."

"Have you been here long?" she enquired. She was relieved to hear that he had not.

It was John who had suggested they meet at this place. Knowing that it would be too dangerous to be seen together on the high moor or in the town, he had come across the wood in his early days at Marley. He had explored the area on either side of the river, the slopes of the hills, the hamlets and villages. Hearing the noise of cascading water he had followed the sound into the wood that winter day, the trees naked, the spring angrily boiling. Tasting the water he found it to be sweet. He had visited it often through all seasons of the year, something of its geography reminding him of his birthplace, the wooded slopes of home.

As Eliza told of her journey that morning and her visit to the widow Bell, John was distracted by the movement of her lips, the rise and fall of her dark brows as her voice became animated. Gawthorp, she remarked, was away to Ilkley that morning and unlikely to return before nightfall. John noted that at the mention of his name Eliza's lips drew back slightly in the way that Mab snarled silently at the sight of a cat. She could not linger for she had promised her mother that she would return to assist in the cheese-making. John drew from his waistcoat a small folded slip of paper.

"This is for Ann. I met with George this week and he gave me this."

Laughing, Eliza produced a similar tiny furl of paper from her apron.

"This is for George, Ann hopes that you might deliver it to him. Are we not like angels, winged messengers?" Again she laughed, this time at the gentle blasphemy of her words.

"Indeed we must be."

As Eliza ran her fingers through the quiet flow of the spring she mused aloud on the futility of the situation. Ann had not seen George for three months, and she herself was now afraid to speak with him, all of which was due to the will of Gawthorp.

"Do you read, John?" she enquired.

"I have a little understanding, though Nathan and Jennet do not. I have not seen a book since I left my father's house."

"My father left us many books, though Gawthorp would have them destroyed. Had not my uncle spoken out, he would have thrown them into the fire," she spat.

"He does not read?"

"No. He denies us the church but he cannot take away our knowledge once taught. We can still read the word of God."

At the thought of church, she turned to John.

"Have you seen the Parson Gale of late? Three months have passed since I delivered the note, and still he does not reply to mother."

"I confess I have not, except at a distance. I am certain he would not forsake her." His voice trailed uncertainly; three months was indeed a long time.

A blackbird sang in the high branches and the sound of footsteps trailing and raising dust approached. They locked eyes anxiously, the water continuing its gurgling flow. Almost not daring to breathe, they remained motionless until they heard the traveller's tread pass and retreat.

"I must go, I can delay no longer." She jumped to her feet. "Perhaps we could meet again a fortnight hence, in this place?"

"Yes, I shall let George know of our plan." He marvelled at her gaze which held his determinedly, only breaking off as she turned, took up her basket, and scrambled the slope to the track. He remained seated for ten minutes more, resuming his plucking of leaves. Above, the blackbird continued to trill a complex melody.

As the string of houses of Riddlesden came closer, Eliza quickened her step, not daring to look back. Passing the widow Bell's doorway she wondered how long she had been away. She judged that the sun had still not reached the mid-point of its daily race, and she would be back at Holden within the hour.

Mary had been called back to the parlour; the baby John had managed a restless sleep, swaddled tight at Ann's knee, but had awoken with a fury that his mother was struggling to contain. As she paced the floor, rocking the child violently, his cries juddering and hoarse, she was relieved to see Eliza enter the yard. As she set down her basket at the door, the scent of hills about her, she opened her arms to take the screaming baby.

"The widow Bell sends her regards, I am to tell you that you still make the best butter in all of Airedale."

13

June 1700. Keighley

Miles had not worn his thickest woollen coat for some weeks, following an unexpectedly warm Easter. Instead he had taken to wearing an old light-wool jacket, which in spite of being somewhat tight about the girth, and outmoded in its cut, had been an expensive purchase with much wear in it still. There had been one day, the week previous, when even this light garment had seemed too cumbersome, and his scalp had run with sweat beneath his wig. In his costume of perpetual mourning, he felt like a beetle as he made his way along the high street, envious of the townsfolk in their airy linen shirt-sleeves. Summer had settled upon the valley with the heaviness of sleep, stealing beneath doorways, through narrow alleys and out across the high heath. Each day the sun tarried longer in the sky and by evening the town echoed with the voices of those at leisure.

It was as he packed away his great coat in the cedar wood coffer that he remembered the girl in the market and the note. Reaching inside the breast pocket he felt for the scroll of paper, and recalled with shame that it had been in his possession for many weeks. In mitigation, he mused, there had been much to occupy his time – Easter, one of the busiest times in the Christian calendar, tiresome parish business, a protracted quarrel with the parish overseers (as yet unsolved). There had been the disappointment of the cancellation of the visit of Mr Ralph Thoresby. They had recently begun corresponding upon historical matters, and the good gentleman had expressed an interest in visiting Miles on his progress to Carlisle. With a date in his diary, Miles had made haste to complete the annotation of his vast mineral collection. However, an outbreak of smallpox in Leeds had resulted in the deaths of Thoresby's two eldest daughters. A short letter conveying the news had not indicated that the visit should be rescheduled.

As he unfurled the yellowing scrap of paper, the Rector was at once taken by the tiny hand thereupon. His glasses were at his desk in the study and without them the script would be unreadable. He made his way through the hall across the beamed floor, beeswaxed sleek as a chestnut, the house echoing in unaccustomed silence. Margery had taken the children visiting the Parkers of Marley, and was unlikely to return before supper-time. Drawing up his chair, he turned his back to the window, allowing the sunlight to fall upon the page

Sir,

Please forgive me for writing but I seek your guidance.

1 Peter : 3

I put my trust in the Lord but fear that I shall fail my children. I ask but he answereth not.

Mary of Holden

The first thing that struck Miles was the beautiful, if old-fashioned, script. Although the hand was minuscule, and the page blotted in places, the author had clearly been tutored in her letters. He read the note again, unsure at its meaning and turned over the page in case he had missed something. The reverse was blank. What was he to make of the thing? He cast his mind back to that day in the market, and the raven haired girl who had tugged at his sleeve and handed him the note. Was she Mary? No, impossible, the letter spoke of her children, and the messenger had been but a child herself. He felt unease at the sentiment of the letter, the woman, Mary, was seeking his help, but why send the child in her stead?

Still clasping the note, Miles rose from his chair and walked over to his book slope upon which lay his bible. Carefully lifting the bulk of the heavy pages to the left, he came to the first letter of Peter towards the end of the book. He had not had cause to read the epistles for some time, finding the lessons of the Old Testament more fitting as the basis of his sermons. His flock could follow the tales of Daniel, Noah, David and Goliath, making simple distinctions between good and evil. He reflected, as he had done many times over the years, that his sermon must entertain as well as enlighten; if not, the ale-house next door provided a tempting alternative.

For the next few hours, Miles pored over the text of the epistle. Several times he stood up and walked about his study, deep in thought. On one occasion he consulted his copy of *Enchiridion Militis Christiani*, seeking wisdom and meaning in the words of Erasmus. A picture slowly began to form in his mind of the mysterious author of the note. This was a woman in distress at her circumstances, unable for whatever reason to seek guidance in person. Resolved to help, he realised that he must be circumspect in his method. He rose to his feet and headed towards the kitchen in search of Sarah.

"Sarah, I desire some coffee and perhaps a little sweetmeat."

The girl, busily plucking a chicken at the back door, was taken aback at the sight of the Reverend Gale in the kitchen. She placed the ragged chicken on the step and wiped her hands down the front of her apron causing feathers to float up and catch in her wiry hair.

"Yes, sir, I shall attend to it now. Do you wish me to bring it to your study?"

"Yes, thank you, Sarah." He paused and enquired, idly he hoped: "Do you know of a place called Holden?"

She eyed him quizzically. "Yes, sir, it lies about three miles hence on the Silsden road. It is the old deer park."

"Do you know of the people who live there?"

"Some, there are many houses in the old park."

"Do you know of a Mary?"

By this stage Sarah's interest was piqued, but as she answered, "No, sir," she knew the conversation was at an end.

Miles returned to his study and considered what he had learned. He felt certain that Holden lay without his parish boundaries. This surely begged the question: why had not the woman contacted her own priest, the Reverend Mitton? He resolved to visit the young incumbent of the neighbouring parish of Kildwick the coming day.

He returned to the bible and the third chapter of Peter's letter. It dealt with the duties of husbands and more specifically wives. The writer, afeared to write precisely the nature of her torment, was directing him through the words of the Apostle. At the sound of Sarah's step he shuffled the note into the pocket of his waistcoat, anxious that the girl should not see it. Placing the tray of coffee and cake on the desk, he thanked her and indicated that he would require nothing else until the family returned. She bobbed and returned to the kitchen.

Miles tried to recall the girl who had handed him the note. He felt sure that she had mentioned her mother, in which case the girl herself was perhaps in peril. The note had languished in his pocket for many weeks and with a shudder he prayed that Mary and her children had come to no harm. He must now act with haste to help them. As he sipped his coffee he consoled himself with the words he had read and reread over the course of the afternoon:

The eyes of the Lord are over the righteous, and his ears are open unto their prayers.

The arrival of Margery and the children was proclaimed in a volley of chatter and wailing. John the youngest boy had taken a tumble on the flags at the door to the Rectory. Having skinned his palms, his joyous afternoon spent running with his brother and sister about the gardens at Marley was now forgotten. He could hear Margery clucking and coaxing her son to be brave, but it was the emergence of Sarah with cake that finally silenced the tears. Having settled the children at the parlour table, Margery gently knocked and entered the study.

"Madam Parker sends her kindest regards," she announced, taking his hands into her own.

"We have enjoyed a most convivial afternoon," she continued. "Have you made the most of our absence?"

"Indeed so." He never failed to thank God for the patience and understanding of his wife. Throughout their long years together she never failed to cheer his spirits, even in his most turbulent of humours. Truly she possessed the patience of Job.

"Margery, I must go to Kildwick tomorrow morning." As her mouth opened in protest he continued, "But I shall be sure to be back in time for lunch. I am well aware that we are entertaining your cousin."

"Very well – come speak with your children, they have much to tell you of their afternoon at Marley. Madam does indulge them so."

Having sat too long at his desk, Miles rose to his feet with the stiffness born of age. Meekly he followed Margery out into the hall. He had resolved to say nothing of the note until he had gathered more information, though he supposed that eventually he would take his wife into his confidence.

Much later in the day, Margery and the children having retired to bed, Miles returned to his study. They had dined well that evening, Sarah having produced a fine pie of the unfortunate chicken. Marianne had excitedly recounted her day at Marley, interrupted at intervals by Edmund and John. Their visit to the stable yard to view Mr Parker's fine horses had been a great thrill and privilege. Marianne had asked her father whether she might be allowed some paper as she wished to make some drawings for him of the things she'd seen, whilst the memories were still sharply fixed in her mind. As he sat at his desk, he smiled at Marianne's half completed drawings, abandoned when weariness had overcome her. He reached into his waistcoat pocket and took out the scroll of paper. By the light of his candle, the tiny writing seemed even more poignant. It brought to mind thoughts of Christopher, so far away. Surely there could be no worse thought than to have failed your children. Pray God it was not too late to help this woman. As he tried to summon up Christopher's face, his gaze blurring in reverie, he was startled at the sudden flapping of a large moth testily breaching the arc of candle glow.

He resolved to rise early, and instruct Stephen to make ready his horse for the ride over to the neighbouring parish of Kildwick. He had heard tell that the Reverend Mitton's wife was expecting her first child at any time, and it was likely therefore that the Rector would not stray far from his hearth. As he made his way across the study, leaving the moth to seek another source of light, he reflected that, as a man of God, he must help this woman in her crisis of faith. In his long years within the parish he had never been approached in such a way. In spite of his trepidation he felt a spark of excitement. The greying embers of his intellectual curiosity had been softly raked. The lightness of his tread on the stair belied his years as he made his way up to bed.

14

June 1700. Marley

In the darkest hour of the night John was awoken by a guttural scream. Instinctively and immediately he sat up, ears keen to further noise. From the parlour he could make out sobbing and the gentle voice of Nathan. Sliding from his bed he made his way towards the ladder. Nathan was already clambering up to meet him. From below the sulphur glow of the rush lamp illuminated little.

"The baby is coming," cried Nathan, anxiously glancing back towards the figure of Jennet. "But it's not time. John I need you to make haste. Fetch Martha Wright, she will know what to do."

John clasped Nathan's arm before reaching for his boots and scrambling down the ladder. Nathan had returned to Jennet in the recess of their bed. Though John couldn't make out her form, the noise of her thrashing body, and her howls and whimpers seemed those of a stranger.

As he reached the door the air was rent with another ungodly scream. In terror he ran from the house. Thankfully a half moon hung in a sky untroubled by cloud, lighting the track that meandered like a silent stream towards the town. The Wrights – Isiah and Martha – lived on the outskirts of Keighley in a house as ill-fitting as an inherited hat. Their seven children had all grown, married and moved out, leaving the couple to grow old in their vast drafty parlour. Isiah continued to work at the nearby corn mill though with each passing winter his spine curved and set a little more tightly. Martha was known for her midwifery skills, the townsfolk having great faith in the knowledge that all her own children had survived and prospered. She had witnessed the arrival of countless children, and seen the cruelty and joy of birth in its many forms. Though she now approached her sixtieth year, she was kept busy through all hours of the day, and seasons of the year.

As he ran hard along the lane, to the music of the night creatures in ditches, the sudden shriek of an owl reminded him of Jennet's agony, and he lengthened his stride. In little over fifteen minutes, and with lungs bursting from his chest, he found himself at the Wrights's door. Above, on the low stone lintel, moonlight picked out the date 1620 and the triangulation of letters TS and W, the monograms of Isiah's forebears, in sharp relief. Aware of the lateness of the hour, his initial knock was almost apologetically gentle. When he got no reply, his hammering became faster and louder, and he eventually resorted to shouting up to the chamber window.

"Martha, Martha, please come down."

After what seemed an age, the casement above opened, and John took a couple of steps backward. Martha's head with its soft corona of white downy hair appeared.

"Is that you John Asquith?"

"Yes, Martha, please come quickly, Jennet's baby is coming. Nathan says it's too early. Please hurry!"

"Wait there!" and with that the head retreated and the window rattled shut.

As he waited at her door, nervously kicking at the dust, John could make out the sound of a distant dog bark, answered shortly by another bark at closer quarters. He tried not the think what might be happening back at Marley; would they be too late? From inside the house he heard the creaking of floorboards as Martha dressed, and after a short time which John was powerless to hasten, the door opened. Martha appeared carrying a small bag, shrouded in a cape intended for a figure of twice her stature. Barely reaching his shoulders in height, she felt for his arm.

"My eyesight leaves me with the setting of the sun," she stated. "Come, I shall walk better on your arm."

They turned and set off back towards Marley. In panic and irritation at the slowness of their progress, John fought the urge to pick up the tiny woman and run with her. Conserving her energy, and mindful of her step in the dark, she made no conversation. The night was now the domain of the wild creatures, busy in the fields and hedgerows, invisible and silent.

Eventually the dim light of the cottage emerged from the gloom. As they approached the threshold, they heard low moaning from within. Nathan leapt from the bed to greet them as they entered the parlour.

"Martha, thank God you are here. The baby is coming and Jennet grows weak. I'm sorry I don't ..." Nathan's words tripped from his mouth in a torrent of distress.

Martha gently shed her cloak and lay her hand upon Nathan's arm.

"You were right to fetch me, and now Nathan, John, I must ask you leave whilst I attend to Jennet."

Nathan paused uncertainly, his eyes tracking back to Jennet, who in her agony seemed oblivious to his presence; he was finally led to the door by John. Martha had already begun to reach into her bag and was heading over to the recessed bed.

Once outside in the still night air, the dew beginning to settle heavy upon the grass margins, Nathan stared back at the door. Each whimper and moan caused him to start.

"Come, let's walk down to the river," said John. "There is nothing we can do here, Martha is about her work."

Nathan stared at him uncomprehendingly, but at length followed his friend down the slope towards the river, pewter-still in the moonlight. John attempted to engage his friend in chat though unsure whether this was a help or irritation. At intervals Nathan muttered prayers, beseeching God to intercede to spare Jennet and the child.

"All will be well," replied John, more in hope than certain knowledge.

The friends found comfort in walking the circuit from the river, back to the cottage, on to the Hall, then back to the cottage. Each time they returned they listened hard at the door. Jennet's unearthly cries continued, sometimes faster, occasionally low and bestial. Light was beginning to leech into the sky above the line of the hill, staining the blackness purple. Seemingly hours had passed and the new day was stealing in. By the strengthening light, Nathan's face creased deep with worry as, for the eleventh time, they approached the cottage door.

Something had changed. The air was filling by the by with the songs of birds alive to the coming of day. Across the valley, cattle rose and began their daily unbidden journey to the milking parlour. From the Hall, a shriek of merriment and the yapping of hounds. Rising above all of the sounds of the dark morning came Jennet's cry, rising in pitch through teeth set hard, dissolving finally in wracked sobbing. A pause, then an alien sound, full of fury and fear, a child's first cry. Nathan swung to face John, gripping his shoulders, his fingers clenching tighter as the child continued its loud complaint. From Jennet there was not a sound.

Inside the parlour they could make out the voice of Martha beneath the infant's cry. At length she opened the door to them. Drying her hands upon her apron she smiled at Nathan.

"You have a son," she said simply. "He is small but strong."

"Jennet?"

"She is weary and has lost much blood."

Stepping aside she allowed Nathan to stride past her to the bed where Jennet lay, the child at her breast. John remained in the doorway, overcome by the warmth of the room and scents, earthy and strange.

"Could I trouble you for a drink, John?" enquired Martha. "It has been a long night."

Eager to be of some small service, John organised small beer for all. Nathan stroked Jennet's brow, her face pale as moonlight about which her hair clung in damp coils. The child slept, its tiny hands clenched and raised about its head, the rest of its body swaddled tight. Martha drank heartily and gathered together bloody rags which she cast upon the fire where they sizzled and shrank.

"I must get home now. Isiah will be at the mill already. I'll return tomorrow to check on Jennet. See that she has a little warm milk and oats and then she must sleep."

John, aware that Nathan should perhaps be alone with Jennet, offered to walk with Martha back to Keighley.

"Thank you, John, you shall be my eyes once more." She chuckled before walking over to the bed and gently taking Jennet's hand. "Rest now."

Nathan rose to his feet and walked with Martha to the door. From a pouch at his waist he produced a scatter of coins. "Martha, thank you," his voice dissolving as emotion rose in his throat. He placed the coins in her hand and folded her fingers about them.

As John and Martha made their way past the Hall, the sun was already casting long shadows in the dust. Away on the hillside the figures of men could be seen walking the high road, and swifts and martins feasted on the plume of insects rising from the long grass. Their pace was leisurely, as they enjoyed the newness of the morning. Though the air still carried the chill remnants of night, it was going to be another warm day.

"Is it always like that, Martha?" enquired John. He was trying to rid his mind of Jennet's screams, to make sense of what he had witnessed that night.

"The mother of every child born has a different story. The priest would have it that this is Eve's punishment. I say it is nature's way."

John considered this for a while. He had witnessed the birth of many animals, most sliding from their mothers silently and secretly. What he had heard that night was something other. Here was danger and pain, nature at its most cruel.

By the time they reached Martha's door the road was busy with people about their day. Martha beckoned John inside. As he stood in the vast parlour, grown chill as the fire struggled in the grate, Martha went to her cupboard. After a moment she handed him a small twist of cloth.

"This is for Jennet's pain. Boil this willow in a little water and allow to stand. Not too much mind, and John, thank you. I have much enjoyed your company."

As he walked the road back to Marley, he thought on Martha's words. Why was it woman's lot to suffer? He had heard of the punishment of Eve but had not known its meaning, and why did Martha reject this? There was much he had to learn he mused, as he approached the Hall to deliver news of the baby.

15

June 1700. Kildwick

Miles Gale was finding it very hard to maintain his temper. The day had begun well, he had breakfasted handsomely, enjoying some particularly well cured bacon. The children had not yet risen, still weary from their trip to Marley the day before, when he had left the house. He had thought better than to wear his thick coat as the weather promised to be warm again. Stephen had saddled up his horse, and, as he had progressed through the streets of the town he found himself smiling. For all his love of intellectual pursuits, there was nothing he enjoyed more than to ride out when the weather was fair. Leaving Keighley behind, the road stretched ahead along the valley floor, shadowing the river's gentle course. On either side the hills rose but slightly, and the landscape became more pleasing to his eye. He was reminded of the countryside of his boyhood home, Farnley, the house there set on a gentle incline, the land spreading away to a distant grey horizon.

The road began to rise as he crossed the river, and the tower of the long church at Kildwick emerged from the treetops. It was not often that he had cause to journey this way, and he could not but admire the handsome church with its improbably long aisle. He recalled the burial of the previous incumbent, the Reverend Pollard, some three years past. A benevolent man, he had been much rooted in the land and the lives of its people. As a curate to the Reverend Little, he had taken up the post of vicar only a couple of years before Miles arrived in Keighley. In the early unsure days of his tenure, the Reverend Pollard had arrived at his door. Keen to make the acquaintance of a fellow man of the cloth, he had welcomed Miles with generous spirit. Together they had enjoyed convivial hours at the fireside, but whilst eager to engage in discourse of matters spiritual, the Reverend Pollard was equivocally not a man of science. As the years had progressed and Miles became bedded in to parish life, their paths had crossed less and less. He had, however, been saddened to hear of the Reverend's death from influenza in the early spring, and had been called to officiate the funeral. He was appropriately interred on Valentine's day, his love for his flock undimmed to the end. The churchyard had been full that cold morning, and Miles had been moved at the sight of so many who had taken time from their labours to pay silent respect.

His hurried replacement had been his curate, Roger Mitton, a young man who Miles had only met on one occasion since the funeral. His memories of that encounter were not entirely agreeable; however, mindful of the purpose of his visit, he avowed to maintain his temper.

As he dismounted at the worn stone block and led his horse towards the Vicarage he was struck by the proximity of the ale-house to the church gate. Was it ever thus? He led his mount through the arch and into a neat stable yard where he was met by a fellow whose face he distantly recalled.

"Good morning, Parson Gale."

"Good morning, em …"

"Henry, sir, Henry Gott."

"Yes, indeed, Henry. Is the Reverend Mitton at home?"

"Indeed, sir, his wife's first child is due any day and he doesn't wish to leave her."

Much as I thought, mused Miles.

"If you hand me your horse I shall go let him know that you are here."

"Very good."

Standing in the small yard Miles studied the back of the house, admiring a fine stone porch, a recent addition to the ancient fabric of the building. Elsewhere he could see where windows had been remodelled and replaced in a less convincing manner, scarring the otherwise neat facade. Presently Henry appeared at the porch doorway and ushered Miles in. Stooping to avoid the low lintel, he found himself in a narrow panelled hall. Henry knocked gently at the pitch-black door to the right, and, when so obliged, indicated that Miles should enter.

Roger Mitton was not an attractive man. Miles was immediately taken by the broadness of his outline, as he stood silhouetted against the window, blocking the light with the effectiveness of shutters. As he stepped forward Miles could see that he was not wearing a coat, instead a waistcoat that strained to remain closed about his vast belly. His countenance had the tight livid appearance of a boil, and his neck, clenched tight by his collar, chafed red.

"Reverend Gale, had I known that you were coming I should have prepared a good breakfast."

Miles was repulsed by the smallness of his voice, which belied his great size, and by his damp flaccid handshake.

"Sir, please beg my intrusion at this importune time. How goes Mrs Mitton?"

"Well, sir, well, though I find that I am unable to sleep these days. I fear that I am completely distracted through want of sleep."

"Indeed so." Already Miles could feel irritation at the man's self-obsession.

"Will you take a little sack, sir?"

"Thank you," replied Miles, taking a seat at the Reverend Mitton's behest.

As he fussed with a bottle and glasses, Miles cast his eyes about the room. Furnished sparsely with fine, if old-fashioned, oak furniture, much of which he remembered, the new incumbent had yet to stamp his personality on the house. Sadly he spied an austere wooden crucifix in the puritan style that the Reverend Pollard had recovered from the church. Its plainness had been a painful reminder of the war, and, during renovations to the church, it had been removed and placed in his parlour. Its replacement had been a far more graphic depiction of Christ's sacrifice.

"I do so dislike the heat, I am want to stay indoors," the Reverend Mitton continued, "so it is likely that you will find me here these summer days."

He continued in much the same manner for a goodly while, bemoaning his lot before finally enquiring as to the purpose of Miles's visit. Not wishing to reveal his true aim he began.

"Are you familiar with Holden, a part of your parish I believe?" Mitton nodded vaguely.

"It is of a personal nature, but I seek a woman named Mary of that place; do you know who that might be?"

The prosaic nature of the request seemed to disappoint the other man.

"Mm, I do not care to visit that part of the parish, the road is so bad. The last time I was there my horse lost its footing. I was lucky not to be cast off."

In irritation at what was likely to be a lengthy tale of misfortune, Miles steered him back to the question.

"Do you know of a Mary of Holden?"

Roger wracked his brains. Mopping his clammy brow as though to dislodge thoughts therein, he replied: "Well, there is the widow Taylor, she is a Mary I believe, and the young Mary Booth whom I married not a month ago, and that, I think, is all."

"Are you quite sure, sir? I believe the woman I seek has a husband and children."

"Oh yes, there may be another. She asked that I baptise her child, a son, as I recall. She was a stranger to me, and does not attend church; I was about to deny her but my curate vouched for her good character. I baptised the child but have not seen the woman since."

"Her name, sir?"

"No, I'm sorry, I cannot bring it to mind. Do you not find it impossible to find a good tailor about these heathen parts? You must let me know where you acquired your coat. I see it is a quality cloth, and the buttonholes, so fine."

Fighting to keep his voice even, Miles replied:

"This is an old coat, sir; as I recall, it was made for me by my father's tailor in York, though I doubt he still plies his trade. But sir, I must press you for the name of the woman, it is a matter of some urgency."

"Ah, that is a shame, one cannot expect to find such workmanship about here, though I hear talk of a decent tailor in Ilkley. Now, the name of the woman." He paused, his eyes rolling ceilingward as though the answer might be writ among the rafters. "No, I cannot recall it."

In a small voice Miles persisted: "Perhaps you might remember the month of the baptism?"

"Now that I can say. It was December. No. January. I was greatly troubled by a cough at the time."

"With your permission, sir, might I see the registers?"

"I do not have them, my curate Mr Topham keeps them. Although his hand is much inferior to my own, he takes much pleasure in maintaining the records."

"Might I enquire where I may find Mr Topham?"

"Well that is hard to say, sir. He could be at the church, or perhaps at home?"

Miles's voice was tightening with impatience, his cheerful humour disappearing like smoke from a chimney.

"I shall try at the church. Perhaps you could let me know where Mr Topham abides?"

"Let me think, it is Thursday is it not, and the hour early? He may have left for his mother's house."

"And where might she live?"

"On the Broad Street in Keighley," the Reverend Mitton replied with some satisfaction.

Miles could do little to stifle the snort of exasperation at this news. Rising abruptly to his feet he spluttered.

"It would seem that my journey has been a fool's errand. I wish you good day, sir." Then remembering his manners added, "Please give my kindest regards to Mrs Mitton. May God protect her." Never had he spoken a truer word.

As the Reverend Mitton trailed him to the door, careful not to step beyond the threshold into the light, he bid farewell.

"It was good to make your acquaintance again, sir. I'm sorry that you have not found the answer you seek. Mr Topham, he will know. Yes, he has a mind for detail. Should you remember the name of that tailor in York …"

Miles had already turned, raising his hand in silent farewell. When he was sure that the Reverend Mitton had returned to his parlour, he sought out Henry at work in the stable.

"Would you know where I might find Mr Topham, Henry?"

"Yes, sir, he left for Keighley not an hour since."

Miles saw that his journey had indeed been in vain, for even were he to locate Mr Topham in Keighley, he would not have the registers about him.

"Thank you, Henry," he managed at last. Taking the reins of his horse he made towards the archway. As he was about to leave the yard, he turned back.

"Henry, do you know of a woman called Mary who lives at Holden. She is married with children."

"Yes, sir, that would be Mary Fowler as was. Her husband died and she married again. She lives at Holden

Gate, the entrance to the park. Her husband's name is Gawthorp." As Henry drew out the last word his lip curled.

Miles at last had a name.

"This Gawthorp, what do you know of him?"

"Forgive me, sir, but the man is a knave, any about here would tell you so."

It was not yet noon, the weather warm and Miles's humour much improved as he resolved to take the Silsden road, as instructed by Henry. The hillside track twisted its way eventually down to Keighley. It would take him through the ancient park, and past the house which had been for years the home to its gamekeeper, Holden Gate.

16

June 1700. Holden Gate

What had become of Ann? Eliza was sensing a harshness in her manner that she had never known. That very morning as they had gathered outside the barn watching the last of the cows making their slow progress down the slope, heads nodding deeply with each heavy step, Ann had snapped at her gentle teasing. Gawthorp walked some distance behind, his dog darting excitedly from side to side, eyes never leaving its quarry. He carried a long willow stripling which he whipped through the air with a breathy whistle. As he walked past the girls he turned to face them without breaking his stride.

"See that you've finished milking sooner than yesterday."

Ann mumbled a reply but Eliza remained silent, her gaze fixed upon him, daring him to chide her. Taking up their pails, they followed him into the barn. He weaved between the cows, tethering the beasts at the manger, each animal taking its familiar place. There was something comforting about their mechanical chewing, the occasional shake of their heads in irritation at a fly's bite, and their warm earthy smell. Gawthorp, having gathered up his scythe, strode out of the barn towards the meadow.

Haymaking had begun early this year, the weather being so fair, and whilst he would have preferred to have done the work alone, he had been obliged to pay for help. Rather than hire local men, which was the common practice, he had instead procured the services of three itinerant Scots. Two were brothers, the other a friend; all had made the long journey down from Ayrshire in search of paid work. Having proved that they could handle the scythe and fork, he had employed all three. It would take a week to mow and turn the hay and, should they prove themselves honest labourers, they might be retained for ricking and storing the harvest.

The three men worked silently, an arrangement which suited Gawthorp well. Mary was instructed to leave their snap at the gate where he would collect it and take it to them. Together they would eat, and afterwards the men would laze a while in the stubbly grass. Gawthorp and his dog remained watchful. As the shadows lengthened and dissolved into the meadow, Gawthorp would signal the end of the long day. Gathering up the tools, he made his way back to the house, leaving the men to their own company. In the gathering gloom of the warm evenings they would bed down in the soft mown mattress of grass and flowers.

There were six cows on the farm, and each day the girls would take equal share of the labour.

To the rhythmic hiss of milk, Eliza enquired: "Is all well, Ann, you have been very quiet this past week."

"I am quite well."

It was quite clear to Eliza that something was amiss. Though they differed greatly in manner, Eliza forthright and questioning, Ann quiet and reserved, they had always enjoyed a sisterly closeness. Eliza would open her heart to Ann, her worries and joys, always anxious to hear Ann's opinions. Her elder sister, in contrast, would not volunteer information in the same easy way, but when asked would be truthful and frank in her reply. This day, she seemed unable to trust herself to retain her temper. Still Eliza persisted.

"Ann, I am certain that you are not, please tell me what troubles you."

"Eliza, I tell you nothing is wrong." Her raised voice, however, put paid to her deceit.

Though the shaggy flank of the cow obscured Eliza's view of her sister, she could readily hear her muffled sobs. Rising from her low stool and making her way around the back of the beast she came upon Ann, continuing bravely in her labour, tears silently falling. Eliza rushed to her and fell to her knees, taking Ann into her arms.

"Please, sister, tell me what it is that pains you so? I cannot bear to see you so upset."

Quite overcome, Ann ceased milking and fell upon Eliza's shoulder sobbing. Eliza stroked her cheek gently and waited for the crying to subside. Eventually Ann raised her head and dried her wet face upon her apron. Taking a shuddering breath and focusing on Eliza's anxious face she began.

"I am being punished, and I don't know that I can endure it." Again tears sprang unbidden and her words were swallowed by wild sobbing. Eliza clasped her sister's hands together as though in prayer and stroked them gently between her own.

"Come now, come. Who is punishing you?"

"God is punishing me for my sins," Ann managed in the smallest of voices.

"I do not understand." Eliza was bewildered, for Ann, like Mary, was pious and meek, and for the life of her, she could not imagine what dreadful sin Ann was now being punished for.

"Father... .... Gawthorp ... I ... I ... deny him." These faltering words seemed to sap every ounce of strength and again she was overcome with distress. Eliza cautiously went on.

"Has he harmed you?" Her slow, carefully chosen words seemed to unlock something in Ann. Again she looked Eliza directly in the eye.

"Many times he tries to force himself upon me. I refuse him, Eliza, but he is strong. Each time it happens, I pray for God's help. This angers him, and he strikes me but then ... he weeps." Eliza's face had frozen, mask-like. Ann continued: "You must not speak of this, Mother can never know, Eliza, you must swear, please swear it, Eliza!"

Like the lighting of a lantern, the meaning of Ann's words began to dawn on Eliza.

"And George ...?"

"George knows nothing of this, nor can he ever know. Gawthorp keeps us apart, he knows nothing of our letters, were he to find out ... So I am punished, God sees my wickedness."

At this final announcement Eliza clasped Ann's hands tightly.

"You are a victim of Gawthorp's wickedness. You must not believe it to be God's punishment!" Such was her anger in that moment that she sprang to her feet, alarming the cow patiently waiting its milking. "Ann, this cannot be endured, George must be told."

"No, that can never happen. Though I fear that we can never be together I still harbour the hope. Should he know then he would never want me ..." The tears that now fell were those of misery together with fear at what Eliza might do. "You must swear it, Eliza, please!"

Deeply troubled by what she had heard yet beholden to her sister's entreaties she nodded.

"George shall hear nothing of this from me. But Ann, this must end. I don't know how but I shall pray to God that he shall deliver us. Come, we must finish our work lest he return to check on us. Dry your tears now. We shall speak more of this tonight."

With a sweet kiss, Eliza returned to her stool and recommenced milking. The mechanical nature of the work allowed her thoughts to range over what Ann had just told her. She found herself clenching her teeth at the thought of Gawthorp and his violation of her sister. The cow voiced its discomfort at her rough handling.

As the sun passed the mid-point in the heavens and the air assumed the wavering haze of a perfect summer's day, a figure on horseback raised a low dust train on the hillside track. The Reverend Gale was making his way through the pleasing wooded landscape of Holden. Though the park was now given over to farms and mills, the managed clusters of trees, like neighbours on market day, leaned in on one another. He was minded to remove his wig which itched at his scalp in the heat, but for appearance's sake, he retained it, instead removing his wide-brimmed hat.

All around him where the land fell away into the valley, he could see men about the business of haymaking, an agreeable occupation on such a fine day as this he mused. The road ahead disappeared and reappeared at intervals as it followed the undulating contours of the hill. Ahead, at what he judged to be the highest point, a pair of buildings came into view. The handsomely proportioned farmhouse was dwarfed by the barn, set gable-end to the road. This was likely Holden Gate. Unsure as to how he would proceed, he eased the reins of his mount, causing it to slow as it approached the gateway. He waited a while in the hope that someone would emerge from the house, but the place seemed deserted. Perhaps they were at work in the barn and had not seen his approach, he thought, as he wheeled his leg about and dismounted. His horse was soon tearing at the long broad-blade grass that fringed the track.

He made his way into the yard across the wide flagged pavement about which chickens languished in tight groups, their wings spread decorously in the sun. Inquisitively, the Reverend Gale made towards the barn. Peering inside he was struck by the cavernous interior, cathedral-like in its shady gloom. There was no one to be seen. He retreated into the yard and made to the low stone-framed door above which "TF" had proudly announced the building of his house in the year 1619. He knocked gently and from within he was sure that he could hear light footsteps, the scraping of wood on stone.

"What is your business here?" boomed a voice at his back which caused Miles to start. Swinging about he was met by the sight of a tall man in shirt-sleeves, hair plastered flat to his tall narrow forehead, hands on hips. The man seemed out of breath.

"Good afternoon, I am the Reverend Gale of Keighley Parish. And you, sir, are?"

"I do not care which parish you belong to, you have no business here, please be gone."

Miles was in no doubt that he was now in the company of Robert Gawthorp; even so, he was take aback by the rudeness of the man, and his air of menace.

"I wondered if I might trouble you for a drink, sir, that is all. I have travelled over from Kildwick and am on my way back to Keighley. I thought I should take a different route but had not thought the distance so far nor the day so hot." Miles felt this explanation would seem entirely plausible and might gain him access to the house. He was wrong.

"Like I say, you have no business here." This time the words were delivered with cold deliberate exaction.

"I shall wish you good day then, sir," Miles retorted, keeping his own temper in check. He moved past Gawthorp and out to the road where he gathered up the reins of his horse, and using a jagged quoin in the wall, remounted. All the while Gawthorp's eyes were upon him. As he drew up his horse, somewhat agitated at being denied its grass, and continued his journey, he was aware that he was being observed. When he had travelled a distance further along the road, he glanced back over his shoulder. Gawthorp stood in the centre of the road, his hands still on his hips, watching until satisfied that Miles was out of sight.

The journey down the road to Keighley took in fine scenery, the full extent of his town laid out beneath him and the swathe of the Aire, a bright ribbon in mellow golden landscape. Miles's thoughts, however, where taken up with other matters. The day which had started out so frustratingly had yet proved to be a fruitful one. He had discovered the name of the letter writer, and could now place her home. He had also been acquainted with the cause of her distress.

There was nothing that he liked more than a conundrum. It reminded him that he was still alive, and that God had a purpose for him, even in a place like Keighley. He could see that he was being posed a problem that would require all of his powers of intelligence. Mary needed his help, but how could he help when Robert Gawthorp stood in his way. He was still struggling with the difficulties of the situation as he crossed the bridge and entered the shaded streets of the town.

Mary had heard the raised voices in the yard but had been afraid to go to the window. Instead she had gathered up the baby and quietly opened the back door to the house and edged her way about the far corner, praying that the baby wouldn't waken. She had seen the departing figure of the Reverend Gale make his slow passage along the road. Hardly daring to breathe, she could make out the figure of Gawthorp only a matter of yards away. She remained motionless until she heard the slide of his dusty step as he returned to the hay field. Down the slope Eliza and Ann were descending towards her as they returned from the well with heavy pails. They could not have seen the Reverend

Gale who was by now out of sight, but yet she feared what Gawthorp may say come supper-time. In spite of this, deep in her stomach she felt a fluttering of excitement like the first quickening of a child. The Reverend Gale had not forsaken them, and God in his mercy would hear her prayer.

17

August 1700. Marley

Martha Wright had seen to it that Jennet was churched in the parish church of Bingley. The Reverend James Roberts officiated, and it had taken much persuasion on Martha's part for the ceremony to take place at all. Jennet was still not fully recovered from the birth of her son. He had been given the name Jonas after her father who had died the previous winter. Though the child was thriving, it was not without the services of a wet nurse who Martha had employed when Jennet's feeble supply of milk seemed not enough to sustain the boy.

In the days following the birth, Jennet had slept for much of the time. John saw to it that the fire in the parlour was well banked. By the third day, it was clear that a fever raged. The wet nurse was called and Martha remained at the bedside, administrating cool wet linen to Jennet's brow. She refused all offers of food, but Martha was able to trickle a little syrup of poppy into her throat to ease the pains which caused her body to curl like a fallen leaf. Nathan, bewildered and afraid, had been unwilling to leave the house for fear that something would occur in his absence. John had petitioned the estate manager that Nathan be allowed a little time to spend with his ailing wife, and had vouched to cover as much of his labour as was practicable. He had also found time to call upon Jennet's widowed mother Joan, who lived with her eldest son and his family in a small cottage at the far side of Bingley. On hearing the news of Jennet and the child, she had insisted on returning with John to offer her services with the running of the house.

It worried Nathan that Martha and Joan broke off from their whispered conversations at his approach. When he questioned them about Jennet's condition, they would glance at each other before Martha spoke, her answers offering little encouragement. While his son slept dreamlessly in his cradle, Jennet communed in an unknown tongue, her eyes wildly seeking figures in the air. Even as he clutched at her waxen hand and whispered endearments that were theirs alone, she seemed not to know him. After the sun had left the sky and the land was bathed in the green half-light of a summer's night, he and John sat outside. Uncertain of how to raise his spirits, John had tried to reassure Nathan, but even as he spoke, the words were hollow vessels, without substance, void of belief. Each night Nathan would drag a straw mattress to the side of the bed where Jennet lay, his sleep so shallow, starting at every small sigh, each feverish turn. Above, John also struggled to surrender to sleep, and in the smallest hours of the night he found himself praying that God would spare Jennet.

On the morning of the eighth day John clambered down the ladder into the parlour to the sound of gentle laughter. Joan held Jonas in her arms, and Martha chuckled as the infant clasped at her finger. Nathan sat at the edge of the bed, carefully administering small spoonfuls of gruel to Jennet. Propped at a shallow angle she seemed as fleeting as a wraith, her colour muted, her eyes dim.

"John!" The effort of speaking his name seemed almost beyond her, and yet John knew that she was returned to them.

"Jennet, thank God!" He could not find further words, as the sight of Nathan tenderly ministering to his wife caused tears to spring forth. Before he was aware of what was happening, he was sobbing as he had the day his mother died. Martha took him into her arms wordlessly where he remained until the great storm of emotion had subsided. Eventually he drew himself away.

"We must all be in need of breakfast."

Jennet's journey back to health was a long road, and Joan had insisted on remaining with the family until she was satisfied that her daughter was strong enough to resume her duties about the house. She had remained in bed for such a time that when she first rose to dress, she found that she hadn't the strength to stand for more than a few moments. She could find little joy in food; even the wild strawberries that Nathan had collected in the woods failed to delight. Almost everything seemed to move her to tears, which she fought vainly to control. She felt shame that she could not adequately feed the child and relied in some measure upon the wet nurse. As she stared at his tiny face screwed in fury, it was fear and not love that she felt in her heart. She tried to commune her feeling to Martha.

"I have seen this many times, and often with first born, but you must not worry. Once you have your strength again all will be well." Though Martha's words soothed, there remained an unease, a prickle of doubt.

One morning Joan encouraged Jennet to stand at the threshold of the house, to take the air. By this hour, men were labouring in the fields and she was unlikely to be observed. As she stood watching a chevron of birds slicing the unblemished sky, feeling the warmth of the sun on her pallid cheek, she was for that instant without care. But as the child awoke, stubbornly demanding attention, she was drawn back to the parlour and her strange new life.

A month had passed since the night that Jonas had arrived and the small party made slow progress down to the church where the Reverend Roberts greeted them in the low stone porch. Though the journey measured but two miles, it had taken almost two hours to arrive at the church gate. Nathan had carried the child in a sling about his chest, and the warmth of the day, the slow procession and gentle murmur of voices ensured Jonas slept the entire distance. John and Joan supported Jennet under her arms, pausing often to allow her to catch her breath, her cheeks glazed with effort. The Reverend Roberts placed a thin gauze veil over Jennet's head and incanted the ancient blessing and prayer of purification. At last they stepped into the cool interior of the church, Jennet following the vicar to the altar rail. Acknowledging her weakness, he carefully took her arm as she eased herself to her knees.

As the prayers began, Jennet stared out through the thin cotton veil, infused with the scent of candle smoke and damp. She tried to hold on to the words being spoken, but the prayers floated as butterflies on a breeze, unconfined, beyond her grasp. At last it was over, the veil removed and coins exchanged for the churching and then the naming of the child. As they made their way back into the whiteness of the morning, Jennet gazed at the Madonna and child frozen in stone. She had known the image since childhood Sundays in church, and had prayed to Mary on her wedding day that she be blessed with children. As she gazed upon the holy family, heads touching, hands raised in benediction, the image was now one of pain and foreboding.

They had rested a while at the old inn which stood on the banks of the river only a short distance from the church, and shared a simple meal. The child grizzled and was removed by the wet nurse to the bank of the river where he was fed in the shade of a sprawling willow. Joan, once reassured by Martha, kissed Jennet tenderly and departed for her son's house, promising to visit later in the week. The clatter of heavy hooves on the bridge delayed their homeward journey a while, and they watched through the window at the file of cattle being led out towards the drovers' road. The journey back to Marley took even longer than the journey out, the sun being at its highest point, and Jennet's energy spent. It was with some relief that they eventually stepped into the stillness of the parlour. Jennet was lain in bed, the curtain drawn.

"It will take time, Nathan," Martha cautioned before leaving. Promising to return the next day at first light, Nathan marvelled at the stamina of the woman, as he watched her down the lane, her bird-like steps carrying her briskly out of view.

In the weeks following the birth, John had only seen Eliza on two occasions. They had intended to meet at the woodland spring to exchange letters between George and Ann, but when the baby made its unexpected arrival, it was clear that John could not attend. Frantic at the thought that Eliza should think herself forsaken, he had volunteered to run to Keighley to seek the wet nurse as instructed by Martha. It was market day, and the hour early when he raced across church green. Eliza was just taking her customary seat at the corner of the square, Margaret in attendance. Her eyes widened at his bold approach, and she glared as though to warn him away.

"I should like some butter," he gulped his words as he caught his breath.

As she lowered her head and reached into her basket he leaned in and whispered.

"Jennet's baby has arrived, she is ill, I cannot get away. Next week I will be here, with news – I'm sorry."

As they rose up Eliza held his eye, and as he handed over his coin her fingers gently brushed his palm.

He turned and made for the house by the river where the wet nurse was to be found. Over the coming week as he worked long hours in the field, his thoughts returned to the moment of Eliza's touch. Again and again he relived the feeling, his cheeks flushing anew at the memory. Unwilling to discuss the matter with Nathan, who was too taken up with worry, he could only contend with private thoughts. Returning to the house as the light faded he worried that his presence was burdensome, as Martha and Joan ministered to Jennet, and Nathan fretted at her side. Unbidden he chopped logs for the fire, carried pails and stacked and turned the peat stack, and all the while he called upon God to spare Jennet.

The following week it was past noon before he arrived at the market. He had risen at dawn to begin his labours, and run as though pursued by the devil himself to the town. His relief at the sight of Eliza was overwhelming, but he lingered in the shade of the lane before making his approach. Margaret fidgeted in the heat and seemed to suggest that she had grown tired; Eliza handed over a coin to her and the child smiled and trotted away. Taking his chance John raced across the green to Eliza.

"I feared you wouldn't come, how is Jennet and the child?"

"Her fever is passed and Martha says she will recover, but I fear it will take some time yet; the baby thrives."

"Praise be!"

"I have not seen George this past week as I am tied to harvest at Marley."

"John, I have much to tell but Margaret cannot find you here. I shall visit the spring this Saturday noon, if you are not there I shall leave a note explaining all. The hawthorn, know it?"

"Yes."

Eliza suddenly flinched. John turned to see Margaret weaving her way towards them. He held Eliza's eye, whispering "Saturday" before running down the nearest dark ginnel.

In the lane the dust hung in the air like spawn in a pond, the sound of the market muffled by the heat. As a couple of women, arms linked, eased past, he felt the heat from their bodies. The bolder of the two winked slyly at John causing him to flush. Remembering the second purpose of his visit to the town, he hurried towards the river and on to Martha's house.

Isiah Wright greeted him at the door, a clay pipe clamped between thin lips, unbolstered by teeth. "You'll be wanting this," he murmured, handing a small cloth bundle. "I'll see Martha when I do then."

Yes, and I'll see Eliza when I do, thought John, despondently.

18

November 1700. Glusburn

The blow when it came had been savage and unprovoked. Philip Parker had been making his way from Glusburn to Marley. Flooding in the valley had meant that the land to the south of the Aire was under many feet of water, and his father had advised him to take the moorland road up through Silsden. Although it would add a good deal of time to his journey, he could be assured that he would reach his destination safely.

He had saddled up the largest of his father's horses, an even-tempered mare, sure-footed and tall. The rain continued to fall though not with the intensity of the past day. The wind still tore at the trees removing the very last of the summer leaves. Philip secured his hat with a woollen scarf which he knotted under his chin. Throwing on his stoutest coat, he was helped onto his mount by the groom. His father sent him away with instructions about the Eastburn land sale for his brother Robert at Marley, and a bottle of finest brandy. His mother waved from the sanctuary of the low porch as he steered his horse out of the yard.

Philip enjoyed the company of his uncle Robert and his amiable wife. As the only son of the family he was very much indulged. He enjoyed nothing more than when his uncle walked him about Marley, his arm through his, and spoke to him not as a child but a man. Philip was seventeen years of age and of a fair clear countenance. He, like other members of the Parker family, was not tall of stature, but made up for this shortcoming with a fine sense of humour and gentle nature.

He was rather dismayed that the weather was so inclement, for riding was his greatest love and horse and rider were unlikely to take pleasure from the conditions that day.

As he made his way up the rising road, water coursed from the moor, and his horse, struggling to maintain purchase, trod cautiously. There were few folk foolhardy enough to venture abroad unless necessity dictated. A shepherd making the same journey to the higher ground raised a wet hand as Philip tapped his hat; the shepherd's dog trudged close at heel, eyes fixed downwards. Presently he reached Silsden. From a distance the smoke from chimneys barrelled wildly before dispersing into the low cloud. In the darkness of the lane, rushlights illuminated gloomy parlours where linen weavers strained to see their work. Rainwater cascaded in long rods from slate and ling. A solitary voice sang plaintively of a lost love, and a dog cringed in a doorway.

Before long the lane broadened out into the sweep of the moor, the track fractured by dips and hollows. At the verge side a buzzard tugged at the entrails of a rabbit as Philip drew his scarf tighter about his chin. The cloud filled the valley like water in a ditch, and the land was a palette of grey. After a couple of miles he had reached the highest part on the road, and the gable of a large barn emerged from the gloom, flanked by a single wind-blasted rowan tree. As he drew level with the barn he observed the roof of a handsome stone house set a little back from the road. In the yard a straggle of red chickens scratched miserably at the tufted grass that sprouted between the flags; otherwise all was silent.

As he passed the house, the land began to gently fall away, but to his left, the moor rose broodily, its summit lost in the heavy distention of cloud. A little further along a figure began to emerge, walking the track towards him. As they drew close, Philip was somewhat surprised to encounter a young woman, head shrouded in a thick woollen shawl, eyes downcast. The girl carried an open basket looped about one arm, the other encircled her body holding the shawl fast.

"Good morning," Philip volunteered.

The girl seemed not to hear, not even raising her eyes from the road.

"I said good morning," he repeated in a louder yet cheery voice.

Still the girl ignored him and continued on her way without a word. Somewhat affronted at her ill manner, Philip muttered to himself. After only a couple more paces, he heard a small cry, and turned to see the girl sprawled upon the track, her basket and its contents scattered about her. In an instant he sprang from his mount and taking the reins, walked back towards the girl who was now on her knees frantically gathering up her sorry goods from the mud. He approached gently.

"Let me help you. Are you hurt?"

With every word the girl's movements became more rapid and panic stricken. Philip could see that her basket had contained eggs, many of which lay smashed and ruined, splashes of colour upon a drab canvas. There were also small packages bound with twine, some of which had been thrown into the grass verge by the violence of her fall. Crouching, he retrieved a couple and replaced them in her basket. Glancing up into her face, their eyes momentarily met, and he was shocked at the fear he encountered in her gaze. It was the terror of a trapped animal.

"You are hurt. Tell me where are you going? You can ride with me. I fear that your misfortune is my fault – I startled you."

Still the girl would not speak, but simply shook her head violently. It was as he leant forward for a last small parcel flung almost as far as the hawthorn hedge that he heard a scream, felt a lightning bolt of pain at the base of his skull, and the light was extinguished.

As if awakening in a strange bed, Philip was first aware of the ripping of grass, and felt the warmth of breath on his cheek. Opening his eyes he encountered the soft muzzle of his horse and the rhythmic champ of her teeth. The mare stood over him, stooping at intervals to tear at the coarse grass. He was then aware that he lay prone in the margin of the track, his clothes saturated, his skin cold as the earth upon which he lay. Gingerly lifting himself to his knees, he was overcome with a sickness and an intense pain which clamped his skull. Reaching back to the point at the base of his hat, he discovered a great swelling, alien and painful.

Drawing his hand back in alarm he was fascinated to see it streaked with fresh blood. As though fishing in the shallows to retrieve a lost coin, he tried to recall what had happened, and twisting himself into a sitting position in the grass, his eyes fixed on the litter of broken eggs.

After a little time during which he expelled his breakfast into the mud, he carefully rose to his feet. The rain was now a soft gauze curtain softening the sparse features of the moor. Gathering the reins of his horse, Philip, with no small effort, hauled himself back into the saddle. Screwing his eyes, he wheeled a full circle about, seeking both the girl and his attacker, but aside from the mournful cry of birds, the moor was deserted.

His passage down to Marley over the broiling waters at Keighley bridge was otherwise without incident. With each step of his horse, pain bloomed like an angry flower from the wound at the back of his head. He felt overcome with weariness and had not the strength to raise his hand in greeting at his few fellow travellers. It was only the tolling of the church bell that alerted him to the hour; the morning had passed and from chimneys and doors the smell of cooking food rose to meet the rain.

As he rode through the gates at Marley he was met by his uncle's groom who was at once alarmed by Philip's deathly pallor. Dried blood arranged about his throat in a jagged necklace.

"Master Philip, what in God's name has happened?"

Philip slid from his horse, his knees almost buckling as he touched down. The groom shouted for his lad and together they supported Philip into the house.

Remembering about the land sale papers and brandy, Philip murmured instructions and the lad was sent back to collect his saddlebag.

Robert Parker had been waiting on his nephew since breakfast and was beginning to fear that the road to Glusburn had proved impassable. On hearing the commotion in the hall he flung open the doors to his study to be met by the sight of Philip, pale as a wraith and soaked to the skin.

"Uncle ..." The word hung in the air as his head slumped forward and he lost consciousness.

It was not until the following morning that Philip awoke, once again unsure of his surroundings. After his collapse, he had been taken to the guest chamber where his sodden filthy garments had been gently removed. At Robert's insistence, the fire had been steeply banked and word was sent to Dr Barrett at Bingley, who was in attendance throughout the night. As the grey light filtered in broad stripes through the shuttered window, Philip finally opened his eyes. At the sight of his uncle's anxious face he raised himself in the bed and at once felt a dull throb of pain at the back of his head.

"Philip, thank God! We have been so worried. Did you fall? Were you thrown? Dr Barrett says that your skull might have been smashed like an egg were not the ground so soft."

At the word egg the events of the day rushed back at Philip with the ferocity of a storm.

"Sir, this was no accident, I was set upon."

"Thieves? Are you sure Philip? Your saddlebag is here, what has been taken?"

Reaching inside the leather bag, still cold and stained black with damp, Philip was astounded to find the papers and the brandy. Over the course of the next few hours, he tried to recollect what had happened to him. A hearty breakfast was delivered, and Dr Barrett dismissed from his bedside once it had been established that no lasting damage had been done. Answering Robert's questions to the best of his ability, Philip began to reconstruct his journey.

"There was a girl, she fell and I went to her aid. I was struck from behind. I did not see my assailant."

By the late afternoon, the housemaid who had attended to Philip and the doctor had spoken to the cook of what she had overheard. The cook had then spoken to the groom who in turn had spoken to the stable lads. As John was returning to the yard with Mab in the dying light of the day, a stable boy rushed to him, bursting with the news of Philip's attack. As he listened grimly to the details grown more embellished through the course of the day, he wondered at who could be responsible. It had been no robbery, but a vicious unprovoked attack. Having witnessed his anger at first hand, John could not but imagine that this was Gawthorp's handiwork.

19

November 1700. Holden Gate

The door flew open and Ann tumbled into the parlour accompanied by an eddy of dead leaves. Mary, Eliza and the younger children were about the table, salting a section of beef from a cow past milking and too old to overwinter.

"He's killed him!" she stated blankly.

The family remained rooted as statues, aghast at the sight of Ann. Her pale hair clung to her face, streaked like woodgrain with tears and mud. As she placed the basket on the floor, broken eggs seeped from its fabric, pooling in the muddy water that dripped from every part of Ann.

"Child, what do you mean?" cried Mary, stepping forward and taking Ann by the shoulders. Her daughter's eyes seemed to stare through her as though she were a spectre.

"Ann, Ann?"

At the sound of footsteps in the yard the family froze and Ann's eyes rolled wildly. The dogs barked and grew fainter as the steps receded. The frenzy of dogs indicated their passage up the slope towards Ghyllgrange. Collectively they all breathed anew. Ann began to weep silently, and without the slightest movement. At the sight, Eliza stepped forward and gently led Ann towards the seat in the hearth.

"Margaret, take the children out to the barn, I must speak with your sister," said Mary, her eyes still fixed on Ann. Horrified and afraid, Margaret did her mother's bidding, gathering up shawls and capes at the door. When finally they were gone, Eliza crouched at Ann's feet and began to speak.

"What has happened? You must tell it!" but Ann just shook her head as though trying to dislodge for ever the thoughts therein. Eliza tried again.

"Who is dead? What has happened?" Mary tenderly bent in and stroked her arm.

"You must confess it, Ann, in God's sight." The look with which Ann returned Mary's words almost broke Eliza's heart. It was as though it pained her to speak the words, though she could not deny her mother nor God. The girl was in purgatory.

The three remained in silence for the longest time, the chatter of the hens and the temper of the wind in the chimney being the only sound to punctuate the peace. Finally Ann began to speak. She recounted her journey back from Widdop's farm at Upwood that morning. She had been sent at the behest of Mary to sell as much butter and as many eggs as she could among the ageing farmers of the hamlet, who had been prevented from making the journey to market by the flooding in the valley. Gawthorp had agreed to this on the understanding that she return within the hour to help with the salting. That she had been

145

allowed to go at all was due to Eliza having turned her ankle the day before on the slippery flags of the yard.

Ann's journey had resulted in the sale of only a small amount of butter and no eggs. As she had made her way back along the road to Holden a rider had passed her, on his way down to Keighley. She had not known his face, and when he had spoken to her, she had thought it best not to reply. As she had passed him, he had spoken again, and as she turned, unsure as to whether to speak, she had lost her footing and fallen. The man had immediately come to her assistance, anxious to know that she had not injured herself. At this point in her tale she fell silent and inhaled deeply.

"And then?"

"And then he appeared from nowhere and struck him, struck him with his staff."

Mary's expression was one of frozen horror as Ann's tears continued to flow, and in the tension of the moment it was Eliza who spoke.

"And then? Did he strike you?"

Ann's head snapped up. "No, no! He screamed at me to run ... run ... and I did his bidding, God forgive me, I did his bidding, and ... and ... a man is dead because of me ...", at which point words became too difficult as the scene played out again in her mind. Stung by these words, Mary finally spoke.

"Ann, you are not to blame. God sees everything."

"Then God has seen his handiwork and should punish him," spat Eliza. "How can God allow this?", a question to which Mary had no immediate answer. Jumping to her feet

Eliza added, "I am going to find the man, he cannot be left to die."

"No, Eliza, no! If he were to see you … I cannot allow it!" cried Mary, but Eliza was already at the door

"I'm sorry, Mother", and with that she was gone.

As she passed the barn she could make out the nervous voices of the young children, and Margaret's vain attempts to silence them. The dogs were gone and could not be heard on the distant moor. Eliza turned left and set off along the road. Her ankle pained her greatly, and her gait was uneven and tentative. The rain, carried on a cold gathering wind, punched at her shoulders. Water gathered in hollows creating polished pavements which Eliza skirted to avoid. Ann had come from Upwood, a distance of only half a mile, but where the attack had occurred she knew not as she had forgotten to ask. After only a short time she noticed crows gathering on the track like priests in conversation. She hastened towards them. As she approached the birds took to the air, voicing their irritation. The scatter of broken shells upon the track marked the scene of the attack, but of the man there was no sign. Wandering onto the grass verge as far as the hawthorn, Eliza frantically scoured the area for signs of him. Satisfied that he was gone, she offered up a silent prayer, turned and hobbled back towards Holden.

The children had been readmitted and toiled busily at the table at the business of salting. John was in his cradle, and Mary sat with Ann at the fireside. As she flung open the door, the family froze like figures in the church window, fearful at her news.

"He is gone, the man is gone. He is not dead," panted Eliza. Ann failed to swallow a grateful sob.

The children had been in bed many hours when Mary heard the approach of the dogs. Eliza had taken Ann's hand, and together they had kissed Mary. Eliza had wanted to be with Mary at Gawthorp's return, but Mary had forbidden it. When she was certain that the children slept, she had fallen to her knees and prayed. Gawthorp could not find her reading from the bible, and, much as she longed to seek comfort among its verses, she could not take the risk. Instead, she recited silent prayers, so much a part of her being they were as necessary as breathing. She called upon God to forgive her. She had not found the way to lead her husband to God and thus must bear responsibility for his sins. He knows not what he does.

As he entered the parlour, Mary was at the hearth struggling at her sewing in the dim light. Robert placed his staff at the door and removed his cloak and hat. With that staff had he almost killed a man, she wondered?

"Do you want supper, husband?" she asked, struggling to hide the quiver in her voice. He seemed not to hear, instead he walked towards the hearth and turned to warm himself, hands clenched at his back. Though she knew him to be a man of few words, his silence terrified her. She lowered her head and made a pretence of stitching. Time stretched uncomfortably before at last he spoke.

"Has the beast been salted?"

"Yes, it is barrelled and hung."

She waited for the words that didn't come until he turned and drew a rush lamp from its cradle.

"Come then", which signalled the end of her day, and like the dogs she was bound to follow him.

Ann had cried herself to sleep, which came suddenly, as though the events of the day had drained her spirit like whey from curds. In the blackness of the chamber Eliza lay, eyes open. The wind moaned its wild passage, the hiss of rain spoke of its unfinished business. Something was growing within her, a seed germinating in the dark. The roots of her hatred had begun to grow with the first arrival of Gawthorp many years ago, but she had left them untended for her mother's sake. Now, however, she felt tendrils gaining, grasping, constricting her heart, her stomach, her liver. She imagined herself raising the staff and bringing it down on Gawthorp's head, again and again, until finally he twitched and breathed his last. But no, she could not allow these wicked thoughts. God knows the devices and desires of the heart, and can recognise sin. How could she learn to forgive he that trespass against her? How could her mother find that strength, that belief? The more she dwelt, the more miserable she became. The only crumbs of comfort she could find were that the man was not dead, and the beast had not raised his staff to Ann.

Now another thought occurred to her. Who was the man that Gawthorp had assailed? This act could surely not go unpunished. What would be the consequences, for him, for the family?

She was still wrestling with questions when she heard the return of the dogs, their claws rasping on the flags. She heard their complaint as Robert led them to the barn and fastened them in for the night. The door of the house opened and she held her breath as Gawthorp entered the parlour. She waited for the recriminations to begin, but none came. In the shortest time the faint glow of rush flame that pierced the boarded ceiling was extinguished, the blackness was complete. She imagined that she heard Mary cry out, though perhaps she imagined it.

By her side Ann shifted and turned, troubled by dreams, and although the air was chill, her skin burned as though a fever raged. Eliza reached over the floor to her shawl and placed it over Ann's shoulders; her sister murmured something like a prayer at her touch. Through the darkest hours of the night, sleep remained an elusive prey, so with all the stealth she could muster, Eliza rose from her mattress. Shuffling on her knees, her muscles tensed, she eased herself towards the small slit window in the gable wall. She drew aside the shutter and gazed out. The night was moonless and though the rain had ceased, the cloud draped the land like a shorn fleece. She could just make out the road, falling away towards Keighley. A little distance along she saw a fleeting movement, and then stillness. A fox, its eyes trained towards her, seemed to sense her presence. As she continued to watch, the animal was joined by its cubs, scrambling through the grass and onto the track. Even at a distance she could feel the tension in the fox, its senses alert to any threat. The three cubs remained close, noses raised, tasting the air. For what seemed a long time, they remained transfixed, motionless, before at some unperceived signal they scattered like broken shards. Eliza eased the shutter fast and made slow silent passage back to bed. Sleep, when it finally came, brought troubled dreams.

20

November 1700. Marley

John was anxious to speak with George Snowden. It had been several weeks since they had met. It was an unsettling time and the sudden arrival of winter added to his discomfort. The heavy rains and strong winds which had brought misery and hardship to the valley had moved on with a nonchalance to be replaced with the unwelcome early appearance of winter. He had woken that morning, and before he even opened the shutter he knew that the snow had arrived.

Downstairs in the parlour Jennet was about her work, a fresh harvest of oatcakes above the fire, a sign that she had been up some time. Jonas, in his cradle, slumbered still, his corona of soft fair curls captured in a fine linen cap.

"Nathan has left. He was called to attend the cattle, the snow has come."

Though dawn was just breaking, the light in the parlour belied the hour. There was a blue harshness to it, illuminating every beam and corner of the room.

"Then I should go help him," he said, draining the last of his warmed ale and helping himself to a couple of oatcakes. Jennet smiled gently and wiped her hand upon her apron.

With each passing day she felt a little stronger but though she forced herself to keep active throughout daylight hours, it sapped at her fragile reserves. The girl she once was had gone, replaced by a pale and delicate imitation.

John opened the door about which the snow was gathered in deep drifts. Nathan's early footsteps, which had carved a narrow channel out towards the road, were already filling as the leaves of snow fell from a blank open sky.

The clipped cries of cattle deadened by the snow-filled air directed him towards his friend. Blinking, he could see three figures to the back of the Hall surrounded by a steaming huddle of cows. As he drew close, Nathan called out as he spread hay about himself in a thick carpet.

"John, what have we done to deserve this?" he laughed. "He first sends the flood, and not satisfied, he means to freeze us in our beds."

John marvelled at his friend's good humour; it had failed him but once, the night that Jonas was born.

"An unwelcome gift indeed. I see that you have help here. I shall take the dogs up to the moor and lead the sheep down."

Nathan raised his hand before bending again to draw from the straw stack. John continued towards the Hall.

The stable yard had been cleared of snow by the action of many feet and resembled a black rug cast upon the whiteness of the land. Horses jittered from side to side, taking measure of the cold, their breath fantastic rising plumes of white. The dogs wove between legs and in and out of the stables excited at the prospect of the day. After a word with the groom, John set off from the yard and up the slope with a noisy retinue, Mab and three of her bedmates. The snow lay thick and crumped softly at his step. The track was lost, buried beneath the snow, so John relied on his knowledge of the land to guide him.; each twisted tree and receding rooftop.

At length the land levelled and stretched out, the terrain a mystery of soft purple shadows. In the distance he could see the sheep, scattered like crumbs about a table. The snow overcame his boots as his feet found hidden hollows, and the dogs sprang like deer in frenzied excitement. Since that day when he had first encountered Gawthorp he had kept his distance from the Doubler Stones, anxious to avoid a further confrontation, but looking at the distant flock he could see that he must venture that way, towards the grazing lands of Ghyllgrange.

The snow intensified, flakes catching at his lashes so that he could scarce see the dogs, his lively vanguard. He became disorientated, the whiteness erasing all landmarks so that it was with surprise that he suddenly found himself upon the cluster of houses he knew to be Ghyllgrange. Candles burned in the windows of the main farmstead, the home of William Rishworth. The ancient longhouse, much extended over the years, had an extravagant stone porch, a proud declaration in stone of the Rishworths name. Behind the main house sat a cluster of cottages, home to the Snowdens, Lamberts, Dixons and Fosters, tenant farmers of centuries standing.

"John Asquith, is that you?" A familiar voice was at his shoulder.

"George, praise be! A man would struggle to know his own father in this weather." The two friends clasped hands and stamped their feet for fear of freezing to the spot.

"Sheep?"

"We have all been out since dawn and they are now all in the folds." Scattered across the very highest moor, ancient hands had created round dry stone pens, offering shelter for the hardy sheep, and convenient feeding points for the hill farmers.

"Where are you headed?"

"Chasing the stragglers down the hill. Will you walk with me a while?" John queried, anxious to put distance between himself and Ghyllgrange for fear they might again encounter Gawthorp.

"Yes, I am going down to the town and will be glad of the company."

The house quickly receded in the great bank of white as the boys retraced John's footsteps. His dogs had incited a vocal rebellion from the dogs about the hamlet but soon this too was swallowed up by the snow.

As they walked John recounted the story of the attack upon Philip Parker, word of which had already reached George's ear. It had been the work of Gawthorp, they grimly agreed. The boy was recovered well enough to return home, but Mr Parker was determined that the act should not go unpunished. He had accompanied Philip on the same moorland road, together with his groom, but by this stage the snow had begun to fall. The landscape was so much altered that Philip was unable to state with any conviction where the attack had taken place. They walked on some distance in silence before George began,

"Gawthorp was seen that day at Ghyllgrange, much agitated. I was securing the barn door, nearly torn off by the wind, when I saw him coming. I made sure that he didn't see me, but I heard him cursing and raving like a madman."

"And Rishworth opened his door to him?"

"I cannot explain it!" cried an incredulous George. "He has a hold over him!"

As they walked, the dogs rushed ahead, jaggedly cutting across their path, rounding up the sheep. As the land began to fall away their train of sheep grew progressively larger.

"Have you seen Eliza?"

"Yes, but briefly. It was the day after the attack. We had arranged to meet but she stayed only a moment to recount the tale to me. Gawthorp had seen Ann fall, and the Parker boy came to her aid. Gawthorp came from nowhere and became a devil as he beat the boy. Ann tried to stop it but, so afraid that she would receive the same treatment, she ran. She was convinced that he had killed the boy."

"He didn't harm her?" cried George anxiously.

"No, she swears it."

The boys were suddenly alerted by the wild barking of the dogs to the plight of an old ewe that had wandered into a deep drift. For some time talk was abandoned as they laboured to free her. As she stumbled to an ungainly freedom, they blew on their hands grown livid red with cold.

"Eliza means to see him punished, George. She would go to Mr Parker herself, but she fears for Mary."

"People in the town are talking. They know who is responsible, and it will come to the ear of Mr Parker soon enough."

"But it will come to naught – he will deny it! The only person who could prove it is Ann, and she will never tell," concluded John miserably.

The roof line of Marley Hall came into view, its chimneys festooned with smoke which rolled and fell like water from a spring. The sheep rushed at the untidy mound of hay that John had earlier deposited.

"I am meeting with Eliza on Saturday. If you have word for Ann I shall deliver it."

"I think perhaps it would be a mistake to write. What you say is true, John, she is the only one who knows the truth of the business, and he will see to it that she will never tell."

Kicking at the snow in irritation, he added, "Just let her know that she is ever in my heart. The day will come when we can be together."

John nodded in acknowledgement though could find little conviction in his friend's words. The future was as obscured as their path through the snowstorm.

At the gates of the Hall the dogs rushed ahead to the warmth of the stables and the promise of food. John had been deep in thought for some moments, but before bidding his friend farewell as he continued his journey on to the town, he enquired: "How well do you know Rishworth?"

"He is our landlord, and I have known him all my life."

"Perhaps he holds the answer. George, you must become his shadow, your ears open to his every word, because it is through idle talk and hidden gesture that secrets are revealed."

George considered John's words. "I know that you speak the truth, but I cannot risk his displeasure. I must think of my family …"

"Speak of this to no one. You will be safe, I swear it."

"Very well, I shall find out what I can."

The friends clasped icy hands and parted ways. The snow continued to fall with a building ferocity as Nathan waved from the courtyard. Thoughts of Rishworth were dispelled by the promise of scalded ale in the warmth of the kitchen.

21

January 1701. Keighley

There were times when Miles had cause to question his faith, and this day he felt his beliefs sorely tempted. Upstairs Margery continued to weep: the two had exchanged unkind words over breakfast. Not even the presence of the younger children had cautioned her vitriol. Marianne had glanced nervously at her father awaiting his response.

"Madam, you should have a care, I do not seek to drive the boys away!"

With this rebuke, Margery had pushed back her chair and rushed from the room, sobbing. Marianne's eyes widened and searched her father's face beseechingly.

"Father?"

"Go child, go!" he snapped. With the swiftest of nods she fled the room, her footsteps racing up the stone stairs. Edmund and John continued eating in unison, their heads much lowered.

"Sarah, mind the children, I am away to my study."

Once in the refuge of his own room he sank into his chair and exhaled loudly. What in God's name did she want of him?

A letter had arrived that morning from Christopher which had, amongst other things, announced his imminent marriage to the widowed daughter of a local dignitary. Her late husband had been the deputy governor of the county, and though Miles could only wonder at the meaning of such a title, it was clear that Christopher was now moving in elevated circles. His wife to be, Sally was described in loving terms as being of a sweet disposition and robust good health. It was the observation that his mother would find her most agreeable which had perhaps seemed to have upset Margery the most.

"He is so far away," she wailed. "It was always my dearest hope to see him married, but that is now cruelly denied."

Christopher had written diligently and often since his arrival in the colonies, and it was clear that he was now well established. Through the likes of Lawson he had forged trade links with the natives and had acquired "a good house and sizeable estate" with the proceeds of his newly earned fortune. To Miles's great delight, his letters came well furnished with details of the local flora and fauna, enhanced with delicate illustrations guaranteed to excite his father's curiosity. Miles's replies were, by necessity, more prosaic, containing, at Margery's insistence, earnest enquiries as to Christopher's health, and mundane minutiae of life within the Rectory.

It came as little surprise to Miles, but a huge shock to Margery, when Miles the younger and Edmund expressed their desire to follow their older brother over the Atlantic. Though a despairing Margery pleaded with them to reconsider, their ideas were firmly fixed. Only Thomas, a solemn boy of sixteen years, was able to state, with some certainty, that he had no intention of heading overseas, preferring instead to continue his studies and follow his father into the church. Edmund, an impatient child, had at least four more years of schooling, and it vexed him no end that he would not be sailing from Tilbury in the spring with his older brother Miles. The letters from Christopher awakened that part of his father that delighted in the new; how he wished that he were there to share the experience. Sadly he resigned himself to the fact that he had grown too old, and he could now only hope to enjoy such opportunities vicariously through the lives of his children.

How different were the circumstances of Mary and her children through the will of Gawthorp, their lives confined within the walls of Holden Gate. No matter that their learning offered them possibilities even beyond the town, they were bound like hobbled goats to the house. If only Margery could see what it meant to be denied the freedom to make one's way in the world. Did she really wish this for her own children?

Having recalled the plight of Mary, Miles was once again exasperated and though not often minded to, reached for his pipe and tamped a bud of tobacco into its bowl. Drawing a taper from the candle, he puffed rhythmically until the pipe glowed orange. Exhaling loudly, he thought back to the day, summer past, when he had first encountered Gawthorp. Proprietorial as a dog fox, he had ensured that Miles had got nowhere near the family. His contempt had been plain, and it had mattered not that Miles was a man of God.

Glancing at the soft flakes that slid in courses down the casements and gathered in soft drifts at the sill, Miles thought miserably at how he had failed Mary. After that day at Holden Gate he had returned to the Rectory indignant and upset at his treatment, and mystified as to the motives of the man. Though farmers of the district initially bluff and uncertain at his purpose, none had been so openly hostile. Having satisfied most that his aim was improve their lot through education, they had come to appreciate his efforts. Literacy had begun to spread like a benign virus through the parish, brother to brother, father to son and daughter. His well thumbed cache of books had journeyed the length of the valley, passing through hands old and young. Whilst many still viewed him with suspicion as an outsider even after twenty years among them, they did acknowledge his efforts as a force for good.

In the later summer days, the harvest gathered, fruit ripening in the hedgerow, Miles begn to fear that helping Mary was a lost cause. She was not even his parishioner, he reminded himself. There was, however, nothing to be gained from raising the matter with the Reverend Mitton now so taken up with his young daughter. In the vaguest of terms he had written to his Bishop seeking guidance, but only the vaguest of insights had been forthcoming; he was at a loss as to what he might do next.

As the days grew shorter and winter blew in from the north, Miles's days were taken up with church and parish business. A ferocious November storm had brought flooding to the valley, and cottagers on the ings had watched their livelihoods washed away, subsumed into the swollen brown body of the Aire. Heated meetings of the overseers had become inevitable as they had battled over how best to relieve those most deserving with funds that were woefully inadequate. Mercifully the flood waters had subsided, only to be replaced by keen and early frosts, and, as midwinter approached, the snow began to blanket the land. In the long hours of darkness, the people of the valley took to their beds to preserve their rushlights, and clung to each other like burrowing animals for warmth.

Christmas morning had dawned so cold that only the most pious of his flock came to celebrate Christ's birth. His sermon had concentrated on the shepherds who had journeyed to witness the nativity, given the same prominence as the Magi in the story. In the sepulchral cold of the pulpit he had delivered his address speedily, and had not lingered long at the church gate. So now in January of the new year his thoughts turned back to Mary. It was obvious that a direct approach would be futile. Perhaps he would be better advised talking to the girl, the daughter from the market. On the few Wednesdays that he had been at home, he had wandered about the church green in search of her. He had asked the meat sellers at the market cross what had become of the Holden girl who sat at the corner, but no one had seen her. If anything the cold drew more people into market, serving as it did a social as well as practical purpose – a couple of hours' company before the cold beat them back to their hearths.

From the upstairs chamber he could hear the groan of floorboards, Margery was in conversation with Marianne. The light tones of his daughter could not be discerned, only

Margery's replies. He marvelled at Marianne's wisdom in spite of her tender years. She seemed not to possess his own temper nor her mother's anxious nature, instead a calmness and practicality which acted as a balm to both of them. Presently footsteps could be heard in the hall and a light tap at his door.

"Husband, may I sit a while with you?"

"Of course. Margery – I am sorry for my unkind words. Know you that I do understand how it pains you for the boys to go." At this tears glistened at the margins of her eyes, and he gently took her hand.

"I am a selfish woman, Miles. I should want nothing less than the best for the children. I should feel joy for Christopher, not wish him here. Forgive me."

"Margery, how would I live without you?" he smiled at his heartfelt words. "Were we younger I should take you far from here, out to the colonies where we would live out our days with the children about us, but I fear it is now too late for us."

A fat teardrop fell into her lap, but composing herself she replied: "We are grateful that Christopher prospers and keeps us in his thoughts." Tenderly Miles stroked her hair, observing the craze of lines about her eyes through which her tears channelled.

"And Edmund's wings are clipped a good few years yet, and Marianne and John, they need us still. May God grant us health and strength my dearest."

They remained unspeaking for several moments, the silence broken only by the lively crackle of green wood in the grate. At length, and in a cautious manner, Miles looked at his wife.

"Do you ever have cause to visit Kildwick, my dear?"

"Kildwick? Not really. I have once taken supper with Mrs Mitton in the company of Madam Parker. A silly woman, head full of thistledown I thought. I must entertain her here, but at the moment she is much distracted with the new baby."

"Anyone else?" She pondered hard, unsure as to why she was being questioned.

"No, indeed. After leaving the Vicarage that day, myself and Madam rode over the hills and out to the strange stones on top of the moor; know you of them?" He nodded. "It was a fine day and Madam said we could see Lancashire at a distance. On the way back to Marley she pointed out the house of Rishworth, hard by the stones. We did call, but the family was not at home. It was such a day as I have not known." She smiled at the memory.

"So Madam knows the Rishworths?"

"Not so well though both families have deep roots in the area."

"Perhaps you might have cause to be introduced, Madam being so fond of you."

"Indeed yes, Madam insists upon it, though not until the spring I fear. Only sheep can survive up there in such weather."

"God will see to it that the sun will shine again, and you shall ride out with Madam." Glancing towards the window now half obscured with snow he laughed. "Difficult to countenance, I know."

With a gentle kiss to his head Margery left him to his thoughts and his pipe. He could not leave the problem of

Mary until the spring. He must find the daughter and speak with her. The market would convene early the next day, and he would leave his parish business until after lunch.

It was a much refreshed Miles who sat at his desk later that morning to begin his letter to Christopher. It was with regret that his son Miles would not be in attendance for the wedding but would arrive, God willing, in the early summer. It was in absolute truth and conviction that he penned his congratulations at the forthcoming nuptials. Both he and Margery sent their blessings.

22

January 1701. Keighley

The upper chamber of the Old Sun was a room unremarkable but for the carving over its fireplace. A macabre tableau represented the Dance of Death, replete with leering skeletons merrily leading the figures of a pope, a king, a labourer and a child to their inevitable demise. For the purpose of cruel amusement, children were sometimes taken to the room to view the fireplace. At the sight most would scream and many would flee. Its history had been lost, with none alive to attest to its true provenance. Theories abounded: some said that the ancient inn had been the seat of a great family fallen on hard times, others that the chimney piece had been stolen from a great house and placed in the upper chamber in distant times. What was universally agreed was that the carving was an incongruous feature in an otherwise humble ale-house.

A fire had been lit in an attempt to rid the room of its fetid chill, and the flames reflected orange on the high points of the bas-relief, the grinning skulls and the arms flung wide in riotous dance. Goss, the innkeeper, proud of his attraction, ensured that his wife maintained its glossy black facade with beeswax and a daily polish.

Miles was not the first to arrive; as he made his way up the narrow staircase, he could hear the drone of voices in quiet conversation. It was with some trepidation that he pushed open the door and entered the chamber. He was greeted by Newsholme and Drake, fellow overseers of the parish, gathered like himself for the first meeting of the year. The three men shook hands and exchanged niceties that passed the time as they waited for the rest of their number to arrive.

They had been forced to meet in the inn as they were expecting more people that day than could be comfortably accommodated at the Rectory. Miles had woken that morning with a cheeriness brought on by an unusually unbroken night's sleep. This was, however, quickly dispelled as he recalled what he had to do that day. Parish meetings often began with civility and manners but quickly descended into raised voices, accusations and acrimony. The distribution of the poor relief always proved the most contentious issue. Not a day went by when he was not petitioned for help. Firewood for the bed-ridden widow, boots for the child, bread for the starving, the sexton's due. He would dutifully record their pitiful requests in the parish book which he would present each month at the meeting. The overseers then had to assess the most deserving of the causes, the coffers never stretching to relieve all.

Voices at the door heralded the arrival of Brown, the parish constable, together with Goss, bearing flagons of ale which he placed upon the table. His wife followed with a basket of bread. As more of their number began to arrive and gather in front of the fire, Miles studied the carving and considered its message. It mattered not your station in life, riches would not protect you from the inevitability of death. That's as maybe thought Miles grimly, but the passage through life for some, especially the poor and infirm, could be greatly improved through the intervention of others. He was still musing on the injustices of life as the voice of Michael Pighells rose above the low chatter of the group announcing that, with all members present, their meeting could begin.

As he took his place at the table, Miles was surprised to note the presence of the Reverend Mitton and Robert Parker, the former an occasional attendant, the latter never before seen at a parish meeting. Having all charged their tankards the proceedings began with a toast to the continued good health of the King, and another to the coming year being one of prosperity and good health for all present. Formalities completed, the meeting began. The parish clerk commenced with an assessment of finances, the amount of tithe gathered, which showed a slight increase on the month past. As more land was being reclaimed from the moor and new leases being drawn up, so the fledgling farmers became liable for the tax burden levied by the church. By another stroke of good fortune, the parish had received a modest bequest from Mary Savile, one of an ancient landed family who had died unmarried. It had been her dying wish that four pounds of her estate be annually distributed to ease the suffering of the poor until such time as the funds ran out. Miles was beginning to feel that his incipient ill-humour had been somewhat premature.

The clerk, keeper also of the church registers, recited the list of entries for the month, the burials far outnumbering births and marriages. The death of Mary Savile merited a short eulogy from Drake whose property neighboured hers. There was a general agreement that she had been a Godly woman whose days had been undeservedly short, at which Miles glanced again at the chimney piece.

It was now his turn to produce the parish book and recite its long pathetic litany of requests. Many names on the list were familiar, and appeared each month with a dreary regularity. The amounts requested were, on the whole, pitifully small. Three pence for bread for the widow Moreby, still poorly, seven pence for coal for Dorothy Camm, three pence a shirt for the Johnson child. On and on the list went, most items attracting only a murmur of assent. As he progressed, the dated entries reaching the last days of the year, so a pattern emerged. The requests were nearly all pleas for the payment of rents, and the amounts ran to shillings and even pounds. Pighells, at the name of one of his tenants, leapt to his feet, his face pink with indignation.

"No, no, no, that scoundrel shall not receive a penny! Ask Drake here, the man drinks his livelihood away. Goss sees more of him than do his wife and children! No, I cannot allow it!"

"But would you see his wife and children cast out?" countered Miles. He knew the wife as a woman of good character, who listened attentively to his sermons each Sunday, and plied her trade of rabbits each Wednesday at market. The question provoked a flurry of opinions of what should be done. The outcome was an agreement that for the final time the rent should be paid. Pighells snorted with disgust, and vowed to speak with the man at the soonest opportunity.

The mood in the room grew more fractious as Miles proceeded through the list. The last few petitions were flatly denied notwithstanding their merits, on the grounds that, by then, the coffers were empty. Pausing a while in the proceedings for a drink, the men rose from the table and clustered in groups. Robert Parker walked about the table to Miles's side.

"Reverend Gale, it has been many months since I last saw you, I trust that you are well?"

"Indeed, sir, though I confess that parish business does little to improve my humour."

"And Mrs Gale? Madam does so enjoy her company, and that clever daughter of yours, Marianne. She certainly has your intellect," he laughed. Miles blushed slightly in pride rather than modesty.

"You will have heard of this bad business with my nephew?" he continued. "What is to be done?"

Puzzled, Miles confessed he knew not what Mr Parker spoke of. Margery, a source of parish news, had been unable to venture abroad with the coming of the bad weather, and was miserable for want of company, in particular that of Madam. She always returned from Marley animated with gossip, her cheeriness lingering for many days.

Robert related the tale of Philip's attack which had occurred just before the snows arrived. Miles listened with increasing concern, and a sickening recognition.

"It is rumoured that Gawthorp of Holden was responsible," said Parker. "Know you of him? That is why Mitton is here today, the man is one of his parishioners."

Miles felt uncomfortable. Should he confess to his dealings with Gawthorp and so further condemn him in the eyes of Parker?

"I confess I know him not," muttered Miles guiltily, praying that God would see fit to forgive the untruth. In justification, he did not know the man but for a single angry encounter. The shuffling of chairs at the table heralded the recommencement of the meeting. Brown, the parish constable, an amiable man with a face as red and polished as a carnelian began. He had little to report other than the usual removal of vagrants from the town and the theft of two ewes the week before Christmas. The animals had seemingly vanished, their absence not noted for an entire day. He remarked upon a couple of fights at the turn of the year; in the most serious, a man had drawn a knife on his brother. There was nothing that required the hearing of a higher court, fines had been recovered, and for one individual, a short spell in the stocks had been awarded to allow him to reflect on his misdemeanours.

"We are joined today by the Reverend Mitton and Mr Robert Parker of Marley to discuss a most serious incident that occurred since we were last gathered," continued Brown, before recounting in detail what was known of Philip's attack. "Though we are unsure exactly where he was most cruelly set upon, it was on the Silsden road near the parish boundary."

When questioned, Robert thanked them for their concern and was happy to report that Philip was now quite recovered. Pighells was next to speak.

"I think we all know who is responsible for this, do we not?" Heads nodded in wordless agreement. "Then he must be brought before us to answer for his actions."

Mitton shuffled in his chair attempting to avoid the eye of anyone.

"For want of proof?" cried Miles, hearing the controlled anger in his own voice.

"The man keeps his family like caged birds, denies them even the church, is that not so Reverend Mitton?"

Mitton squirmed, clearly wishing he were somewhere else. "I confess, I do not see the family at church."

Pighells made to speak again but was interrupted by Robert Parker.

"It is my intention to speak with the man, and his daughter, to find the truth of this matter. Reverend Mitton, I would ask that you accompany me, and perhaps you too, Brown." The constable nodded in agreement, and with the eyes of all upon him, the Reverend Mitton also acquiesced with as much grace as he could muster.

"Then might I suggest that following church this Sunday we should ride together to Holden. Commitments prevent me from arranging this sooner."

With a triumph that he failed to disguise, Mitton replied in his bird-like voice: "I'm afraid that will not be possible. My wife and I have long planned to visit her family in Nottingham. They have yet to see our new child. We leave two days hence, and will not be returning until the end of the month."

Seeing the evident relief in Mitton's eyes, Miles spoke up.

"Sir, I am happy to take Reverend Mitton's place on Sunday if you would find this an acceptable proposition."

"Yes, Gale, your company as a man of God would be most welcome," replied a smiling Parker.

With the matter resolved, the business of the day gave way to more informal conversation, the continuing bad weather being a topic of much speculation. One by one the committee members rose to their feet and began to disperse, Mitton being the first to depart.

As Miles gathered up his hat and coat, his gaze was again drawn to the chimney carving. At last the chance to meet with Mary Gawthorp presented itself, after so many months. Though she had not approached him for money like those in the parish book, she had asked for his spiritual guidance. Miles sensed that her cause was the most deserving he had ever encountered in his long years of service to the parish. Come Sunday he might finally be able to offer her some relief. With a smile he noted that the carved figure of the king, its grotesque bloated body and crown askew, bore more than a passing resemblance to the Reverend Mitton.

23

January 1701. Holden Gate

M ary startled as the shadows of figures stole across the window, causing a faint flicker of grey light to dance across the flags. A moment later there was a loud knock at the door. The children sat at the table finishing the remains of their soup, dragging coarse bread about their bowls to remove the last smears of moisture. Ann gasped and clung to Eliza's arm. It was Eliza who sprang to her feet to answer the door. She was greeted by the sight of three men, heavily cloaked for the weather, faces mottled with cold. Eliza immediately recognised the Reverend Gale, but it was the shortest of the three men who stepped forward, removing his hat as he did so.

"Good morning, my name is Robert Parker of Marley, this the Reverend Gale of Keighley, and this Thomas Brown, constable of the parish. We wish to speak with the father of the house."

As all three men replaced their hats, Eliza stared transfixed. Behind her the children shuffled noisily, the diversion of food forgotten. Flurries of snow carried in on the air and settled like spilt flour at Eliza's feet. The silence was broken by Mary who stepped away from the fire and smoothed her hands down the length of her apron. Eliza stood to one side as her mother drew close to face the men, her eyes focusing softly away over their heads towards the great barn.

"Good morning to you gentlemen. I fear that your journey has been in vain, Robert is not here." The words were delivered precisely and calmly though Miles detected a slight quaver in her tone which he sometimes recognised in Margery's voice. He also observed the spark in the eye of the girl at the door, the girl he had last encountered all those months ago at the market.

Robert Parker, with the confidence of someone used to running a large house and estate and all that entailed, was not easily deterred.

"Then perhaps we could trouble you for the comfort of your fireside a while. We are happy to wait on his return, as we are here on a matter of great importance."

There was no mistaking the panic with which Mary attempted to dissuade them, but faced with a Gentleman, a Rector and a Constable, she had little choice but to admit them. Eliza made to move the long settle away from its station against the wall and drew it towards the fire. Mary bade them sit and offered them scalded milk or ale.

Miles studied her closely as she warmed the poker in the fire and poured ale from the flagon. She was of slender build with skin cut close about the contours of her face. Her hair drawn back at her nape was the colour of sun-bleached linen. Beneath her eyes, bruise-like shadows spoke of fatigue, worry and the march to later age.

At the table the children observed the strangers at the hearth; a girl, watery pale, bobbed an infant on her knee, its tuneless voice the only sound. Mary plunged the poker into the ale causing it to bubble and fizz angrily. Eliza stepped forward to hand the warmed drink to the visitors. Miles was again taken by the paleness of her skin against the riotous darkness of her curls. He could see nothing of Mary in her at all. Glancing about the generously proportioned parlour, he was struck by the paucity of furniture given the apparent size of the family. The long planked table about which the children were arranged took up a sizeable portion of the space. Aside from a selection of stools and the settle, the only other item of note was a low oak dresser of ancient style and construction. He contrasted the spartan surroundings with the comfort of his own study, a veritable magpie's nest of ephemera.

Robert Parker thanked Mary for the ale and was about to speak when the door was rudely flung open and the gaunt figure of Gawthorp strode into the room propelled by a vicious north wind. The room sucked in a great quantity of jagged flakes that clung to his frame like spider silk. For a brief moment time ceased. It was Parker who seized the moment, rising from the settle and taking a step forward, smiling disarmingly.

"Robert Gawthorp? Please beg the intrusion but we must speak with you on a matter of some urgency."

Gawthorp seemed to require a moment to take in the scene before trusting himself to speak. When he did so it was in a voice that Miles did not recognise, one of calm measure.

"And you, sir, are?"

"Forgive me, Robert Parker of Marley Hall, and the Reverend Gale of Keighley, and Thomas Brown, constable of the same." Miles and Thomas rose to their feet at his introduction. Gawthorp moved to close the door behind him, his eyes fixed on the figure of Parker. Mary and the children remained motionless, even the infant ceasing his babble.

"This matter of which you speak?" Gawthorp continued evenly.

"It concerns a brutal attack on my nephew some weeks ago, you will have heard talk of it I'm sure. Happily Philip is recovered, but the family is keen that this terrible act should not go unpunished." Miles marvelled at Parker's smooth charm that belied a steely resolve.

"Children, be gone!" snapped Gawthorp, at which the group gathered about the table became suddenly animate. Gathering up the baby, disgruntled at the disruption, they headed towards a door at the back of the parlour that led into a small off shut.

"Perhaps we should speak with the older girls, sir, as it may concern them." Parker's words were an order rather than suggestion. Eliza gently took Ann by the hand and led her back into the parlour, shutting the door behind her. Parker indicated that they should all gather about the table. As this was happening Gawthorp slowly removed his hat and coat, and stamped his feet with force to remove clods of snow. He was the last to take his place at the table.

"I am told that the girls sell eggs at market, is this so?" Parker turned, smiling towards Eliza and Ann.

"What of it," interrupted Gawthorp. "They are not the only ones."

"No, indeed, but Philip stopped to aid a young girl with a basket of eggs at some point on this road when he was violently attacked. Perhaps it was one of these two young ladies?" He turned his gaze back towards Gawthorp, his smile still fixed, goading him to reply. "Perhaps we should ask them?"

With all eyes upon them, it was Eliza who finally spoke.

"I cannot understand what kind of a monster would do such a thing!" There was no mistaking the venom in her words, nor the defiant look she gave Gawthorp.

"It was not you?" enquired Parker.

"No," she answered, truthfully.

For a moment all was silence. It was Miles who next spoke.

"Is it the worry of attack that has kept you from the market these past weeks, for I have not seen you there in some time?"

"He thinks it best we do not go." Eliza's words came thick with meaning.

"Can you afford this?" said Miles, turning to study Gawthorp.

"We manage," he answered.

"But this will not do, will it, Brown? After we have spoken with your neighbours to hear what they might know, we shall see to it that this road is well guarded. Brown will see to it, won't you, Brown?"

Brown nodded vigorously, wondering at how this might practically be achieved.

"Then I hope to see you girls at market on Wednesday," said Miles, at once enjoying the sport of baiting Gawthorp.

"Yes, indeed," said Parker. "I would hate to think that your family should suffer over this matter. The good Reverend will let me know should the girls not be there come Wednesday." The warning in his words was implicit, and Gawthorp could find no rejoinder.

Parker rose to his feet, indicating that he had said all that was necessary. Gale and Brown drained the last of their ale and made for the door. The women followed them, pausing at a distance; only Gawthorp remained seated. Parker thanked Mary for her hospitality, pleasantly remarking on the excellence of the scalded ale.

"We will detain you no longer, sir, madam. We are amply refreshed for the walk to Ghyllgrange." At the word Gawthorp's shoulders noticeably stiffened. "It is a while since I last spoke with Rishworth, and I imagine that we have much to discuss. I count him as a good friend, we were boys together." He left the words trailing in the air. "Anyway, come, we must go. Good day to you, sir."

"Sir," muttered Gawthorp, still hunched at the table, his back to the door.

The snow had eased as the three men walked out of the gate and onto the road. The cold bit into their unprotected skin and their breath ballooned about them in clouds. They made their way up the slope and Holden Gate finally disappeared as the track levelled onto the top of the moor. A pheasant bemoaned its lot in an unlovely cry as it dipped into the soft snow in search of food.

"I was not aware that Rishworth was a boyhood friend," said Miles, puffing slightly after the exertion of the climb.

"Indeed he is not, so please forgive the untruth. I am told that Gawthorp spends much time in his company, though no one knows why this should be. Rishworth is a wealthy man of a proud and ancient family. Why he should waste time on this scoundrel is a mystery."

The men walked on, scattering a huddle of sheep ranged over the track.

"Do you think Gawthorp is responsible for the attack?" enquired Brown after a while.

It was Miles who answered with all the conviction of his faith. "That is beyond doubt, though perhaps Rishworth holds the answer as to why."

24

January 1701. Keighley

"I'm afraid," shivered Eliza. "He is an altered man."

It was barely light as she and John shared the poke of roasted chestnuts fresh from the pan. The ice about the church green had glazed the cobbles like apricots, and traders picked their way cautiously towards their pitches. Ann stood at a distance with George Snowden, their heads almost touching, deep in conversation.

Eliza and John had met at the spring Monday past, and in spite of the bitter cold she had lingered just long enough to furnish him with every detail of Parker's unexpected visit the day before.

"It doesn't surprise me that Gawthorp's name comes to the ear of Parker – though you must believe he did not hear it from me, Eliza." She had smiled and taken his hand in reassurance. Since Sunday Gawthorp had barely left the house but to tend the animals. So absorbed in thought was he that even the youngest child knew not to disturb him.

"We are now a family of ghosts!" said Eliza.

After the men had left the house, Gawthorp had remained at the table as Mary and the girls wordlessly went about their duties. It was only when Mary made to put on her cloak to get wood from the barn that he seemed to re-enter the world.

"I shall see to that," he stated with a benevolence that shocked her.

The rest of the day had seen him industrious about the farm, mostly in the arduous but necessary business of hedge laying and repair. The small enclosure immediately behind the house was where the cattle spent their daylight hours during the harsh winter months, and each year the boundary of woven hazel and hawthorn had to be maintained. Mary watched from the yard as he hacked at the summer's growth, and wove its barbed fibre into a living wall. On and on he worked as the snow choked the thin grey light from the land, never pausing to straighten his back nor rest his arms.

At length Mary drew on her cloak and filled a tankard with warmed ale. She made her way out around the back of the house, her soft footfall going seemingly unnoticed by Gawthorp. When she grew close, he finally rose and straightened, allowing his curved blade to fall to earth. For the first time she could remember he seemed to hold her gaze, his expression unreadable. The light was draining fast now, and a nervous red hen at the field's margin was the only dab of colour on a bleached canvas.

"Will you be away to Ghyllgrange before supper?" she enquired gently.

"No, I have much to do here."

As she handed him the ale and turned to leave, she was certain that she must have imagined him murmur "thank you".

The following days had seen a change in the man whose presence so dominated the family even in his long absences from the house. His role was now taken by one who was there at their waking and the fixed points of their days. He laboured long at his hedge work, he mended tools with care and precision, and the family woke each morning to the sound of his staff breaking the ice in the stone trough.

In the orange light of the parlour, the family gathered for supper about the table, eyes lowered as they had grown accustomed. Mary and Ann served the thick stew of beef and barley in silence. When they had finally taken their places, Mary paused for want of a spoken grace, silently thanking God for the food they were about to enjoy. It was with some surprise that she noted Gawthorp, hesitant, at the head of the table. Following his lead, the children also waited until finally Mary raised her spoon and the meal began.

"And he hasn't left but to feed the sheep," Eliza continued. "The dogs howl the night long."

John could not help but smile at this, knowing well the impatience of the dogs at Marley to be free to run the endless moor. At the sound of laughter they turned.

"It is so good to see Ann and George together at last. He feared this day would never come."

The market was now beginning to fill, and for the first time in many weeks the sun, a soft white smudge veiled in cloud, shyly rose above the church's dark form.

From his study window Miles had been observing the green for some time. He extinguished his candle as the watery light infused the room, smoke heavy from the newly lit fire. Sarah, at his request, had brought him a little warmed milk infused with sage which, he felt sure, would ease his bloating. These past days he had been stricken with all manner of small ailments, brought on, he was certain, by his journey to Ghyllgrange with Parker. On his return, Margery had fretted at his pale countenance, fearful that he had caught his death. She had chided him that to have made such a journey in the snow was madness. In truth it had been a folly for which he was now paying the price, but for many reasons it had been a necessity.

The three men had arrived at Ghyllgrange having endured weather that seemed to herald the end of days. The snow, carried on a cruel erratic wind, blew at their faces so that conversation was impossible. It was only the barking of dogs that directed them unseeing towards the growing grey silhouette of Ghyllgrange. It was impossible to know the hour, and, but for the barking, the place seemed abandoned, even hostile. Parker it was who had made his way to the door and hammered loudly. Presently the door was opened by a young woman who might have been considered handsome but for a severe cast in one eye.

Having repeated his introductions and given the purpose of their visit, they had been admitted into a narrow, panelled hallway. The young woman had taken leave of them as the snow that shrouded them dissolved in the warmth of the hall. Assuming that they would be led through to meet Rishworth at his hearth, they were confounded when, with the opening of a door, he stood before them. He was an imposing figure of a solid gait possessing broad shoulders which carried the weight of a fine-featured head. Miles imagined himself as being of a similar age, though a life spent on the land had afforded Rishworth the physique of a much younger man. His long jacket was of the old style and was missing a number of buttons. Clearly the man had not been expecting visitors.

"Good day to you, gentlemen," he began in a steady calm tone. "What business brings you to my door in such weather?"

"Your neighbour, Robert Gawthorp. We are just come from him. We were there to ask what he knows of an attack on my nephew some weeks ago." Again Parker's smiling charm masked his steely purpose.

"What might this have to do with me?" countered Rishworth.

"We have learned that Gawthorp spends much time in your company. Perhaps he has confided in you, as a friend?" The last word hung in the air as though waiting to be claimed.

Finally Rishworth spoke with a level calm. "Sirs, you have been cruelly misinformed, Gawthorp is no friend of mine, merely a neighbour."

At this patent untruth Parker continued: "With the greatest of respect, sir, we know that Gawthorp is responsible for the attack, we also know that you are seen in his company most days. I ask myself why you should seek to deny this?" The words from the mouth of anyone but Parker would have been taken as highly impertinent, but from him merely enquiring.

What flashed across Rishworth's face was most unexpected, and was read by all three men as fear.

"We speak only of farming matters. I repeat, he is no friend of mine. Now will you excuse me for my wife ails and I must attend to her. I'm sorry, gentlemen, for your trouble."

With a nod to the young woman who remained in the hall, the front door was opened and the snow rushed in at their backs. Rishworth was gone and they were dismissed.

Thomas Brown silently cursed the inadequacy of his great coat which had failed to keep his teeth from chattering. His companions that day, though equally exposed to the elements, seemed to fair better than he, a fact he put down to the superior quality of their cloaks. The snow had not eased since their arrival and showed little signs of doing so. They had spent less than five minutes within the sanctuary of Ghyllgrange, insufficient time for feeling to return to their extremities. For a moment the three men stood at the entrance to the house, facing the long return journey to the valley. Parker thought better of it and, with a purposeful stride, made towards the small cottage that stood a little to the left of the farmstead, Miles and Brown trailing in his footsteps. For the third time that day, Parker approached a front door and knocked resolutely.

Some time later with the light beginning to fade and the snow thankfully easing, the men made their way down the hill. Edward Snowden had been a welcoming host, and though unprepared for their arrival had at once catered to their requirements. His wife Rebekah had ushered them to the fireside, removing their outerwear which she hoisted on a drying rack where they dripped and steamed. She had then insisted they share the soup she had prepared for supper to warm them through. Brown in particular was grateful for the kindness.

Miles had met with Edward Snowden before in the town square and had, on one occasion, spoken with him at length on the subject of the fluctuating price of wool. When the couple's children, George and Rebekah, returned from tending the sheep, they startled at the party in the parlour and were at once alarmed that some calamity had befallen. Parker assured them that it had not, and went on to explain the purpose of their visit. Edward at first seemed reticent to disclose anything that might jeopardise his standing with his landlord, Rishworth. George however, was less so, and over the course of an hour the behaviour of Gawthorp was laid bare. It was with Miles's revelations of his note from Mary, and his encounter with Gawthorp, that the Snowdens felt comfortable enough to speak of what they knew.

It seemed that Gawthorp did indeed visit Rishworth each day and, though much of their business was conducted within the walls of Ghyllgrange or out on the moor beyond the ears of others, they had all witnessed Gawthorp's anger. Since Rishworth's marriage to the much younger Elizabeth two years past, and as her pregnancy had progressed, his visits had increased. When questioned on their knowledge of Gawthorp prior to his arrival at Holden Gate, they knew only that his family were farmers out on the Colne road; this much they had established through their own enquiries. What they all agreed on was the change he had wreaked upon the Fowler family, and their fears for Mary and the children at his hands. As they had finally gathered together their warmed cloaks and thanked Rebekah for her kind hospitality, Parker had taken her hand.

"This shall not be allowed to continue, we three shall see to it."

Now, as he noted with some relief the figures of Eliza and Ann taking up their positions at the corner of church green, Miles reflected on Parker's words. He prayed that they could make good on that promise.

25

July 1701. Holden Gate

Mary dragged a comb through her thin hair. The comb had belonged to her mother and she seldom had use of it, thus preserving its delicate bone teeth. Out in the yard she could hear the girls' laughter as they took turns to wash each other's hair in water which, in spite of the heat of the day, splashed ice cold. The door to the house was open, and on the sun-warmed flags John was torn between watching his sisters and playing with his wooden animals.

The playthings had appeared one evening at supper. Gawthorp had called his young son to him as the table was being cleared, and from his pocket had produced a cache of wooden figures. The four sheep and a crouching dog had been whittled from a dark wood, and polished smooth so as no splinter should work into the boy's tender fingers.

"See, son, what your father has made. They are for you."

John was at once hesitant yet fascinated by the tiny animals, until at last he reached out a hand and held a sheep. Turning it in his plump fingers, he could not guess at its purpose, and so after a moment handed it back. Mary, at the hearth, had watched in astonishment as Gawthorp had placed the animals one by one on the table and scooped

John up onto his knee. Carefully, he had grouped the sheep together and the crouching dog at a distance.

"This is Bess guarding the sheep. See how she keeps them close!"

As he patiently tutored his son, Mary felt a sharpness in her throat at this spectacle of fatherly love. Never before had she witnessed this side of the man. She turned away not wishing to intrude on the affectionate scene. Gathering up the bowls she walked out into the fading light, alive with dancing insects, and to the well. As she drew up the water and wiped clean the remnants of their supper, she reflected on the man she had witnessed that evening. Over the past months she had seen the stone edifice of her husband eroded away to reveal another man, another stranger.

His continuous presence about the farm at once reassured and unnerved her. To her knowledge, he had not visited Ghyllgrange since the day of Parker's visit, and though the sheep on the moortop had still to be watched, he would return from them within the hour. The girls had seen a change in him too; even Ann, solemn and silent, was now to be heard singing at her labours. Only Eliza seemed not to rejoice in the transformation. She continued to keep her distance as one might avoid a feral queen with kittens. As they had draped linen about the hawthorn hedge one sparkling blue morning she had mused aloud, "Can we trust him?"

Mary had not replied.

She watched over her sleeping baby son that night, his fingers tight about the crouching dog, and had asked God the same question.

It was Sunday, a week later, at first light, and with all the courage she could command, she had announced her intention to go to church with the children.

"If it pleases you," had been his reply.

She was still awaiting his change of heart as she walked out into the yard and pulled her comb in turn through the girls' wet hair.

"Let us make haste. Margaret, see to John."

Though the hour was still early, Mary was anxious to leave the house fearing Gawthorp would forbid it. In their Sunday finery, the family made its way out onto the road. Baby John, still clutching his wooden dog, was fractious in the heat. Keen to put distance between them and Gawthorp, Mary bade Ann carry the child a little way. Once along the road to Silsden, the roof line of Holden Gate lost in the folds of the land, Mary surprised everyone by leaving the road and cutting back through the carpet of oats swaying feathery gold in the rising heat.

"Come, I have no wish to hear the Reverend Mitton today. I believe the Reverend Gale should be glad to see us!"

Ann shot a surprised glance at Eliza who in return smiled. Down through the ancient park which had once run with deer, and now bristled with crops grown tall, the family eventually found itself at the banks of the Aire.

It occurred to Mary that her son John had never seen the river, nor its valley, and his curiosity rendered him silent. Pausing at the shallow crest of the stone bridge, Ann pointed out the shadows of small fish shivering in the weedy margins of the river. John struggled to see but seemed rapt at the music of the water as it danced across the bed of jagged stones. Mary struggled to remember the last time she had stood in this spot, the last time she had visited the town. As they crossed the common pasture, swallows cut improbable angles in the air between the overhung eaves and the river's larder. The church bell rang out its ponderous slow call to the faithful as they entered the frayed edge of the town. At their backs the sound of horses hooves serried them to single file against the uneven frontage of the lane. Before long the passage had broadened out into the brightness of the church green. The bell's toll seemed to vibrate through their bodies as they gathered at the church gate looking to Mary for direction.

"I think it best we wait a while, to let others take their seats." Only now was there a nervousness to her, as though in stepping over the church threshold would her fate be sealed, her deception complete.

"Mary?" At the sound of his voice she turned. The girls bobbed with varying degrees of certainty. Miles was astonished at the sight of the family and for a moment knew not what to say.

"You are most welcome. This is a joyous day indeed! Come, come let me find you a pew. Come girls, come!"

Mary allowed him to take her arm and lay it softly along his as together they walked the short distance to the church door. The children followed at a polite distance. As their eyes grew accustomed to the dimness, Miles guided them to a long unboxed pew of precarious construction to the right of the nave.

Laughing he apologised, "By next winter these old things will be warming my parlour. Please seat yourselves."

Taking Mary's hand he squeezed it gently. "I trust that I may speak with you after the service?" Mary nodded shyly.

As he took his leave of them to return to the church door to greet his parishioners, his mind raced. His sermon that day was on the subject of the seven deadly sins, with particular emphasis on the vice of adultery, something too many of his flock openly embraced. In spite of the hours he'd spent writing his text, it could wait another day. He felt compelled to deliver an address to Mary and the children. With nothing prepared he prayed that God would guide him to find the necessary words.

The children sat silent and still, hands clasped together in their laps, all but John who sat on Ann's knee, his head turning like a weathervane with the arrival of each family. Eventually the bell fell silent and the west door closed. Some forty souls gathered in the gloom; many more thought Miles, ruefully, would seek salvation at the maltser's door.

Clearing his throat he began his familiar journey through the Eucharist, his flock making their responses with reverent solemnity. At intervals he glanced up and was heartened to see Mary and the older girls mouth the familiar words of the *Credo* and *Agnus Dei*. When at last it came to his sermon, God granted him a moment of clarity, and with confidence he opened his bible to St Luke's gospel.

In reflecting on the words of Jesus in the parable of the lost sheep, he encouraged the congregation to consider the joy of a community reunited with a lost member. The imagery was at once familiar, as many gathered had left their own sheep to attend the act of worship. But beyond the general reassurance that God would protect his own flock and rejoice in the salvation of a lost soul, he was sending a message to Mary.

As he spoke, with a freedom which belied his lack of preparation, he hoped that she would recognise the sanctuary and protection the church offered. Throughout the sermon Mary's eyes remained closed as though communing rapturously with God. As he later administered the bread and wine, her eyes remained closed, only when she rose from the altar rail did she open them. Glancing up to the great altar cross and then directly at Miles she mouthed the word, "Amen".

The children had remained at the back of the church as Mary partook of the host, but John had struggled in Ann's arms attempting to follow his mother. As she returned to the pew the child threw up his arms, and, as she neared, was scooped up and held tight at Mary's breast.

The liturgy completed, Miles nodded to his clerk who tugged open the doors allowing the brilliant tide of morning light to flood the space. The great bell began to resonate anew, dismissing the churchgoers into the rest of their Sabbath. Miles clasped the hand of each and all, and sent them out with the blessing of the Lord. When only Mary and the children remained, she gathered them about her and whispered to Ann that she should take the rest out to the market cross and wait on her. She had need to speak with the Reverend Gale.

Finally they were alone and Miles carefully drew the oak doors to. Taking a seat at her side he began, "I have prayed these many months that I should see this day. God has answered my call!"

"Good Reverend, sir, it is almost ten years since I last shared communion …" Tears flowed and gathered at Mary's chin, dropping softly to her lap. "I ask that you might hear my confession."

"Dear lady, God demands it!"

As they sat about the market cross, its pale stone grown hot in the sun, Eliza felt anxious. Margaret led the youngest children in a slow procession to each corner of the green in turn. The church door remained shut.

"He will wonder at our absence. Make haste Mother!" she worried.

From the ale-house the sound of bawdy laughter erupted from an open window. Startled, John began to cry. Ann walked quickly to him and gathered him up. As she stroked his curls, he sucked at his wooden dog, moaning sorrowfully.

The doors of the church opened with a painful groan and Miles and Mary stepped out into the sunshine, her arm laid delicately upon his. As they grew level with the market cross the girls again curtsied and bobbed.

"Children, today I feel blessed to have welcomed you into my church." Turning, he added: "Mary, go in peace and serve the Lord!"

"Amen," she murmured.

As they journeyed back along the valley road and up the gentle escarpment, a soft breeze lifted their fresh-washed hair as it escaped from bonnets and caps. Margaret and Maria gathered long buttercup sprays as, in Ann's arms, John fitfully slept, his face pinkened by the sun. In spite of Eliza's attempts at conversation, Mary would not be drawn on her business with the Reverend Gale. Even as the outline of Holden Gate appeared and grew, her step did not falter nor her smile fade. From his viewpoint at the well Gawthorp observed their return with an inscrutable stare.

26

July 1701. Keighley

Miles reflected on his day as he allowed his horse to lead him languidly along the valley road. The red dust kicked up rolled outwards catching among the lace mops of cow parsley. The sun remained high in the sky and, if anything, the temperature was rising. At the river margins children splashed about in the shallows, skimming stones that cracked off the larger rocks midstream. A little further along as he approached the town field he recognised a number of his parishioners enjoying a break in their long working days, settled with the cattle in the bumpy parched grass. Some shouted a greeting while most raised an arm in courtesy. Miles acknowledged each contentedly. It had been a good day.

With the departure of his son Miles in the early spring, Margery had sunk into a deep melancholy which, for the sake of the family, she had best tried to conceal. Knowing her pain, he had behaved tenderly towards her, encouraging visitations to friends about the district, most particularly Madam Parker. They had even enjoyed a family visit to the city of York in May, where they had spent some pleasant days with her sister Ann. Miles had used the opportunity to visit his uncle Thomas Gale, the erstwhile dean of the great minster church.

Though Thomas was in poor health and largely confined to his bed, Miles had spent a couple of hours in his company. The old man seemed cheerful, though his frame had been packed tight with blankets in his wainscot chair to maintain an upright position. Over a small glass of claret, the pair had enjoyed a lively discussion on matters of natural philosophy in which Thomas maintained a keen interest. Finally, close by, the great Minster bell chimed the hour and Miles was forced to take his leave. He had clasped the old man's hand tightly, insisting, somewhat unnecessarily, that he remain in his seat. Though his body failed, the mind remained enquiring and gimlet sharp. He prayed that there would be other such afternoons as he made his way over the river to Margery and their lodgings.

Just this morning they had received word from Christopher that young Miles had arrived safe and well in the colonies. His passage had been mercifully calm, and the boy had adapted quickly to life at sea. In spite of Christopher's suggestion that his brother would do well to marry in England to begin his life overseas, the boy had arrived alone. Christopher, now elevated and established in the Americas, would take his father's part in ensuring that Miles would survive and prosper in the same manner. News that Miles's wife Sally was with child had moved both him and Margery to tears. Together they had clasped hands and offered up a prayer to God who had so blessed the family.

As his horse approached the straggle of houses at the town's end he noticed a figure prone at the roadside. He appeared not to be breathing. Miles at once drew upon his reins, and with care, swung his leg about the saddle and dropped to the ground. His horse gratefully sank its head into the long grass as Miles walked towards the man.

He lay face down, one arm stretched out front as though reaching for some unknown entity. From beneath his coat a single leg protruded. As the Rector approached he called out, though convinced the man beyond the earthly realm. He was much taken aback when, at close quarters, he could discern a nasal snore. He then reached out a hand and tugged at the man's shoulder. The action elicited a torrent of murmured obscenity, which in turn provoked a stern rebuke from Miles. The man at once released from his reverie rolled over and squinted at the brightness of the sun and the dark figure towering above him.

"Excusing my language, sir!" he offered.

The man pushed back on his elbows, drawing himself into a seated position. He wore no cravat, and his filthy shirt gaped to reveal an expanse of pink flesh from which tufts of sparse white hair sprouted. A knee protruded from a ragged hole, and his other leg was entirely missing. Miles took the fellow for a vagrant newly expelled from the town, but Christian charity compelled him to enquire.

"Are you quite well, sir?"

"Oh yes, yes sir. I was merely sleeping. It is such a hot day, sir." Indeed so, thought Miles, though perhaps a surfeit of ale would account for his collapsed state. He wore the stench of stale beer like a cloak.

"Then I shall bid you good day, sir, and hope your continued journey be a safe one."

As he turned, drew up the reins of his horse and prepared to remount, the stranger shouted up to him.

"Begging forgiveness, sir, but do you know of a man named Rishworth?"

Miles froze, his attention fully engaged as he turned and walked back to the man.

"I know him, yes – and what business would you have with him?"

"I fear that there has been a dreadful misunderstanding! It was a long time ago … and I was angry … things were said … it was all mischief!" He shook his head in an exaggerated manner as his words drained away.

"Do you wish to confess something?"

"I didn't mean any harm … it was just mischief … I was angry!" The man so lost in thought appeared not to hear Miles so he tried a different tack, offering his hand.

"What is your name?" The man looked up.

"My name? My name is Jeremiah Hide."

"Take my hand, Jeremiah. We cannot speak here. You may take my horse."

It was with some difficulty that Miles pulled Jeremiah upright. In the tall grass he gathered up the rudimentary crutch fashioned from an ash bough. His horse waited patiently as the two men grappled and heaved to get Jeremiah into the saddle. In his thin black coat Miles sweated extravagantly, feeling every one of his fifty-four years. Finally they were able to continue their journey into the narrow shaded lanes of the town.

Thankfully Margery and the children were not at home. As Miles eased the man towards his study, he requested some sweet almond milk, cheese and bread be brought. Turning his attention back to Jeremiah, he indicated that he should take his own chair at the desk while he drew up a stool. Sarah returned with a tray after a few moments, and Miles emphasised that they were not to be disturbed. The stench of the stranger blossomed to fill the room, a mixture of sweat, ale and ordure. He greedily tore at the bread and cheese as though it were his last meal on earth. Miles sat back, wordlessly observing him.

At close quarters he was much younger than at first imagined. His hair, though matted and streaked snow white, was thick and full. In spite of his broken array of teeth set in a spare narrow face, his features were largely unlined. When Jeremiah enquired as to the possibility of a little ale, it required only a look from Miles to answer his question. When the platter between them lay empty, Miles ventured to speak.

"So, Jeremiah, I confess I do not know your face. Where is your home?"

"My life is on the road, but once I had a family. My father was a shepherd, he was a good man, he was an honest man." He emphasised the word "honest" and was at once lost in thought. Miles cleared his throat, and Jeremiah recommenced.

"I was a boy when it happened. I couldn't understand it. One day men came. They stood and watched. They laughed as my mother wept, they laughed …" His eyes filled as he recalled the scene. "They said they knew that my father had sold the sheep, he was a thief. We were turned out onto the moor. They would not listen to my father when he said it was all lies. He had worked the sheep for twenty years, why would he steal?" Jeremiah turned to Miles, holding his eye as though waiting for confirmation. Miles nodded for him to continue.

"That was the end of us. My father and mother and my two young sisters, babies they were, could not stay. The whispering had begun, and no one would employ a thief. They went south to find work but bade me stay as I too was a shepherd and I carried no taint. They said they would return one day, but I never saw them again. I swear, sir, my father was no thief!"

"Jeremiah, I believe you if this is your confession. So what became of you?"

"I found work with a neighbouring farmer who knew me to be honest and good at my work. I would have been happy too but for his son. He was of my age but thought himself not my equal. He baited me about my father until I could stand it no longer and, God forgive me, I wove him the tale."

Intrigued, Miles leaned in closer. "God hears your repentance Jeremiah."

"It was easy really, as he was so unlike his older brothers, so tall. I told him that he had every right to feel above me, as he was not his father's son. He didn't understand at first, so I was forced to name his father. I was angry sir, I was angry with them both, it was just mischief!"

"And then?" Miles's curiosity was now fully engaged.

"And then things changed. He no longer spoke to me, to anyone. I could no longer stay for I feared retribution, so I took to the road and left the valley." His tale increased in pace as though he could not bear to contain the poisonous secret a moment longer.

"For a couple of years I found work in the hills of Lancashire, but I always feared that my sin would find me out, so I joined the militia, and was thankful when I was sent to Ireland to fight for the King against the Popish cause. But my sin did find me out, as it was there that I lost my leg to a cannonball. God took my leg but spared me my life. It was a message, sir, I had to return to put right the wrong. It has taken many years to return, but I am finally here." His shoulders slumped as though the very matter of him was draining away with the effort of recalling his tale.

Miles pondered for a moment before genuflecting and gathering up Jeremiah's hands.

"God has heard your confession and he forgives you. You have sinned but you are now forgiven." At these words Jeremiah's body juddered with sobs. When finally he had composed himself Miles enquired, "You first mentioned the name Rishworth?"

"Yes, sir, he was my father's landlord, he whose sheep were gone. He took the word of others that would call my father a thief. I forgive him now just as God can forgive me."

"Can I ask the name of the boy to whom you lied?"

"You can, sir, his name was Gawthorp, Robert Gawthorp, and I told him that Rishworth was his true father. Since I am returned to the valley I hear terrible things spoken of him. You must help me, sir, you must help me make things right in God's eyes! Can you help me, sir?"

At the mention of Gawthorp's name, Miles's heart quickened, his thought spun, and a sickening truth dawned. As he lay his hands in benediction on Jeremiah's head he felt God reveal himself to him in the clearest way.

"Jeremiah, you are saved. I will help you as I am able."

Rising from his stool he walked to the door and flung it wide. In a voice unbefitting of a man of his station he cried: "Sarah, Sarah, some ale if you please!"

27

July 1701. Marley

Jennet was again with child, though the news had not been greeted with the same joy as had her first pregnancy. Sickness had again overtaken her body, and as she leant heavily at the wall behind the cottage, and drew her sleeve across her lips, tears prickled. Nathan, at the news, had sensed her anxiety, and had held her close, imparting reassurances that even to his own ears rang hollow. Struggling to retain food, she had consulted with Martha Wright who had suggested an infusion of meadowsweet. Nipping her nose to imbibe the potion as she fought the rising bile, she cursed her situation.

Jonas had the past month discovered his feet. Jennet had marvelled at his patient determination as he clung to the settle and pulled himself upright. She had witnessed the surprise that registered on his baby features as he had allowed his feet to bear the weight of his body for the first time. He had immediately fallen back to earth with an unknown sensation of fear and achievement. Undeterred he had continued in his endeavours until within a few short days he was working his way about the parlour with the speed and action of a crab. For all her worries at her own abilities as a mother, he was proving to be a healthy and amiable child.

Another wave of nausea overcame her and she emptied the paltry contents of her stomach into the nettles. She prayed that God would spare her and her unborn child.

Harvest was underway, and in the intack under the overhang of a vast horse chestnut, Nathan and John paused in their labours. This year the fledgling field had been given over to hay, and among its rich golden pelt a rash of poppies was as a sprinkling of spilt blood. John lay back in the crackling dry grass staring up at the sky through the tattered canopy of leaves. Nathan, his back against the tree, screwed his eyes against the brilliance of the light.

"If anything were to happen, John …" His voice trailed off, neither words nor thoughts fully formed.

John rose up on his elbows to observe his friend. He too awoke each morning and, within moments, felt the trickle of dread as to how he should find Jennet that day.

"Nathan, God has spared her once. Do not dwell upon it!" But Nathan could think of little else, and nothing that John could possibly say would alter it. The silence was broken only by the screech of swifts, but the clamour of frustration and fear filled the air. John had a thought.

"I heard the strangest tale yesterday when I was in the stable yard. It concerns William Rishworth. He was seen last week in the company of a beggar."

At last something caught Nathan's attention.

"What's that?"

"Rishworth in the company of a beggar, and a crippled one at that! George Binns saw them in the parlour of the White Hart."

"Did George know the beggar?"

"He had never seen him before, but would not forget him quickly as he only had the one leg! According to Binns, he and Rishworth were dining and chatting like old friends. What do you make of that?"

"I confess I have no explanation. Is Rishworth not now a father?" He had turned the conversation about to the subject that consumed him.

"I hear Elizabeth has given him a girl," stated John simply.

Draining the last of his ale and wiping his mouth, Nathan rose to his feet.

"Come, John, we can finish this side by sundown." Gathering up his scythe John followed.

Jeremiah Hide had spent the past week enjoying a life of comfort he had previously not known. Whatever he had imagined the outcome of his meeting with Rishworth would be, he had not foreseen a feather mattress and a full belly. God had chosen to forgive the repentant sinner just as the Reverend Gale had predicted. His eyes filled with tears. His new abode was with Martha Wright and downstairs in her echoing parlour he could hear she was about her business. An unfixed aroma stole up through the floorboards as a door slammed shut. The hour was early, the day unknown, as Jeremiah eased himself to the edge of the bed.

After he had made his confession to the Rector, he had expressed his desire to speak with Rishworth at the soonest opportunity. The question of his fragile health made it impossible, in Miles's view, that he should attempt the journey to Ghyllgrange. With Jeremiah's agreement, a meeting could be arranged there at the Rectory. He would send word to Rishworth immediately. Writing a hasty missive he became acutely aware of Margery and the children's return. With this in mind he suggested that they should perhaps arrange to meet Rishworth at a nearby ale-house. Upon further reflection, he had settled upon the White Hart, which fell outside his parish boundary. There was no telling how the meeting with Rishworth might go, so he considered it prudent not to invite trouble to his doorstep. Leaving Jeremiah at his desk, he hurried out into the yard where Stephen was enjoying his pipe in the shaded threshold of the stable.

"Make haste to Ghyllgrange, and see that this is delivered into the hand of William Rishworth and none other. Take the young one if you will for speed, and saddle up the mare for me." With a last draw on his tobacco, the lad made busy and Miles returned to his study. He noted with distaste that the room had now taken on Jeremiah's base stench.

"Come, Jeremiah, the lad is saddling up my horse. We do not have far to travel."

With a last glance about the room, Jeremiah allowed Miles to help him to his feet. As they made their way through the hall, Sarah could be heard throwing open the study windows. The temperature had not fallen, so Miles thought it best to abandon his coat at the door, but retained his broad hat.

With the aid of the mounting block, the task of raising Jeremiah astride the horse proved to be a much easier task than earlier that day. Miles led the animal through the archway and out along the valley road. The sun had slid from its apex in the sky, and the way ahead shimmered watery in haze. At length they passed Marley Hall, set like a castle of old on a boil-like mound on the otherwise unblemished valley floor. Jeremiah had little conversation, instead staring ahead at the approaching town, insubstantial as smoke. In very little time they passed under the ancient lintel of a shaded yard where a lad took the reins from Miles in exchange for a coin, and together the two aided Jeremiah down to earth.

Miles was surprised to see that the handsome long case clock in the hall read five-and-twenty past the hour of five. *Tempus fugit*, he mused. It was with some relief that he found the inn almost completely deserted, most of its patrons being still busy in the fields. He led Jeremiah over to a table flanked by two high-backed settles. As the innkeeper brought over a leather jug of ale and two tankards, Miles noted Jeremiah's fingers beating an irregular tattoo on the tabletop. With the infrequent arrival of customers, his eyes searched their faces nervously. Some time later, Miles, whose seat faced the window saw the approach of Rishworth, face flushed atop a fine chestnut mount.

"Jeremiah, he is here!" He witnessed the other man writhe nervously in his seat. "I must speak with him alone, though not of your confession of course. Then I will leave the two of you and will return before nightfall." Laying his hand gently upon the man's shoulder as he rose, he added, "God is with you."

In the yard he noted the lad struggling with Rishworth's horse, which was white striped with sweat and peevish for want of shade and water. Clearly they had made the journey in haste.

"Sir, I received your note." Removing his hat in courtesy and discomfort, Rishworth continued,"I cannot imagine the emergency of which you speak. My wife, she has just given me a daughter, you will have heard. I do not wish to leave her o'er long."

"Sir, I would not have requested the meeting at this most auspicious time for you were it not a matter of gravest importance. I have this day met with someone; he awaits your arrival." Motioning towards the door, the Rector continued: "He has, for many years, borne the weight of a great wrong which today he has confessed in the sight of God. I can say no more, but it is vital that you hear his tale."

Rishworth, unconvinced, nodded, then stooped to enter the low portal of the inn. Seeking the lad who by now had pacified Rishworth's horse, Miles had him bring his own. He alighted with the excited anticipation of a child on Christmas morn, and started back along the road to Keighley.

Independent of the outcome of Jeremiah's encounter, it struck him that he should make provision for the man's immediate welfare. Though he considered himself to be a man of science, and in matters medical would always defer to his physician, Lister, Miles acknowledged that most people had not that privilege. Old medicine was still very much the trusted orthodoxy amongst the people of the valley. Through the endorsement of others, and the proof of healing he himself had witnessed, Martha Wright was its most respected practitioner.

He had spent many hours in her company and was enthralled by her knowledge of plant lore, and the care and expertise with which she exercised it. He had no time for those who muttered of witchcraft and magic; he knew Martha to be a skilled botanist and above all a woman of God.

As he drew close to her house, he observed her knotting bundles of lavender, which she then hung from nails in the stone facade.

"Good day, Martha."

"Oh, Reverend Gale, what a pleasure! Will you join me a while, I am almost finished at my work. My old knees are begging me sit!" She cackled joyfully.

"Indeed, Martha. I am here to call upon your charity and great learning."

The sun grew larger in the sky, its light grown orange bright as Miles and Martha sat in discussion at the door to her house, the air piquant with oil of lavender. At the sight of an approaching figure, Martha disappeared into the darkness of her parlour. She re-emerged to find Miles and John Asquith in conversation.

"Here, John, be sure that Jennet drinks this as often as she is able. I will visit soon. And John, God bless you all!"

"Amen," chimed Miles.

As the shadows cut long channels across the land, Miles took his leave of Martha, promising to return later that evening with the guest. For her troubles he handed over a palmful of coins. In return she insisted he take a bundle of lavender. As he made his way slowly back along the road to Bingley, unsure at what might greet him, he was heartened at the thought that the lavender placed in his study would remove Jeremiah's lingering presence.

28

August 1701. Holden Gate

It had been over a week since Gawthorp had disappeared. Mary had initially not noted his absence. The great barn door stood open like a gaping wound, and though the children ran in and out through the course of the morning, they had all assumed that he would be tending his sheep at the moor's summit. When he didn't appear in the parlour, the sun at its height, Mary had thought him detained with the flock, else some other mundane explanation. As the family had gathered for supper with the going down of the sun, his chair remained empty. Later that evening as the children one by one retired, a rowdy chorus heralded the dogs' return. Allowing time for Gawthorp to feed and water the animals before shuttering them away for the night, she waited his entrance. It never came. Out in the yard the dogs scampered in and out of the barn, senseless with excitement at the prospect of food. In the last vestiges of the light which were sliding from the sky like water down a gully she scanned the tall horizon.

"Husband? Robert? Robert are you there?" In the still night air her words carried like thistledown and fell upon the darkening earth. She was alone.

The whole night through she kept a fireside vigil, catching moments of troubled sleep as her head lolled to her chest. A carnival of birdsong which heralded the first bright spars of morning found her jabbing life into the faltering flames in the hearth. She was joined presently by Eliza.

"Mother?"

"He did not come home," mouthed Mary distractedly. Before Parker's visit this would have merited little concern. On occasions he would return from Ghyllgrange with the crowing of the cock and without explanation or apology. But Gawthorp was a changed man and his absence cast a sinister shadow.

"The dogs returned alone. Eliza, I fear some calamity has befallen him!"

"Mother, you must not fear the worst," she replied without conviction. "I will away to Ghyllgrange and take the dogs."

Mary remained in the doorway her hands clasped together at her mouth as though in prayer as Eliza freed the dogs from the great barn. "I will find him!"

As she strode out, the dogs danced reels about her, scattering skylarks from their hidden bowers. The path rose to a sea of jewel bright heather which stretched and deepened in tone to the point where it met the sky. Had some accident befallen him then surely the hounds would seek him out, she thought. At each excited yelp her pulse quickened, but the fluster of disturbed grouse in their ungainly flight proved a false dawn. On the approach to Ghyllgrange, the wind buffeted and roiled, whipping her dark curls into her eyes, causing tears to run. A figure approached, an arm raised in recognition, and for the briefest of moments she imagined it was Gawthorp.

"Ho, Eliza!"

It was George Snowden. They drew close, and the dogs giddy with joy at a familiar face, as he bent to fuss and stroke them.

"George, have you seen anything of Gawthorp? I am on my way to Ghyllgrange where I imagine I shall find him!"

"I think not, Eliza. Rishworth and his wife left yesterday. They are with family in Addingham and will not be returning for a month."

"Then where can he be? He did not return last night!" Though George well understood Eliza's hostile feelings towards Gawthorp, there was no mistaking her concern.

"Let me get my dogs. I'll take the path to the Doubler Stones, then I'll away down to Marley and tell John; he will help us." In spite of the heat of the day, Eliza felt a shiver like winter's blast at the thought of Mary's anguish.

"Thank you George, I must return to mother, then I shall run down to the town. I am certain to find him there."

Without directions, the dogs had set about the task of rounding up the sheep and driving them back down the slope. In her distraction, Eliza allowed them to do their work.

Great cloud battalions gathered in the skies, marching with haste at some silent command. As Holden Gate came into view, Eliza observed the figure of Mary gazing up towards her, eyes shielded against the sun.

"He has not been seen at Ghyllgrange, and Rishworth has shut up the house. George Snowden is away to Marley and I will go down to the town. Perhaps Ann should walk to Silsden, to Francis, perhaps he is there?" Eliza watched in fascination as her mother's jaw tightened and slackened in rhythm with frantic thoughts. "Yes ... that would be best."

As Eliza walked away from the house, the wild song of the dogs desperate to follow grew fainter until lost on the summer wind. Where could he be? Shamefully she recalled the many occasions when she had wished him gone from their lives, and prayed God forgive her.

Along the road she encountered a number of folk, mostly known to her, none of whom had seen Gawthorp when asked. Before entering the town she walked a long stretch of the riverbank, eyes keen to a glimpse of him. Across the town field she paused to question those she met, the answer from all was the same. No one had seen Gawthorp. Though she had never known him to frequent the ale-houses, she felt it prudent to visit each. The hour was still early and most echoed to the sounds of cooking. This morning ritual was witnessed only by a few solitary travellers or ancient men passing their dotage within such walls for want of company. All enquiries met with the same response: he had not been seen on this day, or any. A tour of the shops resulted in the same unhelpful outcome.

When at last she found herself at the town green there was only one more place she could think of to try. The door was opened by Sarah who declared, with self-importance, "The Reverend Gale is not at home." When Eliza stressed the necessity of speaking with him Sarah pointed sullenly at the church.

The building had now become familiar to her since Mary had first demanded that they should be allowed to attend each Sunday. As she turned the great iron ring, the heavy latch lifted and she stepped inside. Miles knelt in prayer at the altar rail but rose at the sound of her footstep.

"Eliza, is Mary with you?" he enquired pleasantly.

"No, sir, she is at home, much afraid. Gawthorp has gone!"

"Gone where?"

"He did not return last night, and no one has seen him!" At once a flurry of explanations crowded his mind, but linking all were the figures of William Rishworth and Jeremiah Hide. Seeming to recognise his thoughts she added, "He is not at Ghyllgrange."

Only the day before he had seen Jeremiah on his way, his meagre possessions contained within the pockets of his coat. The night before that, Rishworth had sat in his study as together they had charted the future course of Hide's life. Rishworth, an infrequent worshipper, had arrived at the Rectory anxious to speak with Miles of his encounter with Jeremiah. Unsure as to whether he sought his advice as a man or a priest, he said little, encouraging Rishworth to talk freely. The sorry tale already confessed was again recounted. Miles nodded sagely at intervals until Rishworth reached the part of the story hereto untold. It seemed that Gawthorp, under the misapprehension of being Rishworth's son, had attempted to establish himself within his apparently rightful family. Rishworth, in his younger days, had been dissolute and reckless, his time spent drinking and whoring. His memories of the period were as insubstantial as cobwebs. Only now in his middle years had he found happiness and peace with his much younger wife Elizabeth. But for the past nine years Gawthorp had asserted his birthright almost daily, his continued presence at Ghyllgrange tolerated with shame and uncertainty.

With the imminent birth of Rishworth's new daughter, Gawthorp's attitude was much changed, and so too Rishworth's. This had coincided with the attack on Parker's nephew. When Miles, Parker and Brown had visited Ghyllgrange, he had spoken the truth when he stated that Gawthorp was no friend. He had not, however, identified him as an undesired son. Without warning Gawthorp's visits had then ceased and the two men had not since exchanged a word.

The arrival of Jeremiah, and the unburdening of his truth, had at last blown away the flimsy foundations of Gawthorp's folly. Rishworth was free of him. At the same time, he was a penitent soul eager to right the great wrongs that had befallen Jeremiah. He felt it his duty to help, with the wealth and connection at his disposal. Miles considered the question of safety. Though Rishworth wished his tormentor to face Jeremiah, he was dissuaded. Gawthorp was a man of violence, unscrupulous and unpredictable. When faced with the truth, his actions could not be guessed at. It was therefore decided that Jeremiah should be removed from the town at once. Miles it was who lighted upon a solution, the details of which they had settled upon later that night. He would be sent to Waddington, a hospital founded by the Parker family, where he could be put to gentle work in return for alms. Miles sent word with Stephen to Marley, and a letter of acceptance and introduction was immediate.

So it was that the next morning Miles had seen Jeremiah on his way, bound west from the valley, health much restored, conscience cleansed and future comfort guaranteed.

Now the Rector was faced with Eliza's distress. "I do not know where to turn!" she cried, "Can you help us, sir?"

"Yes of course, I shall help in any way I can."

But the days passed, and still Gawthorp had not returned. Miles, true to his word, had used the pulpit as a rallying point for those in attendance. He had contacted his fellow clergy in all neighbouring parishes and, as a precaution, the hospital at Waddington. The word had gone out, spreading like ripples in water and yet the man had vanished like smoke.

Mary could find little joy in food, nor rest in sleep. She spent her days at the open door as though her very presence there should draw him home. Francis, her brother, gave of his time and labour as best he could spare to bring the harvest home. He could find nothing to say of Gawthorp's absence, though grimly, he could only imagine the worst.

In the long hours of the night, alone at the table, Mary fetched forth the great bible and by the star-like glow of rush lamp, she screwed her eyes to follow the familiar lines of scripture. As she returned again and again to the parable of the lost sheep, she prayed to her God that Robert too could be found, and returned unharmed to the fold. She could not allow herself to imagine that he be gone for good, and what that would mean for their future at Holden.

29

September 1701. Marley

John had promised Eliza that at the end of his working day he should come to Holden Gate to offer his services to Mary. Over three weeks had passed since Gawthorp's disappearance, and it was wordlessly assumed by many that he would not return. Francis Stirk, brother to Mary, and Edward Snowden had assisted in the gathering in of the harvest, and George Snowden had attended to the sheep each day. There was, however, much other work to do about the farm beyond the means of Mary and the girls. That evening John was to chop wood for the fire and turn the peat stack. If time allowed, he planned to cut fresh turf for the coming winter days.

Holden Gate was as silent as a nunnery. The girls went about their chores anxiously preserving the peace, mindful of Mary's distress. The bible remained at the table, and throughout the day Mary would be drawn to it as though Gawthorp should be found pressed within its wrinkled pages. Occasionally she would seat herself and open the book to a specific page, inciting familiar words in the smallest of voices. Eliza found her one morning mouthing words of scripture towards the open door, as though they should be carried by the wind until they fell upon Gawthorp's ear and guided him home. The flesh was falling from her bones, her skirt dragging across the flags as it sat low on her hips. Eliza and Ann assumed the roles of providing food for the family, and watched alarmed as their mother eschewed their efforts.

Baby John clung to Mary's skirts, his bewildered cries often going unnoticed. Margaret drew him away and up into her arms, his fingers clasped tight about his wooden animals. In the absence of reason and explanation life continued with the silence of deep water.

John hurried along the valley road. He had snatched a little bread and cheese which he ate as he walked. With luck the light should allow him a couple of hours' labour. In the past week, he had noticed the growing heaviness of the morning dew which whispered at the turning of the season. Though his cloak hung weightily on his shoulders, he would welcome it later on his journey home. From her doorway Martha Wright raised a hand in greeting before closing her door to the world for the day.

The town streets pulsed with the movement of people, and the air was an exotic soup of cooking food. Children, banished from busy parlours, crouched in dusty doorways tossing knuckle bones in the dirt as time settled and slowed.

Out across the town field to the bridge across the Aire, John passed a couple, arm in arm, their faces turned in towards each other, the world about them as unacknowledged as the air they breathed. He imagined himself and Eliza one day walking together, and flushed at the thought.

Seeking to save time, he left the path, and cut across a swathe of oat stubble freshly mown, which would bring him out at the foot of Holden Park. In the distance he could see the stationary figure of a great dog, or so it appeared. Likely someone was hunting rabbit, though its owner could not be seen. As he approached he cursed his eyes, for it was no dog, but the figure of a man on all fours. As he drew closer still, the man seemed not to sense his presence, his head hung low like a grazing animal.

"Ho there!" At the sound of John's voice, the man began to crawl like injured quarry, though after only a couple of yards he stopped and slumped to the ground.

"Leave me be!" he whimpered, and with horror John recognised the voice as that of Gawthorp. The man was unrecognisable, the dun vestment, which he had taken to be a dog's coat, he saw now was a linen shirt, the colour of the earth itself. His britches and stockings were the same hue, his boots entirely missing.

"What in God's name has happened?"

"Leave me be! I wish to die …!" His words grew in crescendo to a great roar of pain. Being familiar with the wrath of Gawthorp, John hesitated, but his fear was swiftly replaced by anger. "Where have you been? Your family are in hell!"

"Family? I have no family …" Each word slid into the next. John recognised the lubrication of strong drink, and was sickened by the man's inebriation. He was filled with a sudden fury which grew in intensity as the crouching figure began to weep.

"I am delivering you to Mary!" he said, while remaining wary, as one tending an injured dog. Gawthorp continued to sob, so John approached and grasped him by the shoulder, at which Robert stiffened then swung to face him. "I said leave me!" he spat.

John was shocked at the change in the man. His eyes were lost in the deep shadows of his skull, his skin flaccid and bristled, a deep gash fresh made at the bridge of his nose. With a resolution he had never before known John retorted, "You will come with me or I shall fetch the Constable!"

For a moment Gawthorp did not move, his eyes locked on John's. At last he stumbled to his feet, swaying as though at sea. "Do not judge me Asquith! Do not dare judge me!" His finger jabbed the rhythm of his words. He turned up the slope and stumbled forward, John in his wake trembling with shock at what had transpired. The journey through the park was a slow lumbering progress. On two occasions Gawthorp stumbled to his knees. John paused without offering assistance until he was upright once more. They approached Holden Gate without a word.

"Papa, Papa, Papa!" screamed Hannah, who had been cradling a kitten by the peat stack and first witnessed their arrival. Her charge was swiftly abandoned as she rushed towards the figure of her father. At the clamour Ann and Margaret appeared from the barn, and at the house threshold Mary was framed in dusky silhouette. For a few brief seconds no one moved. Hannah paused at the gate as though awaiting permission to proceed. Gawthorp slowly raised his eyes towards his daughter and at last held out a hand.

It was late, though John could not begin to guess at the hour. The sky scintillated with the light of a million stars. The moon, half full, turned shyly from the earth, but was bright enough to light his way. As he had walked, he had pondered on what he had witnessed since he had discovered Gawthorp. He was most perplexed at Mary's reaction. What he had anticipated had been joy, relief, perhaps even anger. Her reaction had been far more surprising. It was as though her husband's disappearance had not happened. She seemed not to notice his derelict appearance, and merely ushered everyone to the table for the supper about to be served. As John lingered in the doorway, Gawthorp hesitated before shambling to his chair at the head of the table. The girls looked to Mary for guidance, unsure as what to do. Without a word they took their places as Mary dished out soup with an indifference at odds with the situation. As John stepped silently away towards the barn, confused and angry at what he had seen, a grace was being delivered.

He began by chopping kindling for the fire, as had been his plan, with a ferocity which reflected his mood. Why would Mary act so? Why should she welcome him back without so much as a word? He cursed his small knowledge of the world. Splinters of wood flew off in wild tangents, ricocheting against the ancient barn walls. He toiled alone until each bough was reduced to jagged fingers before turning his attention to the peat store in the yard. The door to the farm stood open but not a voice could be heard nor any sign of movement discerned. The stack was sorely depleted, though he was happy to discover that it had dried well and baked hard as brick during the long August days.

He moved to the business of cutting fresh turf to reveal the damp peat beneath. John had been told the spot above the house where the peat was dug, and it was to this place he then went, spade in hand. By then the light was fading and the air growing chill. He vowed to clear an area the size of a trestle and then head back to Marley. He would not call at the house, for in truth he feared what he might discover. He was drawing his cloak about his shoulders when he heard the soft approach of footsteps. Instinctively his hold tightened upon the handle of the spade.

"John?" It was Eliza.

"I am finished for today, perhaps you can return this." He was shocked at the coldness of his own voice. "I'm sorry, Eliza," he added gently.

"John, I can make no sense of it all but, for my mother's sake, thank you for bringing him home." Suddenly she began to laugh wildly, a great uncontrolled gale which just as suddenly turned to violent sobbing. John dropped the spade and wrapped his arms about her. They stood together still as stone until she regained her composure and drew away from him.

"How goes Mary?"

In a jumble of words Eliza explained how Gawthorp had yet to speak. He had eaten his meal in silence, the children his uncomprehending audience. When at last he was done, Mary dismissed the family with a nod of her head; she spoke not a word. The girls had gathered together in the back parlour, finding small meaningless pastimes to fill the uncomfortable void. Baby John had remonstrated angrily at being banished, and held out his arms to his father.

Gawthorp did not see. He continued to gaze down to the spot on the table where once his bowl had been.

A foot on the stair marked the end to their exile, and when they returned to the parlour Gawthorp was gone. Mary sat at the table, her bible opened as her words echoed soft about the room. All knew better than to disturb her.

"She has taken him back to her bed. How can she forgive him? Where has he been? Why did he go?" John shook his head, for in truth there were no answers. He could, however, relate his discovery of Gawthorp in the field below the park, and the strange words that he had used: "Do not judge me!".

A barn owl cried out close by causing them both to startle. There was nothing left to say for the truth of the day's events was a tangled fleece to be teased.

"Thank you," said Eliza simply.

"Send word if I am needed," then on reflection: "Send word anyway." Awkwardly and swiftly Eliza hopped to deliver a dry kiss to his cheek before dashing away, dangling the heavy spade.

The coming hours and days would doubtless see the unravelling of the mystery. Like the spinning of yarn, a truth would be fashioned from the woolly unknown. He could not dispel the image of Mary on their return to Holden Gate, as she beheld her errant husband. What was it that her eyes betrayed? As he passed the stables at Marley, the dogs awoke with frenzied barking at his step. Amongst their wild chorus he could recognise Mab's familiar howl. In that moment he knew what it was that he had seen in the smallest movement of Mary's eyes. It was fear.

30

September 1701. Keighley

Miles could not recall how he had first heard the news. Most likely it was because he had much to occupy his thoughts with the approach of Michaelmas, and in truth, he was not in the best of health. Lister had encouraged the administration of leeches in combination with regular quantities of syrup of peppermint, to be drunk warmed. He had followed this regime fastidiously, yet his symptoms persisted. He could not help but worry that, like his father, he was falling victim to the stone. Margery dismissed this notion as fanciful, instead suggesting that he would do well to moderate his appetite. He was finding it miserable to comply. Mutton pies and a good strong cheese were, after all, only small vices.

That morning he was faced with preparations for the coming quarter sessions, which fell at the end of the week. The very thought caused the blood to pulse at his temples, for in spite of an excellent harvest, for some, it would be their last. Landlords with rents unpaid would summon Thomas Brown to oversee the sorry spectacle of forced eviction. It mattered not the history, nor years of faithful service, there were always families sent off in search of new homes. Sadly, one man's shilling was as good as the next. For Miles, it represented the most loathsome aspect of his work, and participation was against all notions of charity. The prospect of the coming quarter sessions did nothing to improve the pain in his belly.

But how had the news of Gawthorp's return reached his ears? He struggled to remember. Perhaps all was well after all. Parker had reported that Jeremiah was proving himself to be a capable warden, happy and settled about his work. Martha's administrations had ensured that he had entered employment with more health than should be expected of a man short of a leg. Miles was simply relieved that his darkest imagining of Gawthorp seeking retribution had proved unfounded. A germ of worry lingered, for the tenants of Holden Gate had not been seen at church since Gawthorp's return. He had to speak with Mary.

Margery was in particularly high spirits, thanks largely to a cache of correspondence recently come from her boys. Christopher had penned three long missives, busy with detail of his work and household. He bemoaned the slow progress in establishing a church in the colony. This, he surmised, was due to the fact that they had been unable to attract a priest. Miles wondered if this might have been a pointed invitation to Thomas, still set upon a career in the church. He was grateful that Margery seemed not to notice.

Miles, the younger, was proving himself to be popular and industrious about the town. He had been put to work amongst the trading settlements which now bloomed like mushrooms along the inlets and creeks of the seaboard, edging ever deeper into Indian territories. Christopher was enjoying having his brother within the household, and he was genuinely delighted that his wife liked him so well. He was excited to report that whilst Sally grew ever more heavy with child, she was in excellent health. As her confinement approached, he reminded them that, God willing, they would soon be grandparents. That thought had moved Margery to tears of joy. Christopher had even been mindful to include with his letters a number of seed heads, which he hoped should survive the journey home. His father might wish to plant them as a modest experiment. Could such exotica survive the vicissitudes of a Yorkshire garden?

Young Miles seemed to share Christopher's appreciation of life in the colonies, though his two letters were remarkable for their brevity. This came as no real surprise to his father and mother. Their son had been an impatient scholar, preferring observation and conversation to the business of written narration. Miles had already composed two letters in reply, though, aside from news of the family, he could not hope to match his sons' in terms of revelation.

The Rector's thoughts returned to Mary. Gawthorp was returned, though where he had been was a matter of intense speculation. Some spoke of another woman who had turned his head only to spurn him. He had returned to the saint-like Mary, who had found it in her heart to forgive him. Others said that he had journeyed to London to evade the attentions of some creditor who meant him harm. Other theories were even more preposterous in Miles's view. The truth was likely to involve the revelations of Jeremiah Hide, of that he was sure.

It was market day. He had dwelt long on the matter and thought it unwise to go to Holden to see Mary in Gawthorp's presence. Far better, he resolved, to seek out her daughters who would likely be plying their eggs and butter at their habitual spot. He was minded to speak with them before parish business should detain him.

In the event it was Eliza who sought him out. A frantic knocking at the door was answered tardily by Sarah, annoyed to be called away from her kitchen labours. Miles winced as he heard her chide the visitor for arriving at such an inopportune moment. He would speak with the girl later of her questionable manners. A shuffle of feet in the hall and a rude knock at his door by the surly Sarah announced his visitor. Eliza entered his study cautiously, preferring not to speak until the servant girl was gone. Miles smiled with genuine pleasure at seeing her, wondering that she had not read his thoughts.

"Might I speak with you, sir?" she began softly. He nodded and gestured towards a chair. She shook her head. "I cannot stay, sir, as my sisters wait at the market corner. I had to speak with you as you might wish to know of Gawthorp's return." Her words tumbled forth on a single breath. "You had heard of his return?"

"Yes, child, though in truth I cannot recall how it was that I heard it. Tell me, how is your mother? I missed her in church on Sunday."

"Oh sir, I scarce know where to begin! It was John who found him and brought him home. Forgive me, sir, but it might have been better that he left him be!"

Miles smiled reassuringly, for the girl wore her worries like a showy bonnet. "Has he offered an explanation for his disappearance?"

"Sir, he does little else but weep, and speaks to no one aside mother and the baby. She will tell us nothing of what he says though we beg her tell. Why does she keep secrets from us? People are talking, sir, they ask us about him or else whisper behind our backs." A tear sprang unbidden, wrought of frustration rather than sadness. Miles felt wretched. His knowledge of the matter was as a heavy stone that he longed to set down. It was not his place to speak of what he knew, but it was impossible not to be moved by Eliza's plight. He gathered up her hand and held it between his own.

"Perhaps Mary would speak with me on the matter. Do you think it?" Eliza nodded meekly but stopped abruptly as a thought entered her head. "I fear she will not leave his side. That is why we were not at church, she will not leave him for fear he runs away again. You must come to Holden, sir."

"Will he allow it?" asked Miles cautiously.

"He need not know as he has much to occupy him. He has yet to finish ploughing, and I worry that he has left it too late to sow. Uncle Francis no longer comes to help us, nor do I blame him. He must now pay for his folly, uncle says." Indeed so, thought Miles, though the family might yet suffer should next year's harvest fail on his account.

"Very well, I shall come the morrow. Let Mary know, but if she does not desire it then please send word." He loosened his hold of her hand.

"He is undeserving of her charity!" she added contemptuously.

Miles swallowed down the words that sprang to his tongue, instead he gestured towards the door. "I must not keep you from your sisters. Tomorrow morning, then."

Eliza nodded politely as he led her along the hall. Thankfully Sarah could be heard clattering about her business, oblivious of their presence. Miles watched Eliza thread her way through the market sellers about the green until he lost sight of her among the bobbing heads. He closed the door with an exaggerated sigh.

Margery appeared at the head of the stairs arranging her hair by drawing down on the tight curls recently released from their rag bindings. She was wearing a dress of palest blue which had been in her possession for many years. Miles always commented that it reflected the colour of her eyes prettily. It was also a barometer of her humour. It seemed that cheerfulness continued to reign.

"Do we have company? I thought I heard voices."

"Yes, my dear, it was Mary Gawthorp's daughter. She is now gone."

"Gawthorp, why do I know that name?" She advanced down the stairs, running her hand languidly along the length of the oak rail, a frown darkening her brow. As she drew level with him her expression changed. "But of course, Madam Parker spoke of Gawthorp just the other day. He was the devil who attacked their nephew. I heard that the scoundrel has deserted his family. Was the daughter here seeking charity?"

Miles understood in that moment what Eliza and her sisters were enduring. He must caution their mother on the dangers of pride. "No, my dear, he is returned, she desires that I counsel her mother."

"Mm," snorted Margery, "you would do well to counsel her husband." She marched with purpose down the hall. "With your permission I shall go to Teal's. Marianne requires some scarlet twist to complete the kerchiefs for the boys. She can likely finish them this afternoon."

Under Margery's careful tutelage, Marianne had embroidered in the smallest of blood red stitches her brothers' initials on finest silk squares. The letters and their intricate inter-weavings were to designs entirely her own. Miles had long recognised in his daughter an artistic flowering which could be seen in her every action, down to the elaborate way that she preferred to arrange her hair. She had worked hard to complete the eight handkerchiefs to accompany the embroidered robe which had occupied her mother since the news of Sally's pregnancy. Each day Margery had moved her chair close to the casement to harvest the light. Her fairy sized stitches, almost invisible like milk on snow, caused her to frown as she focused, and caused her eyes to run by the end of the afternoon. The robe had been completed almost ten days, and she was growing impatient with Marianne who found much to distract her from her task.

"Come, Marianne, the baby will have quite outgrown my robe if you do not make haste."

"Give my best wishes to Teal, my dear. I have parish business to attend to so I shall be at my desk all morning."

Margery swung her lightweight cape about her shoulders and opened the door. Pausing, she turned to the retreating figure of Miles.

"Then do not be tempted to eat, sir, especially not the last of the pie!"

With a laugh she was gone.

Thoughts of food and a loud crashing from behind the kitchen door reminded him that he must speak with Sarah of her discourtesy. Heeding Margery's words however, he resolved to do it that evening after supper, and with a sigh, closed his study door to temptation.

31

October 1701. Marley

There was something of the air and the bright chill of the low sun that caused John to reflect that two full years had passed since his first arrival at Marley. He had risen from his bed in darkness and made the familiar journey to the Hall to collect Mab. Together they had walked to the crest of the slope where they encountered the first livid glow at the horizon. The air was without movement and the voices of birds carried far across the heath. The face of his mother suddenly returned to him with a clarity he thought forever lost. He wiped away a tear and grew impatient at the thought that there were three more days remaining before his return to his father and kin.

Nathan Gill had been back to the valley of his birth with news of the arrival of his first child and another on its way four months since. He had taken time to visit the Asquith homestead as a kindness to his friend, to furnish John's father and brothers with news of John's progress at Marley.

They had sat a morning about the table, a low fire maintained in the hearth though the day had been warm. In the yard, the children of Benjamin and Susanna amused themselves noisily. The brothers had paused in their labours to hear the news, and Benjamin, in particular, had many questions of Nathan. Was Parker happy with John's work? Had he grown into a man? Was there a sweetheart? Nathan answered honestly that John had proved himself an excellent worker who Parker was ever trusting with further responsibilities.

He paused at this point in his narrative to recount the drama of Jonas's birth, and the essential role that John had played in ensuring that Jennet and the child had survived. For this, Nathan should ever consider him his finest friend. Samuel impatiently pressed Nathan on details of Parker's lands and management with a curiosity born of ambition. Nathan obliged, making particular mention of their success with the intack, hard achieved though now productive. Benjamin and Samuel murmured in admiration. Only the patriarch, Richard, at the head of the table remained silent. Nathan could see that the old man had grown very thin, like fruit left too long on the branch. There was a dullness to his eyes which he had seen many times in animals ailing and in pain. He fretted about how, or if, he should relay this to John.

Having gathered news of the Asquith family, the two new sons of Benjamin, the fine harvest past, and the acquisition of three new cows, Nathan made ready to take his leave. As he rose to his feet the old man spoke. "Is there a sweetheart, Nathan?"

Though he had never admitted it, even to his closest friend, it was clear to Nathan that John was sweet on Eliza. He remembered fondly his first encounters with Jennet, how she drew him like a lodestone, how he introduced her name artfully into every conversation. His friend was exhibiting the same symptoms.

"I believe there is a girl who has caught his eye, sir. Her name is Eliza."

"Tell me something of her."

Not wishing to touch upon the domestic difficulties and scandals swirling about Holden Gate, he thought it best to concentrate on the person of Eliza herself.

"I believe that she is seventeen, and has a lovely face, dark curls and a pretty figure."

The old man shifted his position in his chair. Clearly these details were not enough to satisfy him.

"She reads and writes skilfully, and knows her bible well. Her parents set great store by this." Still the old man seemed unmoved, so as a parting shot he added, "Sir, she has great spirit for one so young."

For the first time in the course of the morning a smile formed quietly at Richard's lips as though shaped by memories of another girl.

"Then he must match her spirit with his own resolve, would you not say, Nathan?"

"I believe so, sir". Unsure as to the meaning of the sentiment, he bade farewell to the family, promising to relay their news to John once back at Marley. As he lowered his head to clear the low door lintel, he imagined he heard the old man mouth the name Ann, though perhaps he was merely clearing his throat.

Nathan returned to Marley after three days, which to John seemed far longer. He had done his best to care for Jennet in his friend's absence; her sickness, whilst not constant, was violent and unpredictable. Martha had called daily to help with Jonas when John was at his work, but as the light departed, and the child slept, the parlour fell silent. He pined for the gentle companionship of his friend as, once supper ended, Jennet drew the curtain about her bed in the vain hope of finding unbroken rest. As he gazed into the hearth, the flames became Eliza's wild curls, and he yearned for the chance to meet with her on Nathan's return.

The news of his family gladdened his heart, particularly the arrival of his two nephews. Though Nathan did not shy from details of the father's appearance, he did not dwell upon the old man's unwillingness to speak. John was, however, no fool, and recalled the way in which his mother had withered, her pain drawing her down into silence. That his father had asked so little of Nathan was an ominous sign. He resolved to return to his family at the soonest opportunity.

That had been four months ago, and the gathering of the harvest and the sowing for next year had prevented him from making the journey. He could delay no longer, and, remembering the speed of his mother's passing, he had approached Parker. He had requested that he be allowed a couple of days' leave to visit his family. His wish had been granted without stipulation by his employer who had recognised in the boy an honesty and capacity for hard work. He had certainly earned this small kindness.

John had planned to journey home at the end of the week. He could work until the town clock rang the Angelus, and walk in the remaining hours of daylight. By nightfall he should be approaching the familiar terrain of home. He would return to Marley after church on Sunday.

As he and Mab paced the wide sweep of moor he willed the hours to his departure to speed by, but ever his thoughts returned to Eliza and what might happen in his absence. Gawthorp had been returned a few weeks now, and though he seemed restored to physical strength there was much to suggest that a malignancy persisted. Eliza had spoken forthrightly upon the matter. In her opinion he was out of his mind. But this was not the madness of Old Ned, the simple-minded beggar whose benign simperings and gentle ways fostered charity from all that knew him. No, to Eliza this was a different madness, malevolent and unpredictable. Mary saw it too, of this she was sure. Though her mother would never speak of what it was that might ail her husband, each day the bible lay open at the same pages, the truth of the matter in the wisdom of the prophet Samuel.

Its chapters told of King Saul, anointed King of the Israelites, and the chaos of his life whose fall was marked by jealousy, madness and suicide. This was a tale hitherto unknown to Eliza. Mary had long schooled her children in the words of the gospels and Christ's teachings. Her occasional forays into the Old Testament were to the tales of the likes of Daniel and Jonah, stories with enough colour and excitement to entertain the very young. Through the words of the prophet, Mary could see the truth of her husband's condition, though she was powerless to help. Only the acceptance of God and love of God could cure him. To Eliza, that seemed as unlikely as snow at midsummer.

John assured Eliza that he would only be gone for two days, and would call by Holden on his way back down to Marley. Should anything happen in his absence Eliza should seek the help of George Snowden, being at closest hand. Feeling that he may have caused her undue worry, he fell silent.

"I spoke with the Reverend Gale. He came to Holden and spoke with mother two weeks past," she suddenly volunteered. This was something she had kept hidden from him. It was soon apparent why. Eliza snorted with distain. "It has changed nothing!"

Her mother and the Rector had spoken together for a couple of hours. The children had been banished from their presence and had gathered together like birds on a rooftop on the slope behind the farmstead. They had passed the time weaving long dry grass into animal forms for the amusement of baby John. All the while Eliza had kept an eye on the figure of Gawthorp far below. He did not pause in his labours and seemed oblivious to the visitation. The grating of hooves heralded Gale's departure, and they watched his shrinking figure raising dust in the lane. Shortly afterwards Mary strode out into the yard and beckoned the children to her. She made no reference to her visitor and instead issued a list of tasks she wished completed in preparation for the midday meal. If Eliza had expected thanks for inviting the Reverend Gale to attend Mary, then she had been disappointed. The bible, pushed to the end of the long table, still lay open at Samuel's history of Saul.

"Were he my husband, I should not countenance him!" Eliza's words were sharp with frustration, anger and impotence. There was nothing John could say that could change things; instead he turned the conversation to something hitherto unaddressed.

"Do you remember your own father, Eliza?" His thoughts were drifting homewards and he was fearful of what awaited him. Though Nathan had couched his words carefully, it was what went unsaid that told him that his father's life was ebbing away.

"As though he were still with us! I think of him every day, and curse the stranger that has taken his place at our table. I curse the fact that I was not born a man, either me or Ann, or any one of us, for were it so she would have never married him." In her outburst was the truth of the matter. God had seen fit to bestow Mary with a healthy family of girls, but in return had taken Thomas from her before his time.

"She was not to know the truth of the man," said John "You must not blame her nor yourself." He took up her hand and cradled it in his own. He wondered at the will of a God who should bless his own mother with three sons and yet not be so merciful to Mary, a woman who had lived her entire life in His name.

"I should have liked to have met your father, I'm told by those who knew him you resemble him greatly." His smile drew from her a smile of her own as she recalled her father's features.

Now, as his thoughts raced across the high moor and down into the gentle slopes of the dale, finding the track to the familiar low doorway of home, John had but one wish. God grant that his own father should live to meet Eliza.

32

October 1701. Ghyllgrange

Elizabeth Rishworth could not hide her relief at being home. She ran her fingers along the narrow oak table in the panelled hall, and noted that the long case clock by the stair had ticked itself into silence in their absence. William's voice could be heard at her back issuing orders for the fires to be lit throughout the house. Though the air was chill and musty she was comforted by its smell, and for the first time in five weeks she felt happy.

Agnes, whose squint gaze had so alarmed her in the earliest days, took baby Ann from her. The child was tightly swaddled, and in spite of the roughness of the terrain had slept soundly the entire journey back to Ghyllgrange. As though she too recognised the familiar scent of home, the child became restless. Agnes cradled her close, and began to sing in a low honeyed voice a song of her own devising. It was all that was needed to draw the infant back into slumber. Elizabeth had much to be thankful for, not least Ann, who had arrived so effortlessly into the world, and whose serenity could be maintained simply with a melody. On the morning of her birth, William had entered the chamber and kissed his wife's head tenderly as she cradled the newborn. She had sensed his faint disappointment that the baby was not a son, but as the process had proved so easy, she had no fear in contemplating more children.

That had been a year ago, and despite her willingness and his vigour a second pregnancy had not been forthcoming. No matter, she thought, if it be God's will then she should accept it. She had grown fond of her husband in the two years of their marriage in ways she would not have imagined on their wedding day. Though he was the same age as her own father, she had learned to see beyond his ageing features. She closed her ears to his groans as he rose from their bed in the pale morning light. His lined face was to her smooth, his sparse hair was to her full. Though she herself was unpossessing of great beauty and lively wit, she considered herself blessed. Elizabeth was content with the smallness of her world, this she recognised in her joy at their return to Ghyllgrange. Here it was she felt safe.

Five weeks past, William had suddenly announced his intention to lock up the house, and take Elizabeth and the baby to visit his younger brother Thomas at Addingham. His demeanour that day had unsettled her in ways she could not fathom. He had returned from Bingley at a late hour, which in itself was unusual, and a strange agitation was evident in the way he had not taken his seat at the fire. He had paced about the parlour in a slow measured manner asking to hear of the small business of her day. She had recalled each detail as was habitual, but sensed he was not hearing her words. At length he had announced that they would journey to Addingham the next morning. They would be away from Ghyllgrange for some time, the reasons for which he did not explain.

The following morning she had awoken to the sounds of voices in the yard. William was already abroad. In a matter of hours a cart was loaded with belongings, carefully packed in two large chests. She, Agnes and the baby had jostled uncomfortably into one another as the cart had bumped along the rough road across the moor. William and his man, Smith, rode ahead, dark silhouettes against the low sun. She recalled the single rowan tree heavy with fruit at the roadside, and wondered that it might foretell a harsh winter ahead. The journey passed without a word.

She had met Thomas only once before, that being the day of her wedding. Though her father's house, her childhood home, was barely a mile from Thomas's, she had never before encountered him. She and William had married in the church at Addingham, and Thomas and his wife Jane had been there to witness it. She remembered only that Thomas did not resemble her husband but for his fine nose and dark eyes. Of Jane, she had no recollection at all.

They arrived at Thomas Rishworth's house as the sun was just beginning its descent from its high point in the heavens. Here the land had a softness to it, like linen gathered but not creased. Thomas stood in the doorway shielding his eyes to the brightness of the day. As a groom gathered the reins of William's horse, the two brothers embraced. Elizabeth had been suddenly overcome with a great dread as Jane appeared at her husband's side and beckoned her forth. She was become a child again. Her hosts were in their middle years and she a girl of twenty. In that moment she was no longer blind to the reality of William's being; he was an old man once more. She felt foolish and stumbled over her words as Jane and Thomas took turns to embrace her and welcome her to their home.

In those first few hours Elizabeth felt herself growing smaller and younger, unwilling to speak for fear she would damn herself in their eyes. Her shoulders grew stiff as she cradled Ann and relinquished the child clumsily when Jane asked to hold her that she might get a better look. At close quarters Elizabeth felt ashamed that she had judged Jane hastily. Though at least ten years older than herself, it was her pale hair and milky skin that had given the first impression of a much older woman. Her initial mistake was further overturned by the revelation that Jane had also a daughter barely a year old who by happy coincidence was also named Ann. Jane had laughed good-heartedly, and Elizabeth smiled feeling that they would have little else in common.

Feigning a headache as the result of the journey, she asked that she might lie down a while in darkness. Guided by a servant at Jane's direction, she was shown to her chamber where the shutters were drawn noisily against the light. At last she was alone. As the low chatter of voices seeped up through the floorboards, tears rolled down her round cheeks, dampening the woollen bolster. As she cursed her youth and her other shortcomings, a pain at her temples became a reality, and a shallow sleep overcame her.

Some hours later she felt William's hand in hers. A candle guttered in a draught from below the shutters; the room was grown chill. He enquired kindly as to her wellbeing, and wondered that she might feel better were she to join them in the parlour for an early supper. In the dim light William became her young man again, and she could imagine they were in their chamber at Ghyllgrange. Buoyed by this thought she agreed to follow him down.

In truth, there was little about Thomas and Jane that was not agreeable. He, like his brother, possessed an even gentle voice, which only became animated when he spoke of matters relating to the land. Jane mirrored her husband well, and kindly sought to draw Elizabeth into discussion of the raising of children. When her words were as stones on her tongue, Elizabeth resorted to nodding in agreement. Later that evening as they retired, Elizabeth finally rediscovered her voice. When asked by William what troubled her, words tumbled forth.

"They must think me stupid! They must wonder why you should ever have chosen to marry such a dolt. Husband, I shame you!" Her words were washed away by tears of frustration.

Then, for the first time, his words had taken on a brittle tone. "Elizabeth, you are a wife and a mother, no longer a child. You are amongst family who wish you no harm. I ask nothing else of you ..." His words tailed away, as he rolled away from her and blew out the light.

The following morning he awoke, and kissed her gently above her brow as was his custom. What had passed between them was forgotten. She vowed that she would heed his words, and indeed through effort of will, she found herself lingering at the table with Jane, as together they pinched off morsels of bread soaked in milk to feed their daughters. She even found herself silently rejoicing that her own Ann was such a placid child compared to Jane's who was peevish and restless. Like the thawing of river ice, Elizabeth began to relax in Jane's company, and found herself sharing the small intimacies of motherhood. That night at supper she was emboldened enough to venture her thoughts on the profusion of rowan fruit. Thomas nodded and shared her worries at the promise of a harsh winter.

As the days progressed, William and Thomas were little in attendance, riding out at an early hour, and not returning until supper. This did not worry Elizabeth who had come to relish the company of Jane and the babies. Her yearning for Ghyllgrange had faded to an ancient scorch mark. Thus it continued until the eighth day.

The night before, supper had been a protracted yet genial affair. Earlier, she and Jane had wandered together to the edge of the moor, which draped the land like a carpet, enjoying the stillness of the autumn day. When she fell into bed that night, sleep overcame her at once. Rising the next day, she had gathered up the baby, and hurried to the parlour, keen to share the morning with Jane. To her dismay it was Agnes who greeted her, with the news that Jane was away with William and Thomas, and that she would assist for the day with the business of the children.

With no idea as to where the others could be, she found herself snapping at Agnes, and felt aggrieved that her baby should drift so quickly into sleep, depriving her of company. It had begun to rain in angry bursts which reflected her mood. In the absence of any other pastime, she took up her needlework which both bored and frustrated her. She drew her stitches too tight and was obliged to unpick them, the fabric becoming grubby and misshapen. There was nothing in which she excelled, she thought miserably.

When at last William, Thomas and Jane did arrive she sprang to her feet like a prisoner shown an open door. Though they remarked on the foul nature of the weather and the supper in prospect, they said nothing of where they had been, nor enquired after her wellbeing in their absence. Later she had questioned William in the privacy of their chamber. He would say naught but that there was family business to attend to. But I am family as you wont to remind me, she thought sourly.

The days passed into weeks, and though she could not help but like Jane and the times that they spent together, those moments became ever more fleeting. One night William explained firmly that he, Thomas and Jane had to journey away, and would not return for two nights. She was to remain with the children and servants. When she begged to be allowed to accompany them, his refusal was absolute. In their absence she wandered about the house, learning every inch of its fabric, investigating the secrets of each cupboard and press. It was an act of defiance which shamed her, but she reasoned they saw her as a child, so who could blame her for acting as one. On their return, William presented her with a length of satin ribbon of a chamomile green, and Jane threaded it through her auburn hair with care and dexterity. It tempered the anger she felt at their silence just as William knew it would.

Over breakfast one morning, William announced his resolve to return to Ghyllgrange the following day. Elizabeth could only guess at his reasoning. She had begun to prepare herself for the possibility that they would abide in Addingham until Christmas was passed. As she sat with

Jane at the fireside, the babies slumbering in their laps, Elizabeth began to chatter excitedly about Ghyllgrange, animated at the thought of their return. Perhaps Jane and Thomas might one day come to visit? Thomas had been born there, and would surely delight in revisiting his cherished childhood home.

"Perhaps," replied Jane carefully. After a pause she continued, "My sister lives not far hence."

Elizabeth raised her head in surprise. "Indeed? Might I know of her? You would have a chance to see her."

"No," said Jane, shaking her head gravely. "Her husband would not allow it."

"Oh, who might he be?"

"Robert Gawthorp."

At the mention of his name Elizabeth had involuntarily clenched at her sleeping child, causing her to stir. Though she yearned to return to the sanctuary of her home, she would also be returning to the man who haunted their lives, like a fly circling carrion, Robert Gawthorp. She would say nothing to Jane of her distaste for the man. It seemed her opinions counted for nought anyway. Why else had she been so excluded these past weeks?

"You must teach me the clever way you thread ribbon, that I might remember it when I am home," she chirped with a brightness she did not feel.

The next day as she walked into the dusty parlour of home, the clatter of chests being carried into the passage, she felt for the ribbon in her hair. She thought of Jane, and though she was at last returned to Ghyllgrange, she awaited the heavy footstep that should surely come, announcing the arrival of Gawthorp.

33

October 1701. Keighley

The morning of the fair dawned in a white fleece of fog that wadded the streets of the town. The sounds of the morning were muffled flat in its dense fibre. By and by, horses and carts emerged onto the wide flank of the church green where braziers glowed and dogs barked. Since forgotten times the feast day of St Jude and St Simon had been celebrated in the town with a fair of ancient charter. For most it marked a day of diversion and holiday, to bolster the spirits before the coming of winter. Over the stone bridge, above the river bloated and boiling with recent rain, a procession of people were making their way down from the hills. Among their number came Mary and Robert Gawthorp.

In his study, Miles Gale was making a poor attempt at trimming his quill. He reminded himself, that with less haste came speed, but as he abandoned a second feather split and ruined, he set the blame squarely on his blunt blade. He was resolute in his plan to finish his correspondence before he ventured out into the fair. He was minded to complete the letter to Christopher begun the night before, but abandoned when weariness had overcome him. He must also write to Thoresby of the new instrument he was devising, which, he felt sure, would greatly pique his friend's interest. He had not yet given up hope that the estimable gentleman would one day make good on his promise to visit. It would do no harm to further extend the invitation.

In the parlour Margery could be heard chastising Marianne, Edmund and John for their choice of apparel. Edmund could not wear those britches, for surely they should now be passed to John. How he had grown this summer! John's shirt was speckled with smuts from the grate, though on reflection, it would not be seen under his coat. And Marianne, oh Marianne, let me attend to your hair! Miles rasped his blade across the small whetstone that he had retrieved from the drawer of his desk, and in doing so could no longer make out Margery's words. A thunder of footsteps above his head was Edmund at the business of finding alternative britches. Miles's sharpened blade scored through the quill with ease. As he napped the nib to a precise satisfaction and dipped it into his inkwell, there was a commotion in the hall. After a swift knock, the door opened and Margery blustered into the room.

"Husband dearest, the children wish to know how much longer your business should detain you? Though I have done my best to entertain them, they grow impatient to see the fair." Miles raked his fingers up across his brow and under his wig in an exaggerated show of exasperation.

"I had rather hoped that I should be allowed some small time to finish my letters, dear," he sighed. Seeing her face fall he added, "No matter, we should best make haste before the crowds grow too populous. I shall return to my work later."

Secretly, Miles was happy at the diversion. The fair was a gaudy flower that bloomed for but one day in a season of drear monotony. In a rush of colour, the number of market traders was swelled by a wave of incomers – sellers of the strange, the foreign, the dubious. Though he was both scornful of, and incensed at, the mountebanks and the tricksters who plied their trade in potions and elixirs to the gullible, he was also fascinated. In one small bottle they would have you believe lay the cure for the fever, the gout, the pox. It would restore the ruined complexion, the waning fertility, the lost hair. Though outraged at their deceit, Miles couldn't but admire their well practised cant, and the ease with which they lined their pockets.

Glancing out of the study window he struggled to make out the shadow of the church, so dense was the fog. "Be sure that the children are well cloaked my dear, for I fear that this mist shall not lift." He set down his quill and advanced towards the fire, rubbing his paper dry hands together for warmth. He would wear his thickest coat today for the damp worked into his very bones, seizing them like rusted iron. Joining the family in the hall, Marianne jittered in anticipation of the fair's delights, her memories of the past year still sharp in her mind.

"Very well, let us go," Miles declared, opening the door and ushering in the chill damp air.

From out of the gloom, figures emerged in drifts, their breath adding to the dank white cloud which filled the market place. As they progressed, the sound of a wild melody drew them towards a corner of the green where a fiddler and drummer had drawn a crowd. Miles noticed with some distaste that one of his parishioners, the worse for drink, was attempting to dance a gig in time to the music. As he stumbled and lurched, he was suddenly arrested by a burly woman who pinched him sharply by the ear and led him away, to the great amusement of the crowd. Miles turned from the musicians and the open door of the ale-house, and made towards a long trestle upon which was spread an array of sweetmeats. Like the soft glistening colours of the archbishop's cope, the table was set with great platters of glazed fruits, nuts, sugar plums and other delicacies. Unable to resist, he bought a quantity of honeyed figs, which, he reasoned, were a medical necessity. Margery shot him a wry glance.

Progressing through the fair, he had further cause to dip into his purse, indulging the children with chalks and pencils, and Margery, two plump lemons. Where the lanes broadened out onto the town field, the crowds grew ever thicker, and the smoke from fires and braziers further mired the thick air. Standing proud of the sea of heads, a mountebank in a scarlet coat was addressing his audience from atop a small cart. Miles paused to listen. His stooge, feigning a toothache, mouth padded for effect, was persuaded to sample his potion, and within moments was miraculously relieved of all pain. Miles smiled at the sleight, which convinced at least four gullible souls to part with their money.

Out in the town field, close to the river, the fog was at its thickest, and the crowd at its most raucous. Stopping to watch at a fellow with a collection of small caged birds, he was sorely tempted to buy. Marianne set her heart upon a linnet, scarlet chested and fleet, and had to be led sadly away when Margery vetoed the notion.

"Come, let us find the tinker. I shall send Sarah with the knives. They are so blunt they will barely slice cheese."

They snaked a slow passage through the back lane where a bevy of hawkers plied chestnuts and pies, apples and roasted meats. Miles salivated and wondered at the hour. Breakfast seemed a distant memory. Presently the broad back of Michael Pighells loomed into focus. He was berating one of his tenants with such venom that he drew onlookers as to a sideshow. Not wishing to engage in conversation, particularly when the man was evidently in a ferocious temper, he led Margery and the children through a narrow culvert. The sound of the fiddle and drum grew louder as the alley narrowed to a door frame through which the church green could be reached.

"I see the tinker," cried Margery. "He is over by the pump. But see the queue! Miles, I must go to Sarah at once. Children, come with me, you grow cold in this damp."

Miles nodded in assent, but had already been detained by his sexton who had hurried from the churchyard at his approach. He had spent a busy morning removing traders as they impudently attempted to pitch among the grave flags of the long dead.

"Sir, sir, a rawky day for sure!" He squinted his eyes about the green as though to illustrate his point. The man seldom ventured far from the church precinct other than to walk the short distance to his cottage which adjoined the wall of the churchyard at its furthest corner. His father, and his father before him, had held the same post, from the days of Queen Elizabeth, it was said.

"Sir, there was a man here. Asked to speak with you. I told him that you weren't at home. I'd seen you, sir, with your good lady and children out in the fair. I told him as much. Bethought myself I knew his face."

"Did he state his business?"

"No, sir."

"Then he will find me now at home, for this weather is too disagreeable. Good day to you."

Miles turned towards his front door from which Sarah was emerging clutching a basket of knives. It was likely that she would take a circuitous route to the tinker in order to see something of the fair. He would not begrudge her this small freedom though worried it might delay his lunch. At the sound of Michael Pighells's voice, carried high over the general cacophony, and fearing a lengthy discourse, Miles quickened his pace. As he approached his door he heard hastening steps approach. Snared like a badger in his set, he would now be obliged to entertain the wretched Pighells at his hearth. Experience had taught him that, once comfortably ensconced, Pighells would be in no hurry to leave. His correspondence and figs would have to wait.

"Sir." Such a small voice, and patently not that of Pighells. With some relief, Miles turned to discover the owner of the gentle murmur. His shock was complete as he gazed upon the gaunt face of Robert Gawthorp. This was not, however, the man he had past encountered, angry, sullen or defiant. His expression was unknowable.

"Gawthorp. You seek me?" Miles cast his eyes about in the expectation that he should see Mary and the children. Gawthorp was quite alone.

"Might I speak with you, sir, it is of some importance." His words were delivered calmly and in the same faint tone. Miles hesitated, unsure as to the wisdom of inviting the man into his home. But neither did he wish to conduct any business in the public arena of the church green. Given little choice, he beckoned the man in. Gawthorp followed him hesitantly along the hallway and into his study. A generous fire burned in the grate, and elsewhere in the house; Margery and the children could be heard busy with the morning's purchases and talk of the fair. Miles threw off his heavy coat and took a seat at the fireside. He motioned to the uncertain Gawthorp that he should do the same, and pointed towards the settle. As the man shed his cloak, Miles could find no small talk.

"What is your business with me, sir?" Miles began in a rather aggressive manner which belied his nervousness. Gawthorp was reluctant to look him in the eye, instead finding much of apparent interest among the fibres of the hearth-rug.

"I am damned!" he finally stated flatly. Then, glancing up to look directly at Miles, he added, "But this troubles me not as I have no faith. I see this does not shock you."

"No indeed. In that respect you are not alone. So why then should you worry?"

"My family. I have damned them also." At this Miles was genuinely surprised. Perhaps he had misjudged the man after all.

"You are mistaken. Mary and the children are part of God's family. He sees her piety and love and will not damn them by association. Does she know that you are here?"

"I am here at her request."

"Then how can I be of service to you?"

"You cannot, nor can anyone. I am beyond redemption. My wife, as you state, is a pious woman who blames herself for my Godless state. Her logic I can understand, but her belief I cannot. I am come to you today in the pretence of seeking salvation. Don't look so shocked, sir, what is the harm? If she believes that I have turned to God then she is at peace. I believe that you know something of my circumstances?" He paused before continuing. "My wife does not. I am not without conscience, sir. Let her believe that I am saved that she might not believe herself damned."

Miles was speechless at the man's blasphemy, and the enormity of what was being asked of him. For several moments he struggled to compose himself. Finally, when he trusted himself to speak, he began slowly yet resolutely.

"What you ask of me is a sin. You cannot imagine that I could be party to this monstrous deception." Anger boiled within him as he rose to his feet. "I would ask that you leave, now!"

Slowly Gawthorp rose to his feet and gathered up his cloak. Smiling faintly he took a step towards Miles. "I had much anticipated your reaction, but it is of no consequence. My wife knows that I have met with you at her bidding, and I will have her believe that so potent was your message that I am finally prepared to turn to God, as she so fervently wishes."

"GET OUT, GET OUT!" Miles's voice rose and cracked. He remained rooted to the spot as Gawthorp sauntered from his study.

"I'll see you in church come Sunday," were his parting words as he stepped from the room. With the slam of the front door, he was gone. From his casement window, Miles watched in horror as the dark figure was swallowed up by the lingering fog that would surely now last the duration of the fair. He imagined that he had just gazed upon the features of the devil himself.

34

March 1702. Marley

Jennet beamed at Nathan and pleaded that she be allowed to dress. The new baby slept at her breast, its downy head pulsing with the rapid beat of its tiny heart. Jonas viewed his new sister with wonder and not a little impatience. Nathan stroked her hair and asked that they defer to the wisdom of Martha whose presence was expected within the hour. Jennet requested a little warmed ale. She lifted the sleeping infant gently away from herself and lay her in the folds of the coverlet. Adjusting herself to an upright position, her hand ran across her belly, flaccid and soft where the child, until so recently, had abided.

Jonas trailed after his father, and watched with concentration as he warmed the poker in the fire. Nathan reached up to remove an oatcake from the rack and handed it to the child. With contentment, Jonas began sucking at its edge, and hurried back with it to his mother. Jennet reached over to lift him up, and tucked him into her side. He continued to eye his new sister with suspicion.

Outside a sharp frost was dissolving from branches, roofs and gateposts as the low spring sun rose above the valley rim. Spider lace sagged with pearls of dew as a lone blackbird grubbed daintily among the grass tussocks.

Nathan handed the warmed ale to Jennet and cautioned her gravely that to dress herself before Martha's arrival would be folly.

"I must away, my love, to John, but I will be back before nightfall. Goodbye my little prince." He ruffled Jonas's fine curls but the child was chewing so ardently at his oatcake that he did not acknowledge his father's touch.

Upon the moor, John and Mab stood silently as they observed a ewe tenderly running her tongue across the face of her newborn lamb. Suddenly, as its nose was cleared, the cold air reached its tiny lungs, and with a shudder it breathed its first. As its mother continued to nudge and probe, it opened its eyes, and with a shaky inelegance rose to its feet, the act of balance a tiny miracle of nature. A voice carried thin over the still air, and John turned to see Nathan approaching. When he turned back to the lamb it was aggressively butting at its mother's side in search of milk.

"Come, Mab!" he called as he walked to meet his friend. The season of birth had begun in earnest, and that very morning he had witnessed the arrival of four new lambs. He had thought it somehow fitting that Jennet's baby had arrived with the coming of spring. That the baby had arrived at all was perhaps the greatest miracle.

Mab ran to and fro between Nathan and John, her allegiance tested. When finally they drew close, she settled at their feet, her eyes fixed upon them.

"How goes it?"

"Good, very good. Four singles and a few more before the day is out. I'm over to the Doubler Stones, there's an old ewe I should watch."

"Then let me walk with you."

The day was clear, the air thin and sharp so that in the far distance, some twenty miles away to the east, a battle line of ancient yews marked the horizon. John enquired after Jennet, though he already knew that all danger was now past, and with each morning she grew stronger yet. As they fell into a rhythmic step, John could find little conversation. Though he shared in Nathan and Jennet's joy, the past few months had seen a decline in his own fortunes.

He had rejoiced to return to his family. So moved was he at the first sight of the homestead that tears flowed. He imagined the figure of his mother waving from the path, with an acuity he thought lost for ever. When first he saw his father and felt the frailty of his embrace, he found himself choked into silence. His father sensed his sadness, and with a slight squeeze of his shoulders reassured John that words were unnecessary.

Later that night as he lay in the familiar bed of his youth, in his absence grown smaller, he wondered at the course that his life had taken. In spite of the proximity of family, and his friends back at Marley, he had never felt so alone.

His brothers walked him about the remembered hills and fields, effusive and teasing, questioning and proud. The first day passed with cruel speed and, after pausing long at his mother's graveside, he hurried back to the company of his father. He felt as though he was squandering precious moments as he admired the livestock in the company of his brothers. They were only cows, he thought irritably.

The second evening after supper, they had all lingered about the table as the room had grown warm with food, bodies and conversation. John prayed that this should not be the last time they were all together, but he feared that his father had already one eye on the world to come.

When finally the time came for him to depart, having worshipped at the church so constant a fixture of his youth, he had had not wished to go. After the jibing and fond farewells of his brothers, he stood alone with his father. Samuel was already away to the cows, and from indoors came the sounds and scents of cooking. As he folded into his father's open arms, and felt the butterfly kiss upon his cheek, he again felt the stab of tears.

"I will meet Eliza, I swear it, John," had been his father's parting words, delivered through a smile. He had walked away, his stride lengthening, not daring to look back.

When the hunched back of Holden Gate came into view a gauzy dusk was falling. On the bank overlooking the yard Eliza sat alone. He pursed his lips and mimicked the cry of a barn owl, a secret call that announced his approach. Glancing nervously about that they should not be seen, she had run to him and embraced him with a sureness that outweighed that of his father. Her questions were as unrelenting as a rain squall, his answers, brief and distracted. It was only as they walked a little way from the house did he tell of his father's failing health. He did not mention his father's desire to meet her. As night was but moments away he stopped and, aware of how far they had walked, cautioned that she should return home. In his absence, little had changed at Holden Gate. Eliza had had no cause to call upon George Snowden. He had comforted himself with the fact as he had walked the last distance to Marley.

The day of the fair had dawned, and even the dismal weather had failed to dampen his excitement which fizzed like a trapped bee within him. Nathan and Jennet had forgone the entertainment for the diversion of the new baby, so that he had made the journey to town alone. Confident that he should pass the day in the company of Eliza, he made straight for the church green where she would be found in the company of her sisters. After an hour, and having walked the full circumference of the town field and the church green, he had concluded miserably that she had not come.

On the point of walking up to Holden Gate to discover what might have detained her, he was confounded at the sight of Mary and Gawthorp weaving their way across the town field. He turned about and joined a crowd being entertained by the wild rhetoric of a mountebank. He had no wish to be seen by Gawthorp, and what was the meaning of his unexpected presence at the fair? When he was sure that they had passed and he had not been seen, he wandered on a little without purpose. Perhaps Eliza and her sisters would come later, but the knot of unease he felt at the sight of Gawthorp made him think otherwise.

As he idled about the town field, he had encountered a pedlar. Through the murk he was drawn by the rainbow of clouded ribbons that fluttered limply from his upturned hay rake. The fellow's coat was an exotic plumage of lace, beads and other fripperies. John was reminded that Eliza's birthday fast approached, so with some gentle negotiation he purchased a length of French lace which was sure to delight her. He had lingered until two of the clock by which time he was certain that Eliza would not come, and had spent his remaining money on some candied apple for Jennet and Jonas. The sounds of merriment were quickly swallowed up by the obstinate fog as he made his disconsolate way back to Marley.

Now as he and Nathan marched onwards towards the Doubler Stones, he thrust his hands deep into his coat pockets. In the dark recess of one, his fingers tightened about the thin wad of lace, as yet undelivered, and never likely to be.

In the days after the fair, he had glimpsed more of Gawthorp than he had Eliza. She had failed to keep their appointment at the spring the following week. In irritation he had resolved to tackle her on the matter at market on Wednesday. As he had approached her he was halted by the sight of Gawthorp emerging from the churchyard in conversation with the sexton. If Eliza had seen him at all, she gave no indication. He had attended church the following Sunday having begged to be allowed time off from his labours. Though Bingley was his parish church, he ran the road to Keighley where he knew Mary and the girls worshipped.

As he lingered in the churchyard awaiting their arrival, he was aghast to see the rangy figure of Gawthorp arm in arm with Mary crossing the church green. The children filed wordlessly in their wake. He was bewildered and angry. Had not Eliza persuaded him constantly of the man's Godlessness? Here was the very picture of a Christian family. As they filed past him into the porch of the church, Mary and Gawthorp nodded wordlessly in greeting as did

Margaret and Ann. Eliza did not raise her eyes from the ground and passed him as though he were just another headstone in the churchyard. Feeling foolish and hurt, he could see little point in enduring the Reverend Gale's sermon to be again ignored by Eliza. Nathan and Jennet were surprised at John's premature return, and the manner with which he slammed shut the door dissuaded them from enquiring the reason.

So the short dark days of winter had passed. Christmas, a day of heavy snow, was marked by a fine meal and thankful prayers. For John, surrounded by Nathan's small and loving family, it was a day of sadness and isolation. He truly cherished the scarf of thick coarse wool that Jennet had laboured over, and his words of thanks for their kindness were heartfelt. Deep inside, however, he would have traded all for Eliza's embrace, and his father's parting words seemed now a hopeless premise.

When the first green snowdrop heads forced their fragile way through the frost-crusted earth, John had thought his fortunes due a change. One day out on the Brunthwaite road he had seen a figure at a distance. Knowing with certainty it was Eliza, he had quickened his pace, but at his approach, she had turned, raising her hand slightly before heading back from whence she had come. Since that day, John had actively avoided those places where previously they would meet. The pain he felt was as keen as the January wind.

The menacing form of the Doubler Stones swelled at their approach and, aided by Mab, John and Nathan soon came upon the old ewe, off her feet and breathing rapidly through parted lips. As they crouched at a distance, the stillness of the morning was interrupted by the distant yet urgent peeling of bells. Within moments it was an orchestra of sound from steeples far and near. The ewe, unnerved at the commotion, attempted to struggle to her feet, but the moment of birth was upon her. A cluster of figures congregated in the doorway of the nearby inn drawn out from the darkness by the thunder of bells. Satisfied that the ewe was safely delivered of her lamb, Nathan and John walked towards the knot of men, sombrely supping the sharp morning sun.

"Are we at war?" enquired Nathan anxiously.

"No, lad, the King is dead. God bless us all!"

35

May 1702. Holden Gate

The May blossom was carried by the gentle spinning breeze and alighted upon the green-lichened slates like first snow. Inside the house, the copper still was being prepared for laundry, for conditions were perfect for the drying of linen and cloth. Eliza climbed the bank to the wind-ruined hedges under which the hens furtively lay. She knew the habits of each, and they scattered indignantly as she reached down for the eggs, fresh and warm. She knew already the course of her day, and she was joyless at the thought. Gawthorp emerged from the great barn as she had gathered up the final egg and was about to walk back to the house. From her lofty station, she stared at him defiantly and without moving. He viewed her steadily until finally he snatched up his rake and strode out through the gate and towards the sward of green oats. Satisfied that he would not return, she walked the last distance to the house and entered. Mary and Ann were about the business of sorting through the rick of soiled garments. Eliza deposited the basket of eggs on the table.

"I'll begin the butter then?" Mary nodded.

How was it that they were grown so distant? Eliza remembered the day that Mary had entrusted her with the letter to the Reverend Gale – she, above all her sisters. Perhaps because she so resembled her father in both looks and manner, Mary had favoured her. The deception had bound them together like the weft of mistletoe that ran through the hawthorn hedge. She had been Mary's protector in her father's stead against the devil who had taken his place. Bitterly she recalled the day when everything had changed.

One evening after supper as the light in the parlour grew grainy and the rush lamps were lit, Gawthorp had risen from his chair and walked about the table until his hands alighted upon the spread pages of the bible. The fixture that hitherto had been invisible to him now drew his gaze, and his fingers caressed its uneven fabric. With Mary's eyes upon him, he had drawn up a chair and pushed the book into the soft penumbra of lamplight. For several minutes he stared down at the page, still opened at the sorry tale of Saul.

Eliza, busy spinning at the fireside, had dared to glance at him through her thick curtain of hair, confident that he had not observed her. Anxious that he should not choose this occasion to cast the book into the fire, she tensed herself, ready to spring to its salvation. Instead, Gawthorp had called Mary to his side. She too, fearing his intentions, had placed herself between the table and hearth. What had happened next had been extraordinary. He had beckoned her sit, and bemoaning his illiteracy, asked that she read to him from the book of Samuel.

Fearing it to be a cruel mockery, Mary had hesitated, but when he had gazed imploringly into her eyes and encouraged her to begin, she had done so with joyful relish. As the ancient words had risen and fallen with a graceful cadence, Gawthorp had closed his eyes as though better to absorb the meaning of the text. When the words were exhausted, she fell silent. The only noise in the parlour was the angry spit of green wood in the grate. Then it was that he had thanked her and asked her forgiveness, in a low measured voice. Her reply was addressed not to him, but to God in the form of a prayer, pent with emotion.

Yes, that had been the beginning of the unravelling of it all. In the coming days he had transformed himself into the penitent, desperate to cast off the weight of sin. As the family gathered at supper, with the encouragement of Mary, he would speak the grace over the food that they would then share. Afterwards, as the girls cleared and tidied, he and Mary would remain at the table, crouched over the bible, heads almost touching. Though he had claimed a lack of learning, he was not totally illiterate. As a child, he had received a rudimentary education, but through lack of care and practice it was but a dark memory. With the encouragement of Mary, who guided with her slender finger his ponderous passage across the dense lines of scripture, the neglected faculty was again sharpened. He questioned and considered, bowed to her understanding, and gave the outward appearance of one who cared.

For Eliza, however, this Damascene event was as hollow as a blown egg at Easter. She could see what Mary chose not to. No matter that he announced his intention to speak with the Reverend Gale, and to join them at church each Sunday, his nature was unchanged. She had begun to notice the way he eyed Ann again. It was not a look of paternal concern, but a dangerous concentration. She shuddered at the thought of what it might herald.

The cool disregard he had hereto shown towards all of Thomas's children had now given way to an intrusive regime of control. He demanded to know of their whereabouts, their business, and the company they kept. Once again, their lives at Holden Gate were growing smaller. His daily trips to Gyllgrange were a thing of the past, and Rishworth's name was never mentioned. Though he could tolerate the presence of George Snowden, who had cause to visit regularly, he ensured that he and Ann were never alone. John Asquith was, however, a different matter. If Gawthorp viewed Ann as biddable, then Eliza he did not. He soon ensured that her independence be curtailed. John seemed to represent a threat, which left unattended would spread like blight through a crop. It was clear that he was aware of John and Eliza's assignations, for he did all in his power to thwart them. The day she had arranged to meet John at the spring, he had seen to it that she had not. He had demanded that she help him weave hurdles for a winter fold. Margaret was sent to the widow Bell in her stead. That night she had cried frustrated tears at the thought of John alone, and his hurt at her absence.

The following week the house had crackled with excitement at the forthcoming fair. For the older girls, it marked a long anticipated diversion in their otherwise mundane existence. The youngest were caught up by the promise of its delights. The despair that greeted Gawthorp's announcement that only he and Mary would be attending that day was absolute. His justification was that both Hannah and John were recently recovered from a fever which the dank fog could well reignite. In addition, he and Mary had business with the Reverend Gale, and the presence of the children would be a distraction. Looking to Mary for support, they had been sorely disappointed. When she had sided with her husband, any protest at the injustice of their plight had died on their lips. The day had been spent in miserable resignation and private imagining of what might be happening in the valley below. The weather was a mirror of their mood.

Winter had given over to spring, and with the drawing out of the days Eliza had felt her mother drifting away from her like fry in a stream, and into the sway of Gawthorp. Deprived of John's company, and denied Mary's confidence, she felt truly alone. It seemed that even Ann was convinced of Gawthorp's new-found devotion to God, and was happy to go along with the new family order. Perhaps then, it was she herself who was the sinner for questioning Gawthorp's integrity and begrudging Mary's happiness.

Eliza made her way across to the great barn where Margaret was busy skimming cream from the pails of milk ranged about the threshing floor. With great care she tipped the heavy liquid into the wooden churn which awaited Eliza's hands. With all of the cows delivered of calves, it was a busy time for dairy work. Today as she pounded the heavy dash up and down, awaiting the moment when through secret alchemy the cream became butter, she tried to imagine the future. She was now a woman of eighteen years, but without the freedoms that adulthood had promised. Bitterly she wondered that this was her future, for ever a dairymaid. Her movements quickened, and she felt the thickening of the cream. In wilder moments she imagined herself escaping so that she should never again be forced to breathe the same air as Gawthorp. In darker moments still, she wished him dead.

Margaret hurried back and forth between the house and barn, inexpertly slopping the milk pails in her haste, leaving oily splashes on the flags. When the washing was done, Mary would scald the milk to begin the making of the cheese. This would occupy all of them over the coming week. The very last round of previous year's labours sat on the chill dairy shelf. Soon it would be joined by a nursery of new ones which would see the family through the coming year.

The week past, May Day had dawned, and from first light she had heard voices and laughter carried up from the valley slopes as the young had indulged in the ancient customs which marked the arrival of spring. She had joined with her sisters in the collection of buttercups, lady's mantle and clover, which they had presented to Mary to be set in water.

At first light, Eliza and Ann had scampered to the top of the bank and run their hands through the grass and moistened their faces with the dew. For the briefest of moments they had laughed together as they awaited the miraculous enhancement of their beauty. It was the only time she could recall such merriment in many weeks.

The day for Eliza had ended in restless worry. Had John presented flowers to another sweetheart? Was he now lost to her? Would she ever speak with him again? Sleep when it finally came was as insubstantial as that morning's dew.

Eliza paused a while for the fat in the churn to separate. The process was nearing completion, then she and Margaret would drain off the buttermilk. Heavy footsteps interrupted her thoughts, and she turned distractedly expecting to see Margaret tripping clumsily with her pail. Instead Gawthorp approached her with a slow swagger. Instinctively Eliza took a step backwards, angry to find herself alone with him.

"Margaret, Margaret?" Her voice grew louder.

"I am in need of her assistance to pour off the buttermilk." Even to her own ears the words sounded desperate.

Gawthrop took a step closer but uttered not a word. Instead he reached out and raised the wooden dash from the churn. Eliza hesitantly placed an empty pail in front of him, and slowly he drained off the liquid. All the while his eyes never left her face. With a flurry of footsteps Margaret returned and, at the sight of Gawthorp, stopped in her tracks, uncertain at what she was witnessing. Her presence did not interrupt his deliberate pouring nor break his gaze. With a final upending, the churn was drained and he placed it precisely in front of Eliza. Her cheeks flushed with a rush of blood as he abruptly turned and, without a word, swerved purposefully around the figure of Margaret. Eliza heard the amplified thud of her heart so loud that surely her sister had heard it too.

Something had changed and though she did not yet know its meaning, she was fearful. Up beneath the ancient stone slates, house martins recently arrived were busy resurrecting nests from memory. Their industrious chatter and the speed with which they darted in and out of the barn as though pursued by the devil himself, stirred Eliza to action. She plunged a ladle into the churn to remove the fat which she aggressively slapped into a shallow wooden tray. Like the martins, her movements became more urgent. Margaret turned away, unnerved at the sight of Eliza's tears which gathered at her nose tip and fell. She gathered up the final two pails and attempted the distance back to the house without mishap or spillage.

Alone again Eliza stopped to gather up her apron with which to dry her face. She clenched her teeth until the muscles in her face strained. Does God see this, she wondered? Does he see anything of it?

36

July 1702. Keighley

Thoughts of Miles own mortality still crouched in the corner of his mind, like mice behind a wainscot. It had been a troubling few weeks which had brought him low and confined him to his bed for the past three days. Aside from the inherent issues of his troublesome digestion which, as Margery had prophesised, had yet to result in the stone, this had been an affliction as yet unknown.

He had risen from the table after a particularly fine supper of bacon collops and eggs, minded to speak with Sarah kindly and with encouragement. Earlier in the day he had scolded her, having caught her idling lasciviously with the young groom at his back door. He had made it clear that such behaviour could not be tolerated, given his standing in the town, and besides, his children might have witnessed it. As he rose to his feet, he was at once stricken with a great pain at his right temple, and such a dizziness and confusion that he feared he might fall.

He had grasped the arms of the carver and lowered himself uncertainly. Margery had at once noticed his predicament and had sprung to his aid. He had been unable to answer any one of her frantic questions, but she must have read immediately the gravity of the situation.

Marianne, panic-stricken, had burst into tears, but when Margery had run from the room to fetch Sarah, she had come to her father's side and gently stroked his hand. He had not dared look at her for fear that she should read his own terror at the situation.

With the assistance of the parish clerk and two stable lads, Miles had been transported gently to his chamber where Sarah opened the window to let in a little air. The day had been shimmering hot and still, and the house radiated heat like a loaf fresh from the oven. When at last he and Margery were alone, and she had observed him with such tenderness, he was able to account, with some hesitation, what had happened. The pain in his head persisted, though with less intensity. He had a fearful thirst, yet anything other than a little cordial he could not entertain. The manner with which Margery attended his every word without a hint of a smile confirmed to him that she shared his anxiety at the turn of events.

Sleep had eluded him that night, and as he lay awake listening to the reedy rise and fall of Margery's breath, he had found little respite from the pain which waxed with a pounding intensity behind his eyes. Eventually, he had discovered that by keeping his eyes open the pain was slightly eased. By the glow of the hazy moon sheathed in its soft corona, he could make out the furrows of the beamed ceiling above. Unseen, a civilisation of spiders were building cities in the joints and shadows.

Morning arrived seamlessly, the light growing brighter, the heat intensifying. A blackbird on the guttering improvised airs which were answered from a distance by a rival. Miles adjusted himself amongst the tangle of linen sheets, and in doing so awoke Margery. When she enquired if sleep had eased his pain, he had been unwilling to lie. His situation was little changed, and he was minded to remain in his bed. Despite his protestations, she abandoned her plans to visit Madam Parker that day. A note was sent begging forgiveness for her absence at short notice but citing her reasons.

She had dressed swiftly and encouraged him to attempt a little breakfast. He had assured her that all he required was a drop more cordial, but then asked that she bring him up some of Martha Wright's lavender which was to be found in his study. Lister's belief in the healing properties of sleep had proved themselves again and again to be well founded. He had only to think of his own children's ailments and the way a fever would dissipate through the mysterious inertia of rest. He had placed the bunch of lavender beneath his bolster and, to his great relief, after some little time, sleep had finally come.

It was with some confusion that his eyes stuttered open to the back-lit figure of Margery at his side. She was busy at her needlework, but cast it aside and took up his hand as he awoke. He was greatly heartened to find that the pain in his head had almost completely subsided. It had, however, been replaced with an unexpected surge of sickness. Motioning with agitation for the pot, disaster was narrowly averted as he evacuated the meagre contents of his stomach. Through his tears, he was able to reassure Margery that this was a favourable sign, and that the ill humours resident within him were being driven out. Her expression was of one not entirely convinced.

When once again composed, he had enquired of the hour and was somewhat surprised to discover it only a little before noon. With persuasion, he had agreed to a small bowl of thin broth, after which he felt well enough to speak with the children for a short while. Marianne had brought him a precise and very beautiful line drawing over which she had laboured for the past few hours. It was the blackbird of that morning's serenade, placed among the briars in a neat nest of her own imagination. Even as he spoke to them, he could feel his mind wandering, which Margery read as weariness in his features. With a kiss they were dismissed with a promise that he would speak with them again before supper. Margery too, once satisfied of his comfort, left him to further slumber.

The chamber with its dark linen fold panelling and heavy velvet drapery seemed sepulchral and stifling. Sarah had ensured that the shutters had remained open since his confinement, yet the stale air was without movement, and bided hesitant at the sill. Sleep would not return; instead worries stole uninvited to his mind. Christopher and Miles, and – thanks be to God – the new baby, his namesake, his first grandchild, had arrived safely, but as he even considered this great blessing, it was with some sadness. Would he ever stare upon the child's features, or feel the curl of his soft fingers about his own? He and Margery had spoken of making the journey out to the Carolinas, but their plans were all puff and fancy as they both well knew. Miles would be as much a child of dreams and imaginations as Marianne's illustrations.

And yet? What was it that kept him here? An obligation of over twenty years' standing. Truthfully it had not been without its compensations. There were few amongst the townsfolk who still marked the register with a wavering cross on their wedding day. Through his efforts, attitudes had changed, literacy now thrived and spread like spores carried on the wind. In time, though he should not live to see it, the people of the valley would see learning as fundamental as baptism, the second step along the road to God. Yes, he should celebrate this achievement with pride. There had recently even been talk of school.

There was something of the people too. At first their coarseness had shocked him. Although mostly courteous, they were not afraid to speak as directly to Miles as they would the ploughman or beggar. Over the years he had come to view this as a virtue; after all, are we not all equal in God's eyes? Besides, he had little time for flattery as a currency. There were, however, exceptions. Michael Pighells for one – a man so convinced of his own elevated status in the world that he had cultivated a voice and manner of grotesque proportions. His attitude towards Miles was both pompous and proprietorial. If he was assuming that his place in heaven was assured, it pleased Miles to think of his fury come the day of reckoning.

The house was unusually silent, Margery and the children passing the afternoon in wordless pursuits below. Even Sarah moved about the kitchen with an unknown grace. Snatches of conversation stole in through the open window. Still sleep eluded him. Thoughts crowded urgently, and try as he might, he could not expel them. Chief among his torments was the issue of Gawthorp. Since the day he had come to Miles with his blasphemous deception, he had made good on his word. To the town, he presented himself as the repentant sinner who took his seat amid the congregation each Sunday, the lost sheep returned and forgiven.

That first Sunday, Miles had intended to announce the truth of the deception from the pulpit, and drive the devil out. Gawthorp had arrived with Mary and the children, and taken his place at the end of the nave. Throughout the liturgy, Miles had been uncomfortably aware of Gawthorp's unblinking eye upon him, as if daring him to reveal the truth. It had been Mary who had unknowingly persuaded him to hold his tongue. The expression on her face had been that of utter peace and gratitude. She had accepted the host, eyes closed in thankful prayer, and in that very moment Miles had resolved to say nothing. Gawthorp could not hope to maintain the pretence indefinitely, and in time his downfall would be of his own making.

So it had had been from that day hence. To any observer, the family presented the outward appearance of God-fearing respectability, but beneath the surface, a monstrous sin was being perpetrated. The longer Miles thought on it, the more distant a solution became. He was complicit in the masquerade, bound like a fly in the webbed rafters. On days when his misery at the situation became too much, he imagined himself with Margery and the children heading west across the ocean. So it was that day.

Christopher had written miserably that, for want of a priest, his young son had yet to be baptised. The Quakers and their ilk, having fled England and censure, were now thriving like weeds in the untended garden of the colonies. There was a role for Miles yet, in these his latter years, would that he had the strength or the courage.

The day was growing even hotter, so that he cast aside the counterpane until only a linen sheet grown lacy with wear preserved his modesty. He sipped at the remaining cordial and imagined that he was perhaps in need of food. He reached out for the staff that Margery had left at his bedside, and hammered firmly at the floor. Margery attended him at once, though she lingered anxiously at the door before entering. He called for a little beef broth which he tackled cautiously, but the sickness did not return.

As the sun retreated below the rooftops and the light in the chamber thickened, Miles began to hope that his malaise was perhaps retreating. Margery had remarked upon his returning colour, and the cold film of sweat at his upper lip had at last evaporated. Best of all, he had received word late that afternoon from Ralph Thoresby; the estimable gentleman had penned a short letter enquiring as to his health and that of his family. He was planning to take an extended trip to Lancashire within the coming weeks, and wondered if he might prevail upon Miles to accommodate him for a night along the journey. Miles had, after all, extended an open invitation on more than one occasion. He awaited news, and forwarded greetings from Dr Lister with whom he had supped two nights previously.

Margery had had cause to scold Miles when he asked for his robe, and demanded that a fire be lit in his study, for he was minded to reply straight away. Reminding him sternly that he had been off his feet for two days, and should not even consider alighting his bed, not to say the stairs, she had fetched her own small writing slope. She had insisted that any correspondence be made from the sanctuary of his bed.

It had taken three drafts to compose a reply with which he was satisfied, for his hand wavered and blotted. Margery sought a guarantee that their guest should not arrive before Miles was restored to full health. Secretly she rejoiced that at last Miles had something to look forward to. Since the beginning of the year, she had seen him preoccupied with parish affairs which he carried about with him like a beast of burden. He had fretted over the unexpected death of the King in the springtime, and had wondered at the upheaval and uncertainty of the new Queen's tenure. These fears were proving to be baseless and their lives were continuing without noticeable change. Above all, the birth of their grandson Miles had proved to be both a joy and a sadness. Though she prayed that one day she should see him, her heart was prepared for disappointment. She channelled her sadness through short letters, some of which she declined to send, and seldom spoke of the matter with her husband.

The act of letter writing had brought upon a great weariness, and sleep, when it came, was deep and sudden. His hands lay slack upon the counterpane, ink stained as though charred by fire. As she gazed upon his sleeping features, carved with deep shadows, she felt relief that the danger was receding. They were growing old, and the past days had been a keen reminder. Let not his later days be blighted by cares, concerns and ailments, she prayed. With a purposeful exhalation she extinguished the light.

37

August 1702. Marley

It was the summer of his most distant memory, or so it seemed. John retained thin fragile images of days with his mother, and a cat, a grey striped presence, the name of which was long lost. He had only pictures and feelings of the sun warming his thin hair, and the tall grass through which he ran his fingers. There had to have been rain, the slap of autumn gale, ice, but in those memories he had grown older and they came to him in narratives involving his father, brothers and minor calamities about the farmstead.

He lay back in the grass and wondered at the dragonflies which cut through the sky as the flash of angels throwing light shadows across his skin. He felt the stroke of his mother's soft fingers. It was such a day.

Nathan and Jennet had recently headed back to the cottage. Jonas had grown fractious with the heat, and had wailed with frustration when Nathan had removed from him a hawthorn strip with which he was making mischief. It was about five of the clock, and the shadows had yet to stretch the breadth of the riverbank. There was much to celebrate in the community of Marley, indeed the valley as a whole.

The summer had been remarkable for its warmth, interspersed with a sufficiency of gentle rain. The harvest, already almost gathered, was bountiful and unblighted. Some said it was the new Queen whose ascension had portended the coming of better times. John dismissed the notion: after all, the poor woman could hardly be considered lucky having lost so many of her children. Nonetheless, and for whatever reason, the year, for most, was proving auspicious. For John, it seemed anything but.

He was restless and questioning. Though he loved Nathan and Jennet dearly, and could never hope to repay their kindness; he was feeling increasingly like the cuckoo in the nest. Before long there would be more children, and the cottage already struggled to accommodate them all. When he had spoken on the matter with Nathan, his friend had reassured him that he was free to remain with them for as long as he chose. His friend had not looked him in the eye as he spoke, and John had sensed at the hollowness of his words.

He felt a sharp sting as a horse-fly feasted at his flesh, and he sat up irritably to brush it from his bare shin. His boots lay cast by his side, as the carcasses of rabbits at the field's edge. His skin was tanned the colour of the earth, but for the white chevron scar above his right ankle where, in the first summer of his arrival at Marley, when set to mow, he had swung too wild with the scythe. But for the friends he had made and the experience gained, was the scar all he had to show for his time at Marley?

He tried not to think of Eliza, for even the mention of Holden caused a pain like the bite of the horse-fly, where once excitement had stirred. George Snowden knew better than to talk of it with the passing of days. At first John had hungered for news of Eliza, and had sought George out in anticipation of a note or word from her. When nothing had been forthcoming, and she had seemed to avoid him, hope, like the flapping of an exhausted wick, faded to darkness.

The word about the town, which John could hardly ignore, was that Gawthorp was a man come late to God. Through the error of his ways and the patience of Mary, he was working towards salvation. People were coming to know him, and felt shame at having misjudged the man. It was true that he kept his family close, but he would be the first to offer charity in times of hardship. Had he not helped to plough Harrop's land when his horse fell lame, and been the first to offer his labour when the wind carried off the roof of Lambert's barn? No, every man should be judged by his deeds and, since turning to God, his acts of charity were plentiful.

John screwed up his eyes as, in the distance, two figures approached, seeming to move without legs or feet in the lambent wet haze. As they neared him, their forms became whole, and he recognised the Gott sisters, Ruth and Rachel, arms entwined, heads together, whispering conspiratorially. He had made their acquaintance through Jennet, who had known them since girlhood, and their father had been present at her baptism. Ruth, the elder of the two, carried a trug hooked over her free arm, emptied of what it had carried earlier in the day. They were making their way along the valley road to Bingley. As they drew alongside, they greeted him coyly. John noticed Ruth's cheeks flush with a violence which flooded her pale countenance. She, as her sister, was tall of stature and slight of frame. Her hair, the colour of bark, curled prettily in damp coils from the overhang of her bonnet. As they passed him and receded towards the cottage, he heard a trill of laughter. In irritation he laid his head back down into the wiry grass, and thought of Ruth.

The Gott sisters lived in the town where their father owned a smithy, as had three generations of his family. His son Jacob would inherit the business with the passing of years. Ruth and Rachel were regarded and admired as beauties in the mould of their mother. In recent months, Nathan had teased that Ruth paid more attention to John at Sunday worship than to the Reverend Roberts. The bright flush of her cheek as he took his place across the aisle was an undisguised signal as to her feelings. As the Gott family rose to make their way to the altar rail, John observed her. He could not dispute her loveliness nor her dainty deportment, but he viewed her with a strange involuntary detachment as one might a painting. There was something in her shyness which reminded him of a deer disturbed in a clearing. He could not understand what possible interest she could have in him, having never spoken more than a greeting with her, though he could not argue against his friend's observations. Nathan had encouraged him to make her acquaintance in the hope that she might supplant Eliza in his thoughts, and raise his low spirits. Though he knew the depths of John's feelings for Eliza, he could see no future in the match. Respectfully, he kept these thoughts to himself, but hoped that, with some encouragement, Ruth might prove a distraction. His scheme to date had proved fruitless.

John closed his eyes, allowing the sun's warmth to find the softness of his lids and the hollows beneath his brow. He had decisions to make, which as yet floated formless like an eddy of autumn leaves. The day before he had spoken with Robert Parker of the opportunities of work outside the valley. The Parker estates were extensive, with holdings to the east and west which likely held possibilities for one such as John, who had proved himself able in his time at Marley. When Mr Parker had asked him directly as to the reason for his enquiry, and wondered that perhaps John was unhappy, he was at once undone. He had stuttered and muttered some nonsense about a friend from his home valley in need of employment. He had flushed with shame at the deceit, and trusted that Mr Parker had taken him at his word. Parker had further added to his discomfort by clasping his shoulder as he led him from the Hall, and thanked him for his efforts in his time at Marley, which had not gone without notice. He had every trust in John, and, if he could vouch for his friend, he would be happy to meet him. John had walked away feeling wretched.

In the crisp brown grass, desiccated by the long weeks of sun, John felt the itch of insects over his skin. He allowed them to march aimlessly about his arms before shaking them away. He was reminded of his father. When John was very young, he had, for a time, found sport in crushing insects between stones. One day his father had come upon him in the act of dispatching a ladybird as it warmed itself upon the mullion sill. He could still recall the anger with which his father had chastised him. This tiny soul was just as much a miracle of God's creation as he or his brothers. To destroy a life was to dishonour God. John had wept, not only for himself, but for all the tiny killings his father had not witnessed. His shame revisited him over the years, at unexpected moments, prickling like the sweep of nettles. He could now no longer abide cruelty in any form. At the sight of a whipped dog, a snared hare, the fighting of cocks, the truth of his father's words returned. But horse-flies and wasps, he thought, wryly, were perhaps the devil's creations.

He would see the year out before making a decision. There was much work to be done before the coming of winter. The intack could now be ploughed over, once the cattle had grazed the last of the summer pasture. Mr Parker was keen to sow the land with oats, and the long ditch which he and Nathan had carved out at the end of spring now drained the heavy soil of its standing pools. Like the white scar above his ankle, this was an indelible sign of his time at Marley, he supposed.

He could hear the build-up of traffic upon the road, and even without opening his eyes could picture who passed by. The tuneless creak of a cart and the yap of a familiar dog told of the approach of Parker's groom, heading back to the Hall. He recognised the excited tomfoolery of the Bartlett boys, and there was no mistaking the incessant whine of Michael Pighells astride his horse in the company of his much quieter brother, Peter. The subject of his ire that day was the Reverend Gale who it seemed wished to avoid his company. There was much the two men needed to discuss, particularly the matter of repairs to the town bridge. Each time he had sought a moment to speak on the matter, he had been frustrated by either the man himself, his wife, or even his maid. It would not do. The diatribe faded to a modulating drone as the riders receded. Peter seemed not to speak a word.

In the company of nature once more, John opened his eyes. In the highest blue reach of the heavens, a buzzard soared, wings motionless in a curling arc. Far below, the comic flap of three mallards startled in the reeds stirred him from his reverie. He sat up, allowing his eyes to grow accustomed to his surroundings, his world turned blue by the harshness of the light.

He eased his feet back into his boots and rose to his feet. The grass retained the impression of his form like a handprint on fogged glass. He began to gather up kindling from below the chestnut tree. Here and there miniature spined chestnut cases had fallen before their time. He picked one up, its green spines bending beneath his fingers, before casting it out towards the river.

As he turned out onto the road, armed with an awkward tangle of branches and sticks, a horse and rider approached, slowing as they reached him. John recognised at once the person of William Rishworth. He nodded shyly, and with some embarrassment, his arms being full meaning that to touch his cap in politeness was impossible. Rishworth seemed not to notice.

"You are John Asquith?"

"Yes, sir." As the man clearly wished to speak with him, John released the kindling with a clatter to the ground.

"I believe that you are acquainted with the Fowlers," he checked himself, "and Gawthorps of Holden Gate."

"Yes, sir, though not of late."

"Indeed so?" Rishworth seemed genuinely sympathetic, which encouraged John to continue. "My presence there is no longer welcomed." Even to his own ears the sentiment sounded bleak.

"John, may I speak with you? I do not wish to keep you from your labours." He glanced about to establish that John did not have company.

"No, sir, I am at leisure." He felt an inexplicable excitement given that Rishworth appeared to have sought him out. He could not begin to imagine what reason he might have, but such was his state of mind he was keen to find out. The mention of Holden Gate was like the striking of a flint, so that when Rishworth asked that he walk with him to the nearby inn, he did not hesitate for a second.

38

October 1702. Holden Gate

Eliza lingered in the shadows at the back of the parlour employed with the business of sweeping up the rushes. From this vantage point she eyed Gawthorp. He was leafing through her father's bible, in search of that evening's reading. Mary was at the fireside repairing Hannah's apron which had rent when caught upon a nail. Drawing her thread with speed and accuracy through the linen, the gaping tear was almost resealed. Eliza, whose own skills with the needle were wanting, always marvelled at her mother's patience. Much of her life was given over to the monotony of sewing, of cleaning and of cooking, the results of which went mostly unnoticed. Where was the joy, thought Eliza?

She recalled a conversation she had had with Mary some weeks ago when she had challenged her mother directly. On that occasion she had been emboldened by a frustration at the weather. The long summer's end had been marked by a day of biblical rain and a tugging vicious wind. The children performed their necessary duties, venturing the short distance between the house and barn with haste and economy. Mary had seen to it that they should use the opportunity presented by the weather to practise their letters.

Margaret and Ann, both proficient readers, were tasked with assisting Maria and Jane with their schooling. Maria, though only a year older than her sister Jane, far surpassed her tender years in terms of enthusiasm and quickness of intellect. The last of Thomas's children, she, like Eliza, most resembled him in manner and appearance. Her hair, once pale, was darkening with the passing of the years; her mind was very much her own. Jane would have preferred to be allowed the freedom granted Hannah and John, the youngest children, who amused themselves with the wooden animals in the corner. Lacking in patience, she fidgeted and moaned, and was easily distracted by her brother's laughter. Ann remarked that the Day of Judgement would arrive before Jane should learn her letters, but if this was intended as a threat, it did nothing to focus her attentions.

Eliza had been asked to prepare the day's oatcakes, as Mary picked through the sack of dried peas, pulling out a choice sprinkling to add to the pot. It was then that Eliza had asked her mother if she was happy. She had not planned to do so, but something of the day's morose weather and her own irascibility caused her to pose the question. Mary did not immediately answer, and for a time, Eliza imagined that she had not been heard.

"I have much to thank God for," she replied as she continued to pick through a handful of grey pulses, deliberately not engaging Eliza's gaze.

"But surely, Mother, that is not the same thing at all! I too am thankful, but counting my blessings does not make me happy." Whilst Eliza continued to turn the oatcakes on the griddle with a jabbing impatience that reflected her mood, Mary had paused and angrily eyed her daughter. At her mother's silence, Eliza looked up.

"What do you imagine you deserve, child?" Mary's words were delivered in a flat steady tone which Eliza had not heard since the day of her father's funeral. On that occasion, Mary, on the arm of her brother Francis, had led her children away from the graveside as the sexton began to infill his labours of the previous day. Eliza, barely six, was uncomprehending of why they should be leaving their father in the ground, and had refused to move away. Mary had turned and walked back to her young daughter, whose cheeks ran wet with tears. In a voice that barely rose above the sound of the wind through the summer leaves, she explained that Thomas was no longer theirs, that he had been called to God. When Eliza had protested that God had no right to her father, Mary had silenced her with the words "Do not dare question God's will!"

Over the years Eliza had recalled that moment often. As a child, she had not understood how Mary could be so accepting of a God who would punish her so cruelly in spite of her life having been given over to Christian devotion. Over the years, and with the arrival of Gawthorp, she had begun to question her own beliefs. Where was the design, the reward? Fortune was as unpredictable as the weather, which, in its own turn, was also the work of God. Why was he so capricious, so cruel? Did it please him to see crops fail, children die, disease stalk and to select victims without thought or care? It may please her mother to imagine that Gawthorp was the reward for her loss and a life of piety, but to Eliza it seemed yet another example of God's cruelty. On occasions such as this, she was minded to speak out of what she knew of Gawthorp, the things he took care to ensure Mary never saw.

It had not gone unnoticed that Gawthorp no longer made his daily walks up to Ghyllgrange. Instead, George Snowden, hitherto unwelcomed by Gawthorp, tended the flock on the high moor. Each day he would report to Gawthorp of their welfare, a task for which he was doubly recompensed – coin, and time spent in the company of Ann. This turn of events had unhappy consequences for Eliza. Gawthorp now shadowed her as he had once Ann, like a dog about a young ewe. Though she longed to speak with Ann of her worries as at night they clung together for warmth under the dark rafters, she did not dare. Ann was now changed from the silent wraith who, if it were possible, should dissolve into the shadows. Her eyes, once downcast, now sparkled at George's approach. Her gentle song had become a constant accompaniment to her daily labours. She had shed her former shadowy countenance as a butterfly freed from its case. Eliza rejoiced in Ann's happiness even though she now took the place of her sister as the focus of Gawthorp's advances. He had yet to lay his hands upon her, yet she felt defiled by his gaze. She was repelled by his sour breath as he stood over her in the barn, unseemingly close, unnervingly silent. Though she yearned to speak of her worries with Ann, in the dark hours of the night she kept her counsel. Ann had endured years of his unwanted scrutiny with a miserable stoicism. Eliza could not trust herself to do the same, she would sooner see him dead, and hang for the deed.

When sleep would not come, in spite of her willing it, she thought of John. It had been almost a year since she had last shared his company. Her last sight of him had been on the Brunthwaite road, but in the company of Gawthorp she had not dared acknowledge him. Even to enquire of George Snowden how John fared seemed too dangerous an enterprise. Though she could not fathom the reason, she knew beyond doubt that Gawthorp despised John, and perhaps even feared him. To mention his name in Gawthorp's presence was as foolish as to prod at a wasps nest. Eliza could only wonder miserably at how John now spent his leisure hours, and in whose company.

Since the day that she and her mother had exchanged cold words on the subject of happiness, Eliza had become increasingly fearful. She felt out of kilter with a universe which now revolved about Gawthorp. In the darkness of space she seemed to drift alone without purpose or company. In her most wretched moments she wondered whether this was what death felt like.

Gawthorp seemed to have settled upon a chapter of scripture that satisfied him, and called upon Mary to make haste with the meal. Obligingly Mary set aside the apron not fully mended, and turned her attention to the pot which bubbled away the day long above the flames of the hearth. Eliza gathered up the soiled rushes which she had drawn together at the back of the parlour and cast them down into the fire. The flames rose and spat angrily. She felt Gawthorp's eyes trace her movement across the room back to the darkness of the shadows, where she stretched to collect the flat ware from the rack. As she hesitated, she was greatly relieved when Margaret took the plates from her, smiling cheerfully that she should set the table in Eliza's stead. Eliza retreated into the back parlour and gathered up cheese and butter from the stone shelf. When she returned to the parlour, her heart gladdened to see Gawthorp pulling on his cloak, announcing his departure to check on the livestock before supper.

The room was gilded with a soft golden sheen as the sun sank over the distant hills to the west. Great spars of light cast dramatic shadows about the flags and angled sharply across the tabletop. Was it but chance, thought Eliza, that the house should be filled with such beauty at the very moment of the devil's departure?

Some hours later, the meal having been negotiated, Gawthorp began his scripture reading from the gospel of Mark. It was Jesus prophesising the destruction of the temple. As he spoke of the darkening of the sun, the disappearance of the moon, and the stars falling from the heavens, the mood about the table grew tense. Even the baby, John, oblivious to the full meaning of the words clung to Ann's sleeve, fearful at the reaction the verses had had upon his sisters. After a pause Gawthorp slammed the great book shut.

"We should be ever watchful should we not?" Seeing John's tear-bright eyes unblinking in the candlelight, he then attempted to lift the mood. "Come, my little man, do not be afraid, Papa is here!"

With that, John raced to his father's side and was at once swept up into his lap. As the girls began to clear away the table in silence and puzzled contemplation at the evening's reading, Gawthorp suddenly raised his head.

"By the by, the fair approaches, and this year, given that we are free from illness, we shall all attend!" At the news, the younger children clapped their hands and squealed with joy. Mary, Ann and Eliza were so stunned they froze in their labours.

"Husband, thank you." Mary seemed almost moved to tears by his gesture, and dabbed at her eyes with her apron. Only Eliza seemed to struggle with accepting the kindness at face value. In truth she had almost forgotten about the fair, or rather had pushed it from her thoughts to soften the inevitable disappointment. She thought back to her conversation with Mary on the subject of happiness and saw that perhaps her expectations had been too extravagant.

"Indeed, this young fellow has yet to witness the fair, is that not so, my boy?" The child squirmed with a bemused delight in his father's lap. "Let us pray for weather finer than last year!"

Much later that evening as they lay in each other's arms, Ann turned to Eliza and whispered in the blackness.

"Eliza, are you not glad that we shall see the fair?"

For a moment Eliza struggled to find the words to best express her feelings.

"We must count our blessings."

39

October 1702. Keighley

The long case in the hall stood taller than all other inhabitants of the house. Over the years, tides of water, and the sweep of countless brooms, had eroded at its base so that it rocked precariously with the passage of bodies. Miles had had it in mind to speak with Widdop about sawing away an inch, perhaps two, from its base to ensure that it should not topple.

He had known the clock since boyhood days, when it had been purchased by his father to stand in the passageway at Farnley. He cited the clock as inspiring his lifelong fascination with all things mechanical. He had watched his father each Sunday before supper take the key from his fob and set it in turn into the two small holes in the dial. Miles had seen the weights ratchet up until they almost disappeared into the dark mechanism. All the while, the dome's brass pendulum swung, stately on its small axis marking the measure of their days. There had been other clocks at Farnley, some of greater complexity and finer decoration, but none so captured Miles's imagination as the long case.

His father had purchased the clock in York on the occasion of his first wedding anniversary. Of oak construction, surmounted by a simple carved frieze, there was something of its rugged charm that spoke of longevity. It had proved itself on that score having survived the best part of sixty years and a rough transit over the hills to its current abode.

Miles recalled his father, almost twenty years dead, as he turned the key in the dial, and imagined sentimentally that perhaps, one day, one of his sons should also take pleasure in doing the same.

Margery had taken the children to family in York for a few days, though would be returning in the morning in time for the forthcoming fair. Aside from Sarah, who was preparing a modest supper with a quite unnecessary din, the house echoed and creaked. Miles made his way into his study and placed the long case key into the top drawer of his desk. The past day's angry wind had eased so that the casements no longer rattled. The sky above the church was pale and featureless as muslin.

What a strange day it had been, he reflected. It had begun in the customary fashion, his body in tune with the sound and light of the hour. He had opened the shutters onto the new day and dressed with haste, noticing a distinct chill to the chamber, due, in part, to the absence of Margery, but also the first promise of winter. He had eaten in his study, breaking the night's fast with a plate of eggs and a quantity of bread that would have earned Margery's stern reproach had she been there to witness it. He had excused his gluttony on the grounds that he was feeling the chill and that it should need to sustain him through that morning's long service.

The church that day had seemed unusually full, but over the years he recalled a similar pattern as the days shortened, and folk seemed to crave spiritual reassurance for the forthcoming hardships of winter to be faced. That, or perhaps they sought the opportunity to gossip before the cold confined them to their hearths, he thought wryly.

His sermon that day had been on the importance of the family, citing the Commandments which spoke of honouring parents and the evils of adultery. It was a subject to which over the years he had returned to many times. Though in essence the messages were simple, it seemed, among his parishioners at least, they were not always attainable. Nevertheless, Miles saw it as fundamental to a Christian life, and would continue to visit the theme with determination and evangelical zeal. He drew upon the experiences of his sons out in the colonies where, through want of spiritual guidance, the indigenous peoples lived lives of sinful savagery. He noted that whenever he spoke of the Americas, he had the full attention of his flock, who seemed to relish in tales of a life beyond their comprehension. Often he would be detained at the church door at the end of the service by men eager to know of the New World. What plants thrived there? What of the beasts? Was it true that the natives ran shameless without clothes as Adam in Eden? Miles saw little merit in dissuading them of their wilder imaginings, but always cautioned them on the dangers of a Godless society.

As he stood in the church doorway, shaking hands with the faithful shuffling out from the gloom of the church into the square, he heard a voice.

"Reverend Gale, sir?"

Miles turned to see the figure of John Asquith peering at him from the lee of the porch. His eyes darted nervously about the green. Clearly he had chosen a moment when the last of the churchgoers had departed, either for home, or to the ale-house. A few continued to congregate about the market cross, exchanging pleasantries and prattle.

"Good morning, John," he replied but sensing at the boy's nervous demeanour added, "Perhaps you would like to come into the church with me. I have some business to finish here."

Miles had sensed trouble, and the speed with which John darted forth and into the porch seemed to confirm it. The Rector closed the heavy door and turned to face the boy.

"Well, John, how can I be of assistance to you? Surely the Reverend Roberts has not finished communion so soon!" His attempt at levity seemed to go unnoticed. John seemed to struggle to find words and instead produced a letter which he fingered nervously.

"Is this for me, John?" An apparent confusion of purpose seemed to jolt John into clarity.

"Oh no, sir, you misunderstand. This is a letter for Mary Gawthorp."

Interest piqued, Miles gestured towards one of the old pews at the back of the nave. Together they sat and John began to speak, his words coming in an accelerating flurry.

"William Rishworth came to find me. He brought with him a letter, this letter. It is for Mary, and is from her sister in Addingham. Her sister is married to William Rishworth's brother. Oh sir, I hardly know where to begin!"

"Slowly, John," soothed Miles, unsure at what he was about to be told.

"Rishworth took me to an inn and said that he needed my assistance. At first I could not understand his purpose with me, but he insisted that he could turn to no one else. He spoke to me of Gawthorp, Gawthorp who for many years has believed himself to be Rishworth's son."

As John went on to recount the unmasking of Gawthorp and his subsequent disappearance, Miles held his tongue and hoped that his face conveyed some small measure of astonishment.

"… and again he transforms himself, and is become the loving husband and father. But he is the Barghest that stalks the moor!" Miles winced at the mention of the devil dog of legend which many still believed to exist, in spite of his best efforts to disavow them of this vestige of folk hokum.

"But what has this to do with you, John?" asked Miles, genuinely perplexed.

"There is great concern for Mary and her children. Since first Gawthorp took her as his wife, Mary has broken links with her sister. Even her brother Francis now keeps his distance. The devil is their jailor. Her sister writes to caution Mary, and to assure her that her true family pray for her. What else the letter may contain I do not know." John paused momentarily so that the Reverend Gale should have time to assimilate his tale.

"Rishworth cannot go to Holden in person as he never wants to encounter the devil again. His first thought was that George Snowden should be his messenger, but he does not dare for fear it should jeopardise his standing with Ann. I did explain to Rishworth that, whereas once I was close with Mary, after I found her husband and brought him home my presence is no longer welcomed. I am shunned by all since now Gawthorp has turned to God!" Here John's words failed and he blushed that his last statement might have caused the Rector offence.

"Sir, I didn't mean … I just cannot make sense of what I have done to earn such hostility."

Miles's heart lurched with a realisation that he understood fully the reason for John's predicament, but what John could not fathom was not the mystery of God's ways, but the devil's handiwork. Gawthorp's obscene parody of Christian devotion could only succeed if those who could see through it were kept at a distance, and that included Miles himself. Before even John asked the question of him, Miles knew that he could not be the person to assist in delivering Mary's letter.

"I did try to tell Rishworth that it would be difficult, but he was desperate, and … and he exacted a promise from me. Sir, I told him that I am thinking of leaving the valley to seek my fortune elsewhere, for there is no longer anything much to bind me here." John cast his eyes downwards, his thoughts full of Eliza. "So perhaps I am the person, for, whatever may pass, I will soon be gone from here."

Miles leaned in and rested his hand on John's shoulder.

"John, Rishworth has placed his trust in you because he knows you to be a good man. I grant that you have been set a most difficult task but there is perhaps a way."

John looked up, searching the Rector's face for an answer to his dilemma, unaware that even as he replied Miles had yet to divine a solution.

"I grant that it may be impossible to approach Mary directly, but perhaps the way might be with Eliza." At the mention of her name John attempted to interject, but Miles raised his hands. "Hear me out, John! Mary has indicated to me that she intends to bring the children to the fair come Thursday. They were forced to miss it last year, and it pained her greatly to see their disappointment. She has elicited a promise from Gawthorp that this year the children may attend, but you can be sure that he will guard them like a dog about its flock."

"Then how, sir?" murmured John miserably.

"Can you be here, in the church, before ten of the clock?" John nodded. "It is likely they shall arrive after that time. It is important that you are not seen, John. If you are disturbed as you wait, you are to say that you are here at my insistence, on business with Robert Parker. Is that clear John?"

"Yes, sir, but I do not see …"

"Have the letter with you, and I shall engineer the rest. And John, speak with no one of this."

John rose, the confusion of his thoughts writ clearly about his features. He nodded in gratitude, pausing to peer out into the market square through the knife-thin slice of grey light that appeared as he drew the oak door towards him. Satisfied that he was not seen, he was quietly gone. Miles remained seated in the ancient pew, breathing in the sour air of rotting wood and the mossy damp of the stones. What had he embarked upon, he wondered? In the course of the next ten minutes, he had satisfied his conscience that any mischief at Gawthorp's expense was overridden by his charitable desire to help Mary, her children and poor John Asquith. He offered up a silent prayer, and, aware of a cramping about his calves, made a swift passage back to the comparative warmth of the Rectory.

He had spent the afternoon writing at his desk, but thoughts of his conversation with John that morning intruded to such an extent that he could not settle to productive correspondence. The later daylight hours had drawn him to a study of his mineral collection which demanded collation. Even this had failed to engage him, and so it was that he found himself in front of the long case, key in hand. Tomorrow his family would return, and though they had been gone but a matter of days, their absence pained him almost physically. Acknowledging this, he became ever more certain that he was right to assist John.

40

October 1702. Keighley

Gawthorp's wish for clement weather had, in part, been granted. The day had dawned clear and cold, though as the morning progressed heavy clouds gathered like the heads of soldiers above battlements beyond the far hills. As the family made its slow passage down the hillside, the wind began to gather force, tearing at bonnets and caps, and the rain was a spiteful threat. As they crossed over the town bridge, the river below flowed toad brown with silt. John, who had managed to walk and tumble his way down the hill, had grown tired and was being passed among his sisters like a bundle of laundry.

About the town field, people clustered around carts, swaying with lively conversation and laughter. Plumes of smoke from braziers rose like ghost trees about the sweep of the riverbank. The scene resembled a battle encampment in the hours before engagement. A swell of voices in dissonance, fractured, was dispersed upwards upon the wind. Gawthorp motioned at the youngest of the girls to keep up, but the sights of the fair were proving distracting. Eliza linked her arm through Ann's and gently squeezed in an unconscious show of excitement. Though the sisters made this same journey each week to market, it was always in the company of Gawthorp. Taking up his position at the market cross, his eyes never left them, ensuring that any discourse was limited to the business of selling butter and eggs. Like as not, today he would apply the same vigilance, but with so many children to watch, they might perhaps enjoy a little more freedom.

Eliza's attention was captured by a pedlar who had drawn a small crowd of onlookers. He towered above his audience to such an extent that she imagined that he must be on a block or upturned pail. As they drew closer, she saw that in fact his freakish height was an accident of birth. His frame was so slender, it was almost as if his body had been stretched. In a coat of forest green, his was a presence that could scarce be ignored. He was doing brisk business in spoons and pewter plates that had already long-graced tables. Discarded because of dents and worn patches, they were being snapped up by farmers' wives to see out their usefulness in chilly parlours.

As the crowds grew denser, young John, once again on his feet, grew fearful amidst the tangle of legs and heavy skirts. The attentions of a boisterous dog proved to be the final straw, at which point the child began to wail. Before Mary even had the chance to console him, Gawthorp swept his son aloft, and perched him astride his shoulders. From this vantage point he was the very height of the pedlar who winked at the child, turning his tears to laughter.

The sound of an insistent drumbeat grew in intensity as they snaked their way along the narrow lane, and as they approached the church green, a pipe melody and accompanying song were recognised. The sweet aroma of roasting flesh seemed to assail them from every direction, and, at the doors to an ale-house, fragrant steam mushroomed from tankards. Gawthorp ushered the family together so they did not become separated in the bustle of the crowd, and Hannah and Jane, at their father's bidding, clung grimly to Mary's apron with cold pink fists. Once out onto the flank of the green, the noise was such that they struggled to make out Gawthorp's words as he indicated towards a large open cart to one side of the market cross. As they drew closer, the younger girls became animated with wonder for the stall was a carnival of colour. Some items were known to them: apples in hues from russet through to gold, blushed pink to truest green; incomparable in terms of beauty, a confusion of coppery pears; lemons, the very essence of summer sun; and quinces, the colour of an autumn dawn. Mary pointed out posies of herbs, blue spears of lavender, the winter greens of thyme and rosemary, and the fanciful frill of parsley. In crocks ranked closely, and within careful reach of the vendor, were the rarest and most costly of his wares: plums and cherries preserved in honey, brined cabbages and beets, a dark morass of walnuts. Such was the rarity of his goods, he might as well have been touting the Crown Jewels themselves. Eliza was surprised to see that Gawthorp seemed to share in the rest of the family's fascination; this was further compounded when he purchased a quantity of hazelnuts and pears which he presented to Mary without ceremony or reason. At the sight of her mother's delight, Eliza momentarily imagined that Gawthorp was possessed of some measure of kindness after all.

It was as Mary was gathering up her prizes that the Reverend Gale made his approach. He was accompanied by Margery and his own children, who had already spied the treasures of the stall and were attracted as though to a lodestone. Tipping his hat and silently rehearsing the deceit he was about to perpetrate, he settled his face into the most benign of smiles.

"Good morning to you all. I see that you have already made the acquaintance of Mr Taylor, who has journeyed here today from the port of Hull. With such delicacies we might imagine ourselves in Spain itself!" He laughed goodheartedly at his own wit, which did not elicit so much as a smile from Gawthorp.

Miles had spent a good deal of time that morning at Taylor's stall waiting for the arrival of Gawthorp and Mary, and had learned much of the fellow's circumstances. Margery had unwittingly aided him by enquiring the provenance of almost every item of his wares. Miles had indulged her with a quantity of almond comfits for which he had been relieved of, what seemed, a Queen's ransom.

Gawthorp seemed anxious to move onwards, and unwilling to engage in pleasantries. Miles cleared his throat.

"Oh, I almost forgot! Mary, I have something for you. I meant to give it to you after service Sunday past, but I think I had not the opportunity." Despite his clear impatience, Gawthorp was obliged to pause as Miles continued. "Indeed, I have a book in my possession which I know will interest you greatly." Mary glanced nervously towards her husband. "This book I have found to be the most wonderful instructional guide, and written in the most engaging way. My own children are familiar with its every word. I feel certain, Mary, that your own children should benefit greatly from it. Its title is *The Pilgrim's Progress*."

Mary's eyes searched his, her cheeks flushed with barely disguised delight. "Sir, I have indeed heard of this book."

"Then if your husband would allow it, I should be delighted to offer you a copy in my possession. You may return it at your leisure." He glanced purposefully towards Margery and the children, who were still lingering about the wonders of Mr Taylor's stall. "Eliza, perhaps I could prevail upon you to fetch it. I believe that I have left it in my travelling desk." This was a small deceit, for Miles knew it to be in the hands of John Asquith who he had earlier instructed to hand over the book together with the letter. Eliza looked towards Gawthorp, and for a moment it seemed that Miles's plan might come to naught. Eventually Gawthorp nodded his head sharply towards the church, at which Eliza walked away with a sullen expression. All the while Gawthorp's eyes remained trained on her departing figure. In the awkward silence which accompanied her passage through the graveyard Miles picked up the theme of Bunyan's book.

"Indeed, the book is remarkable for its plain truth which is told through the adventures of one humble man. Oh, such was my delight with the book, I sent forth a copy to my son Christopher." He was aware that whilst his dronings held the attention of Mary and Ann, the younger children were growing restless and cold, and Gawthorp was growing impatient at Eliza's continued absence. It was with some relief then that Margery chose that moment to draw away from Taylor's stall and rejoin her husband.

"Good morning, sir, madam. Miles, John is feeling the chill. I think perhaps we should continue on our way, and see the rest of the fair before the rains come."

"Indeed so, my dear, but first, may I introduce Mary and Robert Gawthorp of Holden and their family." At this, Gawthorp was obliged to shift his gaze from the church door and engage in rather perfunctory social niceties. Miles was growing anxious at the time that Eliza was taking, and attempted to prolong the conversation. "You will perhaps recognise Mary and Robert. They sit at the back of the church in the old pews, which, I have assured them, will be replaced this coming year." Where was the girl?

"I must go and see what keeps her," growled Gawthorp, turning back towards the church. Miles's heart began to race, for, in but a few moments, his deception would be found out. There was nothing now he could say to allay Gawthorp's suspicions. Miles fell silent as Gawthorp took a step away from the group. But it was at this precise moment that Michael Pighells appeared from the door of the ale-house and grabbed Gawthorp by the arm with his great meaty fingers.

"Gawthorp, the very man! I had hoped to find you here this morning. We must talk about the Silsden road. Another bad winter like the last and it will be washed away entirely!" Gawthorp could barely disguise his irritation, and attempted to shake his assailant away and continue on his way to the church. Pighells was, however, a man used to getting his own way and not so easily deterred. "This will take no more than a few minutes of your time, and, as I have my brother Peter here together with Reynard and Lambert, let us at least settle on a mutually agreeable time for us to meet to discuss what is to be done. I do not suggest that it should be today, for I see that you are with your family, here to enjoy the fair."

Just as Gawthorp was about to lose his temper, the church door opened and Eliza stepped out into the churchyard clasping a small leather-bound book. Miles hoped that he alone noticed the flush of her cheeks, and the spring in her step. When she saw Gawthorp in conversation with Pighells at the church gate her nerve seemed to fail and she wavered before hurrying past the men back towards her mother and the Reverend Gale.

"Now I think on, perhaps it was not in my travelling desk after all. My apologies Eliza that I put you to such trouble." Eliza mumbled an apology for the delay as she handed the book to Miles, who in turn placed it into Mary's hands.

"Thank you, Eliza. Mary, let me detain you no longer. Enjoy the book with my warmest regards. I'll bid you good-day."

As he took up Margery's arm and made his way onwards across the green, he glanced back over his shoulder. Gawthorp, still in conversation with Pighells, had been joined by Mary and the children. Though he could not be certain from such a distance, he imagined he saw a fleeting smile grace Eliza's pale lips.

"Come, my love, we should walk to the town field to see what delights await us," he said.

He offered up a silent prayer. Never before had he felt glad at the sight of his nemesis Michael Pighells whose

311

intervention had just averted disaster. Gawthorp would likely be detained a while yet, giving Miles the opportunity to slip away, thus avoiding his own confrontation with the man.

Rain began to fall more steadily as they walked out of the lane and onto the fringe of the town field. In spite of the weather, Miles felt elated. It was with the utmost sincerity that he announced, "Come, my dear, children. I think we all deserve a treat. A poke of the biggest roast chestnuts to warm us!" Margery shot her husband a bemused look, surprised at his sanguine humour in the face of such poor weather. She gave his arm a gentle squeeze.

A little way distant above the heads of the slowly thinning crowd, the green-clad pedlar, in an effort to keep dry, and draw custom, was sporting upon his head, an upturned shaving bowl. At the extraordinary sight, and to the bewilderment of Margery, Miles began to laugh uncontrollably.

41

December 1702. Holden Gate

As she walked up the bank towards the hawthorn hedge, the coarse grass crackled with hoar frost. The valley's contours were bleached to the colour of the milk sky. Where the sun's faint rays extended above the moor's edge, the frost steadily dissolved in a languid tide.

Eliza blew on her hands to restore feeling before crouching to peer under the overhang of hawthorn. A muddle of chickens agitated at her presence scattered, feathers shaking and billowing as clouds. She gathered up a couple of small brown eggs, still warm to the touch. With the coming of winter and the shortening of days there would be fewer eggs to be gathered as the hens' bodies responded to the turning of the season.

A little further along she came across the body of a mouse. The tiny creature lay upon its back, its limbs locked in lifeless motion, its mouth a rictus of surprise. There was not a discernible mark upon its body. Eliza observed its black unseeing eyes, and wondered at the manner of its passing. Within the hour it would be gone, carried off as a frozen mouthful. She shuddered, and moved along the flank of the hedge, collecting only another four eggs. As she picked her way cautiously down the slope towards the warmth of the parlour she wondered that the day should finally see a change in Mary.

It had been three weeks since her surprise encounter with John in the church. Her shock at seeing him was such that she had almost wept with fear and confusion. In the few short moments that they shared together, he had explained the purpose of his subterfuge, the letter, and the promise he had given to Rishworth. He had handed her the copy of Bunyan's book and reassured her that the Reverend Gale had been instrumental in engineering the meeting. Terrified that they should be found out, she had drawn away from him though for all her heart she had desired to be nowhere else. His final words to her that day replayed again and again in her thoughts.

"Eliza, I am in misery without you! If you do not feel the same of me, I beg you speak it now and I am gone for ever." She studied his face, anxious and pale, his brows drawn up as though in anticipation of a blow, and with a great sigh of joy spoke.

"I could not dream you think of me still! I had not dared hope it. You must believe that I feel the same way!"

Such was the release of her emotion that she had blushed furiously at her own words.

She placed the eggs carefully into her apron pocket and felt for the feathery skein of lace and ran it through her fingers. John had given it to her as she moved to leave the church. For a year he had carried it despondently, imagining the day would never dawn when he could deliver it. The significance of the cobweb scrap was known only to Eliza and John, but it bound them together tighter than chains.

She was relieved to discover that Gawthorp had already departed when she returned to the house. As Michael Pighells had demanded, he had gone to a meeting with Reynard and Lambert. The Silsden road had become so scarred and rutted that some weeks past a cart, making its way to Silsden, had met with a calamity. Its axle had sheared clean through, pitching its unfortunate owner and his load of timber into the marshy ditch. The situation was becoming a growing irritation to Pighells, whose farmstead lay along its length. He knew the futility of making repairs before the scourging frost of winter, but this did not prevent him from returning to the theme like a cur to a rats' nest.

The parlour was clammy with steam from the copper. Mary was using the promise of a clear day to launder linen. The stench of lye was so strong that tears prickled and ran down Eliza's face. Mary had rolled back her sleeves, and the skin on her forearms glistened an angry red. A damp tendril of pale hair hung limply from her headscarf. When Eliza returned from the back parlour having deposited the eggs, she rolled up her sleeves, knowing without being asked the task next expected of her.

In the weeks since the fair, Eliza had waited impatiently to see a change in her mother. Though she did not know precisely the contents of the letter, she was able to guess at a truth which Mary could now scarce ignore. She recalled her anxiety at presenting the letter. Her first instinct had been to secret it amongst the pages of Bunyan's book. This notion had been dismissed before she had even left the church for fear of its discovery by Gawthorp. Instead, she had tucked it with her kerchief within the depths of her apron pocket. She had agonised over what she should say to her mother, and in the event had retained the letter for some days. Eventually, one market day, before setting out with Gawthorp, Margaret and Ann, she had placed it on Mary's fireside chair.

As that morning had worn on, and the town green filled with the tide of traders and buyers she grew fitful with worry at the consequence of her action. On the journey home, Ann had wondered what ailed her sister, for she seemed so pale and silent. Eliza had feigned a slight ague, and, as if to illustrate it, had drawn her shawl tighter about her shoulders. As she crossed the threshold, Eliza had waited for the retribution that would surely come. Her eyes had remained downcast as she shuffled through to the back parlour with her basket and unsold wares. When she re-emerged it was to find Ann voicing her concerns as to Eliza's health. Mary had studied her daughter and agreed that she appeared wan. She had insisted that Eliza seat herself at the hearth until her bones were warmed through. The subject of the letter had not been raised, that day nor any day since.

The Pilgrim's Progress had proved itself a welcome diversion for the entire family. Mary delighted in reading from it each night to the children after supper. Christian's journey to salvation, his encounters and misfortunes along the way, captured the family to silence. Even Gawthorp appeared to relish the tale as he cradled the dozing John on his lap.

The winter sun traversed the heavens in a low sweep, and as the day advanced sunlight flooded the parlour, fierce and cold. The girls ferried the laundry to and fro between the parlour and the hawthorn, harvesting still damp linen to finish its airing before the fire.

It was as the sun had sunk below the far hills, its wake an angry copper flush, that Gawthorp strode into the yard. Eliza had just recovered the last of the aprons, taking care that the thorns which had anchored them did not catch and tear. Before ever he had spoken a word, Eliza could read in his features the trouble to come.

"Inside!" he barked.

As she followed him into the parlour at a safe distance, he paused at the table, his knuckles pressed white into the oak. Mary, alert to his angry demeanour, moved to heat the poker to warm his ale. When finally Eliza handed the last of the aprons to Margaret, Gawthorp raised his eyes to meet hers.

"You will leave this house now, and you shall not return!" His words were delivered with such calmness that, but for Mary and Eliza, the rest of the household continued about their business, oblivious to the drama that was unfolding. Eliza felt the breath catch in her throat, and dared not move for fear that he should strike her. Panic-stricken she glanced towards her mother, but in doing so provoked Gawthorp to continue.

"You shall leave now!" Suddenly all movement in the parlour stopped, and all eyes were upon them, all but Mary's. As she frantically sought her mother's support, Mary hung her head, her clenched hands the only outward sign of the turmoil within.

"Mother?" Eliza's voice, piteously small and broken, caused Gawthorp to advance towards her and Margaret to cry out in fear. Determined that he should not lay a finger upon her, Eliza dashed for the door, sweeping up her cloak and bonnet, before exiting with frantic haste, leaving a silence broken only by the weeping of Margaret.

Barely a minute had passed, and yet for Eliza she was now without basis, removed as a plucked flower. She made haste from the yard, terrified that Gawthorp should pursue her. The light though golden and inviting, was tempered chill by the keen winter air. Before she know it, her pace was quickening as her feet guided her down the pocked track away from Holden Gate. To her left, unseen over the brow of the moor edge, sheep bleated as they gathered in hollows for the coming of darkness. It was only as she smelt the smoke of approaching chimney fires downslope of the falling land that her shock began to harden into an anger and hurt.

The lights of Keighley, fleeting as stars, guided her tread towards the town bridge. The river flowed with a controlled impatience beneath as her pattens clacked across the cobbled span. The night was almost upon her as she made her way across the town field. Even the emergence of two fellows unknown to her, but keen to make her acquaintance, did not alarm her. Something in her step, the fixed even gaze of her progress, halted their saucy approach. They continued their passage towards the dark lanes in lively discussion of their friends' marital woes.

As she picked up the valley road, the noise of the ale-houses and the shrieks of children gave way to the slow grassy sounds of beasts on the ings. The fingernail moon afforded sufficient light to illuminate her way as it ducked and bobbed from uneven clouds. The spectral cry of an owl on the wing caused her to startle. It was the feeling she'd had at Gawthorp's earlier outburst, as though her heart should freeze within her chest.

Who had betrayed her? Her immediate thought had been Michael Pighells with whom Gawthorp had met that day. He had been in the market square the day of her meeting with John. Had John been seen? Though Pighells was a man too fond of the sound of his own voice, she could not imagine him thrilling in gossip of such a trivial nature. He was a practical man, interested only in self-serving matters such as repairs to the bridge or the Silsden road.

Could it be George Snowden, a tenant of Rishworth though in Gawthorp's pay? She had known him all her life, and counted him as a true friend. Had he spoken with John of it, and thence repeated it to Ann, his sweetheart? She attempted to shake off the idea as she might a teasel caught in her cloak, satisfying herself that even were it so, Ann should never betray her.

A low ox-cart rumbled past her, its driver a man she recognised. As it slowed, the fellow enquired as to why she should be abroad alone at such an hour. Hastily she devised an untruth, and reassured him that she was almost at her destination, where she would be staying the night. This part was, she hoped, the truth. Satisfied, he tipped his hat and continued on towards Keighley.

Against the dark sky, the chimneys of Marley belched smoke, and candlelight glowed in an upper chamber window, awaiting the closure of shutters. Not completely sure as to the location of Nathan Gill's house, she fought to recall conversations with John, and details of his home circumstances. By the happiest of chances, a child suddenly began to cry softly within a cottage at some short distance. Remembering that John had remarked that the arrival of Jonas had been the first child to be born at Marley in many years, she suspected that she had reached her destination.

A sickening thought came upon her. Had it been her own mother who had caused her banishment? Had she foreseen the outcome? Above all why had she not interceded? Only then did the tears come in hot fast courses, and a sob caught in her throat. Eliza widened her eyes and stared up at the moon, wiping her cheeks with the coarse edge of her cloak. For a couple of moments she remained until she had again control of her breath, and trusted that words would come unbroken. She stepped forward to the low threshold and, softly at first, and then with greater strength and urgency, began to beat upon the weathered-plank door.

42

March 1703. Keighley

In spite of her many shortcomings, her petulance, clumsiness, and crude turn of phrase, Miles felt only sadness. Sarah had presented breakfast that morning at his desk in the solitude of his study, where a pile of correspondence gathered malevolently demanding his attention. As she had clattered his bowl and tankard with her customary lack of grace, she had hesitated at his shoulder. When the slam of the door behind her had not come, Miles had glanced up from his writing and turned awkwardly in his chair. She flushed and shuffled from foot to foot like a flimsy vessel on a strong tide.

When he enquired as to whether he could be of service to her, the words had bubbled forth like broth from an unwatched pot. She was so very sorry, but she would be forced to leave his service. She was betrothed to be married to Stephen the groom. After the wedding she was to keep house for his elderly widowed father in Bingley. She could not bear the thought of leaving as they had been so very, very good to her. At the sight of her tears, Miles rose and produced a kerchief from his waistcoat into which she trumpeted noisily. What she did not disclose, but which he would soon discover, was that she was already with child. At least Stephen, who planned to continue in Miles's employ, was to legitimise the child. A hastily arranged marriage, over which Miles would officiate, would follow barely a week later, and Sarah would remain with them until a suitable girl could be found to replace her.

The year had started very badly indeed, and although all about was the budding promise of spring, it did nothing to dispel Miles's unease. News of Sarah's imminent departure was yet another worry to add to a list which proliferated like the pile of unanswered letters at his elbow. Word had recently arrived in the form of a tersely worded letter from Christopher. His wife Sally had miscarried a child, and the lack of his customary busy observations of life in Carolina conveyed the depths of his misery. His wife's own survival for a time had been in question, though now, thankfully, she was at least physically restored.

His second son, Miles, was also a growing cause of anxiety. Ever secretive and restless, his infrequent letters provided almost no colour to the substance of his life. It came as an enormous shock to both Miles and Margery when, towards the end of the previous year, he had written, and almost incidentally mentioned that his wife Betty was recently delivered of twins. Miles had charitably made allowances for him. Perhaps letters had gone astray, but Christopher's silence on the matter seemed to confirm his suspicions that the marriage had been one of expediency and shame. In addition, his career had diverged from that of his elder brother, now a respected landowner and attorney at law. Miles the younger was earning a transient living mastering a ship, running the seaboard north to south and trading posts in between. A love of the nautical life had been awakened by his passage from England. There was nothing latent in his lineage that could have predicted the course his life now took. Margery, appalled and self-pitying at these turn of events, chose only to speak of Christopher when in company. Miles, whilst sharing her disappointments, harboured a small and secret admiration for his impetuous son.

When, at Christmastide, Edmund had pleaded with his parents to be allowed to join his older brothers at the soonest convenience, Miles had overridden Margery's flat refusal. With the passing of the years Miles was growing more accepting of God's will. Though oft times perverse, even painful, he now recognised an overall scheme, a perfection which could never be improved upon by the impudent meddlings of man. Edmund should complete two more years of schooling, then, should he still be set on a future in the colonies, be allowed to go.

The events of the past few months had shown him in graphic terms the folly of interference. Looking back on the days and weeks following John Asquith's assignation with Eliza in the church, Miles could only marvel at his own naivety. Had he imagined that with his assistance a rightful order would be restored? He could only curse his own arrogance.

The family had arrived at church the Sunday following the fair, the only discernible sign of a change being Eliza's fixed gaze. Seldom, if ever, would his flock follow his every word with such concentration, eyes never leaving his.

Sermons delivered to the tops of bonnets, under which whispered conversations of a less than sacred nature buzzed, was the reality of service. Mary and Robert had shaken his hand at the church gate. *The Pilgrim's Progress* had fulfilled her expectations, instructive and entertaining. She would be sure to return it presently and, with that, they departed. Miles felt relief. It was only much later, as he lay next to Margery, the smoke curl from the snuffed candle dissolving into the darkness, that he thought on it. Mary had yet to receive the letter. His few remaining teeth tightened within his jaw at the idea.

The repercussions of his actions came in a staggered sequence. January saw the arrival of ugly weather. Sleet whipped in on a pitiless north wind, and the river burst its banks. Snow fell fitfully and dissolved into the mud of the valley floor. Ice, unseen in the thin morning light, shattered the bones of the unwary. The absence of Mary, Gawthorp and family one Sunday seemed unremarkable. The few folk present lived hard by, and those who journeyed further to worship had kept away. The sexton had ashed the path to the church door, but his efforts had mostly been wind whipped into walls and stone corners.

The following week the wind abated and a chalky sun appeared as a fleeting apparition low in the sky. Margery had grown restless at her forced incarceration, and set forth to Marley accompanied by Marianne and John. Madam Parker, whom she had not seen since the beginning of Advent, could always be relied upon to raise her spirits. This day had been no exception. At supper, on their return, the talk had been of Madam's new virginal, a present from her husband Robert. Such a handsome object as Margery had ever seen with its pearled inlay and ebony stringing. Its sound was so sweet and Madam's touch so deft. Miles recalled a similar instrument at Farnley that had been his mothers. He struggled to remember what had become of it. Though he tired of hearing of Madam's latest acquisitions, which Margery would describe in endless detail, he was happy to see his wife's cheerful spirits restored.

Later, as they had warmed themselves at the fireside and drunk a little tea, Margery suddenly remembered the other news she had to impart. It concerned Gawthorp, the man she had first been introduced to at the fair. One of his wife's daughters had been banished from the homestead and had fetched up at Marley. Madam hadn't known anything of the particulars, but Robert Parker had been gripped by a great fury on the matter. The young girl had been found work in the dairy and lodgings with a family nearby. Robert would say no more on the matter but that it was the work of the devil himself. Margery's recollections of her day then returned to a fine seed cake that she had enjoyed and the delicate tone of the virginal. Miles had jolted in horror at the news, but responded with "Indeed so" in a voice that he hoped conveyed disinterest.

Inwardly his mind raced. It had to be the girl Eliza. He felt a flutter within, a racing of his heart that bore witness to his own culpability in the state of affairs. He hastily drew the evening to a premature close, citing a weariness brought on by the weight of parish business he had attended to that day. Margery, with as yet untold tales of her day at Marley, kissed his hand as he levered himself from his chair. Disappointed, she vowed to continue her news over breakfast the next day. He left her at the hearth, draining the remains of her tea and smiling as a Scottish air played again in her thoughts.

The continued absence of Gawthorp and Mary from Sunday service was explained a few days later when Miles had cause to visit the Reverend Mitton. Lady Day was fast approaching, bringing with it a frenzy of paperwork necessitated by the fragmentation and readjustment of tenancies and contracts. Once the feast day had been celebrated, the people of the valley would settle back into the new farming year. Miles's presence was required to witness the transfer of a leasehold of three stony acres to one of his outlying parishioners. Once the business had been completed Miles was, for once, grateful for the hospitality of his fellow clergyman before journeying back from Kildwick in a ferocious downpour. The Reverend Mitton had grown even more stout, and in spite of his relative youth wheezed like old leather bellows as he eased himself into a wainscot chair. Over a small glass of sack and a plate of sugar cakes, he had furnished Miles with a torrent of unrequested and unnecessary detail of the domestic irritations of his household. His wife was again with child, his young daughter's persistent cough continued to keep him awake the night long, doubtless caused by the ill-fitting new windows.

On and on he droned as Miles wondered at the fellow's ever finding satisfaction in anything. His mind turned to finding a means of politely taking his leave, a thorough soaking being preferable to Mitton's litany of complaints, when suddenly he heard the name Gawthorp. He at once focused his attentions on the Reverend Mitton's every word. It seemed that the family had recently returned to worship at the church from which they had begun their married lives. Gawthorp had struck Mitton as taciturn to the point of rudeness, his only explanation as to their reappearance being that the Silsden road was in such a bad state of repair that the journey over the fields to Kildwick was the practical choice. When Mitton then steered the conversation around to the relative merits of a kersey or a twill for a new great coat, Miles took his leave, citing his wife's insistence that he be home before noon.

Miles had subsequently made a point of avoiding the church green on market days. From an upstairs window, he would gaze down on the tall spare figure of Gawthorp at the market cross whose eyes were always trained on Ann and Margaret who sat shivering with their baskets of butter and eggs. Here and there he had picked up strands of gossip, like sheep's wool fast on a gate post. Gawthorp would throw them out one by one save Mary until Holden Gate was his alone. It was not safe to speak with Mary's children for fear that Gawthorp should find cause to exile them too. Those who had previously sought Gawthorp's help as a charitable and practical neighbour now kept their distance. As the girls trudged their way back from market each Wednesday, it seemed as though their baskets were scarce lighter than when they had arrived at first light.

One morning Miles had been removing his coat, which dripped like whey from a muslin having been caught helpless by a violent shower as he returned from the grocers. Sarah had appeared in the hall and helped relieve him of his unwieldily garment. As she hooked it over her arm to be transported to dry at the kitchen fire, she handed him a book.

"Sir, a man came by and gave me this. He said it belonged to you."

Miles held the small brown volume in his damp hands. Once in the gloom of his study he fanned the book rapidly in the vain hope that he should dislodge some note or hidden paper. He then took time to study the pages one by one, unsurprised but disappointed when he failed to find some penned message. He replaced *The Pilgrim's Progress* in its narrow vacated slot amongst the ranks of books on his shelf.

He felt wretched. He had been complicit in John's scheme to deliver the letter to Mary, and the result of his actions had meant disaster for Eliza. He perhaps ought not to involve himself further in the affairs of the family. He was, however, a man of God whose conscience would not allow him to stand aside and allow such injustices to happen. For two days he struggled with the problem, causing Margery to fret at the cause of his short temper.

Tuesday dawned bright and cold as Miles stepped out onto the valley road. The air was heavy with dust raised from the tops of furrows newly turned, and at a distance, with a cloud of following birds, a figure was broadcasting from basket panniers. Stretched between two trees a ragged necklace of dead crows fluttered as a gruesome deterrent. He was on his way to Marley.

43

March 1703. Marley

Jennet brought down her ladle, shattering the lid of ice that had formed on the water in the pail. The jagged fragments jittered before reforming on the surface of the water. Over night a heavy fog had descended and the world seemed to have grown smaller. The ancient beech on the bank of the valley road seemed somehow closer, as though it had lifted its roots in the darkness and heaved itself nearer her door. Nathan was already away to his labours, as was John. Inside the cottage Eliza was spooning porridge into baby Joan whilst Jonas looked on. In between mouthfuls of his own porridge, he encouraged his baby sister to eat up as she clawed at the spoon, eager to feed herself. Lumps of oatmeal spattered Eliza's bodice and she lifted them away before they had chance to harden.

Jennet slid the ladle into the deep pockets of her apron and gathered up an armful of peat blocks. The sound of her skirt crackled as it trailed through the frozen grass, the rise and fall of her breath amplified by the solid air. She hurried back into the parlour and cast the peat onto the fire where it raised a shower of orange sparks. Joan's eyes followed her mother across the floor, her mouth slack with wonder causing a large mouthful of food to drip onto her shift. Eliza scooped up the mess and rubbed a damp cloth across the infant's front. Jonas was already on his feet and at his mother's side. She ruffled his golden curls affectionately, but with much to do she continued about her tasks without a word.

"Will your mother be here presently?" enquired Eliza as she rose, baby Joan balanced on her hip.

"Yes. Here, hand me her. You'd best be away." Eliza smiled shyly as Joan stretched out her arms to Jennet, then threw her cloak about her shoulders and adjusted her linen scarf. The walk to Marley Hall was a short one, but stepping away from the hearth she felt the knife-sharp draught as the fog stole in beneath the door and at the window margin. As she closed the door behind her she glimpsed the tableau of Jennet with baby in arms and Jonas, one hand clutching at his mother's skirt, his other thumb lodged in his mouth.

Jennet felt hopeless irritation that her mother was not yet arrived. She had much to do, and encumbered by the children was not likely to meet her ends. She was also beginning to wonder that she was again with child. Her body recalled those sensations, and though there was no sickness she could find no enjoyment in her food. Was this the reason for her fatigue, her bones seemingly ice bound? With no option but to wait on her mother, she sat at the hearth, cradling Joan who reached up to pull at her curls.

She felt irritable and tearful at circumstances which had developed beyond her control. It had begun with Eliza's arrival that December night. No one could have anticipated Gawthorp's actions in banishing the girl, though for weeks before John had worn the expression of one awaiting the hangman. He had shared with Nathan the details of Rishworth's letter, and guessed at the repercussions with the certainty of a gypsy seer. With the wild hammering on the door, the extent of Gawthorp's cruelty had been revealed, and it far surpassed John's imaginings.

They had ushered the girl in, the commotion having caused Jonas to wake. The baby had not yet settled, at her cheek a rosy moon signalling the eruption of a tooth. Supper was left to congeal at the table as Eliza walked blinking into the light. John was in turns delighted and afraid at her presence. Jennet was struck by how very young she seemed, her round pale face not yet sculpted by experience. John guided her to the fireside, and warmed ale was placed between her blue-tipped fingers. Words followed at John's prompting, for the truth of her situation was just dawning. Joan's sorry mewling distracted, so that Jennet was forced to withdraw to join Jonas at his pallet bed, and hush the children as best she could. When finally Joan's eyes rolled back in her head, and her breathing slowed to a nasal purr, she placed the baby in her cradle. Jonas too sensed that, despite the excitement, he should succumb to sleep. All the while John and Nathan coaxed Eliza to speak, though, frustratingly, at a distance Jennet could not make out a word. When she moved to join them at the fireside, Eliza startled like a deer in a clearing.

Long minutes passed in silence, Eliza cradling her ale until it cooled untouched in its vessel. When Jennet suggested that she might join them in supper, Eliza turned distractedly to face her and shook her head. Eventually the table was cleared, the uneaten food scraped into a pancheon. At Nathan's insistence, it was settled that Eliza should take John's place in the upper chamber and rest. John guided her towards the ladder, and with a stuttering rushlight followed her to the space below the rafters. Moments later he rejoined Nathan and Jennet at the fire. His face was pale with worry and confusion.

"Thank you both. I shall speak with Parker on the morrow."

A short time later they took their leave of him, picking their way carefully over the sleeping Jonas, and drawing the curtain. John remained at the fireside, willing a sleep that would not come, his eyes unfocusing on the subsiding flames.

He made good on his promise the following day by heading up to the Hall at first light. Robert Parker was an early riser, and, though not yet fully attired, was agreeable to welcoming John into his parlour. As John recounted the events of the previous evening, Parker grew solemn, rubbing at his unshaven chin.

"And where is she now?" he enquired.

"With Nathan and Jennet Gill, sir."

"Does she wish to return to Holden?"

"I fear that would be impossible, sir," said John bleakly.

Parker seemed lost in thought, striding in a slow furrow between the dresser and the window.

"Bring her here before supper. I will endeavour to right this."

Before heading out to join Nathan in the field, John returned to the cottage. Eliza sat at the table, baby Joan cradled in her lap. As he opened the door, Eliza jumped, purple shadows beneath her eyes suggesting that she had enjoyed little sleep. It was resolved that she should pass the hours before her meeting with Parker aiding Jennet with household tasks. Eliza nodded mutely as though the effort of speaking was beyond her.

As the light faded, John returned to the cottage and found Jennet at the door, sweeping away the limp rushes. Jonas, spying Nathan walking a little distance behind, ran to his father and squealed as he was raised high and fast into the air. Jennet reported quietly that the girl had worked tirelessly through the day with the business of the house and children. She had spoken little and eaten even less, but it was certain to Jennet that she could not yet accept the truth of her situation. As John entered the parlour, Eliza raised a weak smile. He gathered her cloak and placed it gently about her shoulders. Together they walked up to the Hall as snow began to fall, fulfilling its earlier threat. About them birds settled in branches and eaves to wait out the long night.

Parker was at once taken by how young the girl seemed. Standing in his parlour, her eyes remained downcast until he addressed her directly and with warmth and concern. As he spoke of Gawthorp's cruelty, her eyes met his, and in their darkness he saw a rage which belied her child-like appearance.

Until matters could be resolved, Parker offered her work within his dairy. There she could assist in the milking of his cows, and the preparation of butter and cheese. For her services, he could pay her a small wage which, should

Nathan and Jennet be agreeable, would pay her way under their roof. As to her return to Holden, Parker could make no promises, but would do all in his power to right the injustice. He also vouched for her safety at Marley should Gawthorp seek her out. Even as he spoke the words, he was without a thought as to how matters should play out.

So it was that Eliza had taken up residence at Marley, and thus it had remained for the duration of the winter. At times, Jennet grew bitter at the situation. The cottage walls ran wet with the breath of so many, and when one coughed, so did they all. They moved within the confined space with the necessary care of a courtly dance. Jennet recalled the early days of her marriage with a sadness at its passing. The situation could not continue without end. Much as she had grown to like Eliza and value her support about the house and was grateful for the money she supplied, it was small recompense for the inconvenience of their daily living.

John seemed sensitive to her unhappiness, and as the days grew longer he and Eliza would take themselves away from the cottage to spend time alone before returning for supper. Jennet was grateful for these moments when she and Nathan could again embrace without shame. With the children occupied in small play, they would draw the curtain and enjoy each other as the pottage warmed in the pot.

Many times Eliza woke imagining herself at Holden, and wondering where Ann should be that she was so cold beneath her sheets. The truth of the situation was revealed abruptly by Joan's hungry wail and the voices of men passing on the valley road. On such mornings her sadness returned as visceral as hunger. There had been no news from Parker, and the dread that Gawthorp should arrive at her door now seemed fanciful. Her life was now at Marley though her future could only be guessed at.

The day had dawned bright and cold, the fog that had lain stubbornly across the valley the past week finally lifting, and with it, Jennet's spirits. The sniping impatience had been replaced by something approaching happiness, and when she had wished Eliza a good day that morning, it had been heartfelt. Joan lay back in her cot, arms raised, gently snoring, while Jonas was contentedly weaving rushes into a complex world of his own imagining. She had not been aware of the Reverend Gale's approach, and had startled at his loud knock. She had never made his acquaintance being a member of the congregation at Bingley, but knew him immediately by sight. He bowed slightly and touched at his hat.

"Good morning . . ." he hesitated, forgetting the name John had provided.

"Jennet Gill, sir."

"Jennet. Please forgive this intrusion, but I seek Eliza Fowler. I must speak with her on a matter of some urgency. Is she with you?"

Jennet, remembering her manners, but feeling at the same time aggrieved that his presence should disturb the children, beckoned him enter.

"No, sir, she has left for Marley Hall. You will find her there, in the dairy. May I offer you some ale?"

Miles shook his head, and, thanking her for her hospitality, turned to leave without stepping over the threshold. As she watched his departing figure, Jennet's heart raced. A woodpecker's rasp echoed distantly as she closed the door, relieved to see that the children did not require her attention. For a moment she felt fear at what the news the Reverend Gale had could mean for Eliza, for them all.

It did not take Miles long to find Eliza. He picked his way cautiously across the gullied yard towards the open door of the bier. She was one of three girls similarly crouched low below the grunting flank of a red beast. As if to herald his arrival, Eliza's cow raised its tail and deposited a large quantity of steaming ordure which fell with a slap to the stone floor. Miles wrinkled his nose in distaste, but concentrated on the purpose of his visit.

"Eliza!" At first she seemed not to hear him, her cap resting in the soft belly of the animal. He tried again.

"Eliza!" At her name she turned and, though in the doorway his face was in deep shadow, she at once recognised her visitor.

"Reverend Gale." She could barely conceal her disappointment.

"I see that you are busy, but perhaps I might request a moment of your time?" His discomfort at his surroundings was evident, and in spite of any petulance she may have felt, she rose from her milking-stool and indicated that they should step out into the yard. The girl seemed much less of a child. Perhaps it was the weariness in her features.

"Sir, I have only a moment." There was an impatience that seemed to indicate more than just the irritation of being interrupted in her work. For once Miles knew not what to say and as he hesitated, constructing his words in his head, Eliza again spoke.

"Sir, there is nothing that you could possibly say that should make good my situation. I have dwelt upon it these past months, and now see that perhaps Gawthorp was right. God has deserted me; my mother and sisters are now strangers, and but for the love of John I would be alone in this world."

Miles stared at her in astonishment as she continued, her voice rising and clipped.

"Do not waste your breath on me, sir, for I cannot be saved. This is not your doing, but the result of my wickedness. I am wicked and am being punished. I see that you don't believe me, sir! Then know this: I am with child!"

44

May 1703. Ghyllgrange

Ann had returned early to the house, and though she and her sisters had been out at first light to witness the May Day revelries her heart was heavy. She remembered the previous year when she and Eliza had run up the bank to gather flowers for Mary and wash their faces in the dew. It was not simply that Eliza no longer shared her bed or labours, it was as though she had never been. Her name was never mentioned. Her caps and shifts, her patched aprons, had passed to Margaret. It was as if her very being had been scrubbed away as some grassy stain. Her father Thomas had been similarly expunged. All that remained were his books and bible, and the wedding band in the pouch at Mary's waist. Ann had been a child of eight when her father died but she clung like smoke to the vestiges of her memories in the certainty that they should be reunited in death. Amongst the multitudes, it was essential she recognise his face.

There was no sign of her mother, and Margaret could not say more than that she had been entrusted with the mutton bubbling in the pot. Mary had left the house an hour since, and John was already wondering where his mother could be. A slice of oatcake had not quelled his fretfulness, and even his wooden animals lay scattered and fallen in a corner. From the doorway Ann could see the figure of Gawthorp rising and falling as he stooped to pull weeds from amongst his flax. If she was not with him, where could her mother be?

The walk up to Ghyllgrange had been an unexpected pleasure for Mary. The breeze pulsed softly, and there was a gentle warmth to it, the early breath of summer. Lambs scattered at her approach, and the bubbling song of the curlews was all about her as they hung high above, motionless as painted angels. As she drew near the huddle of buildings ranged about Ghyllgrange itself, the smell of woodsmoke drifted towards her. She saw the snaking grey plume of a fire being raked by a man and his young son. Let her thoughts be as clear as the day's sky and not lost in the smoke of fear and indecision.

When her knock was not immediately answered, she began to worry at her folly, turning up unannounced. She knocked again with greater force. This time a shuffle of feet was followed by the drawing back of a great bolt. Agnes smiled obligingly, though the unfortunate cast of her eye gave the unnerving appearance of one simple in mind.

"I wish to speak with Mr Rishworth ..." Her introduction was interrupted by the sight of Rishworth himself, easing on his boots in the darker reaches of the passage. When he recognised the person of Mary, he pulled on his boot with a prolonged wheeze and rose with haste to join Agnes at the door.

"Mary!" Such was his astonishment that he ushered her quickly into his parlour without further pleasantries.

Mary had not set foot within the house since Thomas had been alive. In the early days of their marriage as they had taken up residence at Holden, they had introduced themselves to the landlord of Ghyllgrange, William's father, also called Thomas. By then he was a very old man. The handsome panelled wainscot chair at the fireside recalled memories of him. He had sat in the very chair, a thick fleece about his narrow shoulders in spite of the warmth of the day. He had retained but a memory of hair, wispy as summer clouds, but his eyes shone with the vigour of youth. He had blessed their recent union, and hoped that they should enjoy the longevity of his own marriage. Sadly, this wish had not been realised. The old man had lived to see the death of Thomas Fowler. When his own wife died the following autumn, and he had departed Ghyllgrange for Addingham to see out his final years. His son William who now stood before her seemed a giant of a man, and Mary wondered idly that he should fit in his father's wainscot chair.

Though her husband had spent many hours in this man's company, it was the first occasion that Mary had seen him at close quarters. The resolve with which she had left Holden that morning seemed to evaporate in his presence. Agnes lingered at the door to the parlour and, recognising his visitor's unease, Rishworth bade her fetch ale and cake. As Agnes departed there was, for a short time, silence punctuated only by the distant bleat of sheep and the solemn tick of the long case in the hall.

"Sir." Her voice sounded piteously small. "Sir …" The words swirled unformed in her mind, and she suddenly felt foolish. Sensing her discomfort, Rishworth approached.

"Mary, I think I can guess at the purpose of your visit. The letter from Jane? Eliza?"

At her daughter's name Mary sobbed violently as though stuck with a knife. With unfortunate timing, Agnes returned, and when no one acknowledged her tap, she entered the parlour. Her good eye fixed upon the slight figure of Mary, keening silently, head buried into the shoulder of Rishworth. Awkwardly, and with as little commotion as possible, she placed her tray on a lowboy and withdrew.

Over the course of the next hour, Mary and Rishworth talked, falteringly at first, but with growing candour. For Mary, it felt as though a decade of silence had ended and, with encouragement, her feelings poured forth like water from a hushed stream. Again and again she spoke of her first husband Thomas with a rawness that supposed he was recently deceased. Rishworth noted that as she spoke, she clutched a small pouch at her waist, and knew without seeing what lay within. Her demeanour became more brittle as she spoke of Gawthorp. Whilst she conceded that he had proved himself an able provider in the years since Thomas's death, for other reasons she now questioned the wisdom of her remarriage.

Rishworth listened carefully and without interruption as Mary detailed life at Holden under his dominion. When the incident of his disappearance was raised, and his subsequent return, Rishworth stiffened at the memory. It was only when she began to speak of her own culpability that Rishworth felt bound to interject.

"Mary, you are without blame. You have raised your children in God's good grace, and have endured cruelty at the hands of a man bent on tyranny. He may portray himself as the good husband but there are few about the valley that would recognise it."

Mary shook her head as though to dislodge some sense at what she should do. She could recognise the truth of Rishworth's words but felt powerless to find a solution to her unhappy circumstance. From an upper chamber came the sound of a child's cry and the gentle musical voice of a woman.

"My wife," offered Rishworth. "She is again with child." Mary smiled weakly, her thoughts of Eliza. Again the room fell silent as Mary despaired at the futility of words. The boarded ceiling creaked with the movement of Elizabeth above.

"Eliza …"

"Mary, you will know that she is now at Marley. Robert Parker tells me she fares well."

"I must see her, sir!"

Mary fixed her gaze on Rishworth and in doing so he saw that the moment had come to tell her the sorry tale of Jeremiah Hide. The seeds of mischief this man had sown had borne calamitous fruit which had poisoned the lives of her family and children.

As Rishworth began his tale Mary listened silently, her head bowed. On more than one occasion he felt moved to apologise for his own folly.

"The letter from your sister Jane. It was my idea. I am shamed to say I involved the Reverend Gale, John Asquith and your daughter Eliza. Since I first met with Jeremiah Hide and heard his tale, I have sought to disassociate myself from Gawthorp. Had I come to Holden, I confess, I would have feared for my own safety. The attack on Robert Parker's nephew ..." He left the thread of this tale hanging, its meaning understood.

" I promise you this, Mary, naught shall come between you and Eliza. You must go to her and know that Gawthorp shall not prevent it."

As she walked way from Ghyllgrange she felt the tightness of the skin beneath her eyes where tears had dried. The light wind was at her back, and for the briefest moment she considered knocking at the door of the Snowden homestead as she had so often long ago. Emboldened by her discussion with Rishworth, she resolved to do so, but first she had business at Holden.

The land fell away with a graceful bow, and below the nearing roofs of Holden shimmered in the rising heat. The air was alive with insects on the wing catching at her hair, alighting her skin. The figure of Ann stood atop the bank shielding her eyes into the brightness, her fear and relief palpable even at a distance. As they drew together Mary forestalled the inevitable questions.

"I am returned from Ghyllgrange. Where is Robert?"

Mutely Ann motioned towards the small figure bobbing and rising among a carpet of flax. Mary, with Ann in her wake, strode into the parlour where the children immediately assailed her with a chorus of concerns. Margaret, nursing a burnt wrist, had been tended by Ann with a butter soaked rag. She fretted that the mutton had been spoiled. A glance at the pot told Mary that she had returned not a moment too soon. Kissing her daughter's head and examining the fresh wound, she thanked Margaret for her efforts. The younger children, in particular John, bewildered by Mary's absence rushed to her side, their voices a cacophony of requests. Only Ann, party to her mother's whereabouts, wondered at the purpose of her visit to Ghyllgrange. It was she who flinched when, a short time later, Gawthorp returned from his labours in need of food and rest. Though the day was warm and his face shone with sweat, his skin remained pale as the moon.

As the family gathered about the table, Mary and Ann doled out the mutton which had boiled down to fibres in the pot. Gawthorp eyed his platter with surprise before a mumbled grace. To the clatter of spoons Mary alone did not eat, instead she stared at the bowed head of her husband.

"Robert?" He glanced up and saw something in Mary's face that caused him to replace his spoon on the table. Ann did not dare breathe.

"Robert, I have this morning been to Ghyllgrange. I have spoken with Rishworth." At the mention of this name, Ann saw Gawthorp's jaw tighten, the only outward sign of what fomented within.

"We spoke of many things, but above all we spoke of Eliza." At her name, all eating ceased, even John, hungry as he was, froze. Without giving Gawthorp the chance to respond, and with a calmness that was strange as it was powerful, Mary continued.

"I am told she is with child, my grandchild. It is my desire and will that I see her. Rishworth knows of this and supports me. Husband, I have learned many things this day. I can accept most as God's will, but I cannot accept that I will not see Eliza again. I will go to her with or without your permission."

Ann waited for the fires of hell to ignite, for a violence of which she was acquainted to erupt. Had her mother taken leave of her senses? After an interminable pause during which time Mary's and Gawthorp's eyes locked unblinking, he finally spoke with a wavering uncertainty.

"Mary … I … you must … of course. You must go to her."

As he bowed his head and resumed eating, Mary continued to stare at her husband, pausing only to catch Ann's eye which spilled silent tears. Her heart beat wildly at what had just transpired. It continued to drum even as Gawthorp gave thanks for his food and returned to his labours. When Ann attempted to question Mary she was silenced by her mother's raised hand.

"Ann, I must go to her, but fear not, Robert understands that this must be. Mind your sisters for me. I shall return before nightfall."

If Gawthorp saw Mary leave Holden to take the road to Marley, he did not acknowledge her. His slender frame continued to rise and fall as he removed the choking weeds from his tender crop.

As Holden receded into the haze, Mary's pace quickened. As she passed the wooded spring, the grate of a woodpecker resonated from the shaded green. She felt Thomas at her shoulder.

45

August 1703. Keighley

Miles guided his horse cautiously along the valley road in the direction of Bingley. His mount picked its way between the dark scars, pooled with the night's rain. The sky bulged ominous grey, and in the fetid heat Miles felt his skin prickle with sweat. Either side of the road crops, toppled and bedraggled, signalled troubled times ahead. As the year had progressed, the fine days of May had given over to months of cloud. Farmers eyed the heavens ruefully, praying for sun to gild their sickly-green harvest. Miles had known summers such as this, sunless days presaging blight, disease and hunger. His impotence in such circumstances filled him with despair.

In recent days he had taken to riding out with his portable desk and books, which clattered against the horse's flank in an irregular roll. He had decided to redouble his efforts in the direction of literacy, and set himself a somewhat unthinkable target. It was his dearest wish that on their wedding day, each bride and groom should be equipped able to sign the register with more than a cross. Disillusionment, ill health and the weight of parish business had proved diversions to this good work, and his long held dream of an established school within the town still seemed little more than a fanciful dream. Miles had therefore, after a protracted hiatus, returned to his literary mission with a renewed vigour. It also suited his purposes to be away from the Rectory where he was obliged to entertain all callers, however unwelcome. Michael Pighells, in particular, seemed fixed upon this almost daily pursuit. As he was forced to endure the man's company and litany of complaints in the confines of his study, Miles often felt like a chained bear in a pit. To ride out also served as an opportunity to learn of events within his scattered parish. This was not the contentious business of poor relief, or the arbitration of dispute, but an insight into the lives of his people.

As the mill came into view, he cheered at the thought of spending an hour in the company of Martha Wright whom he had not seen in many months. In the comfort of her cool and cavernous parlour he learned that much had changed since they had last spoken. To his dismay he heard that Martha's sight was beginning to fail her. She imparted the news without a shred of self-pity, but more, irritation that her affliction should cause delays for the people she sought to help. Even self-ministration of eyebright seemed ineffective in relieving her plight. Miles observed sadly the milkiness of her eyes, misted like washhouse windows, but encouraged her to give thanks for her otherwise rude good health. Martha chuckled and nodded in accord. She informed him of the sad demise of the widow Bell of Riddlesden. Her body had lain undiscovered for many days. With a husband long dead, and children even longer departed the valley, Martha had been one of only two mourners to witness her burial.

"A kindly woman, undeserving of such an end," murmured Martha.

Aside from her agreeable company, Miles never failed to wonder at Martha's wisdom. Though she had never been formally schooled, her knowledge of plant lore and the science of childbirth far outweighed that of his most learned acquaintances. The parlour that day was sweet with the scent of woodruff which dried in bundles at the sill. Notes of lavender spiked the heavy incense of wood smoke, and a pot cooled by the open door, its secrets released slowly onto the rising valley air.

"By the by, have you heard, ir? Young John Asquith was married this past week."

"No indeed!"

Martha explained that she had attended the simple ceremony performed by the Reverend Roberts at first light. Although John and Eliza were already espoused, both had been eager to sanctify their union in the sight of God. Eliza, he learned, was by now heavy with child, and it seemed only weeks remained before her confinement.

"They are removed to Thwaites, sir. Robert Parker has granted them a tenancy. It is the cottage by the beech copse where the land rises towards the brow. You will know it."

Miles could picture it well, and Martha's news dictated the course his day would now take. As he rose to leave, she bid him wait a while as she rummaged among a tangle of dried roots and stems at her table. Relying on touch, and raising various stems to her nose, she deftly bound a desiccated bouquet of shrivelled blooms.

"Feverfew. It will help with your digestion."

Miles took the remedy from her and bowed with gratitude. Even Lister himself could learn from this woman, he felt certain.

He had planned to continue his journey to the family of Skirrow who lived in one of the outlying farmsteads, almost at the boundary of the Bingley parish. The hamlet of Thwaites was but a slight diversion. As Miles rode along he encountered familiar faces in unfamiliar pursuits. Fence building, the repair of roofs and other unseasonal tasks were being tackled as men waited with increasing anxiety for the weather to turn. For a distance, he was joined on his journey by a young boy whose legs bowed like worked willow, and moved with an awkward swaying gait. He struggled to keep pace with the horse, but was nonetheless eager to know of Miles's business. His interest was soon lost when they came upon a group of younger children gathering mushrooms at the roadside. Miles continued on towards the beech copse alone.

He guessed that it was two hours past noon though, with the absence of the sun, he could not be sure. A blue finger of smoke that stretched out across the ling roof told him that Eliza was at home. He dismounted noisily, approached the doorway and knocked.

"Reverend Gale!" Eliza seemed genuinely taken aback, though perhaps it was something else. An element of shame at their last encounter. "Please come in."

Miles lowered his head as he entered the cottage and allowed a moment for his eyes to adjust to the dimness. The room seemed scarce bigger than a pantry, and was economically furnished with a pair of chairs and a table. A curtained alcove to the right of the hearth shielded a bed. Eliza pointed towards a chair and offered him some small ale which he politely declined. The girl looked pale as whey but for the blue shadows beneath her eyes. Her black hair was drawn back from her face under a linen scarf, and her sleeves were rolled high as he had disturbed her in the act of washing. A rag lay abandoned on the table next to a shallow bowl of water. He could not help but notice that in spite of the swell of her belly and the ring newly placed upon her finger, she was but a child.

"I am come from Martha Wright," he explained simply. "She tells me that you and John are now wed."

The girl smiled shyly and drew her hand across the dome of her belly. For a time she did not speak, and when finally she did it was her words were faltering and subdued. She did not meet his eye.

"I must apologise, sir. When last we met. I was angry."

Miles nodded, though in truth he felt he should also offer his regrets at the part he had played in her predicament.

"But I was wrong, sir. I had no place to be angry. It made me no better than him. You see I know the truth of Gawthorp now. My mother told me everything."

"You have spoken with Mary?"

Miles listened with growing wonder as Eliza recounted the day Mary had arrived at her door. Though she had rejoiced to see her, she feared dreadful consequences at her mother's action. The woman that stood before her was much altered, her voice steady and measured. She told Eliza of her meeting with Rishworth and his revelations, which had made her determined that, whatever the consequence, she should be reunited with her daughter. Miles twisted uneasily in his chair at the mention of Rishworth and Jeremiah Hide. Seeing his discomfiture, Eliza reassured him that since that day at Marley, a new order now prevailed.

"I am married to John, I carry his child and Gawthorp no longer has hold of me."

Eliza's words were triumphant, yet Miles's face must have conveyed an uncertainty for she continued, "Gawthorp is a devil but he is no fool. Rishworth now minds his every step so that no harm shall come to my mother nor my sisters." Her eyes flashed, yet masked a deep hurt and anger.

"Then may God grant you all peace."

He was not to know it at the time, but these would be the last words he would speak to Eliza for many years. From time to time he would glimpse her traversing the church green or at a distance on the Bingley road. As they parted at the doorway he took her hand and smiled.

"Goodbye, sir."

The rain was beginning to fall as he turned his horse back out onto the valley road. The air was heavy as clay, and in the stillness he could hear little but the dripping trees and the clatter and clop of his horse. The children he had encountered earlier had vanished, and the road was deserted but for a couple of crows picking at the slimy remains of a rabbit. Miles was suddenly overcome with an immense sorrow and a tightening in his throat, a precursor to tears. He drew down the brim of his broad black hat as a precaution should he come upon a fellow traveller.

It had been something in the girl's face that had so upset him, something indefinable yet powerful. Perhaps to many, Eliza's world presented as a capsized vessel now righted. After all she was now married to a good man with a baby soon to be born. Together they were in possession of a home of their own and, above all, Eliza had been reconciled with her mother. And yet . . . He sensed a darkness within, an unhappiness that circumstances had pitched her to this point, which was not of her choosing. As he rode along, conscious of rain finding skin at the turn of his collar, he reasoned that his own life too had progressed on a course he would not have wished in the ambitious days of his youth. In the same way, the lives of his children and all his vicarious dreams could well come to naught. Was this God's design or the abstraction of nature? He battled with the notion as his mount stumbled in the thick mud, pitching him forward in his saddle. Maintaining his seat and his dignity, he found himself approaching the Skirrow household.

They were a family of nine who clung to existence by the slenderest of threads. The father was an itinerant labourer, the mother, a carder of wool. Their clutch of dirt-streaked children gathered wide-eyed and silent in the doorway. Did the Skirrows harbour ambitions? Did they curse their lowly station? Could their children imagine a life of betterment? Miles set aside these morose thoughts and arranged his features into a mask of benevolence. Though the house reeked with the compression of unwashed bodies and the musk of fleeces piled high, he was thankful to be out of the weather for a short time.

46

November 1703. Road to Thwaites.

The land was transformed. Where a few days since, trees had stood, roots clutched at the sky in the throes of a slow death. Water boiled in angry spouts from the hillsides, running and bubbling into narrow channels freshly wrought. Crows picked over the bodies of young rabbits and voles, flushed from the earth by the force of the deluge. The wind still tore across the land, its fury not yet spent. There was further mischief to be had in the tearing off of slates and the toppling of chimneys. Only the sheep remained, ranked in the lee of stone walls which afforded little respite from nature's savagery. It was into this world that John set forth. He could delay his return no longer, and as he turned back towards the homestead, he knew that he had just bid his father farewell for the final time.

Word had come that his father was failing, and John had not known what to do. Eliza was, by then, so heavy with child, that the day of its coming was imminent. She was fearful in the way of all women at the pain and danger to come. Martha Wright had allayed her worries with tales of the many babies she had seen into the world, some of mothers slighter and younger than Eliza herself.

The track rose to meet the moor's russet shroud, and the last of the cottages dissolved into the landscape through the curtain of rain. He now walked into the wind which blinded him with its ferocity and caused anger and pity to rise within him at his plight. Forced to choose between Eliza and his father, the weather mirrored his misery.

He wondered that his father had even been aware of his presence. The chamber had sweltered, the casements stopped with sacking to prevent even the smallest draught reaching the dying man. A fire blazed in the grate through all hours of the day and night. The air was thick with the sour perfume of ashes of broom and decay. The wind forced the peat smoke down the chimney, trapping that thick atmosphere as completely as a corked bottle.

His father had risen only momentarily from sleep as a fish in the shallows, glimpsing the sun before sinking back into darkness. John had sat at his father's bedside and spoken repeatedly of Eliza. He rued the oath he had made that the two should one day meet. It was a promise broken, but he hoped that above the noise of the raging tempest, his father might at least hear of his marriage and the child to come.

Day became night as John and his brothers whispered anxiously of the world they should find once the storm had abated. All felt relief that their father should not witness its destruction. They prayed that he would pass gently from the world into the calm and beauty of the life beyond.

That morning John had awoken from a mockery of sleep in the chair at his father's side. The fire cast dancing shadows across the old man's face, unlined by pain and still but for the barely visible act of breathing. John knew then that his father no longer heard his words. The very moment of his passing would be known only to God, and in this precarious state, he might linger for days. So it was that John had made the decision to return to Eliza.

As he battled towards the highest point of the heath, the sky above him darkened. A terrible sound filled the air, the boom and crack of distant thunder. It was as though the earth itself was being rent apart, the rocks cleaving by the might of an invisible hand. Ahead, great tridents of lightning were being cast down into the valley of the Aire. All about him the sky flashed white with a spectral violence, a warning that nature should not be defied. Yet this was precisely what John was doing, the lone figure in the landscape, battling the elements. He felt afraid, not at the ferocity of the storm, but at what he should find when he returned to Thwaites. He tried, but failed, to forget the birth of Jonas, and Jennet's agony. Death had haunted the chamber that night as so often at the moment of birth. He prayed rhythmically and despairingly with each heavy footstep that Eliza and the child be spared. There was something else too, that prickled and unnerved him, and that was the will of Eliza herself.

He recalled the first time he had seen her, as he and Nathan had left Teal's shop with Jennet's crimson ribbon. He had known her in that very instant, though he had never before glimpsed her face. In ways mysterious, their lives had drawn together like nails to a lodestone. When he had spoken of this with Eliza, suggesting that it had been God's will they should be together, she had not answered him. But then Eliza had little time for God now.

In the first desperate days of her exile, she had demanded God's retribution. She prayed for misfortune to visit Gawthorp as penance for what he had done. She did not have that satisfaction and, in the absence of her family, a change had come about her. He recalled with some disquiet those evenings before supper when he and Eliza had walked alone by the river's deserted reaches. Emboldened one evening, he had once bent to kiss her. She had returned his advance with a savagery for which he had not been prepared. Against the rugged bark of a broad beech they had become one with frenzied surprise and urgency. When, afterwards, he had offered a wretched and shame-faced apology she had merely smiled. They had returned wordless to the cottage, their breath billowing in the clear still darkness. In the days that followed he sensed that their transgression had been somehow preordained.

Eliza had told him she was with child one evening as they walked again by the river. Though but a child herself, she was worldly enough in the ways of women to know. He had stared at her in confusion, his thoughts a tangle, but she had taken his hand, and assured him of her happiness. Feeling as foolish as a child, he had asked her to become his wife. It was not as he had dreamt it, but nonetheless she accepted his proposal.

For two weeks they had not spoken of the matter to anyone, not even Jennet and Nathan. The arrival of the Reverend Gale at Marley towards Easter had changed everything. Eliza had returned from work that evening, her cheeks flushed, her manner sharp. She had taken John's hand and announced boldly their espousal and the coming of a child. Nathan's astonishment was absolute though Jennet had harboured suspicions. Eliza may have thought to have concealed her condition well, but Jennet had witnessed her crouched form at the river's edge and seen the thickening of her waist. Together they had embraced and toasted the future, but behind the Eliza's smiles John sensed an unease, an anger. Neither marriage, nor the coming child seemed likely to supplant her inner torments.

The Doubler Stones approached, silhouetted like brooding demons against the flashing sky. There was a taste of metal to the air, and still the wind battled to remove the cloak from his back. He had not passed a living soul along the track, and even the nearby inn seemed abandoned, its chimney cold and tumbled. From this point, the moor began to fall away and the valley of the Aire came into view. Anxiously, he saw that the snaking river had been swallowed beneath a vast black lake, reflecting back the sky like some monstrous pewter charger. The ridge of Holden Gate in its shallow hollow came into view away to his right. He could not be sure for the force of the wind, but he imagined he saw the whip of smoke from the chimney. A little further along he came upon the tattered remains of a linen bonnet caught upon a gorse, flapping violently like a ravaged standard; it marked the aftermath of a great battle.

A church bell rang wildly from somewhere in the valley below, a voice to the power of the gale. No bells had rung out on their wedding day as the Reverend Roberts had met them at the church door before six of the clock. Mary and Martha had been their only witnesses that early August morning. The air had been restless with the song of birds, the sky combed through with the threat of building cloud. Eliza, tumid with child, could scarce look the priest in the eye, and spoke only when bidden by the ceremony of the service. When John placed the narrow band upon her finger he could not fathom what he saw in her face, joy, perhaps, but something else too. It was only much later as he lay by her side at the end of the sweltering day, and heard her slow shallow breathing, that it came to him. She had left the church with a similar haste to the Reverend Roberts, he to administer last rites to some dying widow, she to be free from the church itself. She had been impatient to be gone from that place; indeed, they had not returned since.

As the town grew closer, John was relieved to see that the stone bridge stood proud of the flood, and the lake that he had seen from high was merely the receding waters pooled upon the ings. He made an uncomfortable and cautious passage across the town field. The storm was moving northwards, its show of lights passing beyond the far horizon. In its wake the rain began to fall with renewed spite. Water coursed down the narrow lanes over a scree of fallen slates. He passed an old man sheltered at the entrance to an ale-house, its door barred against him. If he saw John at all he did not acknowledge it. John crossed the church green, eerie in its emptiness, and noticed a candle at the Reverend Gale's window. A released shutter clattered wildly in the wind. He was almost home.

Along the river's edge, the forlorn skeletons of trees lay toppled upon one another, their branches stretching out into the river's cauldron. The body of a bloated sheep ragged in the current, its fleece snared within a dam of broken willow. He prayed that this was no portent.

His answer came within five yards of home: a child's cry, full of fury, carrying over the tumult of the storm. He ran the last distance to his door. As he fell into the parlour with the thrust of the wind at his back, Mary rose from the hearth and stepped forward, her arms open to him.

"Thank God, John! Thank God you are safe!"

John looked beyond her to the alcove. The child had fallen silent as it lay upon Eliza's breast, feeding greedily. Eliza reached out her hand, her eyes overflowing with tears.

"My love, my true love. We have a daughter."

John fell to his knees at Eliza's bedside and kissed her temple, tasting the salt of her hair. He ran his hand across the dark head of his child, the cold and wet of his touch causing her to jolt and alarm. As the child's cry rose above the storm, John could do nothing to check his thankful tears.

47

Kildwick. June 1707

Eliza shuffled in discomfort, her skirts straining about her distended belly. Her child would arrive in a matter of weeks and she felt forlorn at the inevitability of it being another girl. Her daughters, sat solemnly at her side in the church unknown to them, mute with wonder at the sight of so many folk gathered with unaccustomed cheerfulness. The low murmur of conversations and laughter echoed the length of the long nave. Eliza recalled her own girlhood frustration within the same church, hours spent in needless confinement and enforced silence. No matter the happiness of the occasion, a familiar impatience caused her to shift and resettle in her seat. Her humour, she knew, would be restored with the feeling of the sun on her skin.

It was an early morning of still, blue perfection, the meadows of the valley jewelled extravagantly with sparks of marsh marigold, buttercup and rattle. The air was so still that the bells of Kildwick could be heard from the yard at Holden.

Ann was to become George Snowden's bride, and Eliza thought ruefully on how very different her own wedding day had been. The Reverend Mitton fretted and puffed loudly, eager to begin proceedings, and so be free to cloister with his wife in the cool of his parlour. He paced the nave, his forehead polished with sweat, his balding pate barely concealed by his fanciful wig. In the porch, Ann took the arm of her uncle Francis Stirk. He was to give her away in Gawthorp's stead. At the Reverend Mitton's direction, he squeezed her arm gently that they should begin their procession. He thought to himself how very like Mary she had become. The bells fell silent as they made their stately way towards the altar.

Eliza raised her head to look beyond the edge of the box pew to where her mother sat. At her side, a little removed, was Gawthorp, his head bowed, his eyes closed. The Reverend Mitton began the familiar text of the marriage service after a perfunctory welcome. He reckoned that with haste he would be home within the hour. Gawthorp seemed oblivious to his surroundings and, but for Eliza, those gathered were equally blind to his misery. In her eyes he had no business to be there, but, as his lips moved in silent prayer, she knew that his mind dwelt within another realm. He was not there to celebrate but to grieve.

Eliza recalled the dreadful morning when George Snowden had arrived at her door. Fog filled the valley with its cheerless chill. Candlemass had just passed, and Eliza had been out at first light to bring home snowdrops, a first promise of winter's waning. It was something that her mother had always done, and it brought back memories of Holden. It was at those hopeful, newly plucked blooms that she had looked as William had taken her hand and informed her of her brother John's passing.

She had grown anxious in the weeks before at Mary's absence. When she had spoken with her husband of her worries, he had attempted to calm her: perhaps the road had become too dangerous, it was understandable given the savagery of the weather. Eliza had not been so easily placated. She became convinced that Gawthorp was again set upon punishing her, forbidding Mary her daughter's company. At the thought, anger raged within her like an ember blasted back to flame.

"Do you hear me, Eliza?" George's words had drawn her back to reality in the flinty darkness of the parlour. The snowdrops bowed upon the sill took on a new meaning. She had thanked him for his kindness, and sent him away with messages of love to Mary and her sisters. After his departure she had sat at the table for the longest time, immobilised by the news of John's death. Her girls, unnerved by their mother's silence, picked daintily at their pottage without speaking. Ann, that day, wore a linen cap that Mary had once fashioned for John, its stitches even and fairy small. As she gazed upon it, recalling his golden curls, Eliza began to weep.

The following week John had been buried in the yard at Kildwick church. The sexton had been kept busy in the wake of the fever that had raged through the valley. The churchyard was already scarred with fresh turned earth when the inhabitants of Holden had gathered to bury the child. Gawthorp, mute with sorrow, had placed John's wooden animals within the wool of his shroud, but kept aside the crouching dog. Eliza would much later learn that he carried it close to his heart henceforth, its figure worn smooth as though by the action of John's hands.

Eliza had been absent as they laid the child's pathetic body to rest, afraid at the unpredictability of Gawthorp's grief. She had come to the church some time later. Ranked alongside the other tiny plots, John's grave had sprouted a green shadow of new life. She laid a posy of primroses and could only wonder at her mother's anguish at the death of her only son.

When Mary at last came to Thwaites, Lent was almost over. She had come alone, and had clasped her granddaughters to her breast with a ferocity that Eliza had never before witnessed. Together they had prayed for the soul of John, and given thanks that the rest of the family had been spared. Mary then fell silent, her gaze fixed upon the peat flame. The children, innocent of circumstance, looked to their mother for reassurance. Mary, Eliza's first born, was a strong child, a Fowler in her dark eyes, hair the black down of a marsh chick. She it was who led her younger sister away from the hearth at their mother's mute bidding. The damp peat hissed in the hearth until at last Mary spoke, her words flat and low.

"I'm afraid, Eliza, afraid of what is to become of us, of Holden."

At the mention of Holden, Eliza stiffened. "That is hardly my concern mother!" But as soon as the words had escaped her lips she was filled with remorse. Mary turned to study Eliza, her thin lips working to shape the words that filled her heart.

"Robert … he … is much changed. He cannot accept that John is dead."

Eliza grew tense at what she was about to learn, but refrained from speaking.

"Those who know him see a man about his labours in the wake of his loss, his sorrow, a shadow in his features. But I fear that he has given up on this life."

"Mother! You cannot mean that he is bent of self-destruction!" Eliza had not for a moment considered the possibility, nor its implications for the residents of Holden. When Mary shook her head slowly it was without conviction.

Sleep would not come that night, and though John found words of comfort, he did not confess his own fears. Eliza lay folded against the contours of his body and heard his passage into sleep in the slowing cadence of his breathing. An orange glow from the fading embers illuminated the familiar lines of the room. She at least was unthreatened by Gawthorp, here, within the sanctuary of their humble living, but what of Mary and her sisters?

A small break in the swirling clouds of worry presented itself a short time later when Ann arrived at Eliza's door. It was the afternoon of Ash Wednesday, and Ann's forehead still bore the smudged shadow of ash where the Reverend Mitton had marked her that morning.

"We are to be married Eliza! I am finally to be George's wife!" Ann's words tumbled out in a torrent of happiness. Eliza opened her arms and enfolded her sister, kissing her cheek flushed with excitement.

"At last some good news. I am joyful for you both." The sisters remained locked in an embrace until Ann's namesake tugged at her skirt, eager to know the cause of such celebration. Eliza scooped the child up and, pacing the parlour, explained that there was to be a wedding. It was enough that her mother was smiling again, the cause was somewhat beyond the little girl's understanding.

As they sat together at the table sharing warmed ale, which comforted as the day was raw, Eliza broached the questions that crowded her mind.

"Why now sister? Is this because of John's death?" Ann's smile dissolved and she became solemn.

"You will know that he has changed"

"I am told."

"But you also know that George and I have been promised to each other since childhood days, but until now …" Her voice trailed away. Aye, thought Eliza, until now Gawthorp would have never allowed it.

"George did not ask Gawthorp, he told him of his intention to marry me, with or without his approval. We had waited long enough."

Eliza was full of admiration at the boldness of George, but clearly much had changed that he could dare to be so forthright.

"Do you know what Gawthorp said Eliza? 'So be it!' They are his only words on the matter."

As they sipped at their ale, details of the wedding were scrutinised. Given his indifference, Mary had put it to him that her brother Francis should be the one to give Ann away.

"He was accepting of this?" Ann nodded.

"There is one more thing, sister." Eliza paused, uncertain how to frame her words. She held Ann's eye directly. "Does George know of what Gawthorp did?"

Ann shook her head violently. "He shall never know. I worried for so long that Gawthorp would tell. He held the secret over me these long years, but I know now that he will not." She shrank from the memory of what had transpired behind the doors of the great barn. Eliza knew that her sister was obliged to carry her shame like a closed locket, forged to eternity. There was nothing she could do nor say to relieve her of her burden.

"Will you remain at Holden?"

"No," Ann answered firmly. "We are to abide with Edward and Rebekah, but if mother should ever need us, we are at hand." At the bravery of her words Eliza felt such love towards her sister that tears flooded her vision and overspilled.

"Let us not dwell in the misery of the past. Come, sister, do not weep, be glad for me." Ann gurned unprettily in a way she had not since girlhood days, and together the sisters laughed uncontrollably to the bemusement of the children.

So it was that as the Reverend Mitton declared the couple married in God's sight, the bell again rang out. George winked and grinned his way down the long nave, his new bride on his arm. The door to the church was flung open and the white heat of the morning forced itself into the dimmest reaches of the ancient building. At Eliza's side, her girls scrambled to their feet, eager to be out into the sun. John opened the latched pew and took their hands.

Together they joined the tail of the congregation snaking its way noisily towards the church door. Eliza remained seated until the church fell silent. She found herself offering up a silent prayer for Ann and George. She wished more than anything that her father Thomas had lived to witness the occasion. Guests would be walking the short path down to the ale-house where a breakfast and raucous good humour at the couple's expense would detain them for a couple of hours.

As she rose to leave, she was shocked to see that she was not alone in the echoing church. Across the nave, his head bowed and clasped between his hands, was Gawthorp. She had no desire to speak with him. She realised with unease that this was the first time she had been in his company since the night of her exile. Within, her unborn child squirmed and stretched as though it sensed that it was in the presence of a devil. As she manoeuvred herself from the pew, flinching as the ancient wood creaked, Gawthorp seemed oblivious to her. She began to make for the door, rueing her decision not to leave with John and the children.

"Eliza." She froze at the sound of her name.

"Eliza." She turned slowly to face him. He remained seated though his body was twisted towards her, his eyes glazed with tears.

"I must go to John!" Her words were delivered as a threat, but still he persisted.

"Eliza!"

She closed the church door with a slam and stepped out from the shadow of the porch. A blackbird sang from a hidden bough within a brooding yew. Her breath came fast as she walked the shallow steps down to the ale-house. Four years had passed, and on this day above all others he had wished to speak with her. She would not allow it. Perhaps she would never allow it.

48

Holden Gate. February 1713

The charged silence following bitter words hung in the air between them. Eliza's breath came shallow and fast as she wiped at her mouth. For half a lifetime she had carried her anger within, and as it was finally released, she was overcome with a fatigue that fetched to her very marrow. Gawthorp did not move. His elbows rested slack on the broad sweep of the table. He did not speak a word.

Mary was dying and Eliza knew that her mother's remaining time on earth must be measured in hours. She prayed that Mary was now so close to God that her ears were stopped to what had just transpired. After all the years that had passed, why had she not the patience to have waited another day?

She thought back to the afternoon in the heat of late summer when they had sat together in the shade of a towering beech, and watched the children roll in the long grass. As their laughter had echoed about the copse, Mary had wordlessly taken Eliza's hand. When she had turned to face her, she saw that Mary's eyes were screwed in pain, her skin pale as tallow.

"What ails you, Mother?" she had enquired, worried that the heat of the day had proved too much. "Come let us retire indoors." But Mary had shaken her head, and after a while, her features had uncreased and her grasp softened.

"Eliza, I am being called to God." Eliza's eyes widened and she moved to speak but Mary raised her hand and continued. "There is a cancer grows within me. I have concealed this for some time. Robert does not know of it yet, but I am certain that my time is now short." She smiled with such grace that Eliza found herself silenced. A butterfly danced in front of them, its wings painted with the delicacy of a Book of Hours. At the sight, a tear gathered at the corner of Eliza's eye and caught upon her dark lashes.

"Perhaps Martha …" she began, her thoughts racing.

"No, my dearest daughter, I am beyond even the ministrations of Martha." She chuckled wistfully and turned to face Eliza. "You must not weep for me. Death holds not terror but joy that I shall at last meet my God, but Eliza, I am afraid for Robert."

At the mention of his name she bridled.

"Why should you worry for him. He has Hannah, has he not. He has Holden!"

As soon as the words were spoken Eliza coloured with shame. "I'm sorry, Mother," she mumbled and looked out toward the children who had paused in their play at the sharpness of her voice. She waved them away and forced a smile which, she hoped, would convince at a distance.

"Eliza, as you well know, since John's death not a day passes when I do not worry for Robert. He cannot accept that it was God's will. He is convinced that it was punishment for his sins. For a time I feared that his grief should drive him to self-destruction, but with each passing year I see the opposite to be true. He will cling to life for as long as he is able, for he is convinced that he is bound for eternal damnation. He cannot accept the forgiveness of sin."

"He could atone until the Day of Judgement but I could never forgive him for what he did to me!" Her face darkened with anger, and Eliza's words were brittle as the fallen leaves about them, but her mother's response matched them in intensity.

"You should look to your sister Ann. She has found it in her heart to forgive!"

Eliza was shocked at the revelation, and her breath caught in her throat. Her mother had known of Gawthorp's doings all along, and yet had found it in her heart to forgive. She was chastened into a silence which was to endure throughout Mary's remaining days on earth.

The hours of darkness grew ever longer, and the days between Mary's visits stretched longer still. Christmas morning dawned mild and wet. The house at Thwaites was fragrantly decked with ever greenery, and the Yule bough had been carried within with great good-hearted ceremony by John. The family had attended service at Bingley church already, and the children grew impatient for the promised feast over which Eliza laboured.

Her second son, John, grizzled for attention in the arms of his sister. The parlour grew hot, the chatter and squeals of the children stretching Eliza's patience. She was distracted by thoughts of Mary whom she had not seen in almost two weeks. She had prayed that morning for her mother, that she be spared too great a suffering. Word had come from George that she no longer ventured abroad. Her body's decay could no longer be kept from Gawthorp, who now knew that his wife was dying. To her own surprise Eliza had found herself thinking of Gawthorp with concern. Was Christmas even being celebrated at Holden?

John read the worry in her features as she picked at her food. Her smile at the children's merry banter was unconvincing to his knowing eye.

"You must go to her," he had said at the close of the day as the children slept.

So it was that after Twelfth night was passed, and the greenery had burnt to ash on the fire, George fetched up to Thwaites. He had brought news of Mary's deterioration every couple of days. She was failing rapidly, and George could impart little cheer in the truth of her condition. Martha Wright, learning of Eliza's plight, had been happy to mind her children as, in the company of George, she had set forth for Holden.

The sun sat low in the sky offering no heat, merely a sharpness that illuminated the black folds of the distant hills. A keen wind pushed at their backs as they walked the familiar way to Holden, barely sharing a word. As the house approached Eliza hesitated and became fearful, convinced that her presence there was folly. George reminded that whilst he was in attendance she would come to no harm.

The door was opened by her sister Hannah who had heard their approach. Eliza would scarce have known the young woman who stood before her, for she had been little more than a baby when she had last seen her. She had something of Gawthorp's sharp features, and stood almost as tall as George. The women faced each other uneasily, but Hannah it was who broke the silence, opening her arms in invitation.

"My sister! I thought that I should never see you again. Mother asks for nothing else but to see you!"

Locked in an embrace, the sisters' tears flowed, and George turned away, himself quite overcome at the scene.

"Come." Hannah led Eliza by the hand towards the hearth, where Mary sat in Thomas's fireside chair. Gawthorp, to Eliza's immense relief, had absented himself, in the knowledge of her arrival. The woman whose fragile form seemed dwarfed by the chair was almost unrecognisable as her mother. It was as though her body had been drained of substance, so that only a pale sheath of skin disguised her bones. Eliza gasped at what had become of her. Mary seemed oblivious to her daughter's distress, holding out a wasted hand.

"Eliza, you are home at last."

In the hour they spent together, Mary preferred not to speak of her own condition, instead prompting Eliza to speak of John and the children. She obliged mechanically until Mary grew tired. She glanced to George, who had bided at the table, and nodded.

"Mother, I must go and allow you rest. I shall return, I swear it."

She was not sure that her mother was even aware as she bent to kiss her sunken cheek.

George walked Eliza a good way back along the road before turning up the moor towards Ghyllgrange. They spied Gawthorp a good way distant, a turf spade raked over his shoulder. He had been cutting peat on the moor above Holden and was returning to Mary with their departure.

"Thank you, George. I will return to her when I am able. He shall not prevent it!"

Over the coming weeks Eliza made the journey back to Holden frequently, sometimes in the company of George, sometimes alone. The snow came in faltering starts, but mostly she braved no more than sleet carried on a savage wind. Often she arrived to find one or more of her sisters. Ann and the recently married Jane, both living near Ghyllgrange, were most often at Mary's side together with the ever-present Hannah. Her sister Maria she saw only the once. Given her studious nature as a child, it came as little surprise to anyone that she had married a schoolmaster and removed to the town of Skipton. Amidst the sorrow of Mary's decline, they shared happier recollections of girlhood days, and wondered if their mother listened to their tales and found peace in the memories.

By the turning of January, a litter had been prepared at the fireside, as Mary could no longer be seated in comfort. Her teeth chattered with the absence of insulating flesh, and her finger ends were the colour of the winter sky.

Eliza arrived that February morning alone. She had brought with her a little honey she had spared with which she intended to sweeten warmed milk for her mother. She called out for Hannah and cursed the spite of the wind.

When she got no reply, she looked to the hearth, and to her horror realised that the figure cradling Mary was Gawthorp. They were quite alone. Stricken with panic, she made for the door.

"Eliza, don't go, I beg you!"

She paused. "Please Eliza, I cannot be alone!"

She turned to face him. He clasped Mary's ravaged body to his own, and his eyes, which once carried the same black threat as that of an untrustworthy dog, were haunted and blurred with tears. Cautiously she removed her cloak and bonnet and gathered up the milk ewer from the cold sill. Mechanically she warmed the poker, and prepared the sweet warm milk. She then watched as though in a dream as Gawthorp attempted to spoon the liquid between Mary's cracked lips with a tender patience she had never before seen. At length, his efforts proving futile, he lowered her head and arranged her blankets about her. Mary's breath had become slow and liquid and, with panic and fear, Eliza realised that death was near. She could not leave.

He moved from the hearth and took his seat at the head of the table. There he stared with misery into nothingness. Eliza moved to the far end of the table, and lowered herself into a chair. She studied his face which was that of a stranger.

"Where is Hannah?" she began.

"She had gone to fetch the priest from Kildwick," he mumbled bleakly. "Will you stay with me until they return?" His eyes focused upon her. The absurdity of the request released in Eliza a decade of hurt.

"Why would I leave now? My mother is dying, I shall not leave her. I would always have been here for her were it not for you. I curse the day you arrived at Holden!"

She had no fear now, only strength in the truth of her words. The ensuing silence was broken only by the arrival of Hannah and the Reverend Mitton some short time later. Eliza jumped to her feet at the sound of footsteps, her heart still beating ferociously. Gawthorp had neither spoken nor moved, and only stirred as the Reverend Mitton laid his hand upon his shoulder, dictating that they should come together in prayer for the soul of Mary.

Mary died before the sun had begun its descent. Ann arrived to witness her mother's final moments, her breath leaving her body for the final time in a long low whisper. At the very moment of death, Gawthorp released a great sigh as he clung to her cold fingers. Without hesitation, Mitton began the familiar words of the Lord's Prayer, and invited all present to give thanks for the life of one who had served her God with constant duty and obedience.

After the departure of the Reverend Mitton, who left with the suggestion that burial should be arranged for the coming Friday, the girls spoke together of practical matters. Hannah and Ann would prepare Mary's body for burial, they assured Eliza. She should return to Thwaites in the last of the light, to John and the children. With a nod she agreed and, gathering up her cloak and bonnet, glanced back to the hearth. Gawthorp still remained at the side of Mary's covered form. The desolation of his being seemed complete. She reminded herself that he was not her concern. She imagined that the long walk back to Thwaites would be one of tears and contemplation at the events of the day. She yearned to be in John's arms.

As she opened the door, sending the chill air barrelling into the room, Gawthorp turned towards her, and spoke in the smallest of voices.

"Forgive me."

49

Keighley. May 1713

I f nothing else were to come of the day, Miles could at least give thanks for the most excellent breakfast he had enjoyed in the company of his dear wife and daughter. In truth, over the past months there had been little to cheer, but that morning the three had found themselves laughing joyfully. The cause of their mirth had been the concerns of Constance.

Constance had come to keep house for the Gale family with the departure of her sister Sarah. Aside from their shared parentage, there was nothing else they held in common. Constance, with her unruly red hair, was short and squat, and tackled her labours with a calm orderly determination. She had been with the family for a decade, during which time she had proved herself entirely dependable, and much loved. It was clear from the start that she did not share her sister's wanton ways, and seemed content with a life of domestic servitude.

That morning she had sought to speak with Margery on a matter of great importance. She had wondered whether Margery might step into the kitchen with her for a moment. Clearly, whatever the issue was, it was not for the ears of Miles. As she stuttered and stumbled, not able to meet Margery's eye, the cause of her consternation was slowly revealed. It seemed that whilst cleaning about Miles's study, she had come across the remains of a rabbit. The unfortunate creature had been hung, some days before, in the larder, and was intended to be the contents of a pie that very night.

Did the good Reverend have questions as to the provenance of the animal? Were that the case, she could vouchsafe that she had purchased it earlier that week at the market cross. Also, she related with some discomfort, the rabbit had been opened up along its mid-line and had lain, its inner workings exposed, upon Miles's desk. She had lifted the cloth merely to clean, and had been so shocked to find the carcass that she now pleaded with Margery to defend her against accusations of prying, over and above any suggestion that she had acquired the animal from a questionable source.

Margery had struggled to compose her features as she explained the business of the eviscerated rabbit to the incredulous Constance. The Reverend Gale had lately become preoccupied with the anatomical study of animals, and the mechanics of their living form. His first experiments involved the dissection of spiders and snails, which he had collected about the environs of the Rectory. His new-found enthusiasm for the practice was only tempered by the shortcomings of his eyesight. He had wandered into the larder at first light in search of a little cheese, and spied the dangling rabbit, which offered up the potential for dissection on a more manageable scale.

Constance accepted Margery's explanation with incomprehension and bemusement. Margery had added, with sympathy, that to have come upon such an unexpected sight must have been very troubling. She promised to have words with her husband to ensure that he should not leave his experiments lying so casually about his study in future. Only when Margery assured Constance that they could have no complaints whatsoever with her efforts in the kitchen did the poor girl smile.

Miles had cause to chuckle over the incident as he returned to his study after breakfast, and lifted the cloth to reveal the splayed remains which had caused such upset and subsequent merriment. How Lister would have enjoyed the tale, but sadly his dear friend and trusted physician had passed away the previous spring. He would instead attempt a detailed drawing of his handiwork using ink, perhaps enlivened with a little red chalk. There would be no rabbit pie for supper, he thought sadly, for the poor creature had lain too long away from the cool of the larder.

As he scratched away at his delicate illustration, he found his thoughts turning to his son Christopher. What would he make of his father's new interest? It had been many years since he had seen him and in spite of their regular and detailed correspondence, he would be as a stranger were they to meet. It reassured Miles to think that in the ensuing years his son had lived a life that was both prosperous and full. He had married and sired four children, gone to war and been briefly held captive, established a plantation, and, for his pains, been appointed Chief Justice of the colony. Yet here in England, in half a lifetime more, his father had seen nothing of life beyond his parish, failed, as yet, to establish his much cherished dream of a school, and found pathetic entertainment in the butchery and study of a rabbit.

It was with these bitter and self-indulgent thoughts that Miles set aside his pen, and gathered up the remains of the rabbit in the cloth. He tossed them into the fire together with his drawing, and watched as they shrivelled and burned.

As his children had grown and departed, Miles thoughts had turned increasingly to the legacy of his life. He knew that if his dreams of a school were to be realised, then they would have to be implemented soon. His remaining years could surely not number more than five or ten, and with land not yet acquired, the scheme remained little more than a fantasy.

As a more attainable project, he had turned his thoughts towards the writing of a book, a historical tome that should document the heritage of his line, and culminate in the dazzling career of his son Christopher. This gift to posterity, were he to concentrate his efforts, would be within his capacities. He had already drawn up the framework of his lineage, upon which he was minded to hang the achievements of some of his most illustrious relations. He was to give particular prominence to the life of his uncle Thomas, the late Dean of York. Would that he had lived to have witnessed Christopher's remarkable rise.

There had been no news of his second son Miles in almost six months, and he could only hope that the ominous silence was born of Miles's careless nature. Edmund had left for the Americas some two years past, and had established himself under the auspices of his elder brother as the owner of a small plantation within Albermarle County. The boy had been so eager to follow his brothers to the colonies, that Miles doubted he would waste much time in realising his long cherished ambitions. He was both practical and assured, qualities that should serve him well should he follow Christopher's example.

Miles's only disappointment had been that his two youngest sons had been so lacking in ambition. John, a failed scholar, for want of a career had become lately apprenticed to a cabinet maker, and Thomas had not flinched from his desire to follow his father into the church. He would make only passing reference to both in his family history. Thinking on it, he felt guilty, for he himself could hardly claim a life of extraordinary worth.

How was it, Miles mused, that each child was born possessed of the same inner workings and yet, each would grow to be unique in the manner of their outer appearance and the life they lived? It was a subject that had increasingly come to occupy his thoughts, and piqued that morning by his observations of the rabbit. Was it God's design that marked some men down for greatness whilst others endured lives of ordinary sorrow? The circumstances of birth played their part but, beyond that, what possible forces were at work? What advantages could be gained by accepting God's will, or indeed, defying it?

Miles stared blankly towards the window, where the light fluctuated with the passage of townsfolk, their voices rising and receding as a tide. He had heard of the recent death of Mary Gawthorp, though he could not recall who it was that had told him. She had endured a terrible end, he'd heard tell, which seemed undeserving for a woman who had placed her trust in a merciful God, and lived her life to his teachings. It seemed iniquitous that her husband, who was everything that she was not, should endure and benefit.

He recalled it now: Michael Pighells it was who had told him of Mary's passing. He had seemed to take great pleasure in predicting what should become of Holden. Gawthorp was now quite alone, his remaining daughter Hannah having recently wed. He would be sure to take another wife, but then again, where was the woman with the stomach to take him on? No, in Pighells's view, the house would see new tenants before the year was out.

Miles's gaze reaffixed upon his writing materials, and he tried to shake off his maudlin thoughts. I am becoming a bitter old man, he concluded morosely. He was restless, unable to settle to the writing of his history. He shambled distractedly about his study, pausing to slide a leather-bound volume from the shelf only to replace it without even a glance. Perhaps there was truth in Pighells's predictions. Holden Gate might well pass into new ownership. The house built by the Fowler family a century before would perhaps echo with the voices of some other family who would forge their own history in the decades to come. And in those future years would anyone pause to wonder at the monogrammed lintel of weatherworn stone – the only memorial to lives of joy and sorrow, births and deaths?

Miles drew out his kerchief and blew his nose sonorously. His reflections on the brief transience of life had left him feeling morose. Glancing out onto the town green, he was resolved that a little spring air might improve his humour. Margery and Mary glanced up from their needlepoint as he announced his intention to take a short walk. Stepping out he was relieved to see that the church green was empty but for a couple of old women at the market cross, too engrossed in their animated discussions to notice Miles.

He hadn't a thought to where his walk might take him, but he found himself drawn into the shade of the back lane and out towards the town field. He considered with a smile that these narrows passages and low overhanging eaves were so much a part of his being that he felt sure that he could make the journey from the Rectory to the river with his eyes shut.

From the blue-dappled woods on the far bank of the Aire he heard the echoing call of a cuckoo. Everywhere about was the bright newness of the valley; the grass grown tall, the trees full, rippling gracefully in the soft wind.

A cart croaked for want of grease over the cobbles on the bridge. It was being drawn by heavy rust-hued oxen. The beasts were being led by a boy of perhaps twelve years. As he tugged on the ropes of his charges, his voice was carried across the apron of the riverbank. For nothing but his own pleasure, the lad was singing of his true love and the beauty of her eyes. It was a song that Miles had known since childhood days and, whilst the boy's rendition was not the finest, the joy in its delivery could surely not be matched.

As the cart disappeared into the darkness of the wood, and the song dissolved into the ground of birdsong, Miles paused a while at the side of the river. The air as it carried across the water seemed a little fresher. As he turned back to face the town, the jumble of brick, stone and wood capped by the pinnacle of the church, his eye was diverted. A little way distant in the grass, which moved with the soft flow of a stroked pelt, Miles saw a small movement. As he looked closer, screwing his eyes to focus, he recognised the drawn-back ears and dark flashing eye of a rabbit.

July 1730. Holden Gate

They are all gone now, yet I am not alone. The door is propped open by my body as I press myself against the roughness of the frame. The warmth of the weather-scoured stone reaches deep into my very bones. The sun is wheeling across the heavens; it is midsummer.

I am a woman in my middle years, though already I sense that I have witnessed more than any should in one lifetime. My body has retained its spareness, slight as a tree in winter, though I have not the movement of my younger days. My hair, once dark as my father's, is now moonlight streaked, a testament to the years I have lived. In spite of it all, there are days such as this, when I am still the child, here, in the place of my birth. I can find joy at the sight of swallows as they return to their nests in the rafters of the great barn. Like me they have found their way home.

I glance down at my hands where my wedding band balances slack against my knuckle. My body grows more like Mary's with each passing season, but I shall cling to this life in a way she did not, for I do oft wonder that this is all there is. My father and mother would be angry to hear me talk this way, but when John was taken from me so cruelly, I could find no comfort nor truth in God's promise of the life to come.

My final child, Elizabeth, was but a few weeks old in the early spring of the year. Out on the moor the ewes were heavy with lambs. The nights were long and cold, and John's labours kept him from me most waking hours. We had but brief moments together, illuminated by rushlight and flame. The children scarce saw him at all.

When he did not return that day, I thought of him out on the cold moor, imagining his vigil at the side of some young sheep. The safe delivery of a lamb was reward enough for his night without rest. He would tell me so, though he would stumble over his words for want of sleep. I longed for summer days and was impatient at winter's slow drear passage. The second day when he had still not returned I grew fearful. Late in the afternoon as the light was dying, I opened my door to Parker himself, and knew before even a word was spoken that John was dead. As he spoke to me I did not, would not hear it. George Snowden had found John's body hard by the Doubler Stones. He had lain the night long with his dog at his side, his leg shattered by a fall. I could not, nor still cannot, bear to think on his final moments. I raged that a vengeful God could be so cruel. In my despair I felt fury at John for leaving me. My sister Ann came to me when first she heard the news from George. She tended my children in the confusion and silence of my grief. She lay with me those first terrible nights and heard, without judgement, the bleakness of my being.

For fifteen years John has lain beneath the earth in the yard at Bingley church. It pains me still to recall the day when he was finally taken from me. I gathered my children about me that wretched morning, innocent of circumstance and shivering in the rude wind. I was reminded of the day half a lifetime before, when my father Thomas had been laid to rest. I heard again my mother's harsh words, that Thomas was no longer ours but returned to God. Then, as now, I struggle to understand or accept it.

We remained at John's graveside, my children and I, until my baby Elizabeth screamed in hunger and discomfort. I looked about me where I saw Ann at some short distance, my children gathered about her. When she held out her hand to me, I allowed myself to be led towards the ale-house. As we entered I was blind to the small kindness of men who gave up their settle at the hearth, nodding in mute respect. As Elizabeth angrily fed, and our skin prickled at the warmth of the flame, Gawthorp it was who broke the silence. Gently he spoke my name, and with carefully chosen words begged that we return with him to Holden. Two years had passed since my mother's death and, in that time, I had had no cause to return to the place of my birth.

Though my recollections of that day are keen, I had not been aware of his presence before that moment. I was so blinded by grief that I had not begun to consider the future. Robert Parker, sensitive to my plight, had granted me the house at Thwaites, but without John it offered nothing but bitter memories. It was a memorial to all I had lost.

I had not answered him, perhaps I had not truly heard him. Only when Ann laid her hand gently upon my arm did I think on his words. He too was alone. Hannah, the last of my sisters to wed, had departed Holden soon after the death of Mary. I thought back to that day, and the words that had passed between us. In the intervening years, my fears for the *future of Holden had proved baseless. He had maintained it with a solitary determination, though perhaps without thought to its future.*

When I closed the door and walked out from the beech copse for the last time, it was on the arm of Ann. Together, and with my young children, unsure and afraid, we made our way to Holden. I can still recall that day, the creased green of hawthorn leaf and the flush of pale primroses on the bank. As we approached the house, curlews alarmed as we stepped close to their hidden bowers. As I crossed the threshold my tears began to fall, recalling the last time I had done so. Gawthorp was not there to greet me, and for that courtesy I was grateful. Ann watched as I showed my children the place of which I had so long spoken. My father's desk was still in the corner, the bible on the table, its leather bindings worn smooth as a chestnut. Aside from remembered plates and pots, I struggled to find Mary within the fabric of the parlour. The room seemed larger than remembered in my dreams, though this was perhaps the absence of my sisters.

"I am close by, Eliza." Ann took the baby from me and I walked the children about the corners of the parlour. "This is now our home."

There were many callers in those first days. My sisters, of course, glad at my return and anxious to be of service with the children. Gawthorp was a fleeting presence, about his labours in the hours of light. He found much to detain him in the barn, though I wonder now that it was to allow us ease to find ourselves in this place that was now our home. To my children he was a stranger. They fell silent in his presence, and clung to me though they knew nothing of our troubled history. Over time this was to change. My children grew and Holden was again filled with life. Gawthorp and I never spoke of what had gone before, indeed we spoke of little at all, but the quietness suited us well. I did not see the bonds that grew between him and my children. It was invisible and slow as the raising of a field of oats. It was through no gesture on my part, but once established I did naught to dissuade it.

The Reverend Gale journeyed to Holden soon after my removal there. I had not seen him in many years, and imagined that he was but one amongst many to come and offer help and condolence. I remember thinking that he had grown so old and tired as he removed his hat and entered the parlour; indeed by then he was a man of advanced years. I was surprised to hear of the purpose of his visit. The death of John's father, soon after the birth of our first child, had released a small inheritance for which, in the event of his death, my husband had left no instruction. The future had seemed a foreign land beyond the far hills as we had begun our lives together. How foolish we had been. With patience and sensitivity, the Reverend Gale, who had heard of my plight, explained that he would compile letters of administration to secure John's monies in my name.

He had not forgotten Mary, and the manner in which our lives had woven with his own. His mistrust of Gawthorp had endured, but this small gesture guaranteed my independence and his own peace of mind. When he took his leave of me, Gawthorp was returning from the field, and with some awkwardness we all came together at the mouth of the great barn. The Reverend Gale betrayed his unease at the encounter by making to remove his hat but then, thinking better of it. As he moved away Gawthorp spoke, his words spare yet powerful. For the remainder of his days he vowed to work for the memory of Mary and for the comfort and protection of myself and my children. God was not mentioned, his forgiveness not invoked, but as he looked to me, I know that the Reverend Gale departed satisfied.

Even now, all these years later, I think of him often, the man he was, and the part he played in my life's story. I did not meet with him again, and a few years later he died peacefully in his sleep, his beloved wife at his side. He lived long enough to see the foundation of a first school within the town, a legacy that must have given him the greatest satisfaction.

A year after John's death, Thomas Brown, the town constable, came to my door with the offer of marriage. It was no hardship to refuse him, for I knew then that there would be no second husband. My future belonged to Holden and no other.

From time to time I was troubled by dreams in which my father Thomas stood before me, and though his lips moved to speak, I could not make out his words. I tried to approach that I might hear him, but with each step his figure became a drifting shadow without form. It was as though I could pass through his very being. The dream was always the same, and each time I would wake with a heart full of yearning and regret. Once or twice in the clear light of day I imagined that I glimpsed him if I turned quickly to heed a child's call. One day Gawthorp had witnessed me, staring towards a dark corner, questioning what I imagined I had seen.

"It is Thomas, Eliza. He watches over us. I am grateful for his presence."

In his final years, as my sons took on the working of the land, I came to an understanding of Gawthorp, and together we made the same peace with God. Some evenings after supper, I would open my father's bible and read familiar verses aloud. We did not heed the spiritual comfort it offered, nor did I seek to instruct my children in its wisdom. No, when I spoke those words, it was in remembrance of Mary.

Gawthorp lies now in the churchyard at Kildwick. He died a quiet and swift death, taken by the scarlet fever last winter. Paterfamilias, it reads against his name in the register, and by his end, it was a title I could not deny him. He had made good on his vow to the Reverend Gale, and had finally proved himself the respected father. He lies a little way from where Mary and Thomas repose, his grave next to that of his beloved John.

From this doorway, the valley stretches out before me, shimmering in the hot dust. I watch the slow passage of cloud shadows which patch the land with shifting darkness. My sons Thomas and John stand together, looking out over the swaying crop, their bodies watery in the rising heat. I hear the excited bay of a dog, high beyond the bank above the house, and I am transported back across the years. I am waiting for my father; he is coming home.

Author's Note

I began researching my family history (Asquith) about eight years ago, but like many genealogists, hit a brick wall. I could find nothing of the origins of one John Asquith who died in 1715. With scant available details, I decided to write an imagined story of his life. The majority of characters in the book were real people, the dates of their lives accurate, but to avoid confusion, I have altered some Christian names where necessary. I have also allowed myself poetic licence to imagine the town of Keighley and the Aire valley at the turn of the eighteenth century. Some of the minor characters are entirely fictitious, and the places described not geographically accurate. The framework of births, marriages, deaths and wills were the basis of the entirely imagined narrative.

The book begins with the birth of a child during a storm. This was a real natural catastrophe which became known as The Great Storm of 1703. It is thought to have claimed over 8000 lives in England and those who witnessed it believed it to be the manifestation of God's anger. The following year Daniel Defoe published a book, The Storm, a compilation of eye-witness accounts of the havoc wreaked by this ferocious weather event.

Miles Gale became a hero of mine as I wrote this book, and learned more of his life. The town of Keighley should be very proud of him. He was Rector of the parish from 1680 to his death in 1720. During his tenure, he helped with the founding of a school, improved the water supply to the town, introduced new midwifery techniques and above all promoted the importance of literacy. He was a peripheral figure in the circle of intellectuals known as the York Virtuosi who counted among their number Martin Lister (vice president of the Royal Society), Ralph Thoresby (noted antiquarian and historian), and Henry Gyles (stained glass artist). Their interests included the promotion of ideas of natural philosophy, antiquarian study and topography.

Miles' sons, in particular Christopher, became important historical figures in the colonial history of the American state of North Carolina. Judging by contemporary accounts, Christopher seemed to have inherited something of his father's superior and argumentative nature, dividing opinion amongst those who knew him.

Holden Gate still stands on the edge of the moors overlooking the modern town of Keighley. It was inhabited by members of the Asquith family, direct descendants of John and Eliza well into the twentieth century.

Acknowledgements

I must thank a number of people for helping me finally put pen to paper. I have been threatening to write a book since childhood days.

Firstly, enormous gratitude to Hilary and Robert Allan, the current owners of Holden Gate, for welcoming me into their beautiful home three years ago. I had ventured up onto the moors with my friend Helen to see the area in which my ancestors had lived. We had picked a day of unimaginably bad weather. Robert, seeing two drowned rats with a camera at his gate, kindly invited us in. This led to thoughts of the history of the house, and ultimately the writing of the book. They very graciously allowed me to use their house as the setting for the story. They have been endlessly informative and supportive and I am ever grateful for their kindness.

Victoria Knight, for reading the manuscript and guiding me in the right direction when impatience got the better of me. Also, for her friendship and advice for which I am eternally grateful.

Helen Rhodes, for her good humour in the face of adversity, on two rather eventful trips to the moors above Keighley.

Aunties Peggy and Helen, (members of the Asquith family) for driving me around the sites of significance in the Keighley area, and their genuine enthusiasm for the project.

Donna Hefton and Ann-Marie Akehurst, two friends, who share my love and interest in Miles Gale, and have been endlessly supportive. I must also thank Elizabeth Caissie, local historian and retired curate of Keighley shared church for her unequalled enthusiasm for, and knowledge of, all things Miles Gale!

Darren Curley, for so very kindly allowing me to use his wonderful photograph of the Doubler Stones for my front cover, and also for re-photographing them when he couldn't access his original image. I couldn't be more grateful.

Neil Sturr of Online Digital Archives for allowing me to reproduce the Keighley section of Thomas Jeffrey's 1771 Map of Yorkshire.

John Makin for proofreading my manuscript so brilliantly, and Duncan Beal and all at York Publishing Services for helping me realise my dream.

Finally, Ian Rankin, who, unknowingly, was the catalyst for the whole project.

Thanks to you all